TOMORROW WE RISE

THE KILLING SANDS · BOOK 2

DANIEL P. WILDE

Tomorrow We Rise (The Killing Sands, Book 2)
Daniel P. Wilde
ISBN 978-1-77342-017-2

Produced by IndieBookLauncher.com
www.IndieBookLauncher.com
Cover Design: Saul Bottcher
Interior Design and Typesetting: Saul Bottcher

The body text of this book is set in Adobe Minion.

Also Available
Kindle edition, ISBN 978-1-77342-016-5

CONTENTS

This book is dedicated to those who fall,
only to rise again stronger than before.

PROLOGUE

"They're downstairs!" Sonya whispered anxiously, rushing into the small room.

Enrique quietly pushed the heavy door closed behind his sister, quickly bolting both locks.

"I didn't hear them," Enrique whispered. "Where are they?"

"They're coming up, maybe the thirty-third or thirty-fourth floor by now," Sonya replied, still out of breath after having just run up the stairs and through the open door to the small hotel room on the 35th floor. Sonya fidgeted with her old 2014 Smith & Wesson .38 Crimson Trace handgun. "But there's only two of them, I think."

"I'm going to go down and engage them. If there's only two, I should be able to take care of the problem pretty quick. We can't let them send for others."

Sonya relented. She knew that Enrique was right. They should take care of the problem before things got out of hand. Enrique checked his magazine and released the safety. Sonya unbolted the locks and quietly opened the door; then closed it behind her brother. She didn't lock it in case he had to get back in quickly.

Only seconds later, Sonya heard a painful roar that sounded more like an animal than Enrique; but she couldn't be sure. Anxiously allowing a few more seconds to pass by, and not hearing another sound, Sonya crept over to the closed door. She slowly opened it, just a crack, revealing darkness. *Had the electricity gone out?* She hadn't noticed before.

With increased wariness, Sonya peeked through the crack between the door and its frame, and looked right, then left down the dark hallway. Her vision was limited, so she opened the door further, and stuck her head out. Seeing nothing, she opened the door just enough to slip through, and silently moved out into the hallway. She drew her gun and leveled it, just as her late husband had taught her two months earlier, before he died from the disease.

Sonya wished she had a flashlight, but they had left the lights and most of their other gear in their basement bunker the day before. There had been no time to pack when the hairless, human-like monsters—that had been screaming something about "perversions" and "God"—broke in. Now, a flashlight certainly would have eased her mind and quieted her fears—at least her fear of the dark that she had had since childhood.

Sonya walked slowly, steadily, but with tentative steps, toward the stairwell at the end of the hall. There was no noise. Even the aggressive sounds of the rats and feral cats that had kept them awake half of the night were gone. She had a terrible feeling of dread as she approached the door to the stairwell.

Pulling the door open to no more than a sliver, she peeked into the stairwell. It was even darker than the hallway in which she stood, and it smelled like rotting flesh. But she couldn't see or hear anything. Just as her fingers began to pull on the warm metal of the door handle, the door slammed against her, striking her face and knocking her off balance. Her nose and right cheekbone screamed in agony—probably broken. But she didn't fall. Catching herself against the far wall of the hallway, she raised her gun and instinctively pulled the trigger. The bullet smashed harmlessly into the door frame.

"Wait!" yelled a shadowy figure that had come through the door. "It's me!" the shadow yelled as he slammed the door shut behind him.

"Enrique! Are you alright?"

"No! They're here! And they're coming! Run!"

Sonya turned and ran down the long hallway toward the staircase at the other end, not knowing that Enrique was steadily losing ground behind her. She heard a loud thump and looked back to see Enrique on the floor, facedown. Overwhelming fear coursed through her body as she ran back to her brother who appeared lifeless on the floor. She had known fear over the past few weeks, but this was different and it threatened to immobilize her. If something happened to her brother, she would be alone.

Sonya crouched down next to her brother. Blood pumped through a small, but deep, jagged gash in Enrique's right thigh, spurting in time with the pulse of his heart, and spattering the walls and floor around him. In the darkness of the hallway, her brother's blood looked black. Within seconds, the blood flow began to slow. Enrique slowly lifted his head from the floor. He looked at Sonya with eyes that were not his own. Sonya began to back away as Enrique started dragging his body toward her with his arms.

This isn't right, she thought, as she continued to slowly back away from Enrique's rising body. "Sonya, where are you going? Are you going to just leave me here?" Enrique asked in a calm, detached voice.

"No, no. I was just . . . I'm just going to find the med-kit . . . it looks like you're . . . bleeding . . ." Sonya's voice trailed off as she looked into his dark eyes, made all the darker by the shadows of the hallway.

Enrique rose the rest of the way off the floor and, losing a shoe in the process, jumped farther than any man should have been able to jump. He landed inches away from his terrified sister who was pregnant with her first child. She screamed.

He screamed too, but his was the scream of conquest as he knocked his sister to the floor. He dropped to his knees, and, looking deep into her eyes, slowly lowered his head. Just as Sonya opened her mouth to beg for her life, Enrique clamped his jaw down on her shoulder. Within moments, Sonya fell silent. The heart of the baby in her womb stopped beating. The baby was dead—but her mother was not.

1

"My friends," Dr. Yurgi Shevchuk began as everyone gathered around the base of the iron staircase. "I am a bit envious. Anta and Shift, it seems right that you two are among the first to rise and spread life. If it weren't for your efforts so long ago, perhaps none of us would be alive to see this moment. This is your time to tell our diseased world that we will not be beat! Good luck!"

As Yurgi's short speech ended, several others in the group called out their approval. Hugs began in earnest, placing a temporary pause on the pursuit of the four duffel bags and other gear on the floor.

"Here we go people!" Street called out in that deep, clear voice that every member of the group had grown to love.

The small group of four entered the decontamination chamber at the base of the stairs and the door shut quickly behind them. The chamber whooshed and whirred as it sealed shut from the inside and its occupants were cleansed.

When the chamber had completed its vapor washing of the occupants and gear inside, Dr. John Silitzer entered a code sequence on the small pad beside the chamber and the ceiling above the iron staircase began to rise. Threet "Street" Kimball, Dr. Angel Robertson, Dr. Shift Bader and Dr. Anta Chalthoum filed up the stairs. As they crossed the threshold at the top of the fourth and final flight of iron steps, the ceiling lowered over the hidden staircase, leaving the small group huddled together in the dimly-lit interior of the old hunting cabin. It was almost dark outside, with night coming quickly. They were breathing the outside air—the contaminated air.

Anta reached over and gently touched Shift's waist. Angel and Street, seemingly unable to control their own actions, each took a step closer to Shift and Anta. They were all scared to death.

9:45PM—SHIFT

Yeah, this is a big deal. We've been hiding under this cabin for a long time. The world here on the surface is not the same as the world we left a few months ago. There may be only a few thousand people left alive by the time we wake up tomorrow. Maybe less.

Four months ago, outside El-Alamein, Egypt, an Egyptian scientist, his young daughter, and their tour guide, Mr. Riyad Shafik, entered caves that had been hidden from the world for generations. Their discovery of the cave-tomb of an anonymous Nazi German soldier began a world-wide struggle for survival. It was a quick and painful struggle that nearly every man, woman and child on Earth had lost.

"Anthrax E", a biological weapon, apparently concocted by the Nazis in the 1940's, was released from the hidden cave on the wind. It quickly devoured the human population, and much of the animal population of El-Alamein. While the International World Order— the IWO—was able to contain the disease on Earth in El-Alamein, the disease was unwittingly taken to the moon colonies by the good scientist and his daughter. There, nearly all life was lost, save five anxious, lonely colonists, including Anta's brother Hasani.

A few short weeks later, the plague returned to Earth with the destruction of a Mexican airship headed back to Earth from the moon. Starting in the countries surrounding the Gulf of Mexico, where the Mexican ship was shot down by Cuba, Anthrax E then began a rapid, unrelenting sweep through the Earth's population. Now, just seven days after Dr. Shevchuk's announcement that he and his team had finally created a vaccine for Anthrax E, dubbed "E-rase", the few isolated scientific teams working on the vaccine in secret bunkers around the world have agreed that the surviving world population is probably less than forty million people, and that number will likely decrease significantly over the next two or three weeks. Tonight, we're leaving our safe haven to try to save mankind, or what's left of it.

Two people from El-Alamein, Ms. Neirioui Safar and her daughter Suvan, have been found to be immune. That means that others might also be immune. It is believed that Dr. Steven Porter's son, Jon, may also be immune; but Steve hasn't heard from his son in Nevada for several days now.

Tonight, we're sleeping in the cabin. Anta and I are sharing the lone bedroom upstairs. Angel took the large bedroom on the main floor. Street is probably sound asleep on the couch in the living room, snoring away.

In the morning, we'll walk out the front door, trek down a short trail to a dirt parking lot, and load up one of the hovercraft that was left there when we arrived at the bunker months ago. From there, we'll head north to Canada.

Over the past several weeks, our colleague, Mike Petrovsky, has conducted significant research and observation and has located towns in northern Canada that he believes have a number of survivors, unlike locations closer to home. Perhaps the winter cold staved off the illness for a while; or maybe the relative remoteness of several communities is to be credited. Either way, that's where we're headed.

Anta is asleep on the bed now, breathing deeply. The shape and contour of her body under the covers is mesmerizing. I'm going to try not to wake her as I roll back and forth in my sleeping bag on the floor tonight. Maybe I'll be lucky. Maybe I'll actually sleep too.

9:49PM—DR. ANGEL ROBERTSON

This event is unparalleled—such a global catastrophe has never before occurred. My career has led me down a path by which I now have the opportunity to see, first-hand, the results of world-wide devastation by biological means! I shouldn't be excited, given the nature of the disease and the death toll in our world as a result, but I am. I'm safe, and, although I don't believe I'm a selfish person, this whole situation fascinates me, purely due to my love of biology.

Perhaps, some day in the future, when all that is left of me is my bones, disintegrating in the ground or elsewhere, some person will hear stories of my participation in these events and consider me to be a selfish, vile and dreadful person. But I can't help myself. I can't help the fact that I long to see the effects of this plague first-hand. That starts tomorrow!

Of course, I'm also anxious to see E-rase work. I don't want our world to be left to the cockroaches and mosquitoes, especially since I'm quite certain both will be munching on my body tonight while we sleep in this dirty old cabin.

I want human life to continue. I don't think a disease like Anthrax E will ultimately be good for our world. I don't believe our population needed to be "cleansed" or any of the nonsense that has been spouted by naysayers and dooms-dayers over the past few weeks, including the wretched Latisha Bodily.

I want to find people and help save their lives. Maybe that will be the quality that redeems me in the eyes of those who hear my story in the future—but maybe not.

We haven't come topside unprepared. My colleagues and friends, Shift and Anta, seem more than adequately prepared for this task. As for Mr. Kimball, I believe that his massive body and physical strength could be a tremendous asset, and not bad to look at either during the days ahead. He's a pleasant gentleman, and a good man, even though I'm positive that his robust physique and cosmic stardom alone allowed for his placement in our little haven underground.

Off to bed. Tomorrow is going to be exciting, albeit a little frightening!

2

I slept! And I awakened to the wonderful smell of fresh, morning air coming in through the window. I was a bit surprised. I had assumed the air would be stale or have some kind of odor. I guess I figured Anthrax E must smell bad. Duh.

Anta awoke before me. She was standing at the window with her back toward me, gazing out into the early morning light. Her confident silhouette against the bright morning sky was as beautiful as her covered shape was last night. The rays of light cascading around her figure lit the trails from tiny bugs in the dust on the floor around me.

"Anta," I said softly.

She turned around, and, walking toward me, answered, "Yes, Shift."

I didn't know what to say next. We were breathing real air—albeit contaminated air. There was real sunshine on our skin. I was happy. She looked happy too. Then reality hit.

"We need to get downstairs," I said, stupidly.

"You're right," Anta replied. She was already dressed. She picked up her gear, opened the door, and walked out, closing the door quietly behind her.

When I arrived at the bottom of the stairs less than twenty minutes later, after showering and dressing, Angel, Street and Anta were all standing by the door, bags at their feet, ready to leave. They were waiting for me. I felt even more stupid. Anta smiled and handed me a granola bar. Street opened the door. All three of them walked out. I didn't. I couldn't get my feet to move.

I was scared. I couldn't believe it. Was I going to be the person who slowed us down? Was it a mistake choosing me as the leader of this team? Was I going to be *that* guy—like the proverbial idiot in horror movies that gets killed because he makes stupid decisions?

After several seconds of mental torment, Anta walked back in the front door, a crooked little smile on her lips and sparkle in her eyes. She took my hand and gently pulled me outside. No questions. No jokes.

We walked down the trail, holding hands, toward the parking lot. Birds sang in the trees above us. A light breeze from the north blew drops of dew from the leaves into our hair and eyes. In the distance, through the branches of the trees, I could see the sunlight dancing across the ripples of the lake.

When we arrived at the small parking lot, Street and Angel were looking at maps floating in the air above Street's watch. Several hovers surrounded them, resting lightly on the hard-packed dirt. They had been sitting idle for months, but didn't show any wear. The Chevrolet Fluxor, by which Anta and I had arrived at the compound, was among them. It was dirty, but still shone in the morning sun. The doors to the Fluxor were open. Evidently, it had been chosen for our journey. I thought that was a good choice.

We climbed inside, with Street at the wheel. Angel rode "shotgun". Anta and I sat in the back seat, side-by-side, her hand resting gently on my thigh.

"Anybody here not ready for this?" Street asked, excitedly.

"I may not be," I replied. "But I don't think I have a choice now."

Angel and Anta both laughed good-naturedly.

MAY 21—DR. STEVEN PORTER (WEB POST)

```
Jon, I've been trying to reach you for a
couple of days. There's good news! We finally
have a vaccination for Anthrax E! I have
```

been given a shot which will vaccinate me
and allow me to leave the compound without
risk that I will get sick. I am going to
leave here as soon as I can. Once I leave,
it should take me less than two days to reach
you!

MAY 21, 11:25PM—ANTA

"I am so glad this day is over," I said as I lifted my feet off the floor, one by one, and kicked off my shoes. I laid back on the bed in the small motel room I would be sharing with Shift tonight. We'd be sharing a room, but not a bed.

The walls of the room were painted pastel blue, and the dressings covering the bed matched their hue. Two chairs sat in the corner by an old, round table. Pamphlets covered the table top, inviting us to take a tour of the fall foliage or to visit the waterfalls nearby. If only we had time.

A dresser with broken drawers sat against the wall next to the door. Above it, on the wall, hung an old model viewing screen. A remote control rested in a holster of sorts on the dresser. The old technology and furnishings were cozy. More importantly, the bed was very soft, just the way I liked it.

"Yup, me too," Shift replied.

This has been a very long day. And we've only traveled a hundred miles or so. That was part of the plan though. We took the Fluxor, which has plenty of room for the four of us and our gear, so the ride was nice. But the constant stops were taxing.

Shift, dutifully fulfilling his assignment as travel coordinator with the bunker, kept our speed at a terribly boring pace. Not his fault I guess. At each stop, we used the binocs to scope out buildings and fields in the distance. Getting used to those took some time. Hopefully our speed will pick up as we get better at this, or we'll never get to northern Canada.

The Fluxor can travel at speeds up to 180 miles per hour, but not safely. Most drivers are unable to maintain speeds in excess of 120 miles per hour in a craft like this. We are unlikely to ever get anywhere close to that speed. Because our goal is to find and vaccinate the living, we intend to drastically scale back our speed in all areas but the wide open roads. We need to be able to see signs of human life, even in places where Mike hasn't seen any through the satellite feeds.

Shift will be discussing our travel plans with Mike and Dr. Shevchuk over the MEHDS, or Multi-dimensional Eyeglass Holographic Displays, numerous times throughout each day. The general idea is that we'll travel day-to-day with updated instructions from the bunker about locations of likely human life. Our travel will be slow and methodical as we pass through town after town.

But importantly, today, we wanted to find animals. And we did. We found a huge farm not far from the bunker. Many of the animals were dead, particularly those inside barns and corrals. But some free-roaming animals were still alive—cows mainly. A few animals were sick. We vaccinated every one of them still living; many cows, several chickens, and two pigs. Hopefully some will live and we can use them to produce food in the future. We'll continue looking for farms throughout our travels, studiously logging the locations where immunizations take place.

"So, where are we headed tomorrow Shift?" I asked. After leaving the small parking lot outside the cabin this morning, we had traveled generally northwest toward the Massachusetts-Vermont state line.

"We'll keep traveling the same direction," he answered. "Once we get to Interstate 91, we'll take it north until we reach the Canadian border near Montreal. Then we'll head west through Montreal to Ottawa."

"Are we still going to Churchill?"

"Yeah, that's the plan," he replied. "The goal is to travel northwest from Ottawa."

"Still no plans to go to Toronto?" I asked.

"Yeah. Yurgi told me a little while ago that Toronto's bunker has finally duplicated his research and inoculated some people today. Those people will be leaving the Toronto center in a couple of days heading south and west, hopefully vaccinating along the way. So we won't waste time going over there."

"Makes sense," I said. "So does Churchill still look good?"

"Yup; looks great actually," Shift said.

Before we left the bunker, research and satellite video logs suggested that there were hundreds of people alive in Churchill. Somehow, they'd escaped Anthrax E. If that holds true for the next few days, we hope to vaccinate as many as 1,500 people there!

"Does Mike, or anybody, have any theory about why Churchill seems to have escaped Anthrax E?" I asked.

"Yes, I do," Shift replied, as he reverted to his lecturing voice. Shift is a gifted and renowned anthropological historian, which is why he was asked to get involved in the crisis at El-Alamein in the first place. His knowledge of ancient diseases and their effects on human life proved invaluable in the bunker. Of course, his modesty won't allow him to accept praise to his face. But, without considering it, he often becomes "the professor" when asked to explain something in his specialties. I think it's cute, which is why I encourage him.

"It's isolated from almost everything. There's only one road in and out from the south and one to the west. The only paved road, coming from the south, isn't equipped with energy modules, so travel into the area is restricted to older automobiles or hovers with energy rejuvenation cores. And, for much of the year, that lone road is covered in ice. Then, it's impassable for most vehicles. The dirt road to the west heads off into the wilderness."

"But isn't it next to a huge bay or something? What about boats?" My knowledge of the geography of North Am is obviously dismal.

"Yes, it's sitting on Hudson Bay. But boats don't really operate much during the winter because parts of the bay freeze over. So, before the IWO issued its order shutting down travel and international commerce, very little travel was happening anyway because it was winter. Once travel was shut down, it's likely that trains and boats stopped moving in the area altogether. So, only personal vehicles and hovers could get there; but why would anyone go so far away? Anyway, that's my theory. Isolation and timing."

"That's interesting," I said sincerely. "So, assuming we find people there, what are we going to do with them after they're vaccinated?" We had discussed this topic before, but I hadn't been a part of the final discussions in the bunker. I was tending to other matters.

"Well, that's a little sketchy. Dr. Shevchuk wants to wait and see what we find. But he wants *us* to make that decision on the ground, so to speak."

"There are probably tourists there, right? Not everyone there would be natives. So maybe some of them will want to go home."

"I thought about that," Shift said. "It seems likely. There are polar bears all around the Churchill area, or so I'm told. That would have been a major tourist draw during the winter since they're virtually extinct everywhere else. And the tourists would have been stuck there when travel was halted, if they obeyed the rules. And that's a possibility since no commercial craft would have taken them out of the area."

"Yeah," I said. "If I was stuck in some place where I was isolated, knowing that a crazy disease was destroying the human race, I'd probably want to stay where I was too. So, what do we do about them?"

After a simple discussion, which we ran by Angel and Street, we decided that we should stop in Manitoba to pick up three more large hovercraft, one to be driven by each of us, along with a huge supply of energy rejuvenation cores. Our goal now is to vaccinate and leave the additional hovercraft in Churchill so that any of the non-natives who want to return "home", wherever that might be, can use the machines to facilitate that initial travel back to 'civilization'.

3

Jon, where are you? Please post.

MAY 24—SHIFT

"Shift, this is crazy," Dr. Steven Porter said through the MEHD.

Each person from the Boston bunker was provided a MEHD. These awesome contraptions allow us to communicate with anybody we wish, provided we have their ID number. Basically, the MEHD allows us to communicate via real-time holographic display, which is the MEHD's main purpose. So, not only do we hear each other, we can see each other, standing, sitting, eating, or whatever else the person might be doing during the com. Even more amazingly, the users of a MEHD can smell what each other smells and, if allowed by all users during a com, the participants can actually *feel* what the others are feeling— their emotions, fear, hunger, love. It requires a bit of discretion on the part of the participants.

"What's crazy?" I asked. Steve's face showed genuine concern.

"Well, I got home this morning. Actually, I don't have a home. It's just rubble. But I went over to the house where my son was staying. It was empty."

"That's not too crazy Steve," I replied. "But where is he? Did he leave a note or something?"

"No. That's the crazy part. I'm sure he would have left me something to go on. He's a smart kid."

Steve broke down. It's very difficult for me to watch grown men cry, but not because it makes me think any less of them. Actually the opposite. I just don't like to cry along with them because it makes *me* feel weak. Sometimes, like now, the MEHD provides a little too much sensory information.

"I'm sorry Steve. I'm sure he's around. He's not dead, right? You would see his body if he were dead. Maybe he's just out exploring. Maybe he went shopping or went for a round of golf." I was trying to lighten his spirits.

"Yeah, maybe. I didn't see a single living person on my way here though. It was a little scary to me. Jon's only fourteen years old."

"I can imagine."

"You probably think I'm a wimp or something. But I wasn't scared of any danger to me. I'm sure I'm perfectly safe. The scary thing is that there *isn't* any real danger to me anymore. Any person who might have taken my son or caused him harm is probably dead. It's scary because the world as we know it is no more."

"That is certainly something I understand Steve."

"Anyway, it seems unlikely that Jon left against his will," Dr. Porter said. "But then, where is he and why did he leave?"

"Have you talked to Mike?" I asked. "Maybe he can go back through satellite feeds and try to find him and follow him."

"That's a good idea," Steve said. "I'll talk to Mike; but I don't know how many cameras our little town has. It might be tough."

MAY 25—ANTA

"There ain't nobody left but us, and this guy," Street said, pointing to the road in front of the hover. He sounded a little too much like the thug football player of days gone by. But his point was well taken. It's remarkable what Anthrax E has accomplished in such a short time! There truly "ain't nobody left but us", or so it seems.

The rotting corpses in every town and village are so odiferous as to completely overwhelm our senses, even though we haven't been up close to one yet. We haven't seen more than a couple hundred corpses along our route. But one of them lay in front of us now, in the middle of the road.

"I have to see it!" Dr. Angel Robertson said.

"Let's go then," Shift said. "But it isn't going to be pretty."

We each exited the Fluxor from a different door and slowly walked around to the front of the hover. The sun was directly overhead, and its heat was radiating off the roadway. Hundreds, or thousands, of flies were flying and buzzing around our heads, getting thicker the closer we got to the corpse. I pulled a bandana from my pocket and tied it around the lower half of my face, mostly to keep the flies out, but also for the smell. The others noticed. I'm sure they wished they had thought ahead, as I had done.

With Shift in the lead, we crept toward the body, as if sneaking up on someone still living. Street looked the most nervous. Even though we'd been immunized, we still hadn't had a real test like this, so we didn't *really* know that it would work. This was the closest we'd come to the disease . . . and the smell . . . yuck.

As we walked toward the body, Angel pulled out her MEHD and set it to record. She began to chronicle the event visually and audibly. Her inspection got very close and personal, much closer than any of the rest of us dared approach.

"As the biologist among us," she began, speaking into the MEHD, "it behooves me to diagram and identify the characteristic marks of the beast that is Anthrax E. The skin and bones of the subject body remain relatively intact, but with fissures ranging from mere millimeters to several inches in diameter. Two gaping holes exist along the left side of the lower torso. Their origin is unknown, but appear to have resulted from a bite, perhaps by a wolf or other large carnivore. Through these torsol fissures, we can see the subject's main body cavity. The inner organs and other tissue appear to have dissolved, or in some cases, are presently in a state of decomposition."

Angel kept talking while the rest of us stared at her, swatting flies, watching with fascination as she became more and more animated.

Shift whispered, "This lady is nuts, man." I agreed silently.

"Wet blood is seeping from the decaying organs. It appears to have remained fresh as the tissue around it dissolved, leaving the blood exposed for the first time.

"While the degree of decay on this subject appears to be less pronounced than in other bodies we have seen from a distance through the binocs, the end result is certain—the entirety of the body's organs, muscle and other internal tissues will decay and rot until there is nothing left but an epidermal shell. Then, the skin will certainly dissolve over time as well.

"Certain of the bodies we have seen from a distance have been in a state of relative wholeness, while others are left as only a shell. We have not had the opportunity to get this close to any other body, but this particular shell is not rigid apart from the bony frame which holds the skin in place. The skin is still soft," Angel continued as she poked the body with a gloved hand, "despite the decay process, or possibly due to the decay process. Likely, the skin is softer in fresher bodies, possibly indicating that the slow trickle of blood from within is keeping the skin relatively moist until the time when the last organ has decomposed completely."

Angel was disturbingly fascinated by the spectacle. Three days ago, when we first sat down in the Fluxor outside the cabin, Shift described to Street and Angel the first body we saw in the cave near El-Alamein. Then he showed them the photographs Riyad Shafik took of the desert men and the photos we took back on January 6th—four and a half months ago. From that moment on, Angel's appetite for knowledge and her desire to see one of the bodies up close has been growing.

Well, she's in it up to her wrists now—literally. She just stuck her gloved hands inside the body.

MAY 27—JON PORTER, 14-YEAR-OLD SON OF DR. STEVEN PORTER (WEB POST)

Dad, if you're there, I'm so sorry. I know you must be worried and scared. I just read your posts. I didn't have access to them until now. Let me tell you what happened. But first, everything's okay. I'm fine. I'm not sick, but now I've been around more people with the disease—I know it.

Just after my last post to you on May 14, I heard a sound in the house. It freaked me out. I was so scared that I almost puked. It was so different from the sounds of wind and creaking that I was used to. It sounded like breaking glass, but this house is so big that it was more like an echo of breaking glass. I was a wimp and hid in the closet. I was there for a long time without hearing any more sounds. I don't know how long I sat in there, but I had to pee so bad that I had to get out. I shouldn't have done that. I should have just peed myself.

The closet door squeaked when I opened it to come out. Right away I heard the sounds of footsteps running up the stairs from the basement. I ran to the front door to get away from whoever it was that was running after me, but the lights were off so I didn't notice that the door was locked. While I tried to get the door unlocked in the dark, this dude grabbed me from behind. He was huge, but not that strong. I thought that was weird.

I kicked him and he let go of me, but then there was a second guy after me. They caught me again and dragged me out of the house. I would have tried to bite them, but I thought if they were sick or something, that would have been stupid.

They didn't talk to me or to each other, but one of them—I think it was the guy that first caught me—kept coughing. I knew he was sick and that made me scared cuz I was pretty sure I was about to be kidnapped by these guys. I didn't know what they wanted, and they wouldn't tell me. They put me into an old auto that looked like the "Mystery Machine" from those old Scooby-Do cartoons we used to watch. I think it's called a mini-van or something like that. It stunk sooooo bad. They made me lay down on the floor and I think I was laying in blood or puke. It was so nasty it made me hurl. They didn't even care.

After driving for a long time, when it was almost morning, they stopped the Mystery Machine and made me get out. They pushed me into a hotel, up the stairs, and into a big hotel room with couches and stuff. They made me take off all my clothes and take a shower in front of some other people who were watching me—totally grossing me out. I wouldn't have done it dad, but they had a gun pointed at me. There was tons of food and everyone was eating. I was starving but they wouldn't give me any. Then, the one guy who had been coughing before started coughing again. That made everyone there, like ten people, freak out and start running away. They all took off. I didn't know what was going on, but I think when he coughed, all the other people got afraid that they were going to get sick too.

Within a few seconds, the only people left in the hotel room were me and the dude who coughed who had originally caught me back at the Sorenson's house. I didn't know what to do. I just stood there watching him as he coughed more and more. Then, some blood came out of his mouth which freaked *him* out, so he ran away too, leaving me alone.

I took a shower to get his germs off me and washed my clothes in the same shower. Then, when my clothes had dried (I used the hair dryer on the wall in the bathroom), I got dressed, ate as much as I could, stuffed my pockets with more food and left the hotel. I wasn't too worried about being caught again, but I was quiet and checked around corners, being sneaky, like the actors in the holofilms.

Out on the street, I couldn't tell where I was, so I started walking. This small town, just like our neighborhood, was empty. I didn't see or hear anybody alive, but saw lots of dead people. Most of them looked like they were Mexican or from South AM or

Central AM somewhere. That made me think that we had gone south, close to Mexico, but I still couldn't tell. I wish there were road signs like you said were around when you were a kid, 'cuz then I'd know where I was. I don't have any of my personal tech on me—not a phone, tablet, watch or anything else. They're all at home—well, at the Sorenson's home. So, I couldn't even use GPS to tell where I was. And I sure as heck wasn't going to go snatch one off a dead person. Too disgusting.

I kept walking for a few more days. In each town I passed I tried to find food to eat and to take with me. I believed I was going south because of the way the sun was coming up on my left side and setting on my right side. I went that direction on purpose because, while I was standing there naked in front of all those people, they were talking about a colony in Mexico where there was supposed to be lots of people alive. All I heard was that it was supposed to be on the coast of the Gulf of Mexico near a town called Cabo Rojo. If I had any tech, I would have looked it up and downloaded maps. I think I can find it though, but it might take me forever. But that's where I'm going since I've already been dragged so far by the losers that kidnapped me.

After a few days of walking, I got to an old border checkpoint, or at least that's what it looked like. I remember learning about the Mexico-USA border problems in school. I think I crossed into Mexico. So, today I've been walking southeast.

The road I'm on didn't have any houses or buildings for a long time. It's really the middle of nowhere. But, tonight, I finally came to a little town. I don't know its name, but I broke into a nicer house that had a fridge full of food and a computer. I'm using the computer to write this message.

I want you to come find me dad, but I don't know where I am. I do know where I want to go though. I'm headed, hopefully, to Cabo Rojo. I'm going to find a hovercraft and try to fly it. It will have a mapping system. So, I could be to Cabo Rojo within a few days probably. Come find me there dad! I love you!

LATER—DR. STEVEN PORTER (WEB POST)

Son, I'm so glad you are alive!!! I've been at the Sorenson's house for four days, not knowing where to go to search for you, hoping and praying that you would contact me. I'll be packing up now and leaving in a few minutes. Wherever you are, I'll find you, even if it means I have to go all the way to Cabo Rojo.

4

"I can't believe we've been out here for six days already and haven't seen a single living person," I said during dinner tonight. We arrived in Ottawa last night after traveling slowly and exploring methodically along the way.

Strangely, we've found seven separate farms with edible animals and vaccinated all of them. It's strange because there are animals alive, but not humans. Throughout history, plagues often began with animals and then spread to humans. But here, it's been reversed and the animals aren't dying as quickly as the humans. There's probably some explanation, but I'm more interested in the fact that we may have meat in the future, if we survive.

"Yeah, it's bummin' me out," Street said, as he stuffed another bite of canned corn into his mouth.

"What's the latest on Churchill," Anta asked.

"Mike thinks the people are doing just fine," I replied. "Otherwise, if they were dying, the guys would send us up there post haste. No more of this dilly-dallying."

"Oh, is that what we're doing? Dilly-dallying?" Anta teased.

"Funny. You know what I mean."

During a conference with Mike and several of the people at the bunker a few minutes ago, I learned that original estimates of life in Churchill were likely much too high. Their satellite visuals are very poor in the area due to dense cloud cover and the remote location of the area. Plus, most people in the world still alive are not likely outside moving around, but instead, hoping for a signal or word to arrive that vaccinations are on the way. Estimates are now closer to 300–350 living rather than the previous estimate of as many as 1,500. But they don't think people are sick.

"Has Mike been able to get in touch with anyone up there yet?" Anta asked.

"No. They've tried to contact people up there over and over, with no luck."

Thankfully, even though the world's population has crashed, electronic systems are up and running as if nothing has happened. Technological advancements have allowed for the automated running of systems which, until the 2040's and 2050's, had to be maintained by human hands and minds. This is a wonderful situation of which we hope to take advantage. Of course, communication systems can, and do, still crash, and can be tampered with and shut down. But that hasn't happened and now there is really no person alive to screw anything up . . . we hope.

But even with technology running smoothly, and Mike and others like him around the world broadcasting day and night through every avenue available, nobody in Churchill has responded.

The message being sent informs people that a vaccine has been created. It urges them to stay indoors and contact a central communication databank, developed by Mike, with locations and other information which will help us to locate and vaccinate.

Over the past six days, the databank has recorded the locations of only 1,236 living people, all very far away from us—mostly in Africa and Asia. Of course, it's still early in the game and certainly many more will log on as they learn of the databank's existence, or happen upon it accidentally. Once a person has logged on, he or she is instructed to update their situation daily. If a person fails to update daily, they will be presumed sick or dead and no contact will be attempted.

MAY 29—JON PORTER (WEB POST)

Dad, I'm sorry it's been so long—again. I got your message today. I probably would've got it sooner, but there was no data access along my route after my last post, until I got here. Whatever town I was in last time I messaged you had data, but not the other towns along my road to Cabo Rojo. I didn't know that was even possible. Must be like the ancient times when you were a kid. ☺

I found a hover and learned how to fly it. It wasn't very hard. The mapping system took me right to Cabo Rojo. After a few hours searching along the beach, I found the "secret" bunker. I found some information about the bunker on the web, while I was traveling in the hover. I learned that there was a secret password for access to the bunker; but I couldn't find out what the password was. When I got here, I could see cameras. I stood in front of them for like four hours or something, waving and yelling, trying to get the attention of anybody inside.

Finally, the door opened. It sounded like tons of locks were being opened from the inside. When the door opened, I heard and felt a swoosh of air, and then a little girl fell forward. I barely caught her as she fell. She had blood coming from her mouth and nose and she kept coughing—just like all the other people that are dead now. I was scared to have her so close to me, but I began to think about all the people who had coughed on me, or breathed on me over the past few months, and I never got sick. So, I pulled her inside and shut the door.

I hope you're on your way here because everybody that was here is dead. The girl, named Rosa, is only nine years old and is the last person alive here (that's what she told me anyway). She's able to talk, but just barely, and her English isn't that good. There aren't any translation pads around that I can see. Good thing we lived in Nevada and half my friends spoke Spanish.

Anyway, Rosa told me that there were lots of people here, and they weren't letting anyone else in after the news said that so many people were sick. But a small group of people convinced someone to let them in a few days ago. One of them must have been sick because everybody started getting sick and dying. I've wondered if that was maybe the people from the hotel a few days ago.

I've been trying to help Rosa for the last few hours, but she looks like she won't live very long. It stinks in here and I haven't even explored this place. It seems huge. It's mostly underground I think, and right on the edge of the Gulf of Mexico. But I haven't left this room at the entrance because I've been trying to learn all I can from Rosa. When she dies, I'll look around, but I'm nervous. I don't know what I'll find.

At least it's not dark. It seems like all the
electrical stuff is working. I'm going to
look for a phone or a holo. How can I contact
you to give you coordinates?"

MAY 30—ANTA

We were just com'd by Dr. Porter. He found his son! They're both in some kind of bunker in Mexico, on the Gulf. They're safe, apparently, and he thinks his son must be immune. Apparently, he's been in close physical contact with a lot of sick people and hasn't caught the disease himself. Dr. Porter will be working with Dr. Shevchuk to see whether giving the vaccination to his son could cause any harm in the event his son is immune. Great news!

After our com, I told Shift how I thought any family with more than one survivor is very lucky. He reminded me that I'm in one of those families. The reminder hit me hard. I have been so lucky, or blessed, or whatever in my life. Now, when the entirety of the world has perished, not only am I still alive, but so is my brother.

While I'm not optimistic that I'll ever see Hasani again, it is remarkable to think that I am one of the lucky ones—if only losing half of one's family makes one "lucky".

I've been thinking a great deal lately about the future of our world. It appears that those of us still alive should be able to survive, at least for a while. But unless we can band together with other survivors, it will be difficult to maintain our prior way of life, or anything like it. While some of the brightest minds on our planet have survived—in our bunker and others—are there any people still alive who know how to farm, or maintain electrical grids, or fix machines, or any of the other skills necessary to sustain a society? I hope so. Otherwise, we're in trouble, again.

5

"We're here guys!" Street said.

"How many people?" Mike asked, nearly shouting. The anxiety in his voice betrayed his emotions.

"Well," Shift replied, slowly, "there are 131 people alive."

"No." Mike looked sick. He sat down, hard, and put his face in his hands.

"Mike," Shift said. "Mike, listen to me."

Mike looked up, ghostly white, with tears forming in the corners of his eyes.

"There's 131 people here *alive*! *You* did that! You found this place and watched it. You sent us here, of all places. You're the reason we got here in time to find anybody alive at all!"

Several people murmured assent. John put his hand on Mike's shoulder and squeezed.

"So, Anthrax E reached Churchill?" Dr. Shevchuk said quietly, almost to himself.

"Yes, it did," replied Anta, "but more recently than most of the world, thankfully. We've been told that people started to die only six days ago. Mike, you couldn't see people dying. You were right to have us looking everywhere along the way. How would we all feel if we missed someone in one of those towns? This isn't your fault. We found

131 people Mike! Think of that. That's 131 people who, hopefully, will live to help us save the world."

"That's right, dude," Shift added. "If you hadn't done your job, and hadn't found this place and tracked it so closely, there would be nobody alive here. We've vaccinated every one of them. The only problem is that some of them already show signs of contamination."

"That's something we've been discussing here," John said. "We don't know, because there is no test data to tell us, whether any of those already contaminated will live. But we're all alive, and we were all contaminated before we were immunized. So there's hope."

"That's right," replied Dr. Shevchuk. "I think you four should stay there and see what happens. We need to know whether vaccinating someone who is already sick will do any good. I know it's terrible to think about, but we shouldn't be wasting precious medicine on those who cannot benefit from it. We have a finite supply. Some of the material utilized to create the vaccine cannot be machined. Some of it is living organism which must be harvested. I don't have any more."

"Okay, we'll stay here for a few more days until we can determine who is going to live," Shift said. "But tell us what to look for. We need to know what information to provide you."

"Well, it's rather simple really," Dr. Shevchuk said. "Just document who was vaccinated, how long they had felt sick before inoculation, any transformations or problems seen following the injections, who dies, if any, and when they die. I'll send you a detailed list of other physical signs to look for when we're done here.

"What we want to be able to do is determine if, at any point, it is too late to vaccinate. It may be that they can be sick for a couple of days and still live. Obviously, the vaccination is not a cure. If a body has gone too far in the stages of decomposition, there's no turning back. So I suspect that anybody who has been sick for more than a couple of days will not live. It's your job to help us find out."

"By the way," Street said, "on our way up here, we saw three polar bears, all together. A couple of young ones, probably with their mother. It was awesome!"

"Did you go vaccinate them?" John asked, smiling.

"Uhhh, no," Street replied. "We're not idiots."

"That's important news, Street, and definitely awesome," Dr. Shevchuk said. "As you know, while most animals, including mammals, *can* be infected by Anthrax E, it's still unclear which animals, apart from saltwater fish and other marine animals, are hearty enough to survive."

"Well, so far, at least three polar bears are alive!" Street looked happy, like a small child at the zoo.

JUNE 10—SHIFT

"I'm sorry to be so blunt, but what's the final tally Shift?" John asked.

"Sixty-three," I replied, solemnly.

"Actually dead, or dying?"

"Dead or showing progressive symptoms."

Of the 131 people we vaccinated against Anthrax E, only sixty-eight will live, or at least, we hope that many will live. Dr. Shevchuk has determined that the death rate has more to do with the advancement of the disease within a body at the time of inoculation than it has to do with the vaccination itself. I'm sure he's right. Upon our arrival in Churchill, seventy-one of the 131 people already presented with varying degrees of illness—coughing, blood, headaches, etc. Dr. Shevchuk had theorized, and will now likely conclude that once the actual signs of illness have set in, particularly after the initial twenty-four hours, chances of survival are very low.

But, just because a person has been infected doesn't mean that person will die. While seventy-one people showed signs of illness, certainly many others had been infected by Anthrax E, but just hadn't become symptomatic yet. Of the sixty-three who have died since our arrival, or are close to death, sixty-two of them already showed signs of illness at the time of their vaccination.

"So, are you ready to get out of there?" John asked.

"We're leaving in the morning," I said. "We'll be leaving the three extra hovers here and just taking the Fluxor. And we're not taking anybody else with us either. When we first got here, we had considered taking at least one of the extra hovercraft back with us in case we had a breakdown or something. But we've learned that because roads are so scarce and automotive vehicles aren't really needed here, there are only a handful of vehicles of any type. Only two of them have long-term travel capacity. So we've just decided to leave all the extra hovercraft in Churchill for their future use, for whatever purpose and need may arise."

"That's probably a good idea. Have you and Mike talked about where to go next?" John asked.

"Yup. He's sending us southeast, around the coast of Hudson Bay. He's going to have us stop at all of the small towns along the way. I think he hopes there will be other towns that were insulated from the disease, like Churchill was."

"I hope so too," John said, sincerely. "A.E.'s a bitch."

"A.E.?" I asked.

"Oh yeah," John replied, "Mike started calling Anthrax E 'A.E.' a couple days ago. He thinks it sounds cooler and it's definitely easier to say."

"Sure, I guess," I said. "Maybe it will catch."

"Ultimately," I continued, "our goal is to reach Quebec and then Nova Scotia within a week. Of course, the timing depends on who we meet along the way, if anybody. Luckily, we won't have to stick around after vaccinations, like we did here. We have the data. We know it works. Now we're going to speed up the process."

"Sounds like a good plan," John said. "So, do you want to know the latest on the Toronto folks?"

"Yeah, but let me get the others in here first. Hold on."

It took me a few minutes to find the others. Anta and Angel were packing up and saying goodbye to some of the folks here in Churchill. Street was at the bar, but thankfully, not drunk.

"Okay John, we're all here," I said into the MEHD after I'd gathered Street, Anta and Angel together.

"Hi everyone," John said. "I wanted to give you an update on what's happening with the Toronto people. As you know, twelve of them were inoculated nineteen days ago. Eighteen days ago, eight of those people left their bunker to begin searching for survivors. Four traveled southwest toward Detroit; two traveled west along the U.S.-Canadian border; and two went northwest toward Alaska. You know all of that already.

"Last we heard, two days ago, those three teams combined had vaccinated 141 people—in two and a half weeks. Of those 141 people, 113 survived the next twenty-four hours."

"Wow," Anta said, "That's pretty good odds. Do we know how many of those 141 people were already infected?"

"Yes, we do," John replied. "Thirty-three of them already showed symptoms. So, of those thirty-three, twenty-eight died. The Toronto bunker didn't keep real precise records, but it appears that most of those twenty-eight had already been symptomatic for at least twenty-four hours. So, as we had predicted a couple of days ago, if we can get to people within twenty-four hours of the first physical signs of illness, the person has a good chance of surviving."

"John," Anta said, "you told us a few days ago that the Toronto group was handing out vaccines to those already inoculated, and sending them out too. Is that still happening?"

Anta and I had been concerned about that decision from the start. So far, we don't have any news on whether it's been a good thing or a bad thing.

"Yes Anta, it's still happening," John replied. "And I hate it, from a scientific perspective. From the perspective of the survival of the human race, however, it seems like a good idea. You see, we don't have contact with any of those people who've been inoculated, or the original teams. We only have contact with the Toronto bunker; and the bunker only has contact with the original eight people from their bunker. So we have statistics and information about the original people being inoculated, assuming the information being relayed to us from Toronto is accurate. But we don't have any information about how many people, if any, are being vaccinated by those who received their inoculations from the original eight. That's why the plan sucks from a scientific standpoint. But, as you can imagine, in terms of humanity, the more people who are vaccinated the better."

"I still don't like the idea," Anta said. "If we can't keep tabs on anybody, what happens when we've found everybody still alive and need to regroup and rebuild our society? I guess that's pretty trivial at this point. But those things worry me some. I agree, though, that from the standpoint of human life, it's probably a good idea to spread the vaccine the way they are doing it. And, now that we have some fairly good statistics, maybe keeping all the vaccines in-house, so to speak, isn't necessary."

"Well, should we start handing out vaccines?" Street asked. He has been torn between the two viewpoints as well, just like the rest of us.

"I don't know," replied John. "I know Yurgi doesn't want you to do that. Most of the others here in the bunker agree with Anta's concerns. My thought is this: if you inoculate someone who you believe could, and would be able to safely vaccinate others, and won't waste the precious and scarce resource, let 'em at it. How does that sound?"

"I think that's a good plan," I said. "We still have thousands of doses. Better to use them than to sit around a month from now wondering what to do with them because everybody is already dead. One of the residents here has medical background and appears to be in charge, so maybe we'll leave a package of a hundred vaccinations with him."

"Did Lucky or Yurgi ever figure out how Anthrax E, er . . . A.E., was released into the bunker?" Angel asked.

"Nope. Still a mystery."

"That's crazy," I said. "Are you guys worried about whether you're safe with some maniac running around in there?"

"I'm not," John said. "I'm not a little pansy like you." He smiled, clearly ribbing me.

"Well, don't come crying to us when your heads start getting chopped off," I said. "We're kind of busy out here."

6

"What was that?" Shift asked in a whisper from across the room.

"It sounded like breaking glass," I replied, as I sat up in bed. The sound was strange because we knew there was nobody alive in town. It scared me.

Yesterday afternoon, we arrived at the southern tip of James Bay, at the south end of Hudson Bay. The little town was beautiful, but empty. There were some broken windows and a bit of paper floating down the street on the breeze. Flowers were in bloom everywhere. It just looked like a normal town, but wholly deserted. Really, it was no different than all the other towns we'd traveled through over the past few days.

After arriving, we searched the town for survivors, using some old loudspeakers we picked up a couple days after leaving the bunker. This had become standard protocol, but hadn't produced any results yet. After searching for nearly three hours, nobody responded here either.

Concluding that we were alone, with dark approaching, we found a small, cozy tourist motel for the night. Even though a few of the rooms had dead bodies in them, we easily located two clean and empty adjoining rooms. I quickly fell into a fitful sleep—a form of sleep from which I have suffered nearly every night since January. My sleep is always light, and for good reason I guess.

"Stay there, let me check it out," Shift whispered.

Yeah, right. Shift crept out of bed and slowly tip-toed to the window. I stepped behind him two seconds later.

Feeling my hand on his back, Shift looked back over his shoulder at me. He smiled. He must have known I wouldn't sit in bed while he checked out the noise. Shift reached up and parted the curtains just enough for both of us to peak out.

Street, seemingly brave in the face of all adversity, had left his room and was outside on the balcony near the stairs. As we peered out into the darkness of James Bay, we could see his still form leaning against the railing, looking down to the ground below.

I turned from the window to find my jeans. I was going out there too. Less than twenty seconds later, while I was fastening my belt, Shift jumped back from the window letting out a high-pitched and very unmanly shriek.

"What?" I asked, trying not to laugh at the noise he had made.

Instead of answering, he took two steps toward the door and opened it, letting Street in. Street's face was ashen, and surprisingly fearful. I'd never seen that look on Street's tough-guy face. He was clearly scared of something.

"Dude, what's wrong?" Shift asked as Street turned without speaking and locked the door.

Angel came through the adjoining door to our room. "Angel, go lock the door, then come back." Street's voice was a little shaky.

"Why, what's wrong?"

"There was a guy out there . . ." Street replied.

"So what?" Angel interrupted in the blunt manner that we had all grown accustomed to.

"Just do it . . . now," Street barked. Angel jumped at Street's tone, then hurried into the adjoining room, returning quickly.

"Ok. Locked. What's going on?"

"The guy was naked. Well, mostly naked. He had boxers or something on, and a hat. But that wasn't the freaky part." Street was calming down.

"So what was it?" I asked.

"Well, after I woke up; I guess you all heard the window break? Anyway, I jumped out of bed, grabbed my gun, and ran outside. Probably a stupid thing to do; but I figured since there was nobody around, it was probably just an animal. I thought I might be able to get us some fresh meat. So, I got outside and heard sounds coming from below, on the ground floor. I leaned over the railing to see what was down there. That's when I saw the guy.

"Just as my eyes were finally adjusting to the darkness down there, he jumped back out of the motel through a window. I mean, he literally jumped. He was carrying a human body. Pretty tough dude, I thought. Still, I wasn't too worried. I actually thought it was good cuz maybe it meant there were some people alive here. But then he carried the body, a woman it looked like, across the parking lot and dropped her onto the grass over by the side of the road. Then he bent down over her. I thought that was weird. If she was alive, why would he drop her? So I thought maybe she was already dead. But then, why would he carry her out of the motel if she was dead?"

"So . . ." Angel started to interrupt, but Street went on as if she hadn't.

"Even though it's pretty dark over there on the grass—hard to see—it looked like the naked dude started to eat her. Seriously."

"What are you talking about?" Angel asked, clearly not believing the story.

"He was like a wild animal, Angel. He was eating that girl!"

Even if Street didn't see what he thought he saw, I was concerned. I crept back to the window.

"He's gone Anta," Street said. "I shouted to him and he ran away."

"Yeah, doesn't look like he's out there now; but neither is any woman's body," I said.

"Maybe he came back and got her," Street said, nervous.

"Let's go check it out," I said. "Maybe he's still around."

"Uh, I don't want to go out there Anta," Street replied. "There was something very weird and scary about him. I don't know what it was, and I ain't no wimp, you know, but something tells me we should stay in here, at least until morning."

"Okay Street, if that's what you think we should do, I trust you. Let's stay in here until first light."

Street visibly relaxed after I agreed with him. Frankly, if Street was that scared of something, I wasn't too inclined to argue about it.

If Street did, indeed, see the man eat another human body, I can only speculate regarding the cause of such an atrocity. Of course, my speculation is only that; but if a man has become so desperate that he's now eating diseased, dead, human bodies, then such a man is in awful straits and I don't wish to approach him with a vaccination. I hope that we don't run into him tomorrow on our way out of town.

JUNE 12—SHIFT

The half-naked man from yesterday never reappeared and the only sign that he had been there was the broken window—broken from the inside—and some flattened grass where he had laid the body in the field. There may have been blood on some of the grass, but it was hard to tell.

Our travel went smoothly from Hudson Bay to Mistassini. We were traveling very slowly, past and through small towns and rural villages. As we passed through those fairly isolated communities, I couldn't help but think about all the innocent human life lost.

The people in those towns never did anything to deserve their fate. They probably just led their lives, peacefully, fishing or farming, or whatever it is they do up here in these small Canadian towns. When A.E. arrived, they probably didn't even know what had hit them.

Nobody in any of the towns we've passed through have responded to our calls through the speakers. Seeing no life, and having no report from Mike that any life exists in most of them, we rarely stop, except to get supplies and eat as necessary.

Tonight, Mike informed us that our next stop with people presumably alive will be Labrador City. There, we hope to find as many as 150 living, although those numbers are today's numbers, not tomorrow's. Mike also surprised us with the news that they have finally made contact with Anta's brother on the moon, although the connection was weak and faded in and out. We hope to be linked up with them soon.

7

"Hasani! I'm so glad to see you again!" I said, unable to contain my excitement.

"Anta, you look great!" Hasani replied, obviously equally excited.

"These are my colleagues and friends," I continued. "You know Shift; and this is Dr. Angel Robertson and Mr. Threet "Street" Kimball."

"The American football player?"

"Yes, the American football player. But he's much more than that."

Street ducked his head to try to get out of the Holo image. I didn't know the guy was bashful. A recent development?

"Then let me introduce my friends," Hasani said. "This is Dr. Jonas Sampson, from the United States." Hasani pointed to a handsome man, probably forty-five to fifty years old, wearing wire-rimmed glasses. He had dark brown hair, cut short and parted down the middle. He had an intense, but kind look. "He's an astrophysicist by trade and is the wonderful man who found the rest of us and told us what was going on in the early days.

"This is Dr. Thomas Bird and Misty Bird, also from the United States. Dr. Bird is a physician, specializing in family medicine. Misty is a former CEO of some major corporation and an amazing cook, despite our limited cooking resources here."

The Birds were an older couple, probably in their early seventies. Mrs. Bird had that kind, gentle, grandmotherly look. I liked her without her having said a single word. Dr. Bird was, likewise, a kind-looking older man. As a doctor, I imagined his patients loved and cared for him, and likely trusted him completely.

"And this is Dr. Jerad Beaudoin, from Gorges, France," Hasani continued. "Dr. Beaudoin is a shuttle pilot and aeronautical engineer." Dr. Beaudoin, unlike the others, was stern-looking and stood tall and firm. He had the appearance of one who felt he had earned respect, and thus, demanded it.

"It's nice to meet you all," I said. I meant it.

Previously, I had spoken with my brother, Hasani, through the holos, but all other communications with the group on the moon had been made via the various logs and databases set up for such communication. This was a real treat.

After a few more pleasantries, and catching up a bit, Hasani told us that Dr. Sampson, Dr. Bird and Dr. Beaudoin had just created E-rase utilizing the formulations and methods discovered by Dr. Shevchuk! They told Shevchuk and the others at the bunker yesterday. They're somewhat wary of using it, though, because they have nobody on which to first test it. I get that.

"I don't know much about the formulations," Shift began, "but I thought there was some 'ingredient' that was a little hard to come by, even on Earth. You must have found some of it."

"Yes, we did," Dr. Bird replied. "We had to search all of the unoccupied shells. One of them was a botanical farm. We are very fortunate."

"So, what are you going to do now—I mean, to test it?" Angel asked. "What if the disease manifests in the test subject?" Again, Angel's curiosity in matters of morbidity was fascinating. The look on her face as she asked those questions, which continued as she received an answer, was grossly intriguing.

"I'm going to be injected," Hasani said.

Whoa.

"Hasani, I don't think . . ." I began. But he cut me off mid-sentence.

"Anta, I know what you think," Hasani said. "This is dangerous. I could die. We could all die. I'm all you've got left. I know. But everybody here has lost all of their loved ones. My life is no more valuable than theirs. I feel like, somehow, it's my duty to do this."

I didn't reply, but instead, looked down. I didn't know whether Hasani saw it, but a tear slipped down my check and dropped into my lap.

So Hasani volunteered to be injected with their version of E-rase. He will be isolated, then injected, and will stay locked up until they are sure it did not infect him—five or six days from now—pursuant to detailed instructions from Dr. Shevchuk. Then, Hasani will leave his isolation unit and enter an outpost containing a deceased, diseased body. He will be required to get up close and personal with the body, to be sure the live bacteria has entered his body. He'll stay there for eight more days awaiting infection or proof that the vaccine was properly created.

Within fourteen days, they, and hopefully we, will have the good news that all is well for them and they will be able to travel freely among the moon colonies, for whatever purposes they may have for doing so.

"So, what are you going to do if it works?" Shift asked.

"Well, we've been doing a lot of work up here to try to figure out what resources the various shells have available," Dr. Sampson said. "What we'd like to do is come home."

"Is that possible?" Shift asked.

"I think that it is," replied Dr. Beaudoin with a charming French accent. "It is a simple matter of piloting a craft back to Earth, which I have done and am fully capable of doing again. Assuming there are still operational craft, that is. And we have no reason to believe that the various craft at the international station are in any state of disrepair."

"Wow!" Shift remarked. "That would be amazing! Right Anta?"

"Yes," I choked out. After composing myself a moment, I continued, "Hasani, you have always been the bravest of our family. I'm proud of you. Come home safe to me."

"Thanks Anta. I will."

"How did you guys get back in contact with the bunker anyway?" Shift asked.

"It's a wonderful story, Shift," Hasani replied. "As you know, the connection has been down for a long time—I think it went down in mid-March, if I'm not mistaken. But none of us are so-called 'computer geeks'. We didn't know why or how it had happened. We were eventually able to trace our connection to a central hub somewhere in the international station. But we couldn't see exactly where the line was broken. Of course, even if we knew where the problem was, there's no way for us to get there yet. It's too dangerous without the inoculation. Anyway, two days ago, Mrs. Bird was checking the monitor and saw the line come back on. She called us all in and we watched the line go in and out for a few minutes. Then it stayed on."

"What have you found out about it?" I asked.

"Well, that's the wonderful part of this. There's someone else alive here!"

"Really?" Angel asked.

"Yes, really," Hasani replied. "Because we had a connection again, we started hitting all the channels trying to find someone. We learned afterward that another gentleman was doing the same. Finally, we got him. He's in the German outpost. Alone unfortunately. But he's alive and healthy! He said he has been trying to contact his colleagues in Brazil, but has been unable to do so for some time. He said they abandoned him, whatever he meant by that."

"Yeah, what does that mean?" Shift asked.

"Well," Hasani said, "I asked him but he ignored it. It was kind of like he didn't want to talk about it. So we let it go. We've all been abandoned here after all."

"Maybe he's immune," Angel said.

"Yeah, maybe," Hasani said. "Or maybe he has been using canned air and wearing a space suit all this time. I'll certainly be asking. Anyway, he said he found the connection problem and fixed it and that was when we saw the connection go live again."

"So, what are you going to do about the guy? What do you know about him?" I asked.

"His name is Alan Stein. He's from Connecticut," Dr. Sampson replied. "And we know he's a computer guy with some governmental agency. We know he's healthy, but scared and alone. At least he says he's healthy. We weren't on a holo, so we couldn't actually see the guy. He's been alone for months."

"If he's from Connecticut, why did he say he was trying to contact colleagues in Brazil who abandoned him?" I asked.

"Hmm, we hadn't thought about that," Dr. Sampson replied for Hasani. "We'll ask him a bit more about himself when we talk again. He sounded pretty tired. He wants us to come get him, or to tell him how to get to us."

"But you can't do that yet, right?" I asked. "Not until you know the vaccine works."

"Right," Dr. Sampson replied. "Not until we know the vaccine works. Until then, we'll stay in contact with him. We'll go get him after your brother comes home from his little trip in a few days, healthy and happy."

Meanwhile, here on Earth, we have work to do.

We arrived at Labrador City this afternoon to find only ninety-seven people alive. Of those living, sixty-eight showed signs of illness, and it's quite possible that the remainder have already been infected. Of course, we vaccinated them all. We'll soon know what happens, but not from personal observation.

We're going to continue to move, hoping that we might reach more people before it's too late. We spent too long getting to Churchill, and too long in Churchill. That almost certainly cost the lives of some of the people there, and here. There doesn't seem to be any reason to stay to watch the results when whatever happens will happen regardless of where we are. So, we'll move on in the morning. We're headed to Baie-Comeau, where Mike has seen evidence of life. We're leaving six hundred doses of the vaccine here.

8

"Where'd they go?" Street asked.

"They just disappeared," Angel replied.

"They didn't *disappear*," Street said in exasperation. "That's impossible."

"Is it?" Angel asked, with a slight twitch in the corner of her mouth.

Anta and I sat there quietly listening to this exchange. Dr. Angel Robertson is one of the leading researchers in what has lately been called "supernatural" genetics. I doubted that anybody alive really understood what that term meant, apart from Angel. I certainly didn't. But I read some of her published research weeks ago in the bunker. She believes that there are various genetic mutations within our society that may cause certain individuals to exhibit physical capabilities beyond the "normal" limit of human ability.

"Anyway," Street continued, "whatever happened to them, they're not here anymore."

None of us could argue with that.

Late this morning, as we pulled into a town called Baie-Comeau, on the northwest coast of the Gulf of St. Lawrence, we saw people in the distance, running. We sped after them, but by the time we arrived at the place we'd last seen them, they were gone. We searched all of the buildings in the area to no avail.

Then, and now, I can't understand why they didn't answer our calls or come out to greet our vehicle. Surely we didn't all have the same errant vision of the existence of human life in the distance. They did exist.

JUNE 15, LATE EVENING
BAIE-COMEAU—SHIFT

"Hey guys, we got your message about the disappearing people," Mike said. He looked excited about something. John was sitting next to him, legs bouncing.

Tonight, after losing sight of those people, and searching Baie-Comeau in vain for them, we found a seaside hotel towering over every other building in town. Street broke into the stairway leading up to the roof. We spent a warm evening on the roof looking for signs of human life in the streets below. I sent Mike a message, telling him about what we saw, and asking him to give me a call when he had a minute. We wanted to know whether he could figure out what happened to everybody here.

"Yeah, weird stuff," I said. "What are you two so excited about?"

"Actually, we've been seeing disappearing people for a couple of days, but until now, I couldn't decide if I was seeing glitches in the system or reality. Now I think it's reality."

"What do you mean?" Angel asked.

"Well," Mike continued, "we've observed human activity in your area, as you know, and we continue to do so. That's why we sent you there. But we've been unable to get an accurate count of the numbers of living. The strangest thing is not that the people seem to disappear, but that our surveillance continues to pick them up and then lose them over and over again.

"Baie-Comeau doesn't have cameras, so we've been relying on satellite imagery, which is very detailed and can pinpoint an individual on the street with ease. But the people we've seen there will appear on the street, and then, rounding a corner, disappear. Maybe they go into a building; but I don't think that's always the case."

"Why not?" Anta asked.

"It just seems like there are too many people getting away from us. Every time we see a new person, he or she comes onto the screen, rapidly, and then, just as rapidly, he or she is gone. It's not like they're moving into a building where we lose sight of them. They just get away. One guy actually seemed to just disappear, right off the street—a real big dude."

"Do you have any theories?" Angel asked excitedly, rocking slightly on the balls of her feet.

"Not really," Mike replied. "But some of the people we've observed appear to have strange gait patterns and other bizarre movements too. Some of them have been very quick, running faster than I've ever seen a human run. And lots of them are a bit on the naked side."

"What did you just say?" Anta asked, as if she hadn't actually heard what we all just heard.

"I said some of them aren't wearing much clothing. They're mostly naked."

"Mike, didn't we tell you about that guy a few days ago, who Street saw eating a woman?" I asked.

"Yeah, you did," he replied.

"We must not have told you about him being mostly naked," I said.

"No, you didn't. How interesting."

"Interesting?" Street said. "I'd call it more than interesting. The dude was naked. And he was fast. He totally ate that chick. We're probably not safe, right?"

"This is kind of creepy," I said. My arms were covered with goosebumps, like when I was a kid hearing ghost stories around the campfire during scout camps in Colorado.

After that conversation with Mike and John, none of us can sleep. I'm not too comfortable here, knowing that there are super-fast, disappearing, human-eating people around. It seems too much like a horror story—too much like a zombie movie.

Of course, zombies aren't real. There's no scientific (or spiritualistic) basis for the premise that a human can die, and then come back to life, but not really be alive. Nevertheless, these are the things that keep running through my mind as I sit here tonight watching for these people from the roof. None of us dare go out into the town, and none of us dare go to sleep. We barricaded the door to the roof from the outside using furniture from downstairs. We're scared enough to be more watchful and cautious.

JUNE 16, 12:35AM
BAIE-COMEAU—SHIFT

"Look down there," Angel whispered excitedly. "People."

"Where?" I asked, scanning the dark street below. Angel handed me her binocs, pointed to the park, and then ran over to wake Street and Anta who were trying to sleep nearby, here on the roof. "I see them," I said, looking through the binocs.

Anta, Street and Angel all arrived back at the wall I was huddled behind, just as I pointed to where I could see movement on the grass next to the street. There was a full moon, so with the binocs we could easily see two men as they walked around, in and out of the shadows of a dense tree near the road that wound around the city park. We wouldn't have necessarily known that they were men from this distance, but they weren't wearing shirts, and they didn't look very womanly.

"What are they doing?" Anta asked, wiping the sleep from her eyes. She must have finally dozed off.

"They look like they're just talking to each other," Angel said. "Are they wearing sunglasses? In the middle of the night?"

"Strange," Street said. "And they're both bald."

As we continued to watch the men in the park, a manhole cover in the middle of the road next to them opened up. Two more men and one woman ascended from the depths of the sewer system—all wearing sunglasses, in various states of dress, and all bald.

"The sewers," Anta said. She was now wide awake and was looking through her binocs, too. "That explains Mike's mystery of how they get away from him so quickly. They just drop into a hole."

"Holy . . ." I caught myself. I try not to cuss.

We watched in disbelief, none of us speaking, as the last man to rise from the sewer—a huge man—effortlessly dragged an apparently-lifeless human body behind him with one hand. His strength was remarkable—to be able to drag a human up a ladder from below the street, one-handed.

After a few seconds, one man dove at the body and began to bite at it. "Whoa! That's what I saw before," Street whispered, as if we needed reminding.

We watched in horror as all five of them began to gnaw and chew on the body!

"What's going on?" Angel asked, trying to whisper, her voice betraying disturbing emotion. "Who are these people? Are they even people?"

It was strange to hear surprise and turmoil in Angel's voice. She had handled the events of the last few days with grace, like she knew it could happen. But as she watched human cannibals attack another human, her excitement seemed to give way to fear.

"Whatever they are, I'm sure that I don't want to meet them," I replied very quietly.

As we watched the scene below, we made certain to stay as concealed as possible, and I don't think we were seen. Unfortunately, it's nighttime. We have agreed to wait until morning to take our leave from Baie-Comeau. Our goal has suddenly changed. We just want to get away from here, alive.

While we wait tonight, our friends back at the bunker have begun to research and search for similar patterns of human activity elsewhere in the area. What is going on? Why were they in the sewer? Why were they bald? Why were they all wearing sunglasses? Was the body dead or alive? And why were they eating a human? I hope Mike and John can make sense of it. I'm freaked.

JUNE 16, 6:05AM
BAIE-COMEAU—ANTA

"Anta, get the others up. We have something very important to discuss," Dr. Yurgi Shevchuk said.

It was my turn to be on "watch". That word makes it sound like we're in some kind of horror or war movie, but we're not—this is real life. The fact that somebody is actually on "watch", or that we *have* to be on watch, is daunting. It had started to rain. A light sprinkle partially obscured my view of the street below, but I hadn't seen anything all night.

I kicked Street and nudged Shift gently. Angel was a light sleeper. I knew my words alone would wake her. "Hey, wake up. Mike and Yurgi are on the coms."

Shift, Street and Angel were asleep on the roof, using blankets and pillows we procured from downstairs before blocking the roof access door.

"We're here guys. What's going on?" Shift asked moments later, trying to cover his head with a blanket to keep the rain off.

"We've been tracking the people you saw," Mike replied. "We've tracked them back several days. We know where they came from and Yurgi has a theory about why they may have behaved the way they did."

I'm rather unfamiliar with how Mike's tracking systems operate. Shift tried to explain it to me a while back, but I was too busy watching him to pay attention to what he was saying. I love to watch him "lecture". That's when he's in his element, and he seems to really love it.

Anyway, Mike explained again how he hacked into and reprogrammed existing surveillance systems to locate human movement. When human movement is registered, the system locks onto that person and follows him or her. That is how he's been able to tell us when the human life in a city has decreased before our arrival.

It's not a perfect system. A person has to move outdoors or stand in a window or doorway in order to be seen in the first place. Then, if the person goes back indoors or moves out of sight, he or she is lost. But the system locks onto the building the person entered, waiting for movement to begin outside again. Thus, they've been able to track these five people fairly well.

"Don't keep us in suspense Mike," Shift said.

"Okay. Sorry. All five individuals came east together just south of the United States border with Canada, from Toronto."

"Toronto," I said under my breath.

"They were vaccinated on May 23rd by one of the original Toronto groups in a suburb just south of the Toronto bunker."

"So, did something go wrong with the vaccination or what?" Shift asked.

"Well, the vaccination *process* went smoothly enough. But over the next few days, their movements became more erratic. They began to quarrel with each other. But they still traveled together, eastward.

"In a recording from May 29th, we saw their first approach toward another human body—a dead man. The surveillance system recorded a couple of them licking and nibbling the fingers and other various body parts of the deceased man. But they soon moved on, leaving the body relatively intact."

"That's messed up," Street said, wrinkling his nose.

"It gets worse," John said as he moved into our view on the screen for the first time.

"Yup," Mike said. "On June 2nd, they attacked a lifeless body and ate portions of it. Since that time, they've become faster and more animated in their movements. They've gained tremendous strength, pushing doors down and dragging bodies down the street. On June 3rd, some of them first began to abandon some of their clothing and wear sunglasses, for no apparent reason. Over those days, they were all losing their hair too."

"That's incredible!" Angel said, "And rather disturbing."

"Yes, Angel, it is," Dr. Shevchuk replied. "But in this case, 'incredible' does not denote a positive situation."

"So, what's your theory Yurgi?" Shift asked.

"Remember, it's just a theory at this time, but we will be contacting Toronto to discuss it with them. I believe that the vaccination strain used by the Toronto bunker may not be exactly correct. It is, perhaps, saving the lives of the people into whom it is injected, but perhaps the lives it is saving are not worth living."

Mike picked up where Yurgi left off. "In any event, they certainly aren't 'zombies' Shift. I'm sorry to let you down like that." Mike smiled. Shift smiled too. But the joke wasn't very funny.

"They haven't died and then reanimated," Mike continued. "They're human, and they never died in the first place. They were some of the lucky, or maybe unlucky survivors of A.E."

Mike and his team will continue to monitor the progress and movement of these five whatever-they-are. More importantly, however, they are now going to begin tracking the movements of the three original Toronto groups and all those whom they've vaccinated over the past four weeks. Yurgi also hopes to enlist the help of the Toronto folks to try to figure out what, if anything, went wrong.

I hope—we all hope—that these five humanoids are the only beings of their kind, and that Toronto has not erred in some terrible way. Of course, since Street already saw similar activity five days ago, a long way from here, and Mike observed peculiar movements in others yesterday, I'm afraid these five are not alone.

9

Today, we continued our travel in a generally southwest direction along the coast of the Gulf of St. Lawrence, toward Quebec. There were no major roads, so our travel was relatively slow and we weren't able to make as much progress lacking the constant charging from embedded pulsar energy modules in the streets. We only got as far as La Malbaie, where we had to stop to recharge our craft.

We saw no human—or "subhuman" as we've begun to refer to the five humanoids—activity as we left Baie-Comeau, and I'm not complaining. Angel, on the other hand, seemed quite disappointed to have left town without another glimpse of the skin-headed humans.

Angel seemed to have forgotten her fear from last night. As we passed the town limit, she expressed her desire to see more of "those people from Toronto". She actually wanted to talk to one of them. I was not in her camp. I hoped that those five were all there were, and that we may never see them again—although I had a bad feeling that Toronto, in their quest to save lives, may have altered our human existence again. So few humans are left, and my fear was that some of them were receiving, or had received vaccinations that are transforming them into some new species of human. My fear was well-placed.

We received a com from the bunker as we were just settling in for the night tonight. John, Mike and Dr. Shevchuk looked at us from the lounge area of the bunker. Several people were around, and every one of them was paying rapt attention. The looks on their faces told us that the news was not going to be good.

"We've found several of the groups of people injected with Toronto's version of E-rase, and, unfortunately, in each case, the general progress has mirrored the progress of the people you saw in Baie-Comeau," John explained.

"Not good," I said.

"No, Anta, not good at all," John said. "Toronto's vaccination appears to be errant. And what's worse is that each person 'vaccinated' was given dozens, or even hundreds of doses of the same vaccination and instructions to freely inject every person they came into contact with. That's a logical instruction given the current state of the population of the world, and we knew that was happening. Unfortunately, it can now be presumed that the abnormal vaccination is continuing to spread through Canada and the northern United States."

"Are the crazy suckers still vaccinating others?" Street asked, confused.

"No Street," Yurgi said. "They're not. But they have several days between the time of injection and the time they go crazy. It is during that time that they continue to vaccinate. Before they even know there's a problem."

"Dr. Shevchuk has contacted his counterparts in Toronto and all the other stations and informed them of the situation," John continued. "At first, Toronto was defiant, insisting that their formulations were correct. Even seeing footage of the people we've seen, and studying our data logs, didn't convince them of any error."

"So, they're still producing some form of E-rase, and still injecting people?" I asked, incredulous. "Can't they contact everyone and tell them to stop?"

"Well, thankfully, they've changed their mind. They immediately stopped production," John said. "They also allowed Yurgi to review their research and formulas to look for errors. And Yurgi found the error and fixed it. But they can't contact everybody . . ."

"You mean that all the people out there now with doses of the vaccination are still injecting people without any idea what's going to happen?" Shift asked, interrupting John. "And there isn't any way to contact them and get them to stop?"

"Not really," Mike replied. "The original groups from the bunker had standard-issue MEHDS, like us. And we've been informed that some of the original vaccinees maintained contact with the original vaccinators. But the third and fourth line of vaccinees didn't maintain much contact with anyone, especially since they never even met the first line of vaccinators from the bunker. And now, the first and second wave aren't communicating with the bunker either because they've all gone nuts. Toronto couldn't figure out why everybody stopped talking. Now they know. Once the people started going crazy, they stopped reporting in—obviously."

"So none of these people have, or had any idea what they were doing and no new vaccinees have any idea what fate awaits them either?" I asked.

"That's right. The new vaccinees wouldn't likely even know who to contact, if they were inclined to do so. And Toronto doesn't have records of who receives the vaccinations, so they can't initiate contact either."

Unlike our Toronto fellows, we previously determined that it would be better to have the inoculations come from our own hands, rather than having those we inject continue on with vaccinations. At the time we first learned of Toronto's decision to allow others to vaccinate, I thought that we may have been wrong, and that they made a better decision. Under other circumstances, with a proper vaccination, I still believe that Toronto made a better decision. Now, however, it's clear that if Toronto had followed our protocol, presumably, the first persons inoculated—those from the testing center itself—would likely have ceased vaccination attempts when they began to "dehumanize", or whatever it is that's happening to them.

Instead, people they injected have injected others, and they have injected others, and so forth, continuing the process. Hopefully, they will all run out of the vaccine soon and will have no way of receiving any more. Mike has been unable to get an accurate count of people who have received the problematic vaccine, but his estimates, based upon the ongoing tracking at the center, is over 350 people.

"Does Toronto still have anybody in their bunker who was vaccinated with the original stuff?" Shift asked, astutely.

"No," John replied. "At first, they held some people back, like we did. But after three days, everyone who had been vaccinated was sent out. So they don't have anybody in-house to study. They corrected the formula and have it right now, so, unless they can capture one of the wild ones, there's nothing to study."

"Wow. That sucks," Street said.

Yurgi said that testing facilities all over the world are now re-screening their samples and looking for variations that may have inadvertently occurred. So far, no center has announced any problems. Perhaps it's only Toronto's vaccine that was developed improperly.

Unfortunately, although many other centers have sent out people with vaccinations, no center is having as much luck finding survivors as ourselves and Toronto. Dr. Shevchuk theorizes that the cold climate of Canada and the northern United States throughout the winter may have slowed the progress of the disease enough to save more lives than other places.

Additionally, based upon the United States' history with Russia and Cuba during the Cold War, it seems possible that more bunkers may have been built by government agencies and individual citizens in the United States than anywhere else on Earth. If that's true, and I don't know whether it is, that could explain why there have been more reported survivors here than elsewhere. Perhaps people hid out in bunkers and only resurfaced when hearing of vaccination activities nearby.

In a sad twist of fate, however, the vaccines from Toronto have reached more people than the vaccines from all other centers worldwide combined. Our personal efforts have amounted to about 230 vaccinations, many of which have not survived. All other groups, worldwide, are reporting a combined seventy-six vaccinations, apart from those initially vaccinated within the bunkers. And of those seventy-six, only forty-two have survived.

Toronto, however, according to Mike's estimate, has vaccinated at least 350 people as a result of the manner in which they have conducted the vaccinations. Only twenty-one of them are known to have died within hours or days of the vaccination. The rest of the people are believed to be out and about, ignorantly turning what's left of our human population into super-human, man-eating monsters.

JUNE 17, 5:41AM
LA MALBAIE—SHIFT

"Shift, wake up!" Anta hissed at me. I was already awake. How could I sleep through such noise?

"Where is she?" Angel asked. "It sounds like it's coming through the walls, from every side."

"I'll go see," Street said, as he jumped off the old rickety couch he'd been sleeping on. Having found no large tourist hotel in the town of La Malbaie, we spent the night in a rundown motel, right on the main highway through town. We moved two beds from one room into the adjoining room which already had a bed and a couch. We were scared. Sleeping in the same room was comforting, albeit a little cramped. Anta even took one of the pictures off the wall before climbing into her bed. It depicted a young, pretty, blond girl—a teenager probably—in an orange sundress, walking through a park. It was very nice. Anta said it was too much like what we'd seen in Baie-Comeau. Nobody argued.

The scream continued for only a few seconds until it sounded as though it was right upon us. Street, having arrived at the window, slowly lifted the curtain and peeked out. He waved us over. Arriving at the window with the others, I peeked out into the early morning light.

Seven bald-headed, half naked—or in some cases, completely naked—people were tearing at the flesh of a clothed, haired, writhing woman—a *living* woman—not more than twenty meters from our door! Based upon the fact that she was fully-dressed, not wearing sunglasses at night, that she had a full head of hair, and that she was being attacked, I presumed that she had not been inoculated with Toronto's vaccine, nor ours. Previously, we had made a baseless assumption that the sub-humans only ate the flesh of the dead, but we were clearly wrong. Street has dubbed the sub-humans the "Skins" because of their bald heads.

"We've got to help her!" Anta said, with desperation in her voice. I held her back as she proceeded toward the door.

"That's a very bad idea Anta," I said, as calmly as I could, even though inside, I was far from calm.

"Just look at them," Angel said. She watched the ghastly sight with a look in her eye that I couldn't define. Perhaps the fear has dissipated. I don't think she was happy to see the woman being devoured, but she must have been excited to see the Skins again.

"She looks like the girl from the picture Anta took down last night," Street whispered in my ear. "Maybe she's the hotel owner's kid."

Although I thought he might be right, I didn't say so out loud. I simply nodded.

The tearing and gorging lasted only a couple of minutes; then the group dispersed, traveling different directions in small groups, dark red blood dripping from their chins. One of the women wore a scarf, which was matted with the blood of her victim. That was the only item of clothing on her body.

A revolting scene laid before us as the Skins departed. Blood, bones and torn clothing littered the ground. They had devoured her flesh, leaving only her red-stained bones behind. I fought the urge to vomit. The others looked to be in a similarly-uncomfortable state as they stared at the remnants of the grisly scene outside our door.

A few minutes later, after the sun lightened the sky further, we crept outside to the body—or what was left of it. As it had appeared from the window, she had been nearly-completely consumed. The cement around her was stained with the dark red remains of the feast. It appeared that some of the poor woman's bones were missing, probably eaten by the ferocious horde. Many other bones were broken, as if bitten in half. An acrid smell lingered in the air, but not the smell of death. It was something else.

As before, there was no sign of the Skins. In each of the three instances where we've seen them, it's been dark outside. That may just be a coincidence.

We're preparing to leave, scared and depressed at the prospects of the future. Our journey today will take us through Quebec and back up the southern coast of the Gulf of St. Lawrence. Mike reports that a town called Amqui, almost directly south of Baie-Comeau, but on the south side of the Gulf, has thirty-one living, by current reports. We hope to reach there by this afternoon.

While the route through Quebec is approximately 430 miles, the only other route—a ferry crossing just northeast of here which would have saved nearly eighty miles—is impassible. The ferry, according to Mike's research last night, was sunk by radicals several months ago when international travel was banned. Of course, in the Fluxor, traveling 430 miles will be easy, assuming no restrictions or problems along the way.

JUNE 17, 9:10PM
AMQUI—SHIFT

We're in Amqui. There were no living people here eagerly awaiting our arrival this afternoon. Mike had made contact with a small group of people this morning. They knew we were on our way. But based upon what we've seen of the activities of the Skins, if there are any survivors here, they may be in hiding—or worse.

Mike has continued to track the movements of the Skins, whenever possible, and doesn't believe there are any here, or anywhere within three hundred miles of here. But admittedly, his tracking of the Skins is much more difficult than the tracking of humans. We'll spend the day tomorrow looking more closely for the living. We plan to stay here another night or two as well, just in case the living turn up.

10

"Street," I called out quietly. "Street." Louder this time. Anta woke up and threw a pillow at Street. She missed, but her poorly-aimed throw landed with a thud on Angel's face. Her loud squawk woke up Street.

"Quiet everyone," I said. "Listen."

There was a quiet tapping on the door to our motel room. It sounded like the pecking of a wood-pecker from a distance, but was clearly on our door. Nighttime interruptions were occurring more frequently. We needed sleep.

We were sleeping, or trying to sleep at least, in a small, well-kept, one-story motel in the middle of town. Across the street was a small café with red and white checkered picnic tables outside. Like most other buildings in Amqui, the motel itself was nothing fancy. But unlike our last few nights, the room we occupied here was large and spacious. All four beds, three of which we'd dragged in from nearby rooms, fit comfortably.

Disturbed and alarmed at the knocking on the door, for obvious reasons, I quietly crept to the window. I wasn't sure what I would see. I cautiously peeked out the lower left corner of the curtained window. In my view, to my horror, was a mob of at least twenty Skins, but probably more. My gasp of surprise brought the others quickly to my side.

Each of the Skins outside was standing straight and tall, facing toward the closed door of our motel room. They appeared to be captivated by the proceedings, their heads steady and bodies still. Some were completely naked, which was repulsive under the circumstances. But most wore some clothing. The sparse clothing, however, was ragged and torn in many instances. None that I could see wore shoes or footwear of any kind. Nearly all of the people, save a few of the women, appeared completely hairless—at least on their heads. In the darkness, it was difficult to see the finer hair of their arms, legs and faces. Some of them had thin patches of hair standing out in gross and stark contrast to the remaining baldness illuminated by a nearby streetlamp. All but three sets of eyes, at least that I could see, were covered by sunglasses or goggles of some kind or another.

"How could this happen?" I asked myself aloud.

"How could what happen?" Anta whispered anxiously as she sidled up next to me. "Ouch!"

"What?" I asked.

"I just cut my finger on the window ledge, no biggie," she replied as she stuck her finger in her mouth to suck at the blood that had already begun to form on the tip of her finger.

I turned away from Anta and looked back toward the window. "Look." I lifted the corner of the curtain for Anta to take a peek.

Anta looked carefully at me, then turned and ducked down to peer through the window. Instantly, she gulped aloud, like a cartoon character, and then backed away. Street and Angel took turns as well, each exhibiting audible surprise at what they saw.

Mike had been confident that there was no "Skin" activity anywhere near us. A conference with Mike tonight before bed revealed that the Skins had been, by his best estimate, more than two hundred miles from Amqui. Mike was clearly wrong.

In any event, the quiet tapping on the door, along with a soft rumbling of human voices, continued for several more moments as we considered and discussed our plan of action, or our escape. We had an ample store of guns and ammunition, which we had procured a few days ago after our terrifying night in Baie-Comeau. Unfortunately, most of the items in that vast store were in the rear of the Fluxor, entirely oblivious to our desperate need of them.

We did have, fortunately, six early twenty-first century model handguns between us, each with fully loaded magazines.

"We might have to shoot our way out of here," Street suggested, almost excitedly.

"We can't shoot them," Anta said, disgusted. "They're humans."

"No they're not," Street argued, without offering any supporting evidence.

"Anta," I said, "they may be human, at least in some way; but if they want to do to us what they did to the others, they're not human enough to worry much about."

"That's right," Street added. "I don't want them sticking their raggedy mouths on my body. I'm not food. None of us will be if I have anything to say about it."

Street's boldness and energy was contagious. I started feeling a bit of a desire to shoot our way out as well. I couldn't read Angel's thoughts or feelings, but Anta looked like she was coming around.

After a brief conversation, weighing the options, we still had not decided how to proceed. While none of us actually considered them anything but human, the degree of human-ness was debated for a few minutes more. Ultimately, with heavy hearts, it was finally agreed that, whether human or not, it was probable that our only chance of survival was to fight; even if that meant killing the Skins.

We were working on a plan when the constant knocking finally stopped.

"Are they leaving?" I asked Angel as she bent down to peek out the window.

"No. I think they're talking to each other."

"Can you hear what they're saying?" Street asked.

"No."

We took turns looking out the window, curious about their appearance and about what they might do next. Maybe they would leave. Maybe they thought we had left, although that seemed doubtful.

Then, a gentle, soothing voice called out, "Helllooo in there." It was an eerie voice, but clearly human, with a strong southern accent.

The deep baritone voice hailed us again, "Hello, can you folks hear me?"

"Yes," I replied, although I wasn't sure it was the right thing to do. In fact, Anta and Street both eyed me contemptuously, but didn't speak.

The man responded in such a calm manner, with such assurance, that, had we not seen the Skins in action, he could have easily talked us out of hiding. "Folks, my name is Cain. I just wanna talk. I can't seem to find any help for my sick friends. Perhaps you have meds that can help us out."

Obviously, we weren't going to open that door. It must be that simple language and earnest plea that lured the girl in La Malbaie out into the open. It seemed so easy to do, and I wanted to help. Of course, I knew, as did the others, that this plea for help was not what it seemed.

How could people who seemed more like wild animals, maintain the language? Every zombie movie ever made—and this really was beginning to feel like a zombie movie—depicted creatures that couldn't really think and that certainly couldn't speak. To hear the Skins, or at least this one—Cain—talk, was mystifying. Plus, the rest of them had ceased their grumblings and were, at least outwardly, displaying intelligence that definitely never existed in the movies. This seemed to confirm my thought that, perhaps, they weren't really that different from us.

According to Mike, the Skins move very quickly and are physically powerful, but there are drugs on the market, including prescription drugs, that can alter a human body in that way. Still, their partial or full nakedness, especially for the women, was unusual.

And, of course, the cannibalism was difficult to explain.

Still, they seemed so much like us. Of course, we've only seen the Skins at night, and they're always wearing sunglasses. We've seen them move, and they lurch a bit while moving slowly. Mike says that when moving quickly, their motions are fluid. Standing still, here, on our doorstep, they look perfectly normal physically, albeit without hair or clothes. They're still human—there's no doubt about that.

My grandmother once discussed with me an old proverb that went something like, "desperate times call for desperate measures." On that occasion, my grandmother had been referring to her use of some bizarre herb in a family recipe that called for something entirely different, which she didn't have. To my grandmother, the saying may have been merely a quip, but the proverb took on a more sinister meaning in my head three days ago. These are certainly desperate times—although food is not scarce—so why eat another human. Clearly, while retaining most of their humanistic character traits, Toronto's version of E-rase seems to have affected the way the Skins think and act and may have actually altered their muscle or body structures.

Interestingly, as I stood there contemplating "Cain's" words, I recalled something Dr. Justin Case said back in early May. Just four days after he was injected with the test sample of E-rase, he explained how he felt more 'alive' four days post-injection. He said that, not only did he feel no negative effects from the E-rase injection, but he actually felt invigorated. He thought that, perhaps, E-rase was actually altering the physical aspects or components of his body.

I had thought nothing of it at the time. Dr. Case had taken the test sample which ultimately resulted in our survival. None of us has felt any unusual side-effects from E-rase—at least, not that anyone has shared vocally. Perhaps the property of E-rase which affected Dr. Case, whatever that might have been, was exacerbated by the error in Toronto's vaccine; and, that error caused the bodies and minds of the inoculated to go haywire. I resolved to discuss that theory with Dr. Shevchuk as soon as I was able, if I wasn't eaten by the then-docile nudists outside our door.

In any event, none of us was anxious to open the door, and there was no back door to our room. A window in the bathroom appeared to open into the alley between our building and an adjacent motel building. The distance between the front door and the alley was less than thirty meters.

"Do you think we can make it?" Anta asked, looking toward the back window.

Angel answered. "Based upon what we know of the Skins' speed, strength and endurance, it seems probable that the strength of their senses would also be increased. It would probably not be difficult for them to hear any sound we made opening or breaking the window to escape."

"Is this some wild theory of yours about supernatural abilities?" I asked. I immediately regretted it. Angel hasn't attempted, at any time, to persuade us to believe that the Skins fit into her classic model of supernatural genetics. "I'm sorry," I said quickly.

"That's okay," Angel replied. "And, the answer is 'no'. It just seems logical, that's all."

"I agree," Anta said.

"Then, the only possible ways out of here are to either lure them away from the building somehow, wait and hope they leave, or fight our way out," Street concluded.

After a short break, the baritone voice of Cain on the other side of the door renewed its plea for "help". Soon, other voices began to offer their pleas, which became increasingly angry and ugly.

After another conference, we concluded that our best chance for survival was to suddenly burst from the front door and attempt to shoot our way to the safety of the Fluxor. Only Street had any real experience with guns. More importantly, however, I didn't want to kill any of them. Everything within me told me that such an act would be murder. To kill a human, regardless of whether he or she has an unusual mental capacity or some physical limitation—or, in this case, physical adaptation—is still murder. Nevertheless, we had no other option, and they clearly didn't feel the same way I felt about the value of human life, based upon the prior actions of their fellows in eating human flesh. So, a quick weapons tutorial from Street taught us most of what we needed to know about how to kill and escape with our lives. Then, we attempted our escape.

After a much-too-short "count to three", Street yanked open the door and rushed out in the general direction of the Fluxor, swinging his arms and his gun wildly in the process. His fist first connected with the nose of the man closest to the door. A crunching sound and audible moan escaped from the man's mouth immediately thereafter. He struck a couple other Skins before I finally joined him on the doorstep, gun raised to eye level. The surprise attack had caused the Skins to fall back away from the door, allowing the women to join us outside the room shortly thereafter.

I had already unlocked the doors of the Fluxor remotely from the motel room, and its doors were just waiting for us to open them and climb inside. But first, we had the privilege of witnessing what may be one of the more spectacular displays of gun fighting, and street fighting—no pun intended—our world has witnessed in decades.

Rushing from the door step where I was still standing, Street slammed his body into the first row of Skins, including the man he had already hit, knocking several to the ground. Some were slow to get up, but others jumped right back into the fray. Between punches, Street was "popping" (to use his vernacular) Skins in the foreheads, backs, chests, etc. with whatever type of gun he was carrying.

Street's first few targets went down easily, owing to the surprise attack. Thereafter, however, the fighting became more intense. Street stood bravely in the middle of the naked throng, swinging, shooting, kicking and head-butting. Using the back end of his gun, his fists, his feet and his forehead, Street continued to attack and defend himself with amazing speed and tenacity.

One Skin grabbed Street from the back and wrapped his arms around Street's chest. Street, deftly and accurately, swung his head backward, striking the Skin in the nose. The blow caused the Skin to loosen his grip just enough for Street to spin around and, lifting his left knee upward in the process, catch the Skin between the legs. The man dropped in agony. Another Skin, a female, grabbed Street's arm during the melee, lifting his arm toward her mouth. Just as the woman was about to bite, a shot from beside me caught the Skin in the neck.

I turned to the left and saw a wisp of smoke rising from the barrel of Anta's gun. It was beautiful.

I turned back toward the fray in time to see Street lift a thin, teenaged boy off his feet and then toss him to the ground. A loud crack, and immediate blood in the area of his head told us all we needed to know about that boy's injuries.

During Street's amazing display of fighting prowess, as he continued to lunge, twirl, shift and "pop", Anta, Angel and I attempted to help from the doorway, shooting sporadically; both hoping to hit, and hoping not to hit any of the Skins.

As Street, with a little help from us, rapidly dispatched one Skin after another, though not always fatally, they began to drop back. Those that had not been wounded continued to attack, albeit with less zeal. Because they didn't have weapons, they were clearly out-matched. Those apparently in pain, retreated first. Clearly, the Skins felt pain and would die. Unlike zombies in the movies of the past, those Skins were human enough to retreat when beaten. They didn't appear to have an insatiable urge for human flesh. They were definitely *not* zombies, and most of them weren't fighters, or so it seemed.

As Street made greater progress, we slowly made our way toward the Fluxor. By the time the three of us reached the Fluxor, only twenty or twenty-five meters from the door of our hastily-departed motel room, Street had "cut down" (again, Street's vernacular) at least fifteen of the would-be cannibals. Another four or five were on the ground at the hands, or gun barrels of Anta and I. I'm not positive whether Angel managed to hit any of her targets, but that she fought alongside us, regardless of success, is worth note, and I'm grateful for it.

As Street finally reached the door to the Fluxor, his back toward the remaining Skins, he was hit over the head by what appeared to be a wood mallet—the type that might be used to pound a stake into the ground to hold a tent in place. That was the only weapon I had seen, and it was used at a time most appropriate to be effective. The blow didn't knock Street down, but he was temporarily out of action as he grabbed onto the Fluxor to keep his balance.

Sitting in the driver's seat, I lowered my window and shot the offending Skin in his left temple, instantly killing him. Street then climbed in and we exploded away at a speed not even the Skins, with their amplified physical capabilities, could hope to catch. As we sped away, I realized that I would probably always live with the guilt associated with my purposeful destruction of that man's life—at point blank range; but I did what I believed had to be done. We all did. Still, taking the life of that last man, knowing exactly what I was doing, was eating at me. I thought then, that, until the time I meet my maker, I would be haunted by the memory of what we had just done.

Street's legacy, however, would also be forever remembered—at least among his colleagues on that night—as a fearsome and fearless warrior. His bravery and skill was the foremost cause of our eventual escape from the motel in Amqui.

During the melee, I caught a glimpse of the eyes of one of our attackers, a very tall and muscular man. A fashionable pair of sunglasses had slipped down his nose, but still clung to his moist skin. I thought at the time that he may have been the first man Street hit on his way out the door. There was no color in his eyes. Although it was dark outside, the blackness of his eyes was darker still. It was as if the iris had vanished, leaving a larger pupil alone to fill up nearly the entire eye cavity. That probably explained why the Skins wore sunglasses, and why we had only seen them at night. If the Skins' pupils are really as large as they appeared in that man, perhaps no longer being able to dilate or constrict in bright light, any person with such a condition would need to find ways to minimize the amount of light entering the head. I'm no medical doctor, but that seemed likely the case. Like so many other things, I resolved to ask one of the doctors at the bunker about that later.

More interesting though, was that the man whose eyes I glimpsed, whose shoulder was cut with blood oozing from the ragged wound, had an angry, knowing look on his face. He looked as though he knew something I did not and was displeased with whatever that knowledge included. *Was that "Cain"?* He looked familiar.

About two and a half hours after our hasty exit, we stopped in a town called Shediac, about 250 miles southeast of Amqui. Shediac, or at least the sea adjacent to Shediac, must be lobster territory, based upon the numerous lobster shacks, restaurants and sculptures that line the main streets of this small town.

A faint light was creeping into the eastern sky over Prince Edward Island, in the Gulf of St. Lawrence, as we drove along the narrow main street toward what appeared to be the city center.

Unlike some of the other cities and towns we'd passed through, the town of Shediac didn't appear to have suffered much from human destruction during the early days of the epidemic, when fear and desperation led to confusion, anger and violence. Few of the windows along the main street were broken and there was very little trash on the ground. It really looked as though this town hadn't been affected by the tempest of human fear that swept through the country at the beginning of the epidemic, or the rage which bore down with ferocity during the height of the plague.

With the knowledge that the Skins only came out at night, we relaxed. I hadn't realized how tense my muscles had been until I saw the first sliver of the June sun rise over the calm waves of the Atlantic Ocean. The adrenaline left me and my body felt more tired than it had in many, many days. I needed to sleep, but neither time, nor nature, was on our side.

After grabbing a bit of food from a quaint grocery on the main street, we sat down on some old wooden benches along a coastal strip at the north end of this small fishing village. Former friends and lovers had carved their initials all over the sun-bleached wooden planks. Even though our world had fallen apart, in some towns, this one included, the electricity was still on. We ate pre-packaged lunch meat and slightly-grainy ice cream bars as we watched the sun rise.

The sun reflected off the placid waves as it continued its rise. I pondered our current situation as the glistening waves slowly swam up the sand and then retreated the same way. The only reminder of the current state of affairs was a dead body, or what was left of it, floating in the surf forty or fifty meters to the south, bloated and rotting. It was enough to remind me that the peace surrounding us was not as it seemed. A tear slipped from my eye, but I was content.

The longer we sat there, the more my body relaxed. My mind drifted into peaceful fantasies—surfing, a sand castle contest my nieces and I had joined a couple years ago in San Diego. I wanted so desperately to see that our world had not changed. I took solace in the fact that our Earth was still soaring around the sun, and still waking up each day as it had done for millennia. It was peaceful. I almost felt happy, until the quiet was disturbed by the sound of footsteps on a boardwalk somewhere nearby.

The noise startled me into immediate consciousness, and I simultaneously reached for my gun, slid off the bench, and crouched down. My companions did the same. My eyes darted left and right as I watched for movement, but I soon realized that the sound of footsteps belonged to a person with footwear. The clopping of shoes was strangely beautiful. The Skins we had seen thus far hadn't been wearing shoes. Street apparently had the same thoughts as he slowly stood. Anta, Angel and I followed his example. But our guns were kept in firing position and my eyes never stopped moving.

We still had a tense fifteen-second wait before a young boy, clearly human—and normal—stepped out from behind a small stand of bushes between the boardwalk and the beach twenty or twenty-five meters away from us. He moved toward us very slowly. As I caught his eyes, he hailed us with a raise of his hand. We each reciprocated.

A short dialogue from a distance of approximately fifteen meters (as he wouldn't approach any closer), revealed that he was part of a larger group of survivors—thirteen of them—who were hiding in a small bomb shelter under a local hotel. They heard, through Mike's communication database, that we had arrived in southeastern Canada.

Then, early this morning, Mike broadcast that we had arrived in Shediac. The announcement raised their spirits and they sent several people out to look for us, despite the danger likely still riding on the wind. Luckily, they found us.

The young boy, Julian, led us a block down the street and to the back of a small hotel where we descended a dark staircase. At the bottom of the stairs, Julian opened a thick metal door and ushered us inside. We stepped into a glass chamber just inside the entryway. The chamber closed behind us and a violent whoosh of air surrounded us. Seconds later we were welcomed into the light of a cramped basement bunker full of tired, dirty, anxious faces.

In a matter of seconds, a frail old woman—Agatha, we soon learned—hobbled over to us with a bright, warm smile and gave Angel and Anta hugs. After short introductions, we began vaccinations and continued when the others who had been out searching returned. We inoculated all thirteen of them. Amazingly, none of them were sick with any signs of A.E. at the time of the vaccination, so I had great hope that all of them would live!

After the vaccination process was completed, we sat down on dirty chairs that were offered to us and ate a processed meal from a wall unit with our hosts. We spent the next few hours speaking of the catastrophe on the surface and our efforts in locating survivors. But the more interesting part of the stories told that evening revolved around the conditions and realities these wonderful people had faced over the past couple of months.

Agatha spoke of her life before the plague in this small town. The others in the room gave her all the attention a woman of her years deserved. They clearly respected her and loved her. Agatha regaled us with stories from her youth in Shediac, where she had lived her entire life. We laughed and cried with her. But things became very somber, very quickly when she began to discuss recent events.

In her 116 years of life, Agatha had seen illness, death, wars and other calamities, but nothing the likes of which we all face now. Her husband was one of the first in Shediac to catch the disease. She cried great tears of sorrow as she spoke of the death of her husband from A.E.—the way his body trembled with the pain and seemed to melt away before her eyes. She spoke reverently of his anguished cries as his life quickly faded and was lost to her. In a quiet, remorseful voice, with her eyes lifted toward the heavens, she humbly apologized to her husband. There was nothing she could do for the man with whom she had shared a bed and a life for almost eighty years. Her immense sorrow brought most of us to tears. It was amazing that she was able to remain healthy that close to the illness. She may be immune, but we didn't discuss that. It wasn't the right time.

Agatha was brought to this shelter by a young pregnant woman—Blossom. Blossom was Agatha's neighbor and they had spent many hours together in the years leading up to this crisis, building a wonderful relationship of love and trust. Agatha was like a grandmother to the young woman, and when news of the crisis unfolded in Shediac, Blossom sought out Agatha and her husband to take them with her to her uncle Robert's bomb shelter. But Agatha was alone when Blossom arrived. They didn't fully understand the ramifications of taking Agatha, who had been so close to the disease, into a small room with other people. They were all lucky that Agatha was not sick.

Anta sat next to me, tears running down her face, immersed in the details of the story of this mother and the aged woman. Anta was holding Blossom's newborn baby, Isabella, who had spent her entire seven weeks of life in this underground bunker. Isabella had not yet seen or felt the sun on her face. Her clothes and wispy blond hair were filthy. We learned that the people here have no way to wash. They have water to drink, but no sink or even a bucket in which to bathe or wash clothes. Blossom had nearly died during the baby's birth, but Agatha and the others kept her alive through willpower and prayer. They refused to let another one of them "go the way of the Earth" as Agatha said.

Young Julian sat on the other side of me and held my hand while we spoke of both somber and lighthearted subjects. He is only nine years old. I had at first wondered why he was sent out to greet us until we entered the bunker and saw the other options. Of the thirteen people here, only Julian and three others appeared to have the strength and health to walk more than a few steps.

While the group expressed much sorrow at the loss of the world above them, they also exhibited hope and spoke of the future now that they are free to leave. We warned them, of course, that to leave may be as dangerous as before, but from a new source of danger. We spoke of the Skins. Many seemed to not believe what we were saying, but Blossom's uncle Robert, the owner of the hotel and this bunker, understood. He expressed that, once his leg healed from an accident a few days earlier in the bunker, he would make sure his people were safe. He knew where to find guns and ammunition. He also knew where he could take them to be safe now that they could leave. We imparted all of the wisdom we had to help them on their journey, and in their lives from here forward. We also left them with a supply of E-rase. Hopefully they would have an opportunity to use it.

It is now quite late and I'm tired. We're sleeping in the hotel above the Shediac shelter. We're only a few hours away from our old bunker, where Mike, Dr. Shevchuk, John and the others continue to monitor the world's situation. It's hard to believe that we've been on the road for a month already.

Street is posted as a sentry on the roof of the building to watch for Skins. I'll be taking his place shortly. We moved the Fluxor and three other hovers to the alley next to the staircase leading to this shelter. If the Skins arrive, we'll be ready, with plans set for escape and our entire store of weaponry at our quick disposal. Although I don't believe the Skins will be able to find this bunker.

Beginning tomorrow, even though we are tempted to visit our friends, we'll travel southwest through Boston, New York, Philadelphia, Baltimore, Washington D.C., and hopefully arrive safely in Richmond, Virginia where a large group of survivors is presently believed to be in hiding. I'm excited to cover so much ground in such a short amount of time, to get as far away as possible from the Skins.

Speaking with Mike, Yurgi and John tonight, we learned that the Skins who approached us in Amqui reached us by covering over a hundred miles in a matter of hours. Mike thinks they could have traveled that distance in only a couple of hours, but they didn't appear to be looking for us. They just happened to find us.

The Skins seem to have unlimited endurance and ferocious speed. What is most unfortunate is that any human survivors we expected to find in Amqui this morning, had we not fled, were probably being digested in the vile stomachs of the Skins by the time we were awoken last night. Thankfully, we arrived in time to vaccinate and warn our new friends in Shediac.

11

"Did you find out anything about that guy, Cain; the guy I was telling you about last night?" I asked John over the MEHD.

"No, but he sure looks familiar," John replied. "We traced him back from the attack and got a close up of him a couple days earlier. He looks like someone I've seen before. Otherwise, we've got nothing on him. Sorry."

"Funny, Anta thought he looked familiar too. But I don't think I've ever seen the guy."

"Probably just a coincidence," John said.

We arrived in Richmond late last night. Today, we spent the day visiting several bunkers where a total of 148 people were vaccinated. Not one of them looked sick. It was incredible! Maybe the potency and spread of A.E. is slowing, or the people still alive have figured out how to avoid contamination. Either way, we're hopeful that anybody we find alive moving forward will be able to benefit from an inoculation and ultimately live.

In other news, Dr. Shevchuk contacted us this evening to inform us that bunkers all over the world have released the vaccination to the public—what's left of it—through teams like ours. Those teams are traveling as far and wide as possible. Unfortunately, according to Mike's best estimates, the numbers of people vaccinated with the damaged E-rase from Toronto has likely reached into the thousands. The Toronto groups went into northern and western Canada and Alaska, where the cold seemed to keep the disease at bay and many more people were still alive. Those groups, having no contact with any central communication hub, continue to spread that defective vaccination, traveling in all directions. And worse, as they mutate, they are probably attacking and/or eating the living all along the way.

Mike is tracking a group that's nearing the Bering Strait. Unfortunately, he hasn't seen any of the early signs of rabidity in that group yet. He expects that, if they reach any population center before they all turn crazy, the spread of the damaged E-rase will continue into Asia. At present, there's no apparent way to stop those who are continuing to spread Toronto's E-rase through the northern states either.

There have been multiple attempts, by both Toronto and our bunker, to contact anybody who will answer; but nobody is responding. Toronto even sent out a team, who had been vaccinated with the corrected version or E-rase, to try to kill a small group of Skins nearby, but the two humans were killed and eaten by a mob that was much larger than anticipated. Apparently, we were luckier than them when we escaped from Amqui.

I didn't ask for many details though, knowing that my job is simply to help as many survivors as I can. I'll leave the fixing of *that* problem to someone better able to meet it.

JUNE 24
THE MOON

"Great to have you back!" Jonas said cheerfully as he clapped Hasani on the back.

"It's great to be back, healthy!" Hasani replied. "So, let's go get Alan. That guy's got to be miserable, all alone out there."

"Hasani," Jonas said slowly, "Alan hasn't replied to our calls over the last couple of hours. As soon as you com'd that you were on your way back, I began trying to reach him. I'm a little worried."

"Really? What could have happened to him?" Hasani asked, as he looked around the room at the others.

"We don't know exactly," Jonas replied. "We've been searching all of the sensors and computers in the various shells for any sign of life, anywhere. But over the past two hours, the only person we've seen out there is you. The sensors at the German shell have been acting up though, so he could still be there; and he could be just fine. I just don't want you to get your hopes up."

"How are the sensors acting up?"

"Well, a few hours ago, before you contacted us, the system monitoring the life support system in the German shell started fluctuating, meaning that the atmospheric system may be malfunctioning. The computers say there's still enough atmosphere to sustain life, but just a few minutes ago, the system went into overdrive. If the computers are correct, the system is pumping breathable atmosphere into the shell at an alarming rate. The whole thing could burst if the pressure gets too high."

"How long would that take?"

"I have no idea," Jonas replied. "Anyone else?"

Everyone shook their heads.

"Then let's go. Do we have his last known coordinates?"

"Yeah," Jonas replied. "The rover's ready. Let's go."

Hasani turned and headed toward the port, then turned back around to face the group. "You guys are all vaccinated already, right?" he asked.

"Yes," Tom replied. "We took care of that this morning after our conference."

"Good."

Hasani and Jonas traveled across the moon's surface as quickly as their rover would move.

"So, have you learned anything new about Alan?" Hasani asked as they bumped along the moon's rough surface.

"Actually, yes. I did some digging on the guy, like we had planned. You know, to see why he felt like colleagues in Brazil had abandoned him."

"And?"

"And, not much. But it looks like he is, or was, part of some paramilitary outfit out of Connecticut. Leader by the name of Franconi. I couldn't find much about it on the Net, but there seems to be some kind of connection with the two. I don't know what kind of connection though. Anyway, not much else. But maybe his group was supposed to try to get him home before the communications went out."

"That's assuming there was anybody in his group still alive on Earth," Hasani said.

"Right."

As the rover approached the German shell, the men began to see floating debris. The air was dusty, and they could see only the vague outline of the shell in the distance. Wind—strong wind—was pushing against the front of the rover, slowing their speed.

"What's going on?" Hasani asked. "I didn't think the moon had wind."

"You're right," Jonas replied. "I don't like the look of this."

"We're in the right place?"

"Yes, we're in the right place. That's the German shell. But something isn't right here," Jonas said, slowly. A gust of wind hit the rover and pushed it several inches sideways across the rocky ground.

"Obviously."

Hasani slowed the rover's speed as the clouds of dust became thicker and the winds picked up in intensity. "Whatever is happening here wasn't happening yesterday," he said.

"You were here?" Jonas asked.

"No, but I was close enough to see the shell and to know that this wind and dust weren't here."

"So, whatever happened just barely happened," Jonas said.

As the rover crept closer to the shell, it became clear to the men just what was occurring.

"Look at that hole!" Jonas said.

"Wow, that's what's causing the wind, right? The shell actually broke open!"

"Yes. The atmospheric pressure must have gone too high. A hole that size would be letting out tremendous amounts of air that had, until probably just a few minutes ago, been trapped inside the shell. If Alan was in there, he may be out here now."

"But he hasn't responded to your coms in a couple of hours, right?"

"That's right."

"Then something may have happened to him before the shell cracked open."

"Well, let's see if we can get in there," Jonas said.

They continued their slow approach toward the shell's main outer portal, the wind pushing and pulling the rover laterally several inches at a time. When they finally reached the portal, Jonas punched the codes remotely from the rover. The portal didn't open.

"I'm going out there," Hasani said.

"No, you're not," Jonas replied sternly. "That will get you killed. That wind is too strong. You'll be blown away, even tethered to the rover. I'll never be able to pull you back in. The wind isn't going to stop if the shell's atmospheric system is still functioning. It's going to be working overtime to compensate for lost atmosphere inside and that's going to keep the wind pouring out of the hole until the system gets so overworked that it shuts down, or unless there's an auto-override that recognizes that it's a breach and shuts it down. And who knows how long that will take. You're not going out there. It's suicide."

"But ..." Hasani began. Then he stopped talking, his eyes attempting to focus on something in the distance. Jonas looked in the direction Hasani was looking and gasped.

"That's him, isn't it? That's Alan."

"I think so," Hasani replied quietly.

They watched in silence as a man clinging to the edge of the hole eighty meters in the air was buffeted back and forth, slamming into the sides of the jagged hole. The wind was tearing at him; and his clothes—not a space suit—were ripping apart at the seams.

"He's going to run out of air, even with the machines still pumping," Jonas said.

"He won't be able to hold on long enough to have the chance to run out of air," Hasani replied under his breath.

"Do you think he did this to himself?" Jonas asked. "Committed suicide, I mean?"

"Why would he?"

"I don't know; but holes probably don't just appear in these shells, and portals don't just freeze shut. None of this could have happened by chance."

"Well, maybe..."

Hasani stopped speaking mid-sentence. The men watched in horror as Alan shot out into the darkness beyond the shell. They quickly lost sight of him as his body was surrounded by clouds of dust and debris.

After a moment of stunned silence, Jonas pulled away from the shell and headed in the direction they'd seen the man fly. They didn't speak for nearly three hours as they searched in ever wider bands around the perimeter of the shell. Nearly eight kilometers from the German shell, they finally found Alan Stein's body. His sojourn on the moon was over. They buried his body where they found him.

12

"I can't sleep in this crappy bed," Street said as he tried to roll onto his side in the cramped confines of his bunkbed. His shuffling made the whole trailer shake.

We're "camped" in a huge RV, next to a barn, on a farm outside Vidalia, Georgia. The RV wouldn't start, so we couldn't move it into the barn, as we would have liked to have done. The adjacent farmhouse, like so much of Vidalia and the surrounding towns, is in ruins—burnt to the ground.

The chaos and violence that occurred in the southern states when the plague broke out was evidently terrible. Vidalia is like nearly every town and city we've passed through in North Carolina, South Carolina and Georgia. Windows are broken, vehicles of all types lay in the streets, overturned, and blackened. Trash floats on the breeze and is piled high against fences and the sides of burned-out buildings. Usually pristine walls and sidewalks are littered with graffiti yelling obscenities and curses against the IWO, the U.S. government, various races, and the plague.

Nearly every store and home that isn't burned to the ground now sits with open doors and broken windows, showing us the overwhelming destruction inside. There are thousands of bodies in the streets, rotting. But most of them are no more than skin and bones now. I don't envy the people who lived here prior to their deaths, and my heart aches.

"At least you have a bed," Angel replied. "You want us to stick you up on the roof for the Skins to gnaw at overnight?"

"If the smell doesn't kill him first," I added, solemnly.

The stench here, even outside of town where we are, is awful. It is so different from the north. In the cities and towns of Canada and the northern United States, fewer windows were broken and most doors were still closed. In those northern towns, it seemed like most people either died in their homes or in hospitals, as I had previously thought. With windows and doors closed, the smell of rot and decay stayed mostly inside. Here, though, and throughout these southern towns, the smell is abominable. It's actually hard to breath. And, of course, there's nobody to clean up the mess and bury the bodies. Maybe some day the smells will fade in time.

"Leave Street alone," Anta said, smiling. "He's a big dude."

"Are you calling me fat?" Street joked.

Street has a way of making serious situations a bit lighter. Having him around has made this whole situation bearable. Of course, having Anta around is pretty nice too! If I didn't have Anta to talk to at the end of each day, I'd think this whole enterprise was for nothing. She gives me hope that we can rebuild our society, maybe starting with *us* some day.

"John's calling," I said. "Quiet down, and leave the fat guy alone for a few minutes."

"Hey John," Anta said as she opened my MEHD, snickering at my joke. John's somber face appeared in the air above the MEHD. He looked tired. Mostly, he looked worried. The joviality we had just felt melted away in an instant.

"John, why the glum face man?" I asked. "We're the ones being hunted out here."

"Well, I'd like to say I'm just tired, but that's only part of the problem. Actually Shift, you're right. We think you *are* being hunted."

"What do you mean?" Street asked. Hunting was his game. His eyes showed a bit of intrigue at the prospect of being hunted.

"We're still tracking the Skins, but they're also tracking you. That's what I mean."

"They're *tracking* us?" Anta asked. Her tone voiced the surprise that we all felt.

"Yes," John replied. "The older, more mature Skins, like Cain and others who've been 'Skins' longer, are no longer just randomly looking for people. They seem to be directing the search. They actually look like they're raising armies, so to speak, with the younger Skins doing their bidding."

"That's crazy," I said.

"Yup, but it's worse than that," John continued. "The Skins are no longer eating living people."

"That sounds better, not worse," Street said.

"Oh, it's not 'better' Street. I said they're not *eating* living people any more. Instead, they're just attacking and biting the living. They're only eating corpses."

"Can you tell why they're doing that, the biting I mean?" I asked.

"No, we don't know why," John replied. "But we do know what's happening after someone is bitten."

"The way you said that sounds very bad," Street said.

He was right about that. John's face was turning paler as he continued to talk.

"It *is* very bad. I don't know how to explain this without freaking you out, so I'll just say it and let you freak out. Those who have been bitten change. They morph, somehow, into Skins within a couple of minutes. Sometimes, it only takes a few seconds."

Angel let out a little shriek, but quickly clasped her hand over her mouth. The rest of us just sat there on the checkered cloth seats of the posh motor home, staring, open-mouthed at John's face above the MEHD.

"How do you know, or . . . how can you tell that the people are changing once they're bitten?" I asked quietly, several seconds after John's announcement.

"Well," John began slowly, "before, when we were watching footage of the people who were inoculated with Toronto's vaccine, the change occurred over a period of days. It was only by watching the same group for a long period of time that we could see them getting faster and stronger and see them lose hair and rip their clothes off. But with these new Skins—the people who are bitten rather than injected—the change is nearly instantaneous. Within a matter of seconds, or a couple of minutes at most, they stand up and join the throng. The physical changes aren't obvious right away, until they start to move. The new Skins move as fast and as awkwardly as the Skins who attacked them. Then, over a period of a few hours, they start to lose hair and get naked."

We all sat there quietly for a few seconds. I pondered the implications of John's words.

Seeing that we had nothing to say, John continued. "As the Skins continue to multiply, rather than killing all the remaining human survivors, they'll simply transform the humans into Skins. Those that have already changed join the budding throngs of workers. They have the same dangerous propensities as those who have been injected with Toronto's vaccine. They take directions from the older Skins—the overlords—as Mike has begun to call them. Your old friend Cain is one of those overlords, and his army is growing quickly. He has a couple hundred followers, at least."

"Wow," I whispered.

"So," John continued, "it seems that the Skins must have a way of smelling human scents or something. Or maybe it's some other sense that we don't understand since we don't really understand any of this. But in some way, they're finding survivors much faster and easier than we are. They seem to just walk right up to places where humans are hiding. Sometimes they knock and appear to be speaking. Other times, they break through walls and doors and rush in for the attack.

"And, the Skins have become much more aggressive. They're attacking vehicles and buildings where humans are hiding, in daylight now. We've been watching it happen. Apparently, they don't care that the sun is out any more."

"Maybe, as they continue to mutate, if that's what's happening, their eyes are adjusting to the brightness of the daylight hours," Angel said.

"Well, that's a comforting thought," I replied.

"But this whole thing sounds like a zombie movie," Street said quietly. "Zombies don't act like that. They're not rational. They don't think and make decisions."

"Zombies aren't real Street," Angel said. "You're trying to fit the Skins into your pre-conceived idea of what a fictional zombie acts like. That won't work. The Skins aren't zombies. They're humans. Granted, they're humans with extra-sensory abilities and inhuman strength and skills. But this isn't unprecedented. I've been studying this type of thing for years."

"Angel," John said with exaggerated patience, "your studies are very likely irrelevant here. I don't say that to be mean or inconsiderate, or anything like that. I actually *believe* most of what you've written on the subject. But what may exist within the human genome is not what we're seeing here. This is something different. We're not talking about a human who is born with genes that make him stronger than his friends. We're not talking about a person born with the ability to read minds or leap tall buildings or detect a coming tornado. We're talking about regular humans who have been infected by a mutated form of E-rase. The vaccination is causing them to change."

"I understand what you're saying, John," Angel replied testily. "I think you're right. My point was, these aren't zombies. They're humans with abilities that normal humans don't possess. I wasn't arguing that these humans fit the classical mold of my prior test subjects. I'm just saying that they're living humans, not zombies."

"Good, and I agree," John said a little more calmly. "What we need to know is how to beat them to the remaining survivors. The race is on to find, vaccinate, and warn as many humans as possible before the Skins get them. But that's going to be tough. The Skins look to be gaining ground."

"What about those we've already vaccinated?" Anta asked. Her face betrayed her concern. "Have any of them been bitten, and has the vaccination protected them?"

I suddenly felt the same anxiety.

"Great question Anta," I said, proud of her for thinking of a question that had completely eluded me.

"Yeah, many of them have been bitten, and yes, they've turned too. That means you are also in danger—in case you didn't already know that. The vaccination doesn't stop someone from becoming a Skin."

"Shite," Anta said loudly. It wasn't a funny situation, but hearing her curse made me smile inside. Her speech is usually so proper.

"What about those wonderful people in Shediac—Agatha, Blossom and the others?"

"I'll check on them after we hang up Anta. I'll let you know as soon as I know."

"If everything you say is true," Street said, "then the Skins probably won't stop until they've bitten, or eaten, everybody on the planet. So we've gotta bust our asses, right?"

"That's right," John replied. "But no matter what you do, I'm worried that you won't be able to do enough, quickly enough. There's a group of inoculated folks from western Canada that crossed over the Bering Strait a couple of days ago. They vaccinated a large group of people a few miles from the town of Stansk. That's the town that was covered with HMP Foam back in March. So, the Skins, or the future Skins anyway, have arrived in Asia."

"I assume all the bunkers around the world know about this problem with the Skins, right?" Anta asked.

"Of course. Dr. Shevchuk has talked with the head of every bunker that has answered his coms. They're trying to coordinate a joint response to the problem. But ultimately, anything they come up with may be too late in coming or unfeasible. Most bunkers no longer have access to even a semblance of governmental support and weaponry. It looks like we are in for another fight for our lives. After everything we accomplished to get to this point, I hope it hasn't been for nothing."

"I . . . Wow." *Great, that sounded real intelligent.*

Street seemed to be thinking this through. He mumbled ". . . leading to two separate and distinct races of human. A war is coming . . ." Then his voice trailed off into a whisper.

"John," I said, "you've gotta watch us tonight, and probably every night from here on. Can you set up a team to monitor one hundred miles around our perimeter? Otherwise, we won't know whether we're safe tonight in this motorhome. If the Skins approach, com us and give us a chance to escape, okay."

"Got it boss."

As the com ended, Anta leaned into me and whispered, "All of those wonderful people we've met, dead. Or worse." Then she began to cry. I could feel her body shaking, so I pulled her closer with my arm around her waist. With my other hand I brought her head to rest against my chest.

Angel stepped over to the other side of Anta and sat down. She put her arm around Anta's shoulders, bowed her head, and let her tears join Anta's on the floor below.

Street looked at me briefly. I could tell his eyes were red. He quickly turned away and pulled his blanket over his head. That's what finally got to me . . .

I couldn't hold back my feelings any longer. As we sat there holding each other, I said a quiet prayer for those of us still alive. Whether we would get any sleep tonight, I surely didn't know.

13

"Get in the hover, fast," Anta whispered, waking me. "John called."

"What is it?" Street asked.

"Get. In. The. Car." Anta punctuated each clipped word. She was serious. We're learning to trust each other out here. Anta said move, and we moved.

"Look!" Anta said after all the doors of the Fluxor were closed and locked.

Off to our left, coming directly toward my window, was a lone Skin. She was rapidly approaching the Fluxor. It was frightening to see the speed at which she approached. Even though her movements were less than fluid, her speed was faster than any human I've ever seen.

"Shouldn't we leave?" Street asked.

"She's alone," Angel replied. "Let's see if she'll talk to us."

I thought that idea was crazy; but, it was an interesting proposal and I kept the hover where it was. Each of us checked our guns. I flipped off the safety on mine and assumed the others did the same. Then I cracked the window half an inch as the Skin slowed her speed on approach. Then we waited. It seemed like a very long time.

The "woman" was thin, but muscular. Her head was bald; but a couple small clumps of blond hair were hanging on around her left ear. It looked like her hair had probably fallen out in patches. The woman was naked except for a thin pair of underwear, stained with blood. She looked to be about forty or forty-five years old from the few wrinkles around her face and torso, which were also streaked with dry blood.

Finally, she opened her mouth, slowly. Her voice was eerie, but human. "Your kind is not welcome here. We have come to destroy you, and you must know that your death is for the greater good. Would you continue to foul this Earth with your presence? You are unwholesome, filthy abominations and perversions of nature. Your lives must be taken from you."

"Huh?" Street said from the back seat near the Skin.

On hearing Street's voice, the Skin slowly turned her head. She reached her hand up to her face and tentatively removed her sunglasses. Street shifted uncomfortably in his seat and she quickly turned back to me.

I noticed the eyes were dark and colorless, like Cain's, and wanted to turn away from them. They seemed to peer into my soul. I was scared. But her *words* were much more worrisome than her stare.

Again, she said, "You are abominations and perversions. You must die."

"She thinks *we're* abominations?" Angel asked quietly from the back seat, farthest from the Skin. Then her voice raised as she became more upset. "We, the humans, who have inhabited this earth for millennia, are unwholesome and filthy? *We're* abominations—not her? Is she crazy?"

"Obviously," Street growled.

As Street and Angel discussed the Skin's statements in the back seat, the woman turned her head slightly to the left and stared at Anta sitting next to me in the front of the Fluxor. Her pupils grew in size, and the corners of her mouth turned up as she glared at Anta. She looked as though she were trying to figure something out.

We all sat there, very still, for several seconds. Then, without warning, the Skin smashed her bald head into my window. The window stayed intact, but the Skin fell backward, landing hard on the asphalt at the edge of the road.

"Ouch," Anta said quietly. I turned to look at her. She was holding her forehead as if she too had felt the pain that the Skin had felt. Her eyes registered both pain and surprise. I put that thought on a back burner as I turned back to the woman on the ground outside my window.

The woman had placed her hand on her now-bleeding forehead. She looked dizzy and confused as her pupils dilated and contracted. She shook her head slowly back and forth for several seconds. It was as if she didn't know what had happened.

I didn't know what had just happened either. Maybe she was overcome by some emotion—anger perhaps—and tried to do something about it. She acted after what appeared to be a deliberate and conscious consideration of Anta sitting next to me. But her action clearly didn't have the desired result. What it did do, however, was give us further evidence that the Skins are more human than the archetypal, albeit fictional, zombie.

While the Skin sat on the ground, I lowered my window a couple more inches and asked her what her name was. I hoped that she wouldn't be able to give me a clear, cogent response. I thought that, if she was unable to give a name, she may not be as human as she appeared, perhaps clearing my conscience of the guilt I had felt since our "murder" of the Skins a few days ago in Amqui. I also wondered whether we could have a real conversation and learn a little about what was going on in her mind.

"Sarah," she replied. Then she stood, and, wobbling on her feet, stumbled away from the craft.

Anta, calmly, but with difficulty, said, "Sarah? She still knows her name. How can we kill them if they still know their names?"

"I don't think I can," Angel replied. "Her name is *Sarah?*"

After a few seconds of silence, during which we each pondered this circumstance, Angel asked, "Why did she smash her head into the window? After she did it, she seemed to know how stupid it was. She was thinking, and reacting to pain, and acting, mostly, like a human being."

"I felt her pain," Anta said quietly.

"You what?" Street asked.

"I felt her pain."

"That's not possible, is it?" I asked. Nobody answered.

As I began to think about how that could possibly be true, I heard the quiet, but unmistakable sound of a large number of footsteps pounding on the pavement. I raised my eyes from Anta and turned back to my window. A very large "herd"—for lack of a better word—of Skins was approaching from the direction in which "Sarah" had staggered away. They were moving very, very fast. Just before I hit the thruster, I observed a familiar face at the front of the rapidly-advancing herd.

Cain.

We were off. In hindsight, it might have been interesting to see what Cain had to say, but sticking around to hear him could have cost us our lives. Several minutes later, after traveling nearly fifty miles, I slowed down and pulled the Fluxor into a service station. We needed to eat.

"Let's get some grub and get out of here, fast," I said.

We grabbed sandwiches and chips from the wall machine of the service station. As we ate, we discussed what we had just experienced. It seemed—if we were correct in our understanding of Sarah's words—that the Skins wanted us to die, but not just because we are—or were—food. There is apparently something wrong with us that must be dealt with, and they intend to deal with it.

After debating it for some time, Angel posited a theory that Toronto's E-rase did more than just alter the Skins' *physical* state. She theorized that it must have also altered their *cognitive* state. It has made them believe that they are "normal". It has made them believe that we, those who actually *are* "normal", are perversions of nature. Perhaps they're right. How do we know that *we* aren't the ones who have been negatively affected by E-rase? Perhaps *our* minds lead us to believe that *we* are normal and the Skins are abnormal?

Even the physical characteristics of the Skins, while appearing abnormal to us, might actually be normal, but our minds won't allow us to see that. Perhaps it is *us* that have changed, not them.

"I'm not buying it," I said after a few moments thought. "If we were abnormal, somehow modified by E-rase, we probably wouldn't be having this conversation, right? We probably wouldn't have been capable of developing such a theory and rationally discussing it."

"Everyone thinks of themselves as 'normal,'" Angel countered.

Street barked out a laugh. "They are not normal, period!"

"I'm with you, Street," I added with a smile. "So, until I'm convinced otherwise, I'm normal, and my friends are normal."

"Well then, here's another possibility," Angel suggested. "What if they think they are an improved version of human? And since we haven't evolved as they have, we are now sub-human, therefore an abomination . . . in their way of thinking."

We all stared at her, dumbfounded. I couldn't think of a response. And obviously neither could Anta or Street.

"Ok," Angel said, shrugging her shoulders, "I'm ready to go now."

I turned back facing forward and stepped on the accelerator. We shot forward.

14

JUNE 29, 2093, 11:10PM—ANTA

We've just spoken with our friends on the moon! Hasani is alive and well! Their attempt to create E-rase was successful! The others have now all been inoculated against A.E. They'll be leaving their shell in a few hours, as a group, to explore the major moon colonies, searching for survivors. I'm so excited for them!

The five moon survivors have decided that they're going to attempt to secure and prepare a ship to return to Earth. They're pretty sure they'll be able to find a good ship, but I'm not sure they should come back to Earth. We spoke with them for a long time about the Skins. Hasani promised that they won't attempt a launch without first contacting us to receive word that it's safe to do so, given our current problems with the Skins.

My relationship with Shift is getting serious. He kissed me last night. With all of the stress and fear, I haven't felt much desire to get close to anyone, even Shift. Every night I lie down and fall to sleep. I rarely think of romance. But that kiss . . . wow! It wasn't the first, of course. But it was much more . . . passionate than any others. I hope it won't be the last.

JULY 2, 10:03PM—SHIFT

I'm so tired, laying here trying to sleep. Street's on watch and Mike is monitoring our position from Boston. But I still can't sleep.

We've spent the last three days traveling around Georgia and Alabama, visiting abandoned, desiccated bunkers and other alleged safe-houses. Both Georgia and Alabama are riddled with destruction and debris, along with hundreds of thousands of dead bodies in the streets.

Upon examining some of the bodies, it's clear that all the bodies have succumbed to A.E., but perhaps, not all of them were actually *killed* by the disease. Many of the bodies have crushed skulls, or bullet wounds, or other signs of physical violence. What a difference between these southern states and the northern states and Canada.

In any event, despite the overwhelming destruction around us, over the past three days, we have inoculated twenty-one additional people and helped them arm themselves. We have also been forced to avoid several large groups of Skins who certainly outnumber the remaining non-inoculated souls in these southern states.

It's incredibly sad and frustrating that the Skins, with their speed and their likely increased senses are able to find and lure so many survivors out of hiding before we have a chance to vaccinate and warn them. We're certainly losing the battle with the Skins. Our "human" population is decreasing every day—as much from the Skins as from A.E.

The scariest part of this problem is that the living humans are still supposed to be in hiding. Weeks ago, and even days ago, people only come out of their safe houses when Mike contacted them and told them we had arrived, or when we called them out and explained who we are and what we're doing. If they came out before then, they certainly ran the risk of contracting A.E. But now, before we even arrive, Mike is watching these people come out of hiding at the beckoning of the Skins.

These frightened, yet hopeful people are tragically turned into Skins after surviving the plague, in hiding, for months. It is terrifying to think that the Skins are smart enough, and savvy enough to lure these people out. Or maybe, something else is pulling the humans to the Skins. I haven't forgotten the feeling I had when Sarah looked into my eyes.

Additionally, we continue to learn about groups of our newly-vaccinated friends, despite our admonition to arm themselves and stay in hiding or flee, succumbing to, or falling at the hands of giant herds of Skins. All of them that could be contacted—and contact was maintained as much as possible with our bunker—were continually updated on the activity and dangerous propensities of the Skins. It doesn't seem to have mattered.

Perhaps without ample weaponry or other protection, the humans haven't been able to defend themselves. Of course, according to Mike, the people we have inoculated and warned have not all been lured out of hiding by the Skins, but instead, the Skins have found and attacked them.

Despite our prior vaccinations, those bitten by the Skins are turning. Dr. Shevchuk has no explanation for this phenomenon because it simply defies nature and all known physical and spiritual laws presently known to us.

In any case, of the few hundred people we've been able to vaccinate, Mike estimates that less than a hundred—not including the last three days' efforts—remain "human". Of course, all of those vaccinated with Toronto's vaccine, and all those bitten by those vaccinated by Toronto's vaccine, have turned as well, which equates to several thousand more according to estimates at the bunker.

Mike has still not located our friends from Shediac. They are probably dead, or worse.

Our bunker has been in constant contact with safe havens around the world, who have had relatively minor success locating people for vaccinations in the first place. Unfortunately, they are seeing the same events unfold there as we are here. The Skins who successfully crossed the Bering Strait eleven days ago are moving at such a rapid pace—far outpacing the speed of the human vaccinators—that they are overwhelming and overtaking Asia and Europe as we speak. Much like the A.E. plague before it, the plague of Skins is increasing exponentially as those infected infect others, who infect still others.

But what's bothering me most is Anta's statement a couple of days ago that she "felt" Sarah's pain when Sarah smashed her head into my window. We haven't talked about it again. Anta seemed very embarrassed by that whole scene. What could have caused that reaction in Anta? I've thought about it dozens of times, and secretly asked John to look into it, but we still have no answer.

JULY 3
THE MOON

"Can you tell what's wrong?" Ambassador Hasani Chalthoum asked.

"No," Dr. Jonas Sampson replied. "I can feel all these wires sticking out, but they're not attached to anything. It's like someone ripped them out on purpose."

"Why would someone do that?" Hasani asked.

"Maybe they were trying to lock themselves in, or everybody else out," Jonas replied. "Easy enough to get through the blast doors, but getting into the launch bay will be impossible if we can't get these wires back in place."

Jonas and Hasani had been searching the rubble of what was once a great and thriving International Lunar Station. At some point during the onslaught of A.E., someone had apparently destroyed equipment, and perhaps the ships in the launch bay. The United States colony and its shell were still intact, but portions of the international station housed within the shell were in ruins, including the components that controlled the doorway from the electronics station to the shuttle launch bay. The door was jammed, preventing access to the ships that lie beyond the doors.

The two men had easily entered the main protective blast doors on the outside of the compound. But because the launch bay doors appeared to have been sabotaged, they were scared to see what lay beyond those doors, if they ever gained access. If the ships had been destroyed too, they could be stuck on the moon forever.

"Okay, try flipping the switch again," Jonas said a few moments later.

Hasani flipped the main power switch on the wall. Sparks erupted from several points along the landing bay floor and walls beyond the jammed door. Hasani watched through the small, round window in the door as a small fire broke out near a storehouse filled with flammable liquids used to cool ships after they landed at the Station.

"Run!" Hasani yelled.

The two men ran. Jonas slipped through the blast doors leading out into the main terminal just as Hasani slammed his fist into the wall box that controlled the doors. An enormous eruption of heat and sound filled the gap between the two sliding doors moments before they sealed shut. The blast blew Jonas off his feet and propelled him into a small desk near the doors.

"Oh man!" Jonas cried out as the noise from the blast was silenced by the closing of the blast doors.

"Are you okay?" Hasani asked, nervously, as he ran over to Jonas.

"Yeah, I'm good," Jonas replied. "But I'm pretty sure I broke my wrist, or my hand. Probably just a small fracture, but it hurts like crazy."

"Well, let's get back to Tom. Let him cast it. We'll come back later. I hope the others have had more success than we've had."

"At least the bay doors are open now," Jonas said, smiling.

"Yeah, they are. But it could be a disaster in there."

15

I gently tapped Shift on the shoulder. "It's me," I whispered. Shift took a deep breath. It was two o'clock, time to change the watch.

"Ok," Shift mumbled. He stood up slowly and turned to face me. As I looked into his eyes, I could almost see the emotion behind them. Our relationship had deepened significantly over the past few days. We'd been through so much together, and depended on each other so often. It seemed like we'd known each other for years, even though it had only been six months.

I raised my hand and pushed my short, black hair out of my eyes. I smiled as I noticed Shift staring at my lips—again. He moved toward me, but I had a strange feeling that I should move away—that *now* wasn't the right time. I squeezed past him. As I sat down in the chair recently vacated by Shift, I reached for his weapon. Our fingers touched briefly, lightly. It was comfortable. Letting go of the gun, Shift turned away and wandered over to the couch.

Moments later, as I watched Shift's silhouette fade into peaceful oblivion, and wondered why I suddenly felt apprehensive at the suggestion of physical contact with him, the front window shattered. I cried out, startled, and looked out the window, afraid of what I would see. Shift, Angel and Street all jumped up from their resting places, almost involuntarily. Shift reached me just as I started brushing hundreds of glass fragments from my clothing. Street and Angel came quietly, but quickly to the window as well. A large rock rested on the carpet a few feet away from my chair.

"Is it them?" Angel whispered

"Yes!" I whispered in reply. Then I lost control of my emotions. "And there are hundreds of them!" I couldn't disguise the fear in my voice. But there was a longing to see them too.

I felt faint; but I could vaguely hear Street and Shift having some kind of heated discussion. I watched as Street ran to the back bathroom. I watched Shift move from window to window.

Street soon came back. "They're out back, too," he said. "We may have to fight our way out again."

"This is crazy!"

They're at our door again. This time, at a quiet hotel in Baton Rouge, Louisiana.

"Help me!" Shift said, almost angrily. But to whom, I couldn't tell.

Then I felt the splash of cold water. Angel stood in front of me, poised to slap me, as I shook my head to shake the water from my face.

"What was that for?" I asked indignantly; then noticed that Angel stood between me and the outside door, with a stern look on her face. Shift had both arms around me holding me back, and Street stood to the side with an empty ice bucket, dripping water on the floor.

"You were headed for the door, with a glazed look in your eyes," Angel replied questioningly, "and Shift couldn't stop you by himself . . . the wimp."

"Okay. I'm okay. Don't drown me," I said, wiping water from my face.

Satisfied that I was back to my rational self, Angel and Street rushed over to push furniture in front of the door and broken window.

Shift bent at the knees and gazed deep into my eyes. "Are you ok?"

Embarrassed, I looked away and murmured "Yes."

Shift took me by both hands and pulled me toward the others, still looking at me, and still obviously concerned.

In moments, I heard a loud commotion coming from the walkway outside the room.

"There's like 250 of them out there," Street said, fear lacing his words. "I saw some of them coming out of the sewer holes in the street out back."

"Can we still get out over the roof?" I asked. Shift and Street had prepared an escape route, just like we had done for several nights in a row. This time, we might actually have to use it. *Why didn't Mike or John call us?*

"Yeah, I think so," Street replied. "But we'd better hurry."

While we still had time, we gathered our meager belongings, stuffing them into our packs. Then we climbed out the side window and up a short ladder to the roof. On the roof, we were out of sight of any Skins, but our only escape from there was to climb down the fire escape on the far side of the building and get into the Fluxor. And we had to move fast, before we were seen, or smelled, or heard.

The plan was working so far. With the window closed behind us, we could hear only muffled shouts for a moment. Within twenty seconds, however, the window was shattered from inside and voices were calling to climb to the roof. I was again surprised by the humanness of their voices, considering the beastliness of their appetites. Equally surprising was the apparent indication that they knew which way we had gone in a matter of seconds. They may be able to smell us. I slowed down, involuntarily, unable to will my legs to move faster. The others continued to run.

As the others neared the fire escape. Shift looked back and saw me. I had stopped running, but I wasn't sure why. Grabbing Street by the sleeve, Shift spun him around so he could see me too. They rushed to me. Arriving, looking dumbfounded, Street lifted me up off my feet, turned, and ran back toward the fire escape ladder with me bouncing up and down in his muscular arms.

There were no Skins on the street below, yet. Angel was already on her way down the ladder. Street hefted me over his shoulder and began the long climb down the rusted metal ladder. It creaked and squeaked loudly as it tried desperately to support the weight of both Street and me.

As we neared the final landing, I watched Shift, last to climb onto the ladder, duck down below the roofline just in time to avoid being hit in the head with some object thrown at him. Whatever that object was, its velocity was incredible. It shattered against the wall of the adjacent building, sending brick fragments toward the Fluxor waiting below. Angel ducked inside the Fluxor to avoid being struck by the falling debris.

"Faster," Shift hissed. *"Faster!"*

Street jumped off the final landing, over ten feet above the ground. My neck whipped up and back down upon landing, but I didn't feel any pain. Not bearing that extra weight, Shift climbed down a few more steps and then jumped. He bent his legs at the knee as he landed, then ran to the Fluxor and jumped through the open door. Angel hit the accelerator.

As she opened up the thrusters, the mob still on the ground came tearing around the corner after us. Angel blasted right into them, knocking many out of the way. As we passed, several of them got their hands on the Fluxor, their faces leering at us through the closed windows, before we could get past. It was *that* close. As we sped off, I looked through the back window at the mob gathering behind us. I saw the face and dark eyes of Cain; his big, hard body visibly pulsating with energy, or anger, or whatever it was.

He stared at me.

I knew him, somehow.

I wanted to be with him.

Nobody said a word as we followed the route preprogrammed into the Fluxor the night before. Leaving Baton Rouge, we traveled west at over a hundred and twenty miles per hour, the Fluxor automatically dodging cars and other obstacles lying in the road.

Less than thirty minutes later, we stopped to relieve our highly-agitated bladders. We had arrived at a community park in Lafayette, nearly sixty miles from Baton Rouge. By the time we finished, only minutes later, we could see distant movement on the road from which we'd come. They had caught up to us!

The Skins had traveled sixty miles in less than thirty-five minutes!

"How in the world . . . ?" Angel asked. Tears were in her eyes as she struggled to control her emotions. We were all struggling to keep it together.

They were fast. The fastest man on Earth ran a mile in three minutes and thirty-two seconds in the year 2088. That man (Samwel Casimati, from Tanzania) ran the mile at a rate of approximately seventeen miles per hour. Of course, no human could keep that pace for even two miles, let alone sixty. Yet, the Skins just caught up to us. They must have been running at just over one hundred miles per hour!

"Let's go!" Shift yelled, as if Street wouldn't be able to hear him over the noise of the approaching mob.

We're once again fleeing a mob of sub-humans bent on our destruction. Street drives, but none of us can rest. I fear, now, that wherever we go, they'll find us. Either they will smell us, or hear us, or follow us—who knows? But interlaced with that fear is a feeling I can't describe. The farther we get from the Skins—and Cain—the farther away I want to be. But when we're close . . . it's hard to describe. For now, I'm afraid.

How long can we continue to flee?

We will have to kill again in order to survive, and probably kill a lot. I'm not confident that we can outrun them, even at high speeds in the Fluxor. The war that Street predicted a few days ago is at our doorstep.

JULY 4, 7:15ᴀᴍ—SHIFT

We've been driving for several hours to escape the Skins who miraculously caught up to us in Lafayette. Our situation has become desperate. We've recently been in contact with Dr. Porter and his son who are in some kind of underground bunker in Cabo Rojo, Mexico.

They've been there for a month, and that's where we're headed now. It's a long way from here, south, along the Gulf of Mexico; and we've got to hit a few towns that Mike has identified in Texas, Arizona and Utah first. Then we'll head back east, and go south into Mexico toward the gulf.

I can't foresee us outrunning the Skins for much longer, so we will be tightening our schedule and spending less time in the towns we travel through. It may come down to a weapons battle that we will probably lose given their numbers against our four.

Plus, with Anta's reaction to the Skins yesterday, I'm not sure we can count on her to help us. I haven't dared ask her what happened. Nobody has. This is twice now that Anta has reacted strangely around the Skins. I don't know what to do, but I'd like to keep her away from them. I'd like to stay away from them myself.

16

JULY 6, 2093, 10:19AM
SOMEWHERE IN TEXAS

"We gotta move!" Street shouted as he ran toward the Fluxor.

"Then get your ass in here!" Angel shouted back through the door she was holding open.

"Shoot them!" Street yelled out as he neared the open, waiting back door.

Shift and Angel opened fire as soon as Street was clear. The Skins hot on Street's heels were in the hundreds.

"You're so stupid Street," Angel said as she fired off two more shots at the nearest Skin. The others were beginning to back off, seeing their comrades fall. "I told you not to go out there."

As soon as Street slammed the door closed behind him, Shift hit the thrusters and they sped off.

"But the dog was alive, man," Street replied, trying to catch his breath.

"Yeah, but it's not alive now, and you were almost killed too. Idiot." Angel reached over and hit Street in the arm.

"I'm sorry babe," Street said quietly as he lowered his head. He knew he had a real friend in Angel and he felt an incredible weight knowing that he had almost let her down—and for a dog.

"Just don't do it again Street, or I may kill you myself." Angel smiled. Street smiled too. It had been too close, but they were still alive.

As Street began to scoot over to the right, closer to Angel, the Fluxor suddenly swerved to the right, throwing both Street and Angel into the left side of the hover.

"Get ready to fight guys," Shift said as the two in the back seat regained their balance.

The small group looked up to see another horde, or perhaps the same horde, approaching from the left. Shift had swerved onto a side road, but the going was slower. The road was dirt. Without energy pulsar modules in the ground, the Fluxor didn't operate as quickly.

Sensing the loss of speed in the vehicle they were chasing, the Skins increased their speed.

"Shift, you've gotta get us back on the road, man!" Street said, excitedly.

"I'm trying dude. It looks like a paved road up there, doesn't it?"

"Yeah, I think it is," Anta replied.

"Then get there man!" Street yelled as he began to open his window.

"What are you doing?" Angel asked frantically.

"Killing, babe. It's gotta be done."

Angel and Anta watched as Street began unloading his weapon on the Skins hot in pursuit. Angel watched for only a few seconds before she could see that it wasn't working well enough. She opened her window, leaned out, and joined Street in the slaughter. And it *was* a slaughter. The Skins were falling rapidly. But they weren't necessarily dying—it was hard to tell through the dust circling and whirling around the Skins and the Fluxor. But Skins were falling; and eventually, the group began to fall back again.

A few seconds later, Shift yelled, "hold on!" Then he turned hard to the left, onto the paved road. As the Fluxor hit the pavement, it shot like a bullet and the Skins were soon lost from sight.

JULY 6, 10:41AM
HIDDEN BUNKER NEAR BOSTON

"There's something outside the cabin, on the east perimeter," Mike told the group anxiously staring at the monitors that adorned the walls of the lab. He had called them into the lab over the old PA system. Everyone was present, sitting or standing however they could manage in order to get a better look.

"I can't see anything," John said.

"It's not there anymore, but it was big," Mike replied.

"What do you mean by 'big'?" Dr. Shevchuk asked.

"Well, not big necessarily. But it wasn't a small animal. It looked human."

There shouldn't have been people out there. But they had been hearing sounds coming from the ventilator shafts for several hours. Mr. Carón Blanchard, the bunker's ventilation specialist and electrical engineer had inspected the shafts several times already—from the inside. The ventilation system allowed odors and carbon dioxide to leave the shelter and prevented any substance or particulate from entering. But it wasn't invulnerable to damage from outside. The people were on edge.

"There it is!" Mrs. Chrissy Houghton gasped. All eyes turned to the corner screen where she pointed.

"That's a man," John said.

As they stared in disbelief at the sight of a living, walking man outside the bunker, four more human bodies appeared. Within minutes, nearly every one of the twenty-two camera feeds on the outside of the bunker registered the presence of human forms. It was impossible to tell how many were out there, but most of them were naked, and they were all bald.

Then, although they didn't know it yet, the communication system went down.

JULY 6, 2093

Within hours of the Boston bunker's sighting of humans outside the cabin on the surface, dozens of similar episodes occurred around the world.

17

"I haven't heard from anyone at the bunker since early yesterday morning," I said. "My MEHD can't connect with them. It's like the system is malfunctioning or something."

"Weird," Anta replied. "I wonder what's happened."

"They're probably on vacation," Angel said, smiling. "You know how Yurgi likes to party."

We all laughed, but it was nervous laughter.

"Well, vacation or not, I'd really like to know how far we are from the nearest Skins," I said. "Especially after yesterday's close call."

For several days, we'd been narrowly avoiding mobs of Skins as we traveled from Louisiana through Texas and into New Mexico. We had been lucky. Reports from our friends, while they were still communicating, were that those we'd inoculated, those we'd yet to attend to, and others around the world, were succumbing to the Skins in droves. Most don't have the weaponry we do, the experience using any weaponry they do have, nor the experience we do in outrunning them.

Our plan was to head to Cabo Rojo; but we had to do so without being followed by the Skins. The whereabouts of Jon Porter's "secret" bunker must remain a secret, particularly from the Skins.

"What is that up there?" Street asked two minutes later. Street was driving, and his eyes seemed to be far better than mine. I looked up ahead. Sure enough, there was something in the road.

"Maybe it's a rock slide or something," I offered, hopeful that that was all it was. We were traveling through a low mountain pass—actually, more like big hills. But they were rocky. I thought it was possible.

"No, I don't think so," Street said. "I think I see movement. Pull out the binocs Anta. I'm stopping here."

Anta reached over the seat into the back of the Fluxor. She rummaged through the gear that was scattered around the back as a result of the high-speed twisting and turning of the Fluxor over the past couple of days. Nobody had bothered to clean up the mess. She finally found the binocs and handed them to me in the front seat. I placed them over my head and adjusted the lenses.

"Ohhhh crap," I said quietly, and slowly. I took the binocs off and handed them to Street. After placing them on his head, his lips mouthed a few salty curse words. Then he removed the binocs and handed them to the back seat. Anta and Angel each took a turn leaning over the back of the seat in front of them to see. Angel swore aloud, but a peaceful look came over Anta's face. It wasn't right.

Up ahead, maybe two and a half kilometers at most, was a roadblock composed entirely of Skins—a couple thousand of them, or more. They were more-or-less stationary, standing at attention in orderly rows perhaps fifteen to twenty deep. The rows of Skins stretched across the road and up the hillsides for a hundred meters on either side of the road.

We had stopped moving toward them; but curiosity won the day and a joint decision was made to move closer. We knew we could outrun them in the Fluxor, so we determined to move close enough to see what they were up to. Street released the brake and the Fluxor inched forward.

"Ok, I'll get us closer, but Anta and Angel, you watch for an end run out the sides and rear window," cautioned Street.

We had killed hundreds of Skins over the past few days as we escaped from town after town. Perhaps they wanted peace—a little respite from the deadly guns of Mr. Threet "Street" Kimball—former outside linebacker for the New York Giants. It seemed unlikely. More likely, they wanted revenge.

As we inched closer, still "safely" within the confines of the Fluxor, certain details became more apparent through the binocs. At their front was Cain. He stood alone in front of the group—clearly the leader. I wasn't surprised. On two prior occasions, he had looked wiser, stronger, and more intelligent than the others. On this occasion, he held what appeared to be a semi-automatic rifle in his left hand; but from our distance, it was hard to tell. His right hand was raised in the air, palm toward us, and all five fingers were close together and pointed to the sky.

Most of the others also held weapons, the majority of which appeared to be firearms. Until very recently, we had not seen a single gun carried by any of them. In recent encounters over the past couple of days, however, we observed a handful wielding guns. For the most part, though, the Skins had carried nothing more deadly than clubs and axes. This was a new development, and not a welcome one. But none of them had raised their weapons. Plus, the Fluxor was built to be bullet-proof. I felt pretty safe, so far.

When we were approximately 110 or 120 meters away, Street stopped the Fluxor, but left the thrusters running, with the lever in reverse. The living roadblock was on a shallow rise of the land. On either side of the roadway, steep, rocky hills rose up and away from the roadside. Those rocky hills blocked any means of travel forward except for on the roadway. If we needed to leave quickly, backward was our only route. Luckily, Street and I had each had several opportunities over the past few days to test out and gain confidence with the reverse thrusters as we escaped from smaller hordes of Skins.

Cain appeared to be staring straight into the Fluxor, but I couldn't tell whether he was focused on anything in particular.

"Do you think he wants to talk?" Angel asked.

"Don't care dude," Street replied. "I've heard him talk. I don't want to hear it again."

"We need to let him talk, I think," I said.

Anta's knees began to bounce with nervous energy.

Ultimately, we *needed* to hear what Cain had to say, if anything, or we wouldn't have taken the risk. This appeared to be the moment we had fearfully and anxiously waited for: an opportunity to talk, rather than just run.

Cain spoke, making the decision for us. He didn't have any communication device or other apparatus to amplify his voice, but his voice reached us all the same. It was the same voice we'd heard that night in Amqui, but it was laced with intensity and anger.

"Although you have evaded us in the past," he began, "it is time for this to end. Your existence is an abomination to God. You were not created by Him, but rather, are a perversion of his Holy Plan. He did not intend for you to exist and it falls upon us, his ordained and chosen people, to wipe you from the face of God's Earth. Come forward to be slain!"

For some reason, until this moment, I had not considered the aptness of the name "Cain", and I wondered whether he had taken that name or whether it was given to him at birth. Like Cain from the Biblical story in the book of Genesis—and also the Quran and other ancient texts—this Cain seemed like a bad dude. In Genesis, Cain, one of the sons of Adam and Eve, killed his brother Abel some time shortly after the creation of the world. *That* Cain was the first to kill another human. Now, this man, also Cain, seemed determined to kill the *last* humans. Unlike the story in the Book of Genesis though, this Cain apparently believed he had been called of God and *ordained* to kill. I doubt the Biblical Cain had such motives or aspirations. He was just jealous.

Upon hearing Cain's words, Street placed his hand on the door to exit the Fluxor. Street's a very religious guy, we had learned. I knew that letting him leave the Fluxor would get ugly, quickly. Reaching over, I grabbed his shoulder to restrain him. Although my grasp wasn't strong enough for me to stop Street, he didn't fight me.

"Street, sit down," I growled under my breath. "We don't need you acting like a hero."

"He's right, Street," Angel added. "Jumping out that door and shooting off your mouth, or your guns, would probably provide all the motivation the Skins need to attack or open fire, and we won't have time to get you back in the car before they swarm us. We need to talk. So stay in that seat."

"Why did he bring God into this?" Street asked, through clenched teeth.

I didn't know, of course, but I wanted to find out. Street's attempted rash act would have certainly prevented that, and probably got him, and maybe the rest of us killed.

What I really wanted to figure out was why Anta had begun bouncing up and down like she was about to pee her pants. She was looking forward, seemingly staring at Cain. Every time the Skins had gotten near us over the past few days, Anta started acting weird. Angel, Street and I had talked privately yesterday. Angel suggested that, perhaps, Cain held some kind of psychological influence over Anta. I rejected the notion; but now I'm not sure. I nodded to Angel, giving her a knowing look. She understood and reached over and gently grasped Anta's hand.

"Street," I said very quietly, "keep your finger on the auto locks please. We need Anta to stay here."

Street nodded.

Lowering my window, I shouted Cain's name.

Immediately, Cain said, "There is no reason to cry out. We can hear your words clearly, for we are the Chosen."

So, in a normal voice, I asked, "Why do you believe that we are an abomination before God? Aren't we all God's children? Aren't we human, just like you, created in His image?" I looked over at Street for reassurance.

He nodded again.

Cain replied, with passion and great fervor, "You are *not* human like us. You are a perverted creation of man, not God. The God of the Heavens looks upon you with abhorrence and contempt. He has called upon us, from His throne in the Heavens, to act as His messengers, and to destroy you; just as He has already destroyed the rest of your kind through His great and terrible plague."

After these words, Street could hardly contain himself. "Whoa!" he exclaimed. "Nobody tells me that *my* God wants me to die! Nobody tells me that he is a messenger from *my* God, sent to destroy me! These dudes need to go down!"

I agreed, of course, but would probably have used different language. Now I put *my* finger on the electronic locks. There were now two people I had to keep in the hover.

I electronically rolled up my window so we could discuss what action to take. Obviously, Street wanted to fight. Angel, on the other hand, wanted to flee. She couldn't understand the logic of attempting to face a mass of Skins so great under these circumstances. I believed that the time would come for another fight, but that it was not now. I think Anta would have agreed with me, but her vote, whatever it might be, was forfeited as a result of her agitated, nearly-hypnotic state.

Although this wasn't a democracy, Street understood that he was outnumbered, and I hoped that he also saw our logic. We decided to flee. The Skins were starting to get restless. Every couple of seconds, one or more of them would dart out a few meters, then slowly back up into the lines. Cain's hand had remained in the air. It looked like he was controlling them, but that his control was tenuous.

Before we left, I lowered my window and again called out to Cain.

"Cain! We have no quarrel with you. We believe that we can all live on this Earth, together, in peace. We will leave, and stay away from you and your people. Although we have made this decision, do not mistakenly believe that we cower at your presence or your words. We will fight if we must, but we choose, at this time, to attempt to live in peace." I lied. I was pretty sure we couldn't all live together in peace.

"Nice speech," Angel said, perhaps a little too sarcastically.

Cain replied, in a voice full of fury and rage, "You will die! You will die now!" He dropped his hand. With that motion, the throngs of Skins swept toward us like a tsunami. Street hit the reverse thrusters and we fled, narrowly avoiding a crushing blow of bodies as they jumped toward us and high into the air, to rain down from the sky.

At the same time, Anta threw her body into the right side window. Rearing back, she threw herself at it again and again.

"What is she doing?" Street yelled, trying to concentrate on flying in reverse.

"I can't stop her," Angel screamed as she tried, desperately, to grab hold of Anta's clothing and torso.

I sat there for a moment, unmoving, stunned and scared. A few of the faster, or closer Skins had reached us and successfully clung to the outside of the hover. We could hear them howling; their nails digging into the exterior of the hover as the wind rushed past them.

One Skin, grasping the hood next to the windshield, stared at me, her face crushed against the hood as she fought to stay affixed. Her blood-red saliva slipped from her open mouth and I watched with fascination as it ran across her face and bald head and flew off behind her into the slowly-thinning horde. Her eyes seemed to scream at me. It felt as though her shadowy eyes tore into my mind. I actually felt pain. I wondered if that was what Anta was feeling as she continued to thrash against Angel's arms that were still trying to control her.

Street began to swerve back and forth rapidly, attempting to dislodge the few remaining Skins from their grasp on the hover. It worked as one after another lost his or her grip and tumbled to the road, rolling over and over until gravity and friction finally stopped their motion. Finally, the female in front of me lost her grip too and slid down the hood onto the road, wailing as she went. The pain in my head ended abruptly as she crashed into the ground.

Had the Skins been merely human, such a fall—at over one hundred miles per hour—would have killed or very successfully maimed them. But the Skins, whatever they were, just got up and joined their colleagues in pursuit of our small party still trying to escape, traveling in reverse. The woman who had stared into my soul also rose from the ground. Her bare skin was covered in blood which oozed from the cuts and gashes she had suffered in her fall from the hover.

Bullets began to pierce the shell of the Fluxor as the Skins lost ground; but they didn't penetrate the interior.

Having gained a little distance, Street threw the steering stick to the left and slammed the thrusters to neutral, then from neutral to forward, rapidly turning the Fluxor 180 degrees to the right. It was a beautiful maneuver, but I didn't have time to relish it as a blast tore up the road next to us. Another blast, then another, then another narrowly missed us as the Skins continued to fall away behind us. The last explosion hit so close to our left side that its force rocked the hover fifteen or twenty degrees from horizontal, violently throwing all four of us to the right. When I had a chance, I looked back to see what type of weapon the skins had that could affect the hover like that. I couldn't tell because some of the skins were still chasing us and blocking the view.

After falling back to horizontal, Street again hit the thrusters. He never let off as we continued at an uncomfortably-high speed away from the horde. Although they continued to pursue us for many kilometers, we eventually lost sight of them. That was good. We needed to not only put more distance between us, but we needed to do so without them seeing where we went.

A few minutes later—time which felt like an eternity—Anta finally ceased her attempt to break free of the safe confines of the Fluxor. Her body relaxed and she slumped forward, her seatbelt the only thing keeping her off the floor between the seats. I watched as Angel gently and carefully helped Anta back into an upright position. Angel then wrapped her arm around Anta and began to sing. I didn't recognize the melody or the words, but the effect was magical. Anta's eyes opened slowly, and she began to sing along quietly.

A few minutes later, as Angel's song died out, Anta began to cry. She was bleeding from her forehead and seemed dazed. She hadn't spoken since we first saw the Skins, apart from her fragmented singing.

Her clothes were ripped and her skin was scratched in several places where Angel had tried to grab her in order to still her rabid lurching.

Moments later, Anta fell asleep, blood slowly dripping down the front of her face and onto her ripped tank top.

"How bad is that cut, Angel?" I asked.

"It's hard to tell," she replied as she dabbed at the blood with a red and white striped bandana that had been holding her hair back. "It doesn't look deep. She's going to have a killer headache, but I think she'll be fine."

Anta's action reminded me of Sarah, the Skin that charged at my window many days earlier. I no longer doubted the theory Angel posited a few days ago. Cain surely has, or had, some grasp on Anta's mind, and probably the minds of the Skins. I needed to keep Anta away from the Skins, particularly Cain.

Finally, after a two and a half hour trek of nearly three hundred miles, northeastward—back the way from which we had approached the roadblock—we turned north. Although our destination was to the south, in Mexico, we couldn't let the Skins follow us. We travelled north for about three hours, then turned west, stopping only once to relieve our bladders.

As we traveled through southern Colorado, so close to my former home, memories of my sister and her children flooded my mind. Their deaths, at the hands of A.E., could have been avoided for a while, if the three men who accosted them in the cabin had stayed away. But they would not have lived long. I probably wouldn't have been able to reach them in time to protect them from A.E. *or* the Skins. Tears formed in my eyes. I wished, in a way, that I could join them on the other side, but I knew I had an obligation to both my friends and the human race to survive.

This day had turned out to be very emotional. Even Street looked beat up. I couldn't see any tears, but his face had a look of deep grief and sorrow. We all needed sleep, but where would we be safe?

18

"Well, this looks like a good enough spot," Street said. He had pulled up in front of a large resort hotel in some mountainous, touristy town somewhere in southern Colorado. I hadn't even paid attention to where we were. Maybe Durango or Cortez.

"We haven't seen Skins for five hours," Angel said. "Maybe we're safe here. I need to pee, and eat."

"Okay, but let's comb the town first, just to be safe," I said. "Plus, maybe there are survivors here."

I had tried to reach the bunker several times over the past four or five hours, to no avail. We didn't know whether there were any survivors in this town or any of the others we had passed through in our hasty retreat. I was feeling a bit guilty about not stopping in every town to search for survivors, but Angel had convinced me that our deaths would ultimately be worse in the long run. We should make sure we live to see another day in order to vaccinate others, she argued. I still felt guilt. I wanted to check this town out.

So, we drove up and down the streets. It was dark, and we were afraid to use the megaphones. We looked for lights and listened for the sounds of human activity. There was nothing.

Finally, after two hours, we retired to the hotel, parked the hover next to the rear exit of the underground garage, and took the stairs to the top floor, thirty-seven stories in the air. Although the climb was brutal, we reasoned that we were safer up high than down low. We hoped the Skins would have a more difficult time finding us here if we were thirty-seven stories in the air.

Like nearly every other building in most of the other towns we had gone into, the electricity worked, but was sporadic—intermittently switching on and off. We'd been stuck in an elevator once before, and didn't relish the idea of that happening again.

At the top of the hotel, we found a large, beautifully-decorated suite with no bodies. The room was slightly dusty, but otherwise, it was in a condition ready to accommodate high-paying guests like us. As usual, we spent some time preparing an escape route up and over the roof. Of course, this high in the air, the climb down fire escape ladders would be unpleasant, and maybe impossible.

After eating three cheese sandwiches and a bag of Doritos from the wall unit, in an attempt to allay some of the guilt I felt having not searched all the towns we passed through today, I determined to, at least, check out this hotel. There were no signs of Skins, and I felt safe enough.

"I'm going to check out the hotel," I said. "There are hundreds of rooms and maybe someone is alive somewhere."

"I'll go with you," Anta said. She had come out of her funk slowly over the last few hours. She seemed herself again, so I consented.

Anta and I left the room, guns ready. Anta closed the door behind us and we heard the soft click of the manual lock from the inside. We had learned, days ago, to not use the electronic locks on the doors to hotel rooms, just in case the power shut off. Just then, the lights flickered off. I was glad I had eaten before the wall unit shut off.

We started on the 37th floor where we were camped and worked our way down, lighting the way with our flashlights. The 37th and 36th floors were empty. We knocked on each door and received no response. Stepping out of the stairwell onto the 35th floor, Anta stopped abruptly. I ran into her back and almost knocked her over.

"Sorry," I whispered, nervously. "What's wrong?"

"Look," she replied, shining the flashlight onto the floor at her feet.

I peeked around her shoulder into the hallway, placing my hand on the door frame. My little finger slipped into a small hole, about the size of a pea. Dried blood stained the floor immediately at our feet, and the walls on both sides of the hall. Anta and I each took a small step backward away from it. Several seconds later, having gathered my nerves, I quietly stepped around Anta and entered the hallway.

A short way down the hall to the right I came upon the shadowy remains of conflict. Two long streaks of dark, dry blood ran parallel to each other along the hallway floor for several meters. At the end of the left-most streak sat a lone Adidas tennis shoe. Just beyond the shoe, a silver Smith & Wesson handgun lay on the floor in what was once, surely, a large puddle of blood. It looked as though a body had been dragged down the hallway.

"What do you think happened here?" Anta asked, quietly.

"I don't know," I replied. "It looks like it was a while ago though. Should we keep searching?"

"I really don't want to, Shift," Anta said. "I'm very scared."

"Me too. Let's go back. We could both use some rest."

"Thank you," Anta said, and she kissed my cheek.

JULY 9, 6:30PM
CABO ROJO, MEXICO—SHIFT

Our speedy route over the past thirty-four hours took us northwest to the Utah border near Moab, west through central Utah, then south to Las Vegas on I-15. From there, we continued south through the hot, barren Mojave Desert and on to the California coast, near Los Angeles, where we spent the night in another room high atop an expensive hotel. Unlike the last hotel, we didn't bother to search for survivors. We were running for our lives and needed to regroup in Cabo Rojo.

From Los Angeles, we traveled south toward Baja Mexico, passing through Tijuana. Our route continued southeast into central Mexico before finally turning east toward Cabo Rojo. If the Skins had followed us, they never got close to us again. Nor did we see a single living soul; but our searches were hasty.

We finally arrived at a location a few miles south of Cabo Rojo, Mexico. Only Dr. Steve Porter and his son Jon were at the bunker when we arrived. It was difficult to find the place. We hadn't had any communication with the Boston bunker in three days, but finally located Dr. Porter's signal early this morning. He directed us to the bunker, south of town, right on the beach.

Upon opening the door of the large concrete and metal structure, which was locked, redundantly, from the inside, a wave of sickening stench engulfed us—the smell of death. Steve and Jon stood in the opening with masked faces, gloved hands and what appeared to be kitchen aprons on over their clothes. Jon had a box in his hands, which he handed to me when his dad nodded to him.

"You'll want to put these on first thing or you won't be able to smell anything in a few hours." The box contained more cloth masks, which we donned quickly. As we walked inside, Steve told their tale.

Over the past five weeks or so, Steve and Jon had removed the bodies of over 750 people. They told us that there are hundreds more, with which they could really use our help. They haven't been burying the dead, and they expressed great sadness at the fact, but insisted that they felt obligated to remove the bodies first, and then to humanely dispose of them, if possible. To that end, they had located a hollow in the earth about a quarter mile from the bunker, where they had placed all the bodies they were able to extricate.

"How are you getting the bodies to the hollow?" I asked. "It seems like that would wear you out quickly, but you don't look like you've spent the last several weeks carrying hundreds of bodies on your backs."

Steve smiled and said that was part of tomorrow's tour.

"And I've been helping a lot," added Jon.

"You sure have," Steve replied with a chuckle as he ruffled Jon's hair affectionately.

"How are you avoiding catching some disease?" Angel questioned through the cloth mask over her mouth and nose, which reduced the stench to a tolerable level.

"We've been using a lot of disinfectant on any surface we need to touch. The facility is well stocked for medical emergencies and we're taking advantage of that. You're lucky, the smell is lessening as we get rid of the bodies."

"Wow!" Angel said. "I can't imagine a worse smell than this."

Steve believes that the bunker has sufficient resources to support the hundreds of people who were here, seemingly safe, almost indefinitely. We have yet to see how and why he believes that. But our first order of business is to rest.

While the smell of death and decay here is staggering, we at least feel that we're safe. The Skins don't know where we are. Steve and Jon haven't heard or seen anything of them. It seems improbable, even with their exaggerated capacity to smell or see, or whatever it is that drives their ability to locate the living, that they will be able to find us here, underground, surrounded on three sides by sea water and, as Steve described it, some kind of impermeable retaining wall to keep the water out of the bunker.

While it seems impossible that I will sleep *well*, I'm certain I will sleep *long*. As for the others, I'm sure that lying in the comfortable, clean beds here, without the threat of death, or worse, they will also sleep for a long time.

19

JULY 10, 2093
CABO ROJO, MEXICO—ANTA

"Jon, this place is remarkable!" I said.

"I know," Jon Porter replied. "Wait 'til I show you the gardens. And the tunnel. And the docks!"

"The docks?" Shift asked.

"Yeah, the docks. Boats, scuba gear, a submarine."

"You serious bro?" Street asked. "A sub?"

"Yup," Jon replied, a smile playing on his lips as if he were locked in a giant candy store.

We arrived in Jon Porter's bunker yesterday. This massive, underground station in Cabo Rojo, Mexico is amazing, but reeks of death. When we first got here, Dr. Steven Porter and his son Jon welcomed us with open arms and bleeding hearts.

This bunker, according to documents left by the now-deceased occupants and Steve's online research, was originally an antiquated, but functional military installation of some kind. It doesn't have all of the modern life-support systems that have been in use for at least the last two or three decades. It doesn't have food or drink wall units—the food is either canned or freeze-dried. Nor does it have modern waste management systems, but instead, utilizes a septic tank for human waste and a trash compacter and natural gas-fired incinerator for garbage. Nevertheless, it appears to have everything we may need to sustain life here indefinitely. It even has its own submersible power generators, located offshore, that generate power using the flow of salt water. Steve and Jon promised to tell us more about the bunker on our tour.

Over the past few weeks, with help from Mike Petrovsky in Boston, Steve had been able to access remote, hidden files on this station's hard drives and off-location servers. These files, Steve said, detail the purpose for the creation of this installation and its systems, its history, and the functions and uses to which we may put those systems. There are also systems maps and booklets covering most of the operations.

Steve and Jon led us down into the earth through a series of concrete tunnels and metal staircases.

As we descended from ground level, Steve pointed out two levels full of sleeping, eating and sanitation facilities. He showed us the environmental control center on the first level below ground and assured us that the air quality was not harmful. I was wondering why he felt the need to explain about the air quality, when he led us down a hallway to a recreation room and kitchen. They were nice, but there were still dead bodies on these two levels. And the accompanying smell was nauseating, even with the cloth masks Jon had given us. When I pulled out my shirt-tail to cover my face and turned to look at Steve, he was smiling through a handkerchief he held to his mouth and nose.

"That's why I explained about the air quality and why we've been staying up on ground level in a couple of the security apartments," explained Steve.

"I don't blame you," Shift replied.

On the third level down, we stopped again and entered through a large set of double doors.

"Here's the farm!" Steve said. "Jon has been trying to keep the corn alive. Been doing pretty well, haven't you?" Steve looked at Jon with both admiration and love. The father and son may be the only such combo still alive on Earth, and they seem to know how fortunate they are.

"Wow," I said. "Corn? What else is there?"

"Beets, potatoes, watermelon, tomatoes, lots of green stuff," Jon replied, beaming. He had pulled a neckerchief that he wore around his neck, up over his cloth mask. "And way over there against the back wall, you can see the orchard. It's got apples and peaches. There's some raspberry and grape plants too, but they don't look too good."

"That's amazing Jon! You may keep the whole human race alive yourself!" Shift said through the shirt-tail he had pulled out of his pants to cover his mask, exposing a lean and sexy six-pack. He's good at that. I mean—he's good at making people feel appreciated and useful, not at looking lean and sexy—although he's good at that, too. Jon looked proud as can be.

"What other surprises do you have for us Steve," Angel asked. She was clearly impressed, just like the rest of us. A farm, underground, was simply amazing!

"Well, let's keep going down," Steve replied.

We had walked down another long flight of stairs when my nose began to smell the tell-tale signs of animal dung, which was refreshing given what we had been smelling for the past several hours.

"Is that cow crap I smell?" Street asked, wrinkling his nose.

"Yup," Jon replied. "But no cows. They're all dead. But there's chickens, turkeys and a fish pond!"

"It looks like most of the cows died from Anthrax E," Steve said, sadly. "We cut up what's left of the bodies and took them outside with the human bodies. There were a few sheep and pigs too. The cows' 'crap' as Street so eloquently put it, is still around a bit. We've been trying to clean it up too. I don't know whether A.E. is in the feces, and if so, what it would do to plants, so we've tried to clean it up."

"So, the birds and the fish are alive?" Shift asked.

"Not a single dead one among them, that we can see," Steve answered. "It seems like they might be immune."

"That's kind of what we thought, right?" Street asked.

"Yeah, seems to fit our old hypothesis," Shift replied. "The mammals—cows, sheep, pigs—couldn't escape the disease any more than the humans could."

"Anyway," Steve said, "there are chicken coops with hundreds of birds laying tons of eggs every day! The turkeys just run around as they please, and we're not stopping them. The pond is stocked and there's a little fish hatchery over next to the pond. Thousands of eggs and fish in various stages of life. We don't know anything about raising fish, but there are some manuals. Jon's been reading them, trying to figure it out."

"This just keeps getting better," I said, "if you can get past the smell of human rot."

"Luckily, down here on the lower floors, the smell of death is greatly reduced," Steve replied. "Let's keep going."

We followed him down one more level to some mechanical rooms on the fifth floor. A short walk through a maze of huge, old computer systems and other machines took us to another set of large double doors.

"Here's the thing that will impress you most," Steve said.

He opened the doors and flipped a switch on the wall. Within seconds, a string of fluorescent ceiling lights came on, one after another in sequence, leading down a large and very long circular concrete tunnel with a flat, horizontal concrete floor. Several ATVs—All Terrain Vehicles—sat in rows along the right side wall. They were all identical, red, with seating for two, a large wire basket on the back and a spotlight on the front.

"I guess that explains why hauling bodies hasn't worn you out," Shift said. "But how did you get these things up all of those stairs?"

"Ah, that's the trick," Steve replied with a wink.

"We just used the ramps over there behind that big door," Jon added, pointing behind him to the wall. "They go in circles all the way up, with doors on every floor."

"Get on folks," Steve said with a broad smile.

I had never ridden an ATV and was nervous. Shift, likely seeing or sensing my anxiety, pulled me over and helped me sit down behind him. Then he turned it on. The others did likewise, with a little guidance from Jon. I wrapped my arms around Shift's waist. His torso stiffened as I let my hands drop a little lower toward his belt line.

We traveled down the long tunnel, in single file, for about forty minutes. It was loud. At various intervals, green boxes, likely holding electronic equipment, sat next to the tunnel wall. The whole tunnel, as far as I could tell, was in great condition. I couldn't even see dust or spider webs.

Over time, the floor of the tunnel began to rise. We had started several stories below ground, but were obviously moving back up toward the surface. Finally, the tunnel opened up into a small natural cavern rich with the smell of the sea. We passed through a very large set of thick metal doors connecting the tunnel with the small cave, which Steve opened remotely.

The cave was long and wide, with a ceiling approximately eight or nine meters above our heads. Concrete pillars were staggered here and there, probably to help stabilize the ceiling. Steve directed us over to a small area where a couple of other ATVs sat. He motioned for us to turn ours off and get down.

"This is where the fun begins guys!" Steve said after we had gathered around him. "You are now in an underground cave several miles from the bunker. You're also under water."

"Uhhh, that's not good," Street said. His face looked pale.

"Are you afraid of caves Street?" Angel asked. "Or is it the ocean?" The look on Angel's face made it obvious that she thought this was funny.

"It's not funny Angel," Street said. "But it's the water, okay. I can't swim."

Nobody said anything, but I was sure they all thought what I was thinking. *This big, tough dude is afraid of water. He can pound football players into the ground all day, but he can't swim.*

"Well, you shouldn't have to swim," Steve said gently. "And, you've been under water for half an hour now, with no harm. As far as I can tell, the whole tunnel we just rode through is under the sea. But, we'll be leaving the cave now anyway. You can see that there isn't much here to entertain us. It's just a holding block for the ATVs really.

"I imagine the people who lived here also stored goods and supplies on those racks over there," he added, pointing to a corner of the cave roughly fifteen meters away.

"Then let's get out of here," Street said, his voice cracking. He was already headed toward a staircase.

The rest of us caught up and Steve and Jon led us up a wide circular staircase that wound through a manmade hole in the rocky ceiling of the cavern. At the top of the stairs, just above the hole, was a large metal landing with a digital display board affixed prominently on the edge of the railing. Jon hit a button on the wall. A massive metal wall adjacent to the landing parted in the middle and slid into the cave walls, revealing another, much larger cave beyond. We stepped through. The doors sealed shut behind us with a soft hissing sound.

This second cave looked partially man-made. Some portions of the wall were rock, while other portions had been filled in with concrete. The ceiling above was primarily concrete. There were bright lights and other electronic equipment attached to suspended walkways that crisscrossed along the entire length and width of the ceiling.

Near the doors we had just passed through sat a large computer terminal, with three monitors hanging from the walls. In one corner near us, there were various shelves, sheds, boxes and water containers that looked more like a refuse pile than anything useful.

A long wooden pier stretched out across a small, enclosed bay toward a rock wall at the far end of the cavern, perhaps three or four hundred meters away. It was breathtaking, not just for its beauty, but also for its mere existence.

"This cave and the bunker are secret, I think," Steve explained. "No part of this facility is on any map, web posting or data sheet that Mike or I could find. Our only information concerning it comes from internal documents on the servers here in the bunker."

Along the pier were anchored four boats of varying sizes, six wave runners, a good-sized iron-hulled cargo ship, and a submarine! The boats looked like good, fairly-modern speed boats. Three of them were quite large.

"There it is Street," Jon said excitedly. He was pointing to the submarine. Street, with Jon at his heels, jogged over and touched it. I couldn't believe it was real.

"We've been in it, but it might be broken. We'll take it for a spin if we can figure out how to turn it on, right dad?" Jon asked.

"Right," Steve replied. "In fact, maybe you and Street should figure that out."

"Yes!" Street pumped his fist into the air, excitedly, like a child. It was funny to watch. He was only twenty-four or twenty-five after all. Still a kid really.

"How do they get out?" Angel asked, voicing my thoughts exactly. There was no visible exit to the cave.

"That was the great mystery when we first found this place. At first, this obviously man-made cave looked completely hemmed in on all sides. So we took out a couple wave runners and searched all around the outer walls of the cavern. Down there at the end, about 350 meters from here, the cavern wall is a holograph. It isn't real."

"Awesome!" Street said, looking impressed.

"Yeah, that's cool, but a little strange," Shift said. "There's no way this bunker was built with those capabilities. The whole place looks like it was built in the late 1900's."

"That's partially right," Steve said. "According to my research, the main bunker was finished in 1962, during the Cuban Missile Crisis. Then, over the years, various updates included the furnaces down on the bottom level, the fish hatchery, the telecom system, the surveillance system, and finally, the holographic cave wall was installed in 2072."

"Have you gone through it?" Street asked excitedly.

"Yeah," Jon said, equally excited, "it was awesome! A little freaky really, even though we were going super slow. I put my hand out to touch the wall, and my hand disappeared. It was braw! So I stuck my head through and then took the wave runner all the way through. Dad followed me. And we were outside! And my body was tingling all over for a few seconds after."

"What does it look like from the outside?" Shift asked.

"It looks like a natural stone wall," Steve answered. "In fact, the whole structure looks like a small, rocky mountain."

"Can it be seen, do you think?" Shift asked.

"No, I don't think so," Steve replied. "It looks just like a vertical cliff, about as high as this cave. I think anyone boating past would think it's just an inaccessible cliff. It's very natural looking."

"What's outside the holograph?" I asked. I was concerned that they may have been seen. If so, perhaps we weren't as safe here as we thought.

"Miles and miles of ocean. You've probably guessed already; we're on an island right now. Based on the information we found on the computers over at the lab, the Mexican government built the mainland portion of the compound in the 1960's as tension between the U.S. and Cuba escalated. I guess Mexico was worried being so close.

"Anyway, over the next few years, they built the tunnel we just traveled through. At first, it led to this island, *Isla de Lobos*. A large cabin and pier were built up top initially. I don't know why the cabin and pier were built, but I presume they were the initial stages of some larger plan. Then the Cuban Missile Crisis ended. Then the Cold War ended. Over the next few decades, the bunker fell into disuse because it wasn't needed anymore. There's very little information about what happened here, or whether this place was used at all between 1990 and 2050.

"In 2053, though, a doctor from the United States convinced the Mexicans to sell him the two islands north of here—*Arrecife Bianquilla* and *Arrecife Medio*. I imagine the doctor had plans to build on them, but those plans, if any, must have fizzled. We can see both islands from here, outside. With the binocs, they just look like small, flat pieces of land.

"Anyway, he probably didn't build on them because, while he didn't own the island we're on, nobody else seemed to be occupying it either. So he apparently restored the cabin here and discovered the tunnel over to the mainland."

"Is there still a cabin outside on this island?" Shift asked.

"Yes. It's still there, and it's a rather nice building. We haven't cleaned it up. Our time outside has been limited to night time hours.

Obviously, we're trying to keep this place a secret for now, especially from the Skins we've been hearing so much about."

"Yeah, we'll tell you all about them later," Angel said. "We're probably the foremost experts on running away from them."

Shift and Street laughed a little. I was concerned because it was truer than I wanted to admit.

"Good. Anyway, in 2069, the doctor and a conglomerate of wealthy business men and women, whose names I haven't uncovered yet, convinced the Mexicans to sell them this island and the mainland bunker. They restored it, updated it, built this cave and the storm doors, and installed the holograph system. Basically, they made it what it is today. The idea, apparently, was to create a long-stay resort of some kind. But I don't think they finished their plans. Otherwise, we'd probably have wall units and better computer equipment.

"From what I can tell, the resort idea never materialized. There was some kind of scandal and in-fighting between the members of the group as to how to operate the facility. A couple members of the group were actually found dead, by 'suspicious means'. So, by 2073, just twenty years ago, the bunker and this cave were empty again. From my research, nobody occupied this place again until a few months ago when Gortari II was destroyed. Somebody had access to the bunker, probably one of the former members of the conglomerate. Ultimately, it seems that as many as twelve hundred people were in here, living, healthy and safe. We don't know who they were, or how they all got here."

"Then Jon arrived," Shift said.

"Yes, Jon arrived," Steve repeated. "When he got here, only one young girl was still alive, and she was very sick. She soon died. Jon tried to extract as much information as he could about this place before she passed on, but didn't get much. When I got here, a few days later, we spoke with Mike Petrovsky and gained access to the databanks. Everything I just told you was revealed there."

"She didn't speak English very well," Jon added, a little defensively. "Or I would have got more out of her."

"Of course you would have, son," Steve said. "You did a great job. We're here, safe, because of you."

"Agreed," Shift said. "I think you've done wonderfully!"

"What a story," I said. "But really, what an accomplishment. I wonder how this place was kept a secret."

"Maybe it wasn't really a secret," Shift said. "Maybe it was just never publicized because it never amounted to anything. Actually, I imagine many people knew about the place, but they're all dead. Obviously hundreds of people knew about it—maybe thousands even."

"Then why isn't it on the maps, or on the Net?" I asked.

"That's the real question," Shift agreed. "Steve, any theories?"

"Nope. I only know that Jon heard rumors about this place by some bad men who kidnapped him."

"Yeah, we heard about that," Angel said, solemnly. "That must have been awful."

"Ah, it wasn't so bad," Jon said, pulling his shoulders back and lifting his chin.

"So, there was some information out there," Steve continued. "Jon says he came here believing it existed, but not actually knowing what he'd find if he made it."

"Well," Street said, "You're pretty awesome Jon, and brave. I'm certainly impressed."

Jon beamed at receiving a compliment from the big, muscular superstar.

"So, I guess we need to get information out about this place to survivors," Steve said. "People can come here. I think we can start a new life here."

"Yeah, but we gotta keep it a secret from the Skins," Street said.

"Of course," Shift agreed, "but I have a hard time believing the Skins are using the net to get their information."

"Well, let's see if we can get a hold of the bunker then," I said.

"That will be the hard part," Steve replied.

JULY 10
THE MOON

"Are we in position?" Jerad asked from the deck above the ship.

"Yes, ready to go," Hasani said. "I hope this goes better than last time."

"Thanks for bringing it up, again," Jonas joked. "And it will."

"Okay, do it," Jerad said.

The three men had spent several days, after finally securing entrance to the International Station's air base, getting a ship ready for inspection. After inspecting every major shell on the moon, only the International Station, in the United States shell had working transport facilities. And parts of the International facilities were destroyed in the blast seven days earlier. Thankfully, most of the mechanical, electronic and digital equipment was still operational.

Not for the first time, Hasani wondered if someone gave an order to destroy all the ships and transport facilities on the moon; and if so, who and why. If that's what happened, it was a miracle that this one ship was still intact. People wanted to get home to Earth, but destroying the ships prevented that. Clearly, the Mexicans hadn't destroyed their ship, believing they were all healthy still, and see where that got them. Maybe, by the time the order went out to destroy ships, nobody was healthy enough in the International Station or the United States shell. After all, they were the first to be hit by the plague.

Jonas pushed the thruster ignition switch. Nothing happened.

"Did you hit it?" Hasani asked.

"Yes, of course," Jonas replied.

"Jerad, anything up there?" Hasani asked.

"No, the readouts are all fine," Jerad replied. "The computer says the ship should be running. Actually, the computer says the ship *is* running."

"Well, the computer's eyes must be seeing things," Jonas joked.

The men's spirits were still high. The fact that they'd found an intact ship had given them such a rush of relief, that this setback, whatever it was, could not dampen their spirits.

"Get down here and look at it again Jerad."

20

"That's it," John yelled. "The doors won't hold them much longer. Everybody's got to get out *now*!"

"C'mon people," Mike said, trying to maintain a little more order than John was proposing.

"Are they upstairs, mama?" Suvan Safar asked. Suvan was only thirteen years old, by far the youngest person in the bunker. She had witnessed terrible things in her short life. First, she had seen her friends and family die, one by one, and shrivel and rot away, leaving a terrible stink behind. Then, she saw her home—El-Alamein—the only place she had ever lived, buried beneath foam, hiding thousands of dead bodies, including her friends and family. Then, she had been kept in an isolation chamber for months while mechanical arms and other machines pricked and prodded at her. Finally released from her cage a few weeks ago, she and her mother were just beginning to feel normal again. Now, mutant humans—monsters really—were outside the bunker and trying desperately to get inside.

"No honey," her mother Neirioui Safar said. "Charles and Manford are both up there right now, making sure everything is safe. Come, we need to hurry."

"Let's move!" Mike said, now more urgently.

The Skins had arrived at the cabin four days ago. The electrical system at the bunker, which had several redundant back-up systems, had been going in and out since the Skins' arrival. Mike had searched for clues as to what was causing the problem and had found several weeks' worth of surveillance videos from around the USCAN system showing Skins destroying power plants and other electronic equipment in areas where humans lived, or at least, had lived. Apparently, they were smart enough to know that humans needed electricity to live, and without it, they would go outside and become vulnerable prey.

For the past three days, the "Chosen" as they referred to themselves, had been seeking entrance to the underground bunker. They knew the perversions were hiding in there. They could smell their stench. An hour and a half ago, the Chosen had gained entrance through the ventilation system. The smell of the perversions had come from those shafts. That's what led them to the cabin in the first place. Now, the perversions were trapped underground. They had shut the steel doors between the laboratories and the living quarters. But the Chosen would get through; it would just take some time.

The small group of humans, outnumbered at least two to one according to the cameras up top, were making their way up the hidden staircase and gathering in the living room of the small cabin. Charles "Lucky" Rabine and Dr. Manford Stevens had been upstairs for several minutes. It appeared that the Skins had left only two scouts outside. They thought they just might be able to fight off two scouts and get to the hovers waiting down the path before the rest of the Skins broke through downstairs or got back up through the ventilation shafts. That was their hope.

"Ready?" John whispered, "Now. Go, go, go." He practically pushed his friends out the door, one by one. Lucky and Manford were out first, guns pointed toward the rear of the cabin where they believed the scouts were located. As soon as they were out the door, Latisha Bodily pushed her way through the crowd and ran out. One after another, the humans left the cabin and began to sprint toward the small parking lot down the dirt path in front of the building.

Moments later, with several people still trying to exit the cabin, Lucky began to fire at the Skins coming at them from the back. Manford joined him. Sidetracked by the two Skins in front of them, they failed to see the horde coming over the roof and around the other side. The Skins had escaped the basement bunker by climbing back up the ventilator shafts. No human could have performed such a feat.

"Run!" Manford shouted to Dr. Yurgi Shevchuk and the others who were bringing up the rear. They ran.

The Skins, flying through the air in great leaps, and outpacing even the fastest human by a wider margin than was conceivable, began to attack. The humans began to go down, beginning with Dr. Latisha Bodily, who had stopped running at the sound of gunfire. She had turned back to face the cabin and just stood there, in awe, watching the horde swarm toward her. Moments after the attack, she arose, violent rage in her cold, dark eyes. She was on the move.

"Yurgi!" Manford shouted, as he raced toward Dr. Shevchuk. Latisha Bodily, or what was left of her, had Yurgi on the ground, her teeth clenched tight on his shoulder. Blood began to pool on the ground under Yurgi's head. Manford began to back away as Latisha looked up at him with dark, murderous eyes. Manford turned and ran, but had only made it a few steps before he too was cut down.

Others were falling, only to rise moments later to seek the lives of their once-friends from the bunker. Bullets whizzed through the air, in all directions. Once in a while, a Skin was hit. Many that fell rose again as though they had been hit by nothing more than a rock. But some that were hit never got up.

Neirioui had picked up Suvan and run, faster than she had ever run in her life. By the time they reached the parking lot, only two others had arrived. Dr. Andrew Jones and Dr. Nelise Fabrisio were already in a hover, waiting for others. Neirioui and Suvan climbed in and the four sped away to safety.

That was the plan. Each hover would be filled with four people before leaving. The next four to arrive would take the next hover. That way, they would have as many hovers as possible for their escape to Cabo Rojo. This first small group had no idea that the plan would fall apart so quickly.

Soon, Dr. Marilyn Swenson, Mr. Javier Franco, and Dr. John Silitzer arrived, closely followed by Mike Petrovsky and Carón Blanchard. Mike and John began to fire at the Skins who were still wreaking havoc behind them. The whole group was moving toward the parking lot. The humans were fighting valiantly, but were losing. They were no match for the strength and speed of the Skins.

There wasn't much time before it would be too late to leave. Mike fired at a Skin about to overtake Mrs. Chrissy Houghton, but it was too late. She was bitten. Mike watched in horror as she rose, only seconds later, and tackled Ms. Star Lawrence. The two had been close friends in the bunker. That's how they would remain as they pursued others, together.

"We've got to go, now," John said to Mike, as they continued to fire into the crowd.

"Is there anybody left?" Mike asked, tears in his eyes.

"I can't see anybody," John said. "Let's go, while we still can." Emotions were spilling over. John was just about to grab Mike to shove him into the waiting hover.

"Wait," yelled Javier from inside, "Anna is still running this way. Is she still human?" Without waiting for a response, Javier jumped from the hover where he had been anxiously waiting. He ran toward Dr. Anna Wentworth. It was too late to turn around by the time he realized that she, along with nearly everybody else, had her eyes trained on him. He turned to run back to the hover. John and Mike tried desperately to buy him time. It was no use. The Skins overtook Javier and kept going. They were only seconds from the parking lot.

Mike and John jumped in the hover. Carón hit the thrusters. They were gone.

The others watched out the back of the hover as the cabin, and their home underground, faded into the distance. The Skins pursued the hover for a while, but couldn't keep up. They watched, relieved, as the Skins finally stopped their pursuit.

Forty minutes later, Carón pulled up to a small rest area along the highway where Neirioui and Suvan Safar, Dr. Andrew Jones and Dr. Nelise Fabrisio were waiting.

"Where's everybody else?" Nelise asked as the others approached.

"We couldn't help them," Carón replied, lowering his head.

"What? So you just left them there?" Nelise asked, bitterly.

Carón raised his head. "No, we didn't just leave them there," he replied, with equal hostility. "They had all been bitten. What would you have done?"

"I would have saved them!" Nelise yelled.

"How? What would you have done? You took off without even waiting to see what was happening? So don't you give me that crap."

"Guys," John said carefully, "nobody did anything wrong here. We all tried. We all stuck to the plan. None of us could have done more. Let's try to stick together, okay."

"Yeah, sorry man," Carón said a moment later.

Nelise turned around and walked a couple of paces away from the group.

The remainder of the small group huddled together under a shade canopy and cried, and prayed. They were all that was left of the brilliant and brave humans who had saved the world from disaster. Dr. Yurgi Shevchuk, their friend and leader was dead. Worse perhaps. He was probably a Skin; and so were the rest.

JULY 11
HOLOGRAPHIC CONFERENCE

"It all went bad," John said. The small group of survivors had found a holo-café in a town two hundred miles south of the bunker. The electricity was still on. They had stopped to rest, eat and attempt to contact Cabo Rojo, Mexico.

When John hailed the group in Cabo Rojo, Street and Shift had run up from the lab on the bottom level. Steve and Jon Porter were in the gardens, but had dropped their garden tools and run too. Angel was on guard duty at the front doors and walked in, arriving just before the others. Everyone met in the main level communication bay near the front doors.

"What's wrong," Anta asked John, fear beginning to take hold inside her.

"The Skins. They got in. They flushed us out. Almost everybody is dead."

"Or worse," Carón added very quietly from the background.

"Oh no," Anta said. Her body began to shake as she slid to the ground. She hugged her knees close to her chest and rocked back and forth. Nobody else had said a word yet.

"What about Yurgi?" Street asked quietly, moments later. Dr. Yurgi Shevchuk had given Street so much attention and generosity, and had treated Street as an equal. Street had never had a father or friend show such love toward him. Never had anyone loved him for anything more than his athletic ability, not even his own mother.

"I'm sorry Street," John replied.

Street began to cry, great tears of sorrow running down his face. Angel walked over to him and put her arms around his waist, and, laying her head against his strong arm, rubbed her hand up and down his back. Street turned toward Angel, laid his head on top of hers and let the tears fall, wetting Angel's dark, curly hair.

The whole group was moved by the big man's sorrow.

"Actually," Carón said finally, "they didn't die, at least most of them didn't. Although I wish they had." He too had tears in his eyes.

The small group from the Boston bunker had shed many tears over the past couple of hours. Suvan was still dazed, perhaps suffering from shock. She hadn't said a word since she climbed into the hover at the small parking lot outside the cabin. Even now, her mother cradled Suvan's head in her lap, brushing her hair with long, neatly-trimmed fingernails. Suvan began to whimper, again.

"Did they all turn then?" Shift asked, finally getting a grip on his emotions.

"Yes, probably," Mike said. "We couldn't help them. We tried Shift. We tried . . ." Mike's voice trailed off as his head slumped forward.

"Can you get here?" Steve asked. "I can get you coordinates. Actually, I'm sending them now, along with a route that should throw the skins off if they're following you."

"Following us?"

"Yeah, they followed us for days, until we shot ahead to California and approached from there. We think we lost them. The fact that they found you means maybe they gave up on us."

"Ok, we can get there," John said. "Are we safe to travel? We haven't had any communications with outside the bunker for four days. No communications; no satellite; nothing. We don't know what's going on out here now."

"Well, it's bad," Shift said. "But the Skins can't keep up with a hover at full speed. At least none of them that we've encountered."

"Okay, we're on our way," John said solemnly. "Keep the lights on."

21

"That's the last of them," I said, as I folded down the top of the old laptop.

"What's the final tally?" Steve asked.

"Eighteen," I replied.

Over the past day and a half, we had contacted thirty of the thirty-two bunkers Mike and Yurgi had been in contact with from Boston. While there had been several other bunkers at one time, the humans in many of the others had perished when A.E. seeped into their bunkers via the backdraft fiasco a couple months earlier. Mike had sent us contact and location information for each of the remaining thirty-two. We had also logged onto the Anthrax E database, combing it for information. Eighteen of the thirty-two known bunkers had been attacked in very similar fashion to the Boston bunker. And, most of them were attacked within a few hours of the attack in Boston. Clearly, the Skins had orchestrated a coordinated attack. We couldn't fathom how they communicated with each other.

"How many people survived from those eighteen bunkers?" Anta asked.

"Well, it looks like two of them had no survivors," I replied.

"How do you know that?" Angel asked.

"Well, each bunker has been in contact with others through all this time. Some seem to know more about other bunkers than we ever did. Kind of like us and the Toronto bunker. Yurgi had kept in very close contact with Toronto due to proximity. Other bunkers shared similar relationships. When the first of the two German bunkers was attacked, they radioed the other German bunker for help. At just about the time the second German bunker was attacked, they received a final com from the first bunker. The man on the line said he was the last and then screamed as he was attacked. Something similar happened in Japan. So, we know that two of the bunkers had no survivors. Of the other sixteen, based upon the numbers they've given me, only ninety-eight people survived. That's in addition to the six of us and the eight on their way."

"Are there others out there that we haven't reached," Street asked.

"I don't know," I replied. "Mike told us about all the ones he knew of. He doesn't know whether Yurgi might have had contact with others. Plus, only the thirty-two we know of have ever posted anything in the Anthrax E database. So, even though it seems likely that there are others, nobody from any of the thirty-two had information about any others."

"How many people are living in the fourteen bunkers that haven't been attacked?" Anta asked.

"Let's see. I've got those figures here. Um, it looks like there are 203 people between them."

"Wow," Steve said, solemnly. "With those numbers, if that's all the people left in the world, that means we're down to 315 people. That's it."

"That can't be right," Street said. "That can't be all. There's got to be more. We just need to find them, right?"

Angel walked over to Street and put her arms around his bulky frame. She wrapped him in a bear hug so tight that the greatest linebacker in the NFL would have been proud. Street sagged against her small frame.

JULY 12, 8:50PM—ANTA

"Shift, come here please," I called.

"Just a sec," Shift yelled down the hallway from the kitchen.

We had finally cleared out all the dead bodies from the second and third floors, and hopefully everywhere else as well. The stench was beginning to lighten. Once we got the ventilation system running, the smells began to dissipate. But since we now believed that the Skins found Boston and the other bunkers due to smells coming through the ventilation ducts, we shut off the system. We got a few good days of cleaning out of them first though. Hopefully it would be enough and the smell would continue to fade. Getting used to the stench had been the biggest relief. We had even recently begun to sleep in the dorms on the second floor.

Shift discussed the ventilation problem with the people in the other bunkers and suggested that they determine if they can survive without external ventilation, at least until they can locate a backup location. Only a few of the bunkers have air scrubbers and recirculation systems to prevent external venting. And fewer still have any idea where they could go if they have to leave their bunker. The bunkers were supposed to be the safest places to be.

"What's up?" Shift asked as he rounded the corner holding two red apples. He handed one to me.

"Thanks," I said. "Come sit down a minute."

Shift sat down next to me on the couch in the rec room. We were the only ones in there. With only six of us in the whole compound, and one person on watch at all times, there was plenty of opportunity for solitude or privacy, which is what I wanted now.

"What can I do for you miss?" Shift asked, smiling.

"What can I do for *you*?" I asked back.

Shift looked confused for a minute, then looked more closely at me. I gave him my best "come-here-and-kiss-me-you-idiot" look. He got it and scooted closer.

I placed my hand on his leg as he lifted his hand to touch my face. With our thighs touching and my hand on his leg, Shift was unable to resist any longer. He leaned all the way in and kissed me. It was warm and soft. His breath smelled like apple. It felt like I had finally gone home.

We kissed for a long time, hands slowly moving across each others' bodies, slowly feeling and experiencing each other. I had waited for this for a long time. He had too. I was impressed by his ability to control himself.

Finally, after several long, wonderful minutes, I said, "Shift, will you come to my room with me?"

"Absolutely!"

22

"They're almost here," Steve said.

"What's the ETA?" Shift asked.

"Some time after 1:00 probably."

"Let's make sure we're ready," Shift said. "And they're sure they haven't been followed?"

"John said they haven't seen a Skin in over twelve hours. Last ones they saw were back in northern Texas. But there were thousands of them apparently."

"Well then, I certainly hope they weren't followed," Shift said. "That would be the end of all of us."

"Did they ever have to fight anyone, Dad," Jon asked.

"Yes, but only once," Steve replied. Looking directly at his son, who became frightened at even the mention of Skins, he continued, "and they're all fine. They'll all be here safe in a couple of hours."

"Good."

"What's the latest from the other bunkers—the ones that hadn't been attacked yet?" Angel asked.

"Well," Shift began, "we've confirmed that an additional eight of the last fourteen bunkers have been attacked. But each of them was ready with an escape plan. They had the benefit of talking with others before it happened. They were ready."

"So, did all of them survive—from the eight bunkers?" Jon asked.

"No," Shift replied. "But many more of them survived than would have if we hadn't had the opportunity to speak to them."

"What about the rest?"

"The rest may be okay where they are because of their modern ventilation systems. Time will tell."

"How many people are still alive, that we know of?" Angel asked.

"That we know of?" Shift repeated. "Six, plus eight from our bunker, ninety-eight from the first group attacked. Then, with the other attacks . . . It looks like there are 247 at best. The problem is that we don't know what's going on with some of the survivors from the first round of attacks. All we know is that they're attempting to get here, or find some other place to stay."

"We've encouraged them to come here," Anta added. "But that's a bit of a trek for some of them. And most of them can't fly planes."

"Do we expect any of them to actually get here, besides the Boston people?" Street asked. "I mean, what's the chance, really?"

"I'm not too hopeful," Shift replied. "There are a couple of groups from Argentina and northern Brazil that are trying to get here. They don't have to fly over any oceans. Getting here, for them, is a realistic possibility. But that's only fifteen people total between the two groups. Both of those bunkers were hit in the first attack. Brazil has nine people and Argentina has six more. I guess they're trying to hook up and then travel here together, but I haven't heard from them since early yesterday morning. They haven't checked in today like they promised."

"Were they having any problems, other than the Skins?" Anta asked.

"Not that I know of, thank goodness. The Skins are a big enough problem by themselves."

"So, is there any chance of anyone else getting here?" Street asked.

"I don't know," Shift replied. "I really don't. But I do know that we're safe here, for now, and that no other group has anything like this. The only reason we're safe though, is because the Skins didn't follow us and can't smell us through the ventilation system. We need to stay mindful of those things. The rules are still in place: nobody goes outside. If you feel you need to, go through the tunnel. The smell of the salt water from the ocean should disperse our smells sufficiently. But don't leave the cave."

"We know that Shift," Street said.

"I know. I just wanted to remind you. Our lives depend on us remembering that one simple thing. Plus, when our friends arrive, we've got to pound it into their skulls. And some of them, like John, have pretty thick skulls." Shift smiled.

JULY 16, 1:15PM
CABO ROJO, MEXICO

"Welcome!" Shift cried out as he threw his arms around John's neck. John hugged him back, fiercely.

The tired group dragged what little belongings they had through the massive double doors at the front of the compound. While they had picked up some supplies en route, they hadn't spent the time replenishing their wardrobes. Their clothes reeked of sweat and sorrow.

Street, Steve, Jon, Angel and Anta each grabbed bags and helped pull them inside, quickly shutting the large iron doors behind them. The tired group was offered seats and given refreshment. Anta had brought ice water and peaches to the front gallery. They took the food and water greedily.

"Tell me the truth John, were you followed?" Shift asked this question pointedly, looking right into the eyes of his best friend.

"No, we weren't," John replied, looking around. "You know; we weren't sure we were in the right place. Where are your hovers?"

"They're in a huge iron and concrete garage around the side of the compound. We'll move yours too, just in case the skins have been able to follow the heat signature from them. But you're sure you weren't followed?"

"We haven't seen anyone walking, dead, alive, naked, bald, or otherwise, since northern Texas, like fourteen hours ago or something."

"Excellent," Shift said, relaxing. "After you get cleaned up and changed—there are clothes that should fit everyone in the living area—we'll talk some more. There are some rules you need to know . . ."

JULY 16
THE MOON

"Okay, let's try it again," Jonas said wearily. They had been trying to get the ship to start for over a week. They weren't making any progress. The light-hearted mood that had prevailed for the first few days was dissipating quickly.

They needed help, but nobody on Earth seemed able to help. The bunker in Cabo Rojo didn't have anyone with experience in the type of mechanics or electronics required to start up a space ship. Nobody on the Anthrax E database was responding. And, even though Jonas was an astrophysicist and Jerad was both a pilot and an aeronautical engineer, they were missing something.

"Here it goes," Jerad said, unable to hide the hopelessness in his voice.

Nothing happened. They had been tinkering with electronic components today. Other days it had been mechanical components, computer link-ups or software applications. Nothing worked.

"Well, Anta told me this morning that they were expecting the group from Boston to arrive soon," Hasani said. "Let's hope someone in the group can help. Otherwise, we'll probably die here." He smiled, hoping to ease the tension in the huge shuttle bay. It didn't work.

Misty and Tom Bird walked into the shuttle bay with coffee. Dr. Bird and his wife had stayed away from the work the others were doing. The group had made the decision that the elderly couple should stay apart from the work in case an accident happened, like the type of accident that had happened to Jonas almost two weeks earlier. The others needed a physician to help them heal in the event of another accident, and Dr. Bird was that physician. Thankfully, no other injuries had occurred and the group felt healthy and strong.

"How's it going?" Tom called down from the large deck above the cargo hold where the ship sat idle.

"Not well," Hasani called back as he began to descend from the upper deck of the shuttle to the floor of the cargo hold. "We're just going to have to hope someone on Earth can help us remotely."

"Well, I think you guys are doing a great job," Misty called out. "Thank you so much for trying to help us all." The sincerity in her words caused all three men to realize how much she and her husband meant to them. This was a close group. They had been together for months. They were a family. They were closer than a family. And, they had each other, whether they returned to Earth or not.

23

"They're less than fifty miles from here," Mike said simply. "South, down the coast near Tamiahua."

The prior evening, Mike Petrovsky had successfully linked the Cabo Rojo bunker to the USCAN system the group had employed in Boston to look for survivors, and Skins. It wasn't difficult. He had done it before and kept the instructions in his MEHD. While he didn't have nearly as many screens, and thus, not nearly as many simultaneous views, it was something, and they were all grateful. It was easy enough to switch between views on the four monitors in the electronics bay.

"How close are they to the water?" Dr. Andrew Jones asked.

This was an important consideration. Angel and Andrew, both biologists, had developed a theory more than four months earlier. The idea was that A.E., a mutated strain of bacterial anthrax, couldn't survive high doses of salt. The theory hadn't been tested yet, but seemed logical enough given that sea creatures, including mammals and fish, were not catching the disease. Plus, it was already known that typical bacteria couldn't survive high concentrations of salt.

While the inoculation received by the Boston group had worked, and protected the group from A.E., the Toronto vaccine was just a little off. It was believed, at least by Andrew, that the minor variation in the Toronto vaccination not only caused those injected with Toronto's vaccine to physically change, but also that it may not fully protect them from A.E. He hoped that meant that the Skins could not handle salt or, even better, that they would eventually succumb to A.E. and die.

Several days earlier, while still in Boston, Andrew had begun thinking about how, or whether, the Skins would react to salt *water*, clearly lower in salt concentration than pure salt. Now, much closer to salt water in the Gulf of Mexico, he was anxious to see whether the Skins could handle it.

"A few of them have gone down to the beach," Mike replied, "but I haven't seen any go in the water, or even touch the water. Do you want me to go back through the archives and look for any Skins going into the ocean?"

"That could take a lot of time," Andrew said. "If you have the time, it would be excellent, but if not, I understand. Maybe I could help you. I've got some time."

"Actually, maybe this will help," Mike said. "I *have* seen some of the Skins drinking fresh water and once even saw one of them fall into a pond and get back out again. He seemed just fine."

"But no salt water, right?" Andrew asked. "You haven't seen any go into salt water?"

"That's right," Mike replied.

"Okay, so we know they have no problem with fresh water," Andrew thought aloud, "but they still may not like the salt. Yeah Mike, I think you better go back through archives and check. I'll help you."

"What are the Skins doing right now?" Anta asked. "Are they giving any indication that they know we're here, or close by?"

"No, they seem to be wandering a little actually," Mike replied. "It's like they're looking for something, but maybe they don't know what. Maybe there's a human down there still alive in hiding."

"Oh, that would be awful," Marilyn said. Dr. Marilyn Swenson was an obstetrician in her former life, back when people were still having babies. Nowadays, it looked like any chance of performing the work she so dearly loved was gone. It broke her heart every time she learned that another person had died, or turned. She certainly didn't like the idea of helping the Skins give birth, if they were even able to do so. She was afraid, like they all were, that babies would be very difficult to come by now.

Even more, they were all afraid that any human babies born might not live due to A.E. already inside the mother. While the mother may now be immune thanks to the vaccine, the baby could either be immune or catch A.E. Because A.E. was unlike anything they had ever encountered, nobody knew what would happen. And nobody was anxious to try it out.

"Well, keep an eye on them," Shift said. "If they start wandering this way, we need to be ready to take action."

"Mike, have you seen any of them try to drive a vehicle—a hover, or motorcycle, or car, or a boat, or even row a boat? Anything?" Andrew asked.

"Actually, no," Mike replied.

"That's a good question," Anta said. "We never saw any of them drive anything, or even attempt to."

"We didn't either," Andrew said. "So, maybe they can't. Mike, while we're checking footage for salt water contact, let's keep an eye out for any hint of whether they can drive or otherwise operate motorized vehicles."

"Good idea," Shift said. "What about electronics? Do they use phones, MEHDs, holos, anything like that to communicate? Has anyone seen them use any type of technology?"

Nobody answered aloud, but many of them were shaking their heads back and forth.

"I'll take that as a collective 'no,'" Shift said. "How do they communicate?" He wasn't expecting an answer and no one offered an opinion. "Why don't you guys look for that too? If they can't drive, or use communication devices or other technology, we may have a better chance of success against them, I hope."

Following the death of Dr. Shevchuk, the group was without a leader. John and Steve both appeared and often acted as though they could lead this ragtag group. But John, although probably the most intelligent among the group, was not a leader. He was the party animal—the socialite. And even though Steve knew more about the bunker than anybody else, he had always been leery of taking on leadership roles; even though, in the instances in which he had, he had a gift. He was content to follow. Nobody else had ever shown any predisposition to take charge in the few months they had been together. They hadn't had to. Yurgi was always in charge.

That really only left Shift or Anta. Each was capable of making the big decisions. Each was smart enough and respected enough to do the job—and the group really needed someone to fill Dr. Shevchuk's shoes. Anta usually deferred to Shift, a habit she had formed in El-Alamein due to Shift's expertise in communicable diseases; although behind closed doors, Shift wanted, and needed, her advice and assistance. They made decisions together. Thus, when the time came to determine how to handle the Skins if they ever found the bunker, Shift and Anta had formulated a plan.

"So Shift, what are we going to do if they find us?" Mike asked. "Do you have a plan yet?"

"Yes, Anta finally told me what we should do," Shift replied with a crooked smile. Anta rolled her eyes and shook her head, making Shift chuckle. He still wasn't comfortable in this role. "Actually, Anta, Steve and I—and Jon—spent a great deal of time down in the tunnel and over on the island the first few days we were here. This is what we've come up with, but we need some help filling in the details."

The group spent the next couple of hours finalizing their plan for escape, in the event it became necessary. The plan hinged on the belief that the Skins wouldn't, or couldn't cross the water. If they did, or if they could learn to drive a boat, the plan would only buy time.

Finally, reviewing his chicken scratches on the notebook in front of him, Shift looked up and said, "Okay, this is it then. It's still a rough outline. If anyone has any thoughts, or if I get something wrong, just say it.

"Our safe house will be the island, obviously. The island will be stocked with provisions to last as long as possible. And, for as many people as possible, since we don't know yet who will be joining us. All but one ATV will remain on this side of the tunnel so that we have enough of them for each of us to take one in a hurry. That will leave three extra on this side in case there are mechanical problems with any of them. The ATVs don't move near as fast as the Skins, but if we have enough notice, we should be able to cross the channel in time.

"Street and Jon Porter will coordinate the storage of food and water on the island. The supplies will be kept in the underwater cave to help preserve them. They will ask for, and receive help from others as necessary.

"Carón, Steve and Nelise will figure out how to wire explosives from the storage room to destroy the tunnel after we've all safely arrived on the island. There are blast doors that seal at that end of the tunnel. You three will also ensure that those doors will hold fast in the event the tunnel is blown and water flows against those doors. Obviously, the cave has to remain useable, otherwise we lose our provisions and maybe our lives."

"Maybe we should store the supplies up top in the manmade cave," Anta suggested.

"I agree," John said. "The same type of doors sit up there at the top of the staircase. So, the guys can just check them instead and make sure they'll keep water, and hopefully the Skins, out. Steve, don't you think its cool enough up there, back in the corner where those storage sheds are, to keep food chilled for a while?"

"I don't know," Steve replied. "I'll check it out. The other option is to haul some of those big fridges and freezers from the kitchen out there. There's plenty of room and the power supply out there is definitely sufficient. Plus, there are already those massive water tanks out there. Let's make sure they're all full and we should have plenty of water for several weeks."

"Good idea," Shift said. "Let's do that. That will make it easier to blow the tunnel without worrying about whether we'll just die of dehydration three days later. Steve, make sure the explosives won't damage any power cables. I suspect there are separate lines running from the solar power plates to the island and the mainland. If the island gets its power from the plates via the mainland, rather than through a direct link, we could be in trouble. Who wants to figure out how to get the freezers out there?"

"Easy," Carón said. "I just need the muscle to help."

"I got you, man," Street said.

"We can all help when you need us Carón," John added.

"Okay, what else?" Shift mumbled to himself. "Oh yeah, we need to make sure every one of those boats and wave runners are operational. Street, Jon, you've been tinkering with them. What do we know?"

"The sub still don't work," Street said, frowning. "But everything else does. One of the boats is just a pansy sail boat. No motor. Not even worth trying to use. The others have motors, and they all work. All the wave runners work too. That huge cargo ship thing works, but it's too old. It got cracks all along the hull and water inside at the bottom."

"Can you guys make sure everything is charged up?" Shift asked. "Hopefully we won't have to make a getaway from the cave. Hopefully, we'll just be able to hang out on the island in safety for a while. But if not, we need the boats all powered up, with every available extra charging rod ready on the docks to be thrown into whatever boat is used to get away."

"I'll check out the charges, in everything, and get the extra rods charged," John said. "Even an idiot like me can handle that job." He smiled as a few of them chuckled. Not a person among them believed that John was an idiot. He, along with Dr. Shevchuk, had saved their lives with the development of E-rase. He had earned their respect, and their pity laughs when his jokes weren't that funny.

"Good," Shift continued. "Mike, you're going to check out the technology over there, right? To make sure we have the same capabilities there as we have here?"

"Did it this morning," Mike replied. "Everything is set over there."

"Okay, I think that's it," Shift said. "Everybody else will be helping with anything and everything we're asked to do. Remember that, just because something didn't get discussed here, doesn't mean it isn't a good idea. After we've finished these initial jobs, let's continue to brainstorm and figure out what else needs to be done. There's no reason any of us should be sitting around while the Skins are outside and other humans are racing this way trying to get to safety."

"Neirioui," Jon Porter said, tentatively, "can Suvan help me with the garden and getting food ready?" Jon almost whispered the words. His face turned pink as he waited for Suvan's mother to answer him. Everyone knew these two children could be the last people alive from their generation. It was fun for the adults to watch the playful flirtations between them. At only fourteen and thirteen years old, they were both easily embarrassed, especially when any discussion of re-populating the world came up.

"Sure, if she would like to," Neirioui replied.

"I would love to!" Suvan shrieked. Then she clapped her hand over her mouth as everyone in the group tried to stifle their laughter.

JULY 18
HOLOGRAPHIC CONFERENCE

"Boy, it is good to hear from you guys again," Jonas said. "We are literally at our wit's end."

"What's going on?" Shift asked.

"Well, we have a fully-functional ship sitting right here in front of us," Jonas said. "And the computers say it's operational. The computers even tell us it's running. But it's not. There's something wrong that even the great Jerad Beaudoin can't figure out." Jonas smiled as Jerad punched him in the arm.

"Well," Shift said, "let me get a couple of smart dudes over here and talk this through. Hold on."

Ten minutes later, Dr. Nelise Fabrisio and Mike Petrovsky joined Shift and Anta at the holo. Introductions were made.

"Good to see you again Mike," Jonas said. "It's been a while."

"It has," Mike agreed. "So, what's the problem up there?"

Jonas, Jerad and Hasani took turns explaining the different processes they had gone through trying to get the ship to work. There was just nothing left to do. They couldn't figure it out.

"You guys are gonna die when I tell you what you've missed," Mike said. "Although I only found out about it a few days ago."

"What is it," Hasani asked, starting to feel embarrassed, even though he didn't know whether he should have such feelings yet.

"You need clearance codes," Mike said. He looked over to Nelise who was nodding.

"You're joking, right?" Jonas asked rhetorically. "Jerad, you old bugger, why didn't you know that?"

Embarrassed, Jerad began to back away from the holo, hands held out in front of him to prevent a possible attack from Jonas and Hasani. His red face displayed a grin that stretched from ear to ear. It was obvious these guys liked each other. Nobody was really mad.

"Get over here and take it like a man," Jonas said, reaching out for Jerad, but missing him as he slipped away.

Shift and Mike were laughing. Anta smiled as she said, "You gentlemen should probably get back to work now. It looks like you've wasted a lot of time that you could have spent down here running away from Skins." That comment killed the mood, even though that hadn't been Anta's intent.

"Actually Anta," Hasani began, "how is that going?"

They spent some time discussing what they knew about the progress of the other humans, and the preparations underway at the bunker in case the Skins found them. It was a somber discussion.

"Is there any reason for us to come home?" Misty asked. "It sounds like a dreadful place now."

"I don't know," Anta said. "Why don't you guys get that ship working and then let's talk again."

"I can tell you how to hack into the system up there to retrieve the codes, if you need me to," Mike said.

"Actually, I don't need you too, I know exactly where they are," Jerad replied. "I've never been in charge of clearance codes—that's the co-pilot's job. I just forgot."

24

"It's ugly dude," Shift said. "I don't know if anyone else will get here. There aren't any pilots out there, or so I'm told. And even those people who think they can fly haven't been able to figure it all out. Modern planes, and even some of the older ones too, have complex onboard computers and other systems. You can't just jump in and start flying. Jerad is compiling information to send to others, just in case anyone gets an opportunity to attempt to fly, but he doesn't think that will be sufficient. It's much more complicated than just sitting there pushing buttons."

"So what does that mean," John asked. "We're not going to have *anybody* joining us?"

"We haven't heard from the folks down south—the Brazilians or Argentineans—in three days. I don't know where they are. They don't answer the MEHDS. If they had been able to get here as fast as they planned, we could see them as early as tomorrow, but I don't know whether they'll make it, or when. We need to be ready for them though, just in case. Who's on watch tomorrow?"

"I'm on the six o'clock," John replied. "Then Marilyn has the afternoon, Steve has evening, and Anta has the night shift."

"Will you talk to each of them? They need to know that any shapes they see out there could be human, not necessarily Skin. Of course, in the daytime, it will be easy to tell. Even though those Brazilians like their nudity, I don't think this particular group will be showing skin the way the Skins will."

"No, I don't suppose they will," John replied.

JULY 19
PANAMA CANAL, PANAMA

"Jump!" Hubert yelled from across the gaping hole between the massive, broken concrete ribs.

The Brazilians had never made it to the rendezvous point. Hubert didn't know where they were. But he wasn't going to worry about them. He had four people right here who needed his leadership and guidance.

"I can't!" Gemma yelled back. "It's too far." She began to cry, and she felt stupid for it. Sixteen-year-olds shouldn't be afraid of heights.

"You can do it, baby," Gemma's mother whispered, standing next to her. Ange had been afraid of heights too, when she was younger. Now, she worried that her daughter's fear could cost all of them their lives.

Hubert, formerly a military special agent for the Argentinean government, had secured his family a berth in a military bunker outside Buenos Aires when the plague had found its way to his country. Now, months later, he, his wife and daughter, and two others ran for their lives, hoping to get across the old Panama Canal before the monsters finished devouring the others. Or whatever it was the monsters were doing back there. Of the sixty-seven people who had inhabited their bunker, only five were left.

"I'm going," Benoit said. "They're too close. We can't wait for Gemma." Benoit, a sixty-four-year-old politician, jogged back several paces. A few days earlier, he had been hit by a stray bullet as the group fled their bunker during an attack by the Skins. It only grazed his shin, but it was enough to cause him to limp. He began to race forward toward the gulf that separated Hubert from the others. Hubert was safe over there, and Benoit would be too.

Benoit's speed wasn't enough. Hubert could see he wasn't going to make it, but couldn't form the words in time to stop Benoit's rush forward. Benoit leapt. The gap wasn't that far, but the distance to the bottom of the chasm below was as much as one hundred meters or more. In mid-air, Benoit saw that he was short. He reached his hands out for the ledge at Hubert's feet. Hubert dropped to his stomach, reaching toward Benoit. But he wasn't able to react fast enough. Benoit fell. A few short seconds later, his body crumpled against the cracked and dirty concrete far below.

The Skins were coming. Rogelio, the last survivor of the small group, ran forward. He made it, easily. Gemma, seeing the ease at which the young, handsome mechanic made the leap, felt encouraged. Squeezing her mother's hand, she ran forward. As she took the last step toward the gulf that separated her from her father, she heard her mother scream. The effect of that scream, and the gurgling noise of the monsters as they tore into Ange's flesh caused Gemma to lose balance. She stumbled and fell over the edge.

Rogelio ran.

Three seconds later, Hubert stepped off the ledge to join his daughter far below.

JULY 19
CABO ROJO, MEXICO

"Shift, get in here!" Mike yelled through the open door to the computer lab.

"What?" Shift said anxiously as he ran through the doorway into the small room.

"Sorry, I didn't mean to scare you," Mike said. "But look at this, down in Panama."

On the left-middle screen, Mike's camera was following a group of Skins near the old, unused Panama Canal.

"What's going on down there?" Shift asked.

"Those Skins chased down and attacked a group of humans, just now," Mike replied. He was struggling to hold his emotions in check. "I don't know who they were, but they were running. They weren't even in cars or hovers or anything. I just watched some of them fall into the ruins of the canal. They're probably dead."

"How many are still alive?" Shift asked. He began to wonder whether these were the Brazilians or the Argentineans they had been expecting tomorrow.

"Only one. That's him," Mike said, pointing to a lone figure hundreds of meters ahead of a horde of Skins. "He's never going to make it. He'll never get away from them."

"Look how fast they're moving!" Shift said, horrified.

Mike and Shift watched as the Skins closed in on a young man running down a lonely highway. Then they watched, in fascinated terror, as more than two hundred nearly-naked figures began to leap skyward, traveling as far as thirty or thirty-five meters through the air to land all around the poor man. They brought him down swiftly. Within moments, the group fell back as the man arose from the ground, ripping and tearing at his clothing. He was one of them.

"Do you have this recorded? And can you back it up and show me what led up to this?"

"Every camera is recording. But do you really want to see this?"

"We won't show it to anyone else. But we need to know what they're capable of and see if we can find a weakness."

"Ok," Mike said with a sigh. "Happy dreams!"

25

"Street, come in here," Shift called out as Street walked past the door to the small conference room.

"What's going on?" Street asked as he tentatively entered the room.

"We, well Mike actually, has found out something that will be very interesting to you. Can you go gather everyone together please?"

"Okay."

Fifteen minutes later, everyone had gathered in the conference room except Marilyn, who was on watch in the security room by the front entrance. Mike and Shift were standing at the front of the room, patiently waiting. Marilyn was visible on the holo in the corner of the room.

"Thanks for coming everyone," Shift began. "Mike has discovered something that will be very interesting to a few of you."

Nobody spoke.

"Okay, Mike tell us what you've learned please."

"Well," Mike said, "A couple of weeks ago, I began thinking about an issue which I hadn't thought about for a while. So I began to do a little digging. Over the past two weeks, in my downtime, I've been combing through databases and personnel archives from various sources. After a couple of days, I found a few bits of information which led me to focus my search on a small, rogue paramilitary outfit located, well, formerly located in Connecticut. I say 'formerly' because I imagine they're all dead now."

"What's a 'rogue paramilitary'?" Jon Porter asked.

"Good question Jon," Mike replied. "Generally speaking, a paramilitary group is a group of people, often former military, who operate like a military but who don't always have the backing of a specific government. Some paramilitary groups are backed by local governments, but this one doesn't seem to be of that type. This one appears to be rogue, which means, generally, that they are operating on their own, without the backing of any government."

"So what did you learn?" Shift prompted.

"Early on, I found a website that contained various rumors, including that old one about the whole Anthrax E plague being a government conspiracy. As I read through the various postings to that website, I found a rumor about this particular group. They call themselves "ConControl"—short for Connecticut Control. Anyway, according to the rumors, ConControl planned to break into an unnamed lab to secure a vaccination. That got my attention, since we were one of those types of labs.

"The rumored plan called for an attack of some type on that unnamed lab utilizing the services of an insider. The insider had allegedly revealed that a vaccine had been created and was ready for distribution. The informant was supposed to steal the vaccine, escape from the compound, and then reconnect with the group at headquarters somewhere in Connecticut.

"That was all the web posting said. But, naturally, I was interested. The rumor was posted on April 25th, just a few days after that original conspiracy story came out. Among the many other avenues I pursued for information, I also looked back through our bunker's archives from that time. Most of you know, I think, that all of our meetings were recorded and kept in archives. Well, I started checking our archives from that time period, just to remind myself of what was going on in the world at that time.

"As of April 25th, death and infection estimates were somewhere between four and five billion—half of the world's population. But we had some good news that day as well. Does anyone remember what we learned on April 25th?"

"Yeah. That was the day Yurgi told us that the animals Lucky and I caught were immune to Anthrax E," Street replied almost instantly. "He created a vaccine that worked on animals."

"Correct. April 25th was the day of that awesome revelation. But there was more that day. April 25th was also the day I announced to all of you my backdraft theory. The theory about how A.E. was likely being sucked into bunkers like ours through the ventilation systems. We'd just had that ventilation problem a few days earlier and I had come up with my theory.

"Well, there was someone in the group that morning who was displeased with me. She felt I had done something wrong by not telling you guys about the possibility earlier, even though I had just put it all together that morning."

"Bodily," Street growled.

"Correct again. Latisha Bodily was angry that morning when she learned that we were possibly at risk of infection and that other bunkers like ours had probably already been infected. That was the morning Yurgi put her in her place. He humiliated her in front of all of us. You guys remember that?"

Several heads nodded and a few smiles appeared as the memory washed over the group.

"Keep going Mike," Shift encouraged.

"Well, thankfully, we concluded that we were not in danger from infection through our ventilation system, but it put us all a little on edge that morning. So, Bodily's anger was easily dismissed. But, does anyone know where Dr. Bodily is from?"

"The question's too easy now," John replied. "Connecticut."

"Right. So, I was putting the pieces together. I checked out Dr. Bodily's file and everything else I could find out about her in the archives. There's quite a history on all of us in the databases. I followed leads and trails and here's what I've pieced together.

"About six years ago, Dr. Bodily was introduced to a man named Thomas Franconi at a fancy dinner party. They bonded, perhaps were lovers even. Franconi was disenfranchised with the way the IWO was operating in the United States. So he formed ConControl in 2084, without the backing of any government. That's why they're rogue Jon.

"Between 2084 and 2092, ConControl made repeated attempts to peacefully assert itself into the local politics of Connecticut, through elections mainly. They never succeeded. And, of course, without any success locally, they never succeeded in gaining political power nationally or internationally either. In other words, they were very small fish. But size does not always equate with desire or craziness.

"When A.E. began its deadly march through the states, ConControl began stirring up the populace with conspiracies and rumors. They were distributing false information about government cover-ups. ConControl's goal, as I've learned, was to make the government focus on other things while ConControl continued forward with their big plan."

"What was the plan?" John asked.

"It is my belief that Franconi and Bodily were communicating, secretly, while she was in the bunker with us. The logs, which we stopped monitoring as closely after February 9th when Yurgi gave us all the option of leaving the bunker, denote communications from Bodily to Connecticut, and one with Brazil strangely. When I first saw them a couple days ago, I naturally assumed they were coms to family. We all began communicating with our families in those days. And yes, I knew about that, even though you were all trying to keep it on the downlow."

Mike smiled as others in the conference room looked down, bashfully.

"But then, as this information began to surface, I checked out Bodily's coms a little more closely. Bodily didn't have any family in Connecticut. But she did have Franconi. The com numbers were routed from their original destination to an unknown distribution site, and then routed to the Law Offices of Thomas J. Franconi.

"I believe that Bodily was the inside informant I had read about."

Shift and Mike had both prepared for the probability that they would have to reign in the group after that little announcement. Instead, the room remained silent. They were all considering the ramifications of what Mike had told them.

"Anyway," Mike continued after a short pause, "on April 25th, when Yurgi announced the apparent success of the vaccination, at least on animals, Bodily must have been thrilled. She finally had information she could feed to Franconi, and she did place a call that day, after our meeting had ended.

"But only minutes after Yurgi's announcement, I destroyed Bodily's hope, and the hope of most of you as well, when I announced that it was possible we could all be dead within days through the backdraft effect. She must have gone nuts. She yelled at me. She yelled at Yurgi. She was very angry that morning. Remember that it was Bodily who also argued that we should only vaccinate the strongest and the fittest. She was a lunatic."

"So, Mike, tell them what you really wanted to tell them," Shift said.

"There's more than that?" John asked.

"Yeah, there's more," Shift replied.

"Definitely," Mike added. "Seven days later, on May 2nd, Bodily, along with others, volunteered to be among the first humans injected with Yurgi's test vaccine. Later that day, Lucky and Dr. Case were injected with the test vaccine. Bodily was not. She didn't say anything to anyone that I'm aware of, but she did spend the rest of the day in her room. I found several coms throughout the afternoon and evening of May 2nd, from Bodily to Franconi, and again, one to Brazil, which I couldn't figure out.

"The next day, May 3rd, A.E. was released in the bunker."

"Are you saying what I think you're saying?" Street asked quietly.

"I'm saying that I believe Latisha Bodily released Anthrax E into the bunker."

With that announcement, the room finally erupted in a cacophony of voices, all talking to nobody in particular. Shift and Mike let the noise continue for a few moments.

Finally, Shift said, "Alright everybody, get it together."

"I'd like to tell you the rest of my theory," Mike added.

Finally, the noise quieted down.

"Anyway, Bodily must have done it, and here's why: She wanted to be vaccinated the day earlier, even though we knew it was only a test vaccine. She wasn't selected to receive the inoculation. But she needed to be vaccinated in order to get outside the bunker without becoming sick. And she needed to get out soon in order to deliver the vaccine to Franconi and others before they became sick and died. Timing was crucial and time was running out. The only way Bodily could receive the vaccination, and have enough time to get it outside to Franconi, was to release A.E. inside. She'd be sure to be inoculated then, along with the rest of us."

"That's quite a risk," Angel said. "We didn't even know whether it would work on humans yet."

"That's right," John said. "We didn't have that evidence for another ten days."

"Well, like Mike said, she was a lunatic," Steve Porter said.

"But remember that she didn't have the time to wait," Mike continued. "On the outside, everyone was dying. Franconi was obviously still alive, but he may have been sick already. We don't know that. But we also didn't find out that the vaccine had to be administered within the first twenty-four hours after infection until weeks later, after Churchill. So, even if he was sick, she may have thought the vaccine could cure him. Or, if he wasn't sick yet, she knew it was only a matter of time."

"Amazing what love, or perceived love can make a person do," Marilyn said from the security station, through the holo.

"But how did she release A.E.?" Anta asked. "And if she found a way to get into the locked labs to do that, why didn't she just steal the vaccine instead, vaccinate herself and get out with the supply of vaccine?"

"I've been thinking about that for hours," Mike said. "And I discussed it with Shift this morning. We don't have an answer. Maybe Angel and John have a theory, since they had access to the labs."

Everyone looked expectantly at John and Angel.

"Well," Angel began tentatively, "A.E. and the vaccine were not stored in the same place. They were in separate, but adjoining labs. Both labs were locked while any of us were inside; and when we were outside, a passcard was required to gain access."

"And each lab had a different passcard," John added. "So, if she had help from one of us with access, then she could have gained access to both labs. Since she didn't vaccinate herself, she must have gained access on her own, but only to the lab with A.E., not the lab with the vaccine. But how she could accomplish any of it escapes me."

"I don't know either," Angel said. "But I'm impressed with Mike's theory. It sounds reasonable to me."

"I knew there were more reasons to hate Bodily than just the fact that she killed Yurgi," Street said.

Nobody had anything to add to that. Internally, each of them shared Street's sentiments.

26

"Ladies and gentlemen," Shift began in greeting as his friends filed into the conference room for the second time in three days. He knew this would be a very painful meeting. "Is Carón on watch right now? Will you get him on the holo Mike? Thanks."

After Carón had linked up to the conference room, Shift started again. "You all know that I hate these meetings, but we need this one. I have some things to tell you that affect all of us—a lot."

"Over the past eleven days, John and I have contacted—well, in some cases we've only *attempted* to contact—every single contact we have outside the bunker, worldwide," Shift said. "All of the bunkers were silent. Nobody answered a single call or message left at any bunker. Nearly all the individual contact codes we have went unanswered as well. Only two small groups, worldwide, have answered or responded to our calls—in repeated attempts over eleven days."

The group was silent as the ramifications of what Shift just said began to sink in.

"I know this is terrible, frightening information," Shift continued, quietly. "I don't have anything to say that can make any one of you feel any better, so I won't even try. Each of us will need to deal with this information in our own way. I'm sorry."

Several minutes passed in complete silence before Street finally spoke up. "Shift, what did those two say, the ones you reached?"

"It wasn't good," Shift replied. "One group is in Russia. They are being chased by the Skins, relentlessly. There are still several people alive, but every one of them is injured or frightened beyond help. The man I spoke with said they intend to fight or die trying. They aren't even going to attempt to get here. He doesn't think a single one of them is strong enough to make it."

"That's awful," Marilyn said. "Awful," she said a second time, but much more quietly.

"The other group is from Turkey. They were somewhere in the Ural Mountains in Russia two days ago. Only two of them are alive. They're trying to get here because there's nowhere else to go. They've been living and running for their lives in hovers for weeks now. They're hoping to get to the Bering Strait and then south to us, but that's a massive undertaking."

"Is there any chance they'll be able to get here?" Steve asked.

"I don't think so, and neither do they," Shift replied solemnly. "The problem is that they are very young. Two teenage girls." Jon Porter looked up. Suvan looked at Jon, briefly, then looked back down at her lap.

"I think the older girl is seventeen years old. They're scared to death. They can't fly a plane. She told me that every time they stop the hover, they have only a couple of hours before the Skins show up. Even when they've flown hundreds of miles at top speeds, the Skins still show up."

"That's remarkable," Marilyn said, surprise evident in her tone and on her face. "Do they communicate with each other somehow, across distances? Can they sense a human on the way? Is there some other way they have figured out, or some way their bodies have changed to allow them to always know where the girls are? I mean, if so, then we're all in huge trouble."

"It isn't outside the realm of possibility," Angel responded delicately. She turned her head to Andrew, looked him in the eyes, and spoke slowly, as if trying to coax him into discussing a subject she felt so strongly about. The two had formed a bond over the last few days, discussing things that most of the others couldn't understand.

"Those questions are difficult to answer," Angel said in response to Marilyn's questions, still looking at Andrew. "Andrew and I have been discussing questions dealing with the human brain, specifically certain human brains for a long time. The human brain is capable of impressive things."

Andrew nodded almost imperceptibly. Angel continued. "I believe that Toronto's E-rase has unlocked a secret door to the minds of the Skins. What if, what was once an inaccessible part of the human brain is now accessible. Theoretically, a human could fly, or see through walls, or read minds, or control others telepathically. Or any number of other abilities that we've never believed were humanly possible."

"You mean to say that you think the Skins are like Superman?" Carón asked from across the holo.

Angel didn't respond to Carón's question, but instead, again looked into Andrew's eyes, "Andrew, do you think that's a possibility?"

"I . . . I . . ." Andrew began. Andrew knew that, by agreeing with Angel's statements, even in theory, he was stepping into a new world— one which he had purposefully avoided all of his adult life. But this was a new world now anyway, wasn't it? Clearly, what the Skins were doing would be impossible to believe had he not seen it with his own eyes. Even in the short time since he'd been watching the Skins on the monitors with Mike and Angel, trying to sense whether Angel's theories could be accurate, he had seen their almost super-human abilities increase.

After a moment's hesitation, Andrew said, slowly, "Angel, I think your theory is quite possibly accurate. I believe the Skins possess some kind of super-human attribute that allows them to do things none of us could ever dream of."

The volume in the room rose abruptly as each person began to mumble and discuss what they had just heard. For most of them, Andrew's opinion about the matter solidified the likely truth. Now they were afraid.

"Let's quiet down, please," Shift said finally. After the room had quieted, he continued, "Ultimately, whether the Skins are 'supermen' or 'superwomen' doesn't alter the situation we find ourselves in. It's an interesting subject, to be sure. But we need to determine what we're to do next."

Shift paused. "The reality is that we are, probably, alone now."

"But there could be other people, right?" Neirioui Safar asked tentatively. "Maybe we just haven't heard from them yet. You're not giving up, are you?"

"No Neirioui, we're not giving up," John answered for Shift. "It's likely there are others out there. We have messages set on loops across the world on the Net and the USCAN system. If there are others out there, hopefully they'll hear our message and contact us."

"Could someone just show up here?" Street asked.

"No," John replied. "The messages don't relay our position. In fact, Mike set up the signals to broadcast remotely from several different places around the world, none of which are anywhere near us."

"The fear we have," Mike added, "is that the Skins may be listening in. We haven't seen anything to give us any indication that they communicate the way we do, or that they're listening to our broadcasts or accessing the Net. They actually seem quite primitive when it comes to electronics and technology. But they obviously have some kind of ability, like Andrew just said. So, we have the message replaying through remote servers and towers far away from here. Nobody can find us unless we tell them where we are—except maybe the Skins."

"Well, that's not a very comforting way to end such a fine speech," Shift said. "But in any event, that's all correct. Unless and until we hear from someone in response to our broadcasts, we will not be joined by anyone here. I'm hopeful, but not unrealistically so, that someone is still alive."

"Speaking of the Skins and their primitive ways," Steve said, "has anyone seen whether they like the salt water, or whether they can drive or fly hovers?"

"We've been watching for those things very closely," Mike responded. "We've gone back through thousands of video feeds, from all over the world. We haven't seen a single Skin touch salt water, but that doesn't mean they can't. It just means they haven't. We also haven't seen them driving anything. Again, it may just be that they don't need to. They're pretty fast suckers as it is. Also, we haven't seen Skins on any island or in Australia. So, they don't take boats or planes; at least, they haven't yet."

"And that's important news," Shift added. "It means, hopefully, that our escape plan will work, if it comes down to that."

"So, if there are no Skins in Australia," Marilyn began, "doesn't that mean that there could be survivors there, or that we could survive there?"

"Of course that's possible," Shift replied. "But Mike hasn't seen any yet, right?"

"That's right, unfortunately."

Throughout the meeting, Anta sat quietly and listened. While her face may have shown her emotion as various items were discussed, her mouth didn't betray her. Over the past few days, she had grown more and more uncomfortable in the bunker. She loved Shift. They had spent every free moment together, day and night. But her feelings were tugging her in different directions. She longed to be outside, with the Skins, but she didn't know why. And it frightened her beyond words. She wondered if she should tell Shift about her feelings, but she could not have explained it to anyone, nor would she ever try, if she could avoid it.

27

"Yeah, everything is up and running," Hasani said.

"That's wonderful!" Anta replied.

"Yeah, it's good, but we still feel pretty stupid about how long it's taken us."

"I wouldn't feel too stupid about it," Anta said. "What would you have done if you'd fixed it weeks ago?"

"Nothing, I guess," Hasani replied.

"So, what are your thoughts now?" Shift asked.

Anta and Shift had spent considerable time discussing options with Hasani. Others had participated on occasion, but these meetings were special. They openly shared their feelings, holding nothing back. Shift loved these little conferences, and his talks alone with Anta, because he could freely admit his tremendous fear about the unlikelihood of seeing another Christmas. Shift and Hasani began to feel like brothers. Even though they had never met, their common bond—Anta—brought them together.

"Well, Tom and Misty have no problem living the rest of their lives here. They've already been up here for three years. They never expected to go home when they left Earth. So, they're okay with this, especially since things seem much worse there. At least we don't have to deal with monsters up here."

"Yeah, but *we* don't have to deal with fake food and recycled water down here, at least not yet," Shift replied. Hasani laughed.

"But me, and the others—we want to see the moon rise at night, not live on it."

"Hasani, Shift and I were talking last night . . ."

"Whoa sister, I don't need to hear your pillow talk!" Hasani said, chuckling. Shift held his laughter back since he knew Anta was being serious.

"Listen to me, you idiot. Shift and I were talking last *evening*. I don't want you to come here. It's too dangerous."

"But we do want you to be *ready* to come here," Shift added.

"What do you mean?" Hasani asked.

"We want you to be ready in case we need to be rescued," Anta said.

"You mean, you want us to be ready to fly down there, pick you up, and fly back to the moon? Are you crazy?"

"Maybe," Shift responded. "Maybe we're crazy, but you don't know what it's like here. There are no other survivors. If anybody else is alive outside this bunker, we don't know about them. Everybody we know of is dead, or turned. This place we're hiding in may be the only safe place left on the planet. If they find us, we're dead too."

"Wow, you're serious. Could we even do that?" Hasani asked himself aloud.

"Hasani, will you talk to everyone up there and figure out a way?" Shift pleaded. "Find a way to rescue us if we need you to. The time to talk to you and tell you to come would take mere minutes. If the shuttle was ready in advance, what's it take, six hours or something to get here?"

"Well, probably closer to eight hours including takeoff and landing," Hasani replied. "But where would we even land? It would have to be in a place where we could land, turn, and take off, all without trucks and equipment. There aren't many places to do that. According to Jerad, these massive shuttles have to recharge, and they get serviced and cleaned before they take off again. They aren't commercial jets you know."

"Obviously," Anta said.

"Hasani," Shift said, "please consider the possibility of coming to get us before it becomes an emergency."

"Well, let me get back to you. I think you're both crazy, but maybe Jerad can figure out a way."

"Thanks dude," Shift said. "Let us know *when* you've found a way." Shift smiled.

AUGUST 8—SHIFT

We've been here in the Cabo Rojo bunker for a month now. Thirty days that have felt like an eternity. The Skins have destroyed the human race—or at least the remainder of the human race that wasn't already wiped out by A.E.

Our days are marked by routine and sorrow. Very little I say or do cheers anybody up. Very little anybody says cheers others up. John still cracks stupid jokes, but few people laugh. My sole moments of joy come at night, when Anta and I can be together and forget about everything else for a little while.

My despair—our collective despair—comes, not only from the realization that we may become an extinct race at any moment, but from the fact that, even if we live for many months or years, what kind of life will we have? Can we continue to live in Cabo Rojo forever? Could we live on the moon? Maybe we could live in both places.

We need, not only to survive, but to begin to build a new generation. Children. We need children. But nobody, me included, is keen on the idea of bringing a child into this world. I've watched my little group; looked for signs of people connecting in romantic ways. I don't see it though, apart from Street and Angel perhaps. They're all too afraid. Nobody wants to have a child. But more than that, nobody seems to want to get too close to someone who may be taken from them at any time. I understand. I've had that fear for many months.

Jon and Suvan may be the only children left in the world now. The teenage girls from Turkey have not com'd us in many days. I'm certain they're dead.

This life may soon come to an end for all of us, but despite our fear of the future and the present, and despite our sorrow, nobody here at this bunker has given up. We each perform our daily tasks, hopeful that tomorrow will be better.

28

"Watch this!" Mike said.

"What, did you find another funny animal video?" John asked, smiling.

"Yeah, a very big, very strong, very naked and very bald cat," Mike replied.

"Come children, let us be serious for a minute, if we may," I said.

"Okay, seriously, watch this." Mike touched 'play' on the monitor. The digital stamp at the bottom displayed 9 August, 2093—yesterday. 3:42 P.M. central time.

"Hey, it's your friend Cain," John said. "Right?"

"Yeah, my *friend* Cain."

"What's he doing?" John asked.

"I've seen him do that before. I need Angel and Street in here," I replied.

"What about Anta?" Mike asked.

"No, luckily she's on watch right now," I said. "I'd like her to stay there. You remember what I told you about how she acted last time? What if she does it again? I don't want her to see this, okay? Hold on, let me get the others. Tell Mike about Anta while I'm gone, okay. But this is secret Mike. Don't tell a soul."

I left to look for Street and Angel, hoping John would properly update Mike with information about Anta's previous run-ins with the Skin called "Cain". I soon returned with Street and Angel at my heels.

"Restart it Mike," I said. Mike touched "play".

"That's Cain," Street said as his face began to turn red. His fist clenched. It looked almost involuntary. *He really doesn't like that dude,* I thought.

"Watch what he does next," I said.

We all watched as Cain, standing straight and tall, lifted one hand to the sky, palm forward.

"Okay," Mike said, "here's the crazy part." Mike pulled up three other feeds on the remaining monitors. All three showed groups of Skins in different places. Mike paused the feeds.

"See how the times and dates are all identical, except for the difference in time zones?" Mike asked. Not waiting for a response, he continued, "This feed with Cain is just down the road in Mexico City. You can see the crowd of Skins around him."

"These other three feeds," Mike continued, pointing to each in turn, "are from Newark, New Jersey, Hamburg, Germany, and Moscow. There are tons of other feeds just like these, all date stamped the same time. I wanted to show you as many as I could, but I only have the four screens. Sorry.

"Anyway, watch what happens," Mike said. He rewound the four feeds a few seconds then hit play on all four simultaneously.

We watched in disbelief. At the moment Cain raised his hand to the sky, palm facing outward, the Skins with him and in the three cities featured on the monitors all knelt in unison. Every one of them facing the same direction, presumably toward Cain in Mexico City. Then Cain spoke. We couldn't hear him, or read his lips, but as his mouth moved, various Skins on each screen stood up, then knelt back down. Then others stood up, then knelt back down.

"Holy crap Mike. Are you saying this happened all over the world at the same time?" John asked.

"Yup. I've got forty-one feeds displaying groups of Skins doing the exact same thing at the exact same time."

"He's controlling them," Angel said. Her voice was barely audible. The surprise in her eyes shocked me. Angel had already convinced us that Cain and the Skins likely had super human abilities. But this was too much even for her. "He's controlling them on the other side of the world!"

"How is that possible?" I asked, not really expecting an answer. Nobody had one anyway.

"Does Anta know about this?" Street asked. "Does anyone else know about this?"

"Nobody knows yet," Mike said.

"And I don't want Anta to know," I added. "Remember what she did last time we were close to Cain? I don't want her acting crazy just seeing him on the screen. It freaks me out."

"Me too boss," Street said.

"Well, can we keep everyone else in the dark about this?" John asked. "If we don't tell Anta, we can't tell anyone else either. Otherwise, she'll find out. Then she'll find out that you didn't tell her. She would be so pissed."

"I know. Does anyone have any suggestions?"

"Maybe we could just tell everyone about it, but not show them," Street offered.

"Wouldn't work," John said. "They'd just want to see it. So would Anta. She knows Cain as well as the rest of you. She'll want to see it."

"Yeah, she'll want to see it," I confirmed, reluctantly.

"Then what if we got everyone together and showed them the video feeds, just like we've watched," Mike said. "But I'll be ready to shut them down if Anta, or anyone else, starts to freak out."

"But nobody else knows about Anta, right Shift?" Angel asked, obviously concerned about this.

"Nobody knows," I replied.

"Then we need to show Anta first, by herself," John said. "Then we could shut it down for her alone, if she wigs. Nobody would be the wiser. Then, while she's in her little trance, if it comes to that, we get everybody else together to show them. We could just say she's not feeling well or something. Would that work?"

"That's probably the best idea," I replied. "Let's do it. When does she get off watch Mike?"

"Noon."

"Let's all meet back here then. I'll bring Anta."

AUGUST 10, 12:10PM
CABO ROJO, MEXICO

"Okay, are you ready Anta?" Mike asked.

"Yes, but why do you all look so concerned? What are you hiding from me?"

"It's just very shocking, that's all," John lied. "We all saw it an hour ago, so we know what you're in for."

"Hit it Mike," Shift said.

The small group watched the four monitors light up. They watched Anta from the corners of their eyes. Anta's face twitched as Cain's hand rose to the sky. Nothing else happened.

When Mike stopped the feeds, all eyes turned toward Anta.

"Wow. That was crazy. What?" she asked, suddenly suspicious.

"We need to talk," Shift said. He led her out of the room and down to her bedroom to have the first real conversation anybody had had with her about the way she had reacted to Cain in the past. Reactions that she wasn't even aware of.

"That is going to be a tough conversation," John said as Shift and Anta walked away. "I'm glad she's not *my* girlfriend."

"Anta's probably happier than you are about that," Mike joked. They laughed, but not for long.

"At least we know that seeing a re-run of Cain on a video monitor doesn't make her crazy," Street said.

"I'm relieved," Angel said. "I wonder though . . . do we have any video feed of Anta here in the bunker at the date and time of those feeds?"

"Maybe," Mike replied. "Depends on where she was at 3:42 yesterday. Let me look for a minute."

"Got it!" Mike said, three minutes later. "Let's take a look. I'll start it a few minutes earlier though."

"What was she doing on the island yesterday? And by herself?" John asked.

"Actually, she wasn't by herself," Angel replied. "She went over there yesterday with Suvan and Jon. They wanted to fish in the cave. She took them over because neither Neirioui nor Steve wants those two alone."

"Why aren't the kids in the feed then?" John asked.

"Well, the feed doesn't cover the back wall or several meters out from the back wall," Mike said. "Look where Anta is. She's out there about the middle of the docks, by the boats, just walking around. The kids could be anywhere behind her really, and we wouldn't see them."

"But would they see her?" Angel asked. "I mean, I guess it depends on what we see here, but if Anta goes nuts in a couple minutes, we need to talk to those two, right?"

"Yeah, I think so," John replied.

"Okay, here it comes," Mike said.

They waited in silence as the clock on the screen ticked toward 3:42. At 3:42 and thirteen seconds, Anta turned toward the southwest and dropped to her knees on the screen. Angel gasped. Moments later, she stood back up, then abruptly knelt back down. Within seconds, it was over. She stood up, turned back toward the rear of the cave, and walked out of sight.

"What's going on?" Street asked quietly, almost in a whisper.

"Street, go get Shift and Anta," John said.

Street shook his head back and forth, then walked out of the room to find them.

AUGUST 10, 12:37PM
CABO ROJO, MEXICO

"You're not going to like what you see—either of you," John said as Street, Shift and Anta walked back into the computer lab. Anta held her head high, but her checks were stained with dried tears.

"I don't imagine we will," Shift replied. "I have a pretty good idea where this is going. And now, Anta does too." Shift pulled Anta close, keeping his arm tight around her waist.

"I'm so sorry everyone," Anta said as fresh tears filled her eyes. The desperation in her voice was palpable. "Whatever I've put all of you through . . . I am so sorry. I can't explain it. I don't know what's happening."

"You haven't done anything to us Anta," Street said gently.

"We love you girl," Angel added. "Nothing happening here is your fault. But we'll get to the bottom of it. We'll figure this out. Everything's going to be okay."

"I hope you're right Angel," Anta said, trying to stifle her tears. "Let's get this over with."

Two minutes later, Anta was crying again. This time though, there was fear in her eyes and her body was shaking. "How can that possibly be? I don't remember any of that. I don't remember anything Shift told me about either."

"But you should all know, if you're okay with me talking about it Anta . . . ?" Shift looked at Anta and she nodded. "You should all know about the feelings Anta has been having lately. I hope I explain this right."

Nobody said a word. Nobody even looked at Anta. She was grateful.

"It was hard for her to explain it to me," Shift continued. "Over the past few days, or a couple of weeks maybe, Anta has felt a strong pull to the outside. That's why she volunteered to go with Jon and Suvan yesterday. And that's why she was walking down toward the outer wall. She wanted to be outside."

"But I wasn't going out there," Anta added quickly. "I would never go out there alone. I hoped I was just getting cabin fever. I had the same problem back in Boston the whole time we were there. That's all I wanted it to be—just cabin fever."

"Of course babe," Shift said, grasping Anta's hand. "But she also explained to me that she feels like the Skins are calling to her. Like they want her to be with them. But, until a few minutes ago, she thought she was imagining it. It freaked her out, as you can imagine. Anta's been living in fear for days now wondering whether she's going crazy."

"That's insane man," Street said, then added quickly, "Not you Anta. I don't think *you're* insane. I'm sorry. I mean the whole situation is crazy weird."

"That's okay Street," Anta said with a weak, tear-streaked smile. "I know what you meant. It is insane. But maybe I'm insane too."

"No you're not," Shift said lovingly. "There's an explanation for this. Let's figure it out. And while we do, I'm not leaving your side."

"Oh, lucky Anta," John said smiling.

"Shut up dude," Shift replied. Although he tried to look serious, it only lasted a couple moments. Then the corners of his mouth began to twitch and he could no longer repress the chuckle. Laughing, he said, "I mean it John, shut your pie hole."

The others joined in the laughter, although it was a tense laughter. As usual, John had attempted to break the tension. That's why they loved him. But this time, it wasn't quite enough.

"Now, let's get down to business," John began. "Anta, can you remember anything that might shed some light on why, or how, you may have a connection to the Skins?"

"Yeah, it's easy," Anta replied almost immediately. "I've been thinking about it for the last twenty minutes."

"Easy, huh?" Shift asked. "Well, let us have it."

"You guys remember back in Amqui, the day of that first fight with the Skins?"

"How could we forget Street's awesomeness!" Angel replied. Angel looked longingly at Street as she continued. "That was the day Street saved our lives. I won't forget it."

Shift and Anta glanced quickly at each other, acknowledging their suspicions that they were seeing a relationship blossom between Street and Angel. Then Street coughed and the moment was over.

"Anyway," Anta continued, feeling the awkwardness of the situation, "Shift, you remember how I cut my finger?"

"Yeah, you said it was no big deal. Just a little cut, right?"

"That's right," Anta replied. "It wasn't any big deal. But then, a few minutes later we burst out of the motel room and, even though Street took out about ninety percent of the Skins, the rest of us still had a little work to do. One of the Skins I shot was really close. Some of her blood sprayed out onto my arm and hand—the hand with the freshly cut finger. I didn't pay attention to it. Just wiped it off in the Fluxor like the rest of you were doing."

"You think some of the Skin's blood got in your cut?" Angel asked.

"I wouldn't doubt it at all," Anta replied.

They all sat quiet for a moment. Finally Shift broke the silence. "We need to test your blood Anta."

"You're obviously not a Skin," John said aloud. Then, under his breath, he added, "not that we'd mind seeing you naked."

Shift hit him. Anta laughed. Mike, Street and Angel politely attempted to repress smiles.

"Sorry John," Anta said. "Only one man here is that lucky."

"You're talking about me, right?" Shift said hastily. More laughter.

"Guys, let's get our heads out of Anta's boudoir and focus, shall we?" Angel said smiling. "Is there any possibility that Anta could have become infected with Toronto's E-rase but not had the same symptoms?"

"Let's get her tested first, then we'll worry about the 'what-ifs'," Shift said. "Let's go over to the medical center now."

"You are all welcome to join us," Anta added as they stood up. "I don't want to hide this from any of you."

"Let's all go then," Shift said. "But try not to make it too conspicuous. There's no reason anybody else outside this room needs to know about this; at least not until there's something to worry about."

Mike shut down the old video feeds and the group headed out.

29

"Guys, come here!" Steve yelled from the security room where he was on watch.

Anta, Shift, John, Mike, Street and Angel were all passing by the security room, having a phony conversation about chickens, trying to look inconspicuous.

They all turned and walked back toward the security room.

"What is it?" John asked nervously.

"Look!" Steve said.

On the main monitor set to display the front of the bunker where they had all first arrived, a small group of Skins was wandering around, apparently sniffing the air.

"How long have they been there?" Shift asked nervously.

"They're just arriving now," Steve replied. The skin on his arms was raised in goose-flesh. He was scared. They could all see it.

"Steve," Shift said, placing a hand on his shoulder, "why don't you go and gather everyone together. Mike, let's get this feed sent down to the meeting room."

"What should we do?" Street asked.

"Obviously, we need to get everyone ready for evasive action," Shift said. "Let's get to the meeting room and make sure everyone is ready to put the escape plan into action. But I need someone to stay here in the security room to keep an eye on those doors. Any volunteers?"

"Yeah, I'll do it," Street offered.

"Thanks, I was hoping you would say that Street," Shift said. "You're the guy I can always count on."

"Hmmph," Street said awkwardly, a little bashful. Angel stared at him again, reaching out her hand to touch him before abruptly pulling it away and walking out of the room.

Outside, the Chosen sniffed and felt for vibrations in the ground. They knew the human perversions were around somewhere, but their senses were growing too powerful. It was hard to tell whether this ugly, old concrete building was where the perversions were hiding, or whether Cain had sent them on a fool's errand. Perhaps what they smelled and felt came from somewhere else entirely. Cain controlled them, they knew, but even he was beginning to become too powerful. His senses had become too great, and less focused, and he had made mistakes.

Several minutes later, the small group of humans met in the meeting room. Street was absent, sitting upstairs in the security room; but his back was displayed on the holo as he watched the monitors showing the outside of the bunker. The others were all in the room.

Suvan and Jon Porter sat next to each other. Suvan's mother watched them from across the room, clearly nervous about their future. Steve's face displayed his worry about whether these two children, who were obviously fond of each other, had any future worth worrying about. He prayed daily that the children would have the opportunity to grow up and live normal lives. Now, as the group met in the large room off the kitchen, his worry became intense , as demonstrated by visible shaking, had anyone been watching. He had seen the Skins outside, and his body hadn't stopped shaking since.

"Hi everyone," Shift began. "Thanks for coming."

Nobody said a word. Those that didn't know what to expect from this meeting remained quiet, sensing a growing tension in the room.

"Mike, turn on the screens please." Shift said as the old screens began to flicker to life. Then a moment later, he added, "So, this is what's happening outside our doors right now."

Neirioui Safar gasped, placing both arms across her belly as if to protect herself from an imminent attack. Everybody else seemed to expect it. They remained quiet.

"You all know what this means," Shift continued. "We may no longer be safe here. As you can see, they still appear to be wandering around out there. So they may not know we're here. But we need to be ready to evacuate just in case.

"I want everyone to go now and make sure your things are ready. We've prepared for this. We've run the drills. We're ready. If they discover us, they'll likely try to come in through the ventilator shafts. Even though we haven't been running them for weeks, the Skins may know the shafts are there.

"The only other way they could get in, unless their strength has multiplied exponentially, is through the cave. But we haven't seen a single Skin enter a boat or any other motorized craft. And we haven't seen a single Skin go in salt water. So, while the cave is being monitored, we'll be watching the ventilation system more carefully.

"Mike, are all of your surveillance and alarm systems working?"

"Yeah, I checked them all this morning, just like every other morning," Mike replied. "Everything is working fine."

"Good," Shift said. "That means, everybody, that if you hear three short beeps, that will be your sign that we need to evacuate per our plan, toward the cave. If you hear one longer siren, that will mean the Skins are coming through the cave. Either way, we've planned for it.

We're ready to keep them out whichever way they come in. Hopefully though, we won't need to go either way."

Anta screamed. The room erupted in confusion.

"Grab her," John said frantically. "Don't let her hit her head."

Anta dropped to the ground, convulsing, her body rolling and bending as if large hands were grasping and tugging on her limbs.

"Check the screen Mike," Shift said between breaths as he struggled to hold Anta still. "Is Cain out there?" These words made several of the members of the group pause.

"Why does it matter if Cain is out there?" Andrew asked.

"I'll tell you later," Shift replied.

"Yeah Shift, he's out there," Mike said.

Street's voice came over the intercom system. "Shift, Cain's here. Watch Anta."

"Thanks Street, we know," John replied for Shift. "She's struggling, but we've got her."

Anta continued to thrash. Shift, John, Carón, and Steve all held her. But the strength of her convulsions was wearing them out.

"Guys," Mike began apprehensively, looking at the monitors, "he knows we're here."

The group all looked back at the screens. Cain's face was large, filling one of the screens as he peered deep into the mechanics of a digital camera on the outside of the building. He was talking.

"Street," Shift said through the intercom, "Can you turn on the microphones, one way? I want to hear him, but I don't want him to hear us."

"Got it boss," Street said.

Moments later, the deep, calm voice of Cain filled the room. Anta shook violently for a moment, then relaxed completely. Her face turned toward the screen. Cain looked at her, impossibly. It was as though he knew the exact point of the camera outside which would lead his eyes toward Anta's eyes. Then he spoke again.

"Anta," he said. Anta's body jumped. The men had a difficult time holding her. Her eyes lost focus and became black.

"Let us in," Cain whispered, with incredible intensity.

Anta's body jumped again. This time, her left arm broke free of Steve's grasp and she swung it across her body. Her clenched fist hit Shift on the brow above his nose. He let go of her other arm, but immediately grabbed it again. Those that hadn't been holding Anta down before rushed over to help hold her.

"Don't let her up," Shift said tensely. "If she gets free, we may not be able to catch her again."

"What's happening?" Neirioui cried out.

Suvan immediately rushed over to her mother, who had crumpled to the floor in fear. Suvan, crying softly, held tightly to her mother while the others, breathless and through clenched teeth, discussed what to do next.

"How does he know her name?" Andrew Jones asked. Nobody answered. Nobody knew the answer.

"Time to go guys," Street said over the intercom. "They're headed toward the vents."

On the screen, Cain was clearly seen directing an ever-larger force of Skins in different directions. Mike hit a button and the cameras he had installed on the three ventilator shafts all lit up, splitting the monitor in thirds. Skins came into view at each location. The group fell into a hushed silence, except for the heavy breathing of Anta and those holding her down.

"John, we've got to sedate her—now," Shift said.

"Okay, I'm letting go." John let go as others filled his spot. Within moments, John returned with a large needle. He squeezed it and a drop of clear liquid shot out of the end. Then he turned toward Anta, knelt, wiped a small white pad across her upper arm, and plunged the needle into her flesh. Twenty seconds later, Anta was still.

"Let's go!" Shift said. Mike, John, Shift and Carón each grabbed a leg or arm and stood Anta up. She was light, and Shift, with John's help, lifted Anta over his shoulder. She would be easy to carry. But that left a greater burden on the others. Each member of the group began to carry out his or her part of the plan. It was time to get to the island.

AUGUST 10, 1:54PM
CABO ROJO, MEXICO

The Chosen had found the ventilator shafts, all three of them. They had been in this position before, Cain knew. It was only a matter of time before they worked the fittings loose and began to file in. They were struggling though. Cain didn't understand. His mind was as strong as ever, but his body, and the bodies of his soldiers were struggling with simple tasks. They fought with one another as they attempted to shake the fittings loose. Their enormous strength was not the benefit it had been on all prior occasions.

Cain could feel Anta slipping away. She had seen him. She had tried to come to him. She would have let them in, but the perversions stopped her. Now, his grasp on her mind was fading. Within moments, it could be gone. But she was in there. This hole in the ground was no different than the others. But this time, Cain's army was thousands strong.

The perversions, with their guns and their bombs, could not defeat an army this size. They would be reduced to extinction. Then Cain would rule. The perversions would pay for what they had done to him. Shevchuk had already become his slave. The others would too, or die resisting, and this time, Cain would be there to see it.

It had been over six months since those foul creatures had sent him from the bunker at Boston. Sent him out to die. They thought he was dangerous. They thought he was too angry. They thought his theories were the ramblings of a crazy man. Now they would regret that decision. The only thing that had kept them alive this long was the fact that they held Anta captive.

Cain stretched his hand to the sky, again commanding his army to breach the hull. Why they hadn't done it yet was confusing. They were trying, but failing. The perversions were being given precious time to escape, if they had any way to do so. Soon, if his army continued to fail, he would tear this structure down with his bare hands. He would not let them escape again.

30

"Is everyone in place?" Shift asked John through his MEHD.

"Yes, everyone is through the tunnel but you and Street."

"How is Anta? Still knocked out?"

"Yeah, she's out cold," John replied. "And we've got her tied up on one of the boats, just in case. Steve and Mike are with her, also just in case."

"Good."

For some reason, the Skins had not come in yet. They were still outside. The monitors on the walls of the tunnel and on the island showed the Skins trying to rip apart the top of the ventilator shafts, but Mike's alarm system was not yet relaying a breach.

Street and Shift sat in a small control room about mid-way through the tunnel. The others were all on the island. Both groups watched the monitors, frightened, but not panicked.

The arms and chests of the Skins, both men and women, and even children, showed immense muscle mass, rippling and bulging as the Skins tried, in vain so far, to breach the outer walls of the bunker. It looked like the Skins were having trouble with coordination. It was like their minds were having difficulty relaying messages to their bodies. At least that's what Shift thought.

"Maybe Cain is losing his control over them," Shift said.

"Well, he's certainly still trying," John said through the MEHD. "Look at that freakishly large arm up in the air like that."

"But his face is all screwed up," Street said.

"Yeah, like he's having trouble concentrating; or maybe the others are mentally at war with him," Shift said.

"Or maybe that's his normal look . . . all screwed up," Street added sarcastically.

"But they're still trying to get in," John said. "They're still doing what he wants, or at least, they're trying to."

"All I know is that once they get in, and I'm sure they will, we could have thousands crawling around in here within minutes," Shift said. "It won't take them long to figure out where we are."

"But we'll be at the other end of the tunnel before they get here," Street added. "And I can't wait to blow the hell out of 'em! I just hope Cain is in the lead."

"Why does that guy look so familiar?" John asked.

"We've had this conversation before John," Shift replied. "I don't know the guy."

"Hey Andrew, Angel, Mike, come here!" John yelled out. His shout nearly deafened Shift and Street at the other end of the com. "You guys know who this Cain is?"

"Yes," Angel replied bitterly, "he's the guy who's tried to kill us a couple times and now has Anta under some kind of mind control."

"That's not what I mean," John said. "I mean, do you know him from anywhere else?"

"I don't think so," Mike replied.

"I don't know him either," Andrew replied seconds later. "Wait, can we zoom in on him while he's standing still like that?"

"Hold on," John said.

"Actually, he does look familiar," Andrew said. "Doesn't he kind of look like that guy that was at the bunker with us in the early days, before Anta and Shift showed up? Or maybe he left just after they showed up."

"Hmmm, yeah, a little," John replied. "But Cain looks older, a few more wrinkles in his face. That other guy was pretty young, wasn't he?"

"Anta seemed to recognize him too," Shift added.

"Actually," Mike said, reconsidering, "he *does* look like that guy. Was his name Canton? Dr. Canton maybe?"

"Canton?" John asked quietly. "That name sounds right. He was a viral specialist of some kind, wasn't he? Why did he get kicked out again?"

"He was a hothead," Andrew replied. "Plus, every time he talked about A.E., he would go off on tangents about man's ability to make themselves what they wanted to be. Like, men could transform themselves into something else. It was all gibberish, not science."

"Well, if that's him, he certainly made something of himself," Shift said.

"A.E., from Toronto, made him that way Shift," John said.

"A.E. didn't make him six and a half feet tall, handsome, and full of muscle, John," Angel said.

"Well, if that's him, like I said, he's something now," Shift said. "He's leading an army. What makes him so special though, I wonder? Have we seen any other Skins control others the way he does?"

"Not to this extent," Mike replied through the com. "He's the only one that seems to control thousands. But there are a few others who appear to have control over smaller groups in other places. Like maybe they're his generals or something."

"And I think he has a bit to gripe about," John said. "We kicked him out of the bunker. Basically, we sent him out to die—but before we knew how bad it was going to get, of course."

"So you think he has a little vengeance on his mind?" Street asked.

"I think that may be accurate," John replied.

"Anyone there?" came a voice from a different channel on the com.

"Oh, Hasani, sorry. Thanks for calling back. We have a situation here," Shift replied. "The skins are outside, trying to get in."

"Then they've found your hideout."

"Appears so. We're going to evac. We'll have audio only from here on. Got anything for us?"

"Working on it."

Just then, the alarms beeped three times. Street jumped on the four-wheeler next to him as Shift shut down the com.

"Gotta go, Hasani. We'll call again after the situation settles some."

Shift jumped on the other four-wheeler and they plunged down the tunnel at full speed. The Skins were coming in.

AUGUST 10, 3:01PM
CABO ROJO, MEXICO

"Wait until the tunnel's full," Shift ordered as he and Street rushed up the stairs from the underwater cave at the end of the tunnel. After they had entered the main cave, John swiped the switch on the monitor in front of him and the heavy metal doors shut and sealed. He had closed and locked the doors from the tunnel to the underwater portion of the cave moments earlier.

"They took so long getting in the bunker," Shift continued, trying to catch his breath, "they'll probably have a hard time getting through the doors too. The more we can pack in there while they're trying to get through, the better."

"What if the doors don't hold that long?" Street asked. "Or what if the bomb doesn't work?"

"Let's not risk that happening. Let's get everyone on the boats right now. Then, if they somehow get through the tunnel doors before we blast them to pieces, all we have to do is climb on board and shove off before they get through this second set," Shift said, pointing to the doors he and Street had just run through.

"Question?" John began. "Didn't you say that the explosion could breach the outer wall of the tunnel?"

"Yes . . ." replied Shift.

"Well, if sea water enters the tunnel, we should be able to tell if salt water affects the Skins."

"Excellent!" Street said, his enthusiasm apparent.

"Maybe, once the water clears, and if the monitors still work."

Shift gave the orders to the group huddled behind him peering at the large monitors on the wall. They didn't hesitate. Within minutes, everyone but Shift and Street were on one of the three motor boats.

Two days earlier, they had taken the submarine, the sailboat, the iron ship and all but two of the jet skis far out into the cave's harbor and anchored them. If the Skins got into the cave, and the humans had to flee, there weren't going to be any boats conveniently tied to the pier for the Skins to use, assuming they even could. Instead, the Skins would be forced to stay put or risk the salt of the sea. Of course, there was still the risk that the Skins could jump three hundred meters and land safely on the boats. But that risk seemed small. And, in any event, the boats and jet skis anchored in the harbor were much slower than the motor boats the humans would use.

Now, the small group untied the remaining craft and were floating near the pier in the cave. Two jet skis had been left for Street and Shift. If the Skins got through, the whole procession would retreat through the holographic wall at the far end of the tunnel and wait out in the Gulf to see what the Skins were capable of.

"Here they come," Shift said.

"That didn't take them long," Street said.

"Yeah, they may be having a tough time with their bodies, but their minds look sharp as a tack."

"Where's Cain?" Street growled through clenched teeth as a large body of Skins came into view on the monitor. He hadn't entered the tunnel.

The crowd of Skins began the long walk down the tunnel toward the closed doors at the far end, beneath the island.

"Sheesh, at this rate, we'll be sitting here for three hours," Shift said. It had taken him and Street about twenty minutes, at full speed on the ATVs, to reach the island end of the tunnel from the mid-point. The Skins were just walking.

Suddenly, the Skins at the front of the group leapt forward, their legs barely touching the ground, or so it seemed, and their heads narrowly missing the tunnel's ceiling. They quickly reached a speed which made it impossible for the cameras to track. Within three minutes, the leaders were at the double doors closing off the tunnel from the underwater cave under the island.

"Holy crap," Street said.

"Yeah," Shift said.

Before long, the whole tunnel was full of Skins. At the doors, they were heaving and pushing—a mass of naked flesh pulsating and rippling as they attempted to push through the doors. Cain was not among them as his army tried, in vain, to open the blast doors that held them at bay. They looked confused.

"Look at their faces," Street said. "They look constipated."

Shift laughed, but only for a moment. Just then, a loud crack could be heard all the way through the blast doors at the end of the tunnel, through the underground cave, and up through the second set of blast doors separating the island from the cave beneath.

"Blow it!" Shift yelled.

Street hit the switch.

The eruption caused the boats in the hidden marina to shift violently as the water around them danced and moved. Shift and Street both fell to the ground. The large monitor above them on the wall fell from its mounting, narrowly missing Street's outstretched legs as it crashed to the ground. As Street pulled his legs back, he shifted his body to the right. In one motion, he was up on his knees peering at the smaller screen they had been looking at before the blast. Shift was right behind him. Two of the four quadrants of the screen were still on.

"It worked!" Street yelled. "It worked!"

"Look at them," Shift said, more subdued.

As the debris from the underwater blast cleared below them in the cave, the damage became apparent. Only two cameras from the lower cave remained intact: one dangling from the ceiling by a flimsy piece of metal, submerged in the salt water that had flooded the lower cave; the other, slowly spinning as it sank to the bottom of the channel along with the bodies and rubble that failed to survive the explosion.

These two cameras revealed an incredible scene. The tunnel was in ruins, with concrete fragments of all sizes plummeting into the depths of the channel. The sinking camera, miraculously still broadcasting scenes to the surface, revealed the bloody remains of bodies that had been ripped apart in the explosion. Heads, legs, feet, arms, fingers and other body parts, too mangled to distinguish from the general carnage, tumbled into the depths, swept to and fro on the currents created by the blast.

Several Skins, or portions of the bodies of Skins were trapped below, or tangled within the rapidly-sinking remains of the wreckage. Others who had survived the initial detonation, who at first appeared to be trying to swim to the surface, were losing strength. The surface was too far away. They were drowning. The slowly-spinning camera, on each of its revolutions through the murky water, caught the terror-stricken faces of Skins who were running out of air. The men in the cave shuddered as they watched the bodies of these Skins violently shake and thrash as they took final gulps of saltwater in a last attempt to maintain life.

A few of the stronger Skins finally reached the surface of the turbulent sea. Those who made it had kicked and pushed others out of the way to finally reach fresh air. But once on the surface, most had no more strength to begin the swim to land. Having nothing with which, or on which to float, even these stronger Skins began to struggle, their arms flailing, reaching, and grabbing onto others who had made it to the surface. Even with their great strength, the Skins who had survived the destruction below could not keep their heads above water; but it didn't matter.

After three or four minutes, every Skin who had been in the tunnel was dead. Hundreds of them. Those that had not died in the blast or subsequent drowning, were deteriorating from the outside in, their flesh sizzling and boiling from the salt.

31

"So, now what?" Mike called out as he climbed off the boat onto the pier. He knelt down and tied the rope to its anchor so the others could step off. The waves caused by the explosion continued to ripple through the cavern. The other boats followed suit. Eventually, everyone but Anta and Angel were on the pier, rushing over to Street and Shift.

Angel was the last to leave a boat, having first checked on Anta. Once her feet hit the pier, she ran to Street. She wrapped her arms around him and hugged him tightly.

"You should have seen it," Street said to nobody in particular, sorrow lacing his words as Angel squeezed him around the middle. "Those poor suckers."

"Are you actually sympathizing with the Skins," Dr. Andrew Jones asked as he walked up to the monitors to view the aftermath.

"Dude, it was awful," Shift replied as Street lifted his eyes to meet Andrew's. "Skins or not, we were watching people drown. Oh man, I think I'm going to puke."

Shift moved away from the crowd quickly, arriving at the edge of the pier moments later. Everyone watched as he vomited into the water.

"That's how bad it was," Street said slowly, looking directly into Andrew's eyes.

"Okay, I'm sorry," Andrew replied. "I didn't think about it that way. I'm glad I didn't have to see it."

"Let's find Cain," Shift said, standing and wiping his mouth on his sleeve. "Mike, can you get those other cameras back on line and try to find him?"

The blast from the explosives had caused many of the cameras in the bunker to go offline. Hopefully, they would still be operational. Of those that were still on, only a few showed living Skins. Most of them were in the security room by the massive front doors of the compound or still wandering around outside the bunker.

The lower levels of the compound on the mainland were filling with water in the aftermath of the explosion. A few stragglers were struggling to climb the stairs in a race with the rising ocean water. Those in the back were slowly dropping off as the water swam around their ankles, then their legs, and eventually their torsos. They didn't survive the salt any better than their comrades that had been caught in the blast.

On the island, the small group was beginning to feel safe again. They now knew that salt water would cripple the Skins, if not kill them outright. So, unless the Skins decided to use a boat, they were safe on the island. But they couldn't stay there indefinitely. They would run out of food and water. They would have to leave. But where would they go?

"There he is," Mike said, successfully getting a few more cameras back on line.

Cain was inside the building. The Skins had succeeded in opening the large front doors and Cain was standing there, as if waiting patiently for his minions to succeed. Skins were wandering around both outside and inside the bunker, apparently unsure of how to proceed. Cain was not directing them, at least not right then. Perhaps he was still trying to figure out what had happened, or what to do next.

"Angel, how's Anta doing?" Shift asked, not looking away from the monitor.

"She's still out," Angel replied. "But what's going to happen when she wakes up?"

"What was all of that about anyway?" Andrew asked.

"I'll tell you later," Shift replied. "Right now, we've got bigger problems."

"You know, Anta only reacted when Cain was nearby," John said. "But remember how he seemed to be controlling Skins on the other side of the world? I wonder if the link is weaker because she's not a Skin, but just has some of the tainted blood or something."

"Maybe if we get her far enough away, like out in the middle of the Gulf, she won't be affected by him," Street offered.

"Could we do that though," Angel asked. "Could we take her out there and keep her out there until Cain leaves? What if he doesn't leave? What if he sticks around here trying to find a way out to us?"

"I think the Skins are smart enough that they *will* find a way out to us," John said. "We need to find a more permanent solution than just sending Anta out to sea."

"Could we get to the moon?" Street asked.

That question gave them all pause. After a moment, Shift spoke up. "You know, Anta and I talked with her brother Hasani a while back. They finally got a ship working. They decided that they could get back to Earth, but they didn't know where they could land and be able to turn around and take off again if that became necessary. Something about not having the equipment or machinery to do it, and no people to operate that machinery. As of this morning, the moon folks were still trying to find a solution."

"You mean you already considered going to the moon?" Angel asked.

"Yeah, but not very seriously," Shift replied. "We just wanted to know whether it could work as a contingency plan. Hasani com'd just as this latest crisis was starting, so we didn't have a chance to ask if they've found a solution yet."

"I think we should look at that option a bit more closely now," John said. "I'm afraid the Skins will figure out how to get here."

"Me too," Mike said. "Look at them even now. So many of them are looking east. They know we're here. They're trying to solve this problem. I think they'll do it. I'm all for leaving."

"Ok, let's get everything ready and I'll talk to Hasani again," Shift said.

AUGUST 10, 6:59PM
HOLOGRAPHIC CONFERENCE

"Sorry it took so long to get back, Shift," Jonas said. "Hasani and the others are on their way. Hi everyone."

"No problem," Shift replied. "We're just happy to see your face again. We weren't certain the holo would be working after we blasted the tunnel. *And*, we're very glad we're still here to talk to." Everyone surrounding Shift nodded in agreement.

"Ah, here they come," Jonas said. "We've been trying to get the air filters cleaned in the United States shell. Along with just about everything else, it seems like someone tampered with them. Anyway, everyone's here. What's going on?"

"Hi everyone," Hasani said as he walked up to the Holo. "Where's Anta?"

"That's a bit of a story," Shift replied. "We don't have much time, so here's the short version. I'll fill you in on the details later."

Shift gave a quick summation of Anta's "relationship" with the Skins, particularly Cain. The rest, including their theory about who Cain was and the attack on the bunker, would have to wait for another time. Every piece of information was new and terrifying, and now wasn't the time to alarm the people on the moon. The small group on Earth needed help.

When Shift finished, Hasani asked, "So, Anta is still sedated?"

"Yes," Marilyn replied from the background. "But we can't keep her that way any longer. It's not safe. When she comes out of it, we need to be gone."

"What do you think about that Tom?" Jonas asked.

"I agree," Dr. Thomas Bird replied. "If she's been sedated with a dose that heavy, a second one within twenty-four hours will be very unhealthy."

"So, what's your plan?" Hasani asked, looking genuinely concerned. His only living relative, his sister, was being kept sedated and unconscious, intentionally, in order to prevent her from succumbing to the wiles of the Skins. Maybe she was a Skin. Shift had said that was possible. Hasani began to fear that her life might have to be forfeit in order to maintain the lives of the others.

"We don't really have a very good one at this point," Shift said. "Right now, it is very apparent that the Skins can't tolerate salt water. We haven't seen them operate cars, hovers or boats of any kind either. They don't seem to need any of that since they run about a thousand miles an hour."

"So what Shift is saying," John interjected, "is that we're probably safe here on the island for a while, but Anta isn't. Once she wakes up, we believe she'll be too close to Cain and something bad will happen. We don't know what, obviously. Our only plan is to get Anta, at least, away from here, as far as we can."

Nobody had asked the question that they all wanted answered. They had been beating around the bush for a while. Finally, Shift asked, hesitantly, "Jonas, Hasani, what are the chances you can pick us up?"

"I knew that question was coming," Hasani replied.

"The answer is complicated," Jonas said. "We can easily return to Earth. But, as we told you last time, the return trip is the problem. We have determined that the only base close to you that can handle our landing, a turn and then a return take off is the Kennedy Space Center in Florida. Even that location would be difficult though. As we said before, without people to handle the equipment outside the ship during landing and take-off, it would be very difficult."

"But can it be done?" Mike asked, hopeful. "I mean, I can handle the computer and electronic configurations, once I figure out how. Street's got the muscle of ten men, so we can have him outside, right?"

"I think we can do it," Jonas replied. "It will take some coordination and will be tricky; but yes, I think it can be done."

"Jerad can fly the ship," Hasani added. "So, we just need to work out logistics. What do you need from us?"

The two groups spent the next couple of hours discussing logistics, while Mike kept his eyes trained on the monitor in front of him. He switched between cameras every few seconds, keeping close tabs on the Skins, who continued to wander about without direction on the mainland. In particular, he kept his sights on Cain. Cain was smart. If there was a way for the Skins to get to the island, Cain would find it. Several members of the group were armed, prepared for that possibility.

Finally, with a plan in place, the two groups disconnected to begin preparations. It would be difficult. It was believed that Anta had two or three hours before she would awaken. She had to be gone by then. The others, if they weren't ready, could leave later. But they would all need to be to Cape Canaveral, Florida, on the ship and ready for take off by 6:00PM—in approximately twenty-four hours. That was the optimal time for take-off. Any later and the take-off would be even more difficult due to storms approaching the gulf from the southeast.

32

"Shift!" Angel yelled, "Anta's waking up!" The fear in Angel's voice was palpable. Everyone in the man-made cave on Isla de Lobos could feel the tension rise as Angel waited for Shift's response.

"Okay, go," Shift said softly. "Is everyone on board?"

It had been decided only forty-five minutes earlier who would be on the boat with Anta when it departed for Cape Canaveral. Angel, as Anta's closest friend, would be on the boat to comfort Anta when she woke, if necessary. Marilyn Swenson, as an obstetrician, was still a medical doctor, despite her specialization. She would accompany the small group just in case Anta had complications as she came out of her near-comatose condition. Street refused to let Anta out of his sight, so all agreed that he should go. Dr. Nelise Fabrisio was on board. The group was headed to Cape Canaveral to help the ship land. Dr. Fabrisio, an astronomical physicist, was the only person suited for anything close to what would be required of a ground crew at Kennedy. Mike rounded out the group.

"We gotta go now!" Street said frantically as Anta's eyes began to flutter and her body began to shift.

"Go, go!" Shift yelled as he unhooked the remaining tie from the pier.

The boat sped off toward the holographic wall at the far end of the cave. As it neared the wall, it slowed. No boat, and no person had left the cave since Steve and Jon Porter had explored outside the cave when Steve first arrived. In fact, unless one included the island cave as "outside", not one of the members of the group had been outside in over three weeks. This new freedom was scarier than the small group expected as they slowly passed through the holographic wall. The last time any of them had been outdoors, they were being chased by superhuman Skins bent on their destruction. Even Street was nervous.

The boat emerged from the holographic wall very slowly. Once fully outside, they could no longer see the interior of the cave. It was well-hidden.

Street slowly maneuvered the boat along the rock cliff wall heading southward. They would travel southeast for about a hundred and fifty miles and then turn northeast and head back toward Florida. They hoped to fool the Skins as to their ultimate destination.

As the boat moved out from behind the protective shield of the island, and into open water, the Skins on land began to howl and scream. While the smell of the sea had hidden the humans, the Skins' eyes, strengthened by A.E., could easily see the large boat—and its passengers—as it left them behind.

Cain stepped toward the small waves lapping up on the beach. He was beginning to sense Anta's presence, but the sense was dulling as the boat sped away. She was on that boat. He was furious. He stuck his left foot out into the sea to follow. The water caused his skin to burn terribly. Now he understood why his army in the tunnel seemed to be in such pain after the explosion. He couldn't talk to them, but he had felt their pain.

Anta was getting away again, but he would find her.

AUGUST 10, 8:42PM
GULF OF MEXICO

"Where are we?" Anta asked groggily.

"We're on a boat, leaving the bunker," Marilyn replied gently.

"Why?" Anta asked.

"We'll tell you in a minute," Marilyn said. "But for now, how do you feel?"

"I feel fine—on the outside. Why? Was I injured? And why am I tied up?" She was just noticing the leather bindings on her hands and feet.

"No, you weren't injured" Angel said as she moved to Anta's side and began untying the straps wound around her wrists, "But we have a story to tell you, and you probably won't like it."

The small group spent the next several minutes talking about what had occurred. Anta's head hung low and her eyes glistened as she considered the events being described by Marilyn and Angel. The manner in which she had reacted to Cain's presence was mind-boggling. She didn't even know. Her eyes had filled with tears by the time they had finished, and one was slowly maneuvering down the creases in her cheek when she finally looked up.

"I'm so sorry. Maybe you should keep me tied up so I don't do anything rash."

"Don't be sorry," Street said, looking over his shoulder at the others behind him in the boat.

"Thank you. So where are we going now?" Anta asked, quietly.

"We're headed to Florida," Angel said. "We're going to catch a ride to the moon with your brother."

"Really?" Anta said, her sorrow turning quickly to excitement. Her face glowed, both from the wetness of her tears and from her joy. "I'm going to see Hasani!"

"We're all going to see Hasani," Street said. "And we're hoping he'll be able to get us off this rock."

"Where is everyone else? Where's Shift?"

"They're coming," Angel said, laying a hand on Anta's arm. "They're fine. Just getting anything else we may need before they leave."

"Can we com them—just to make sure they're okay?" Anta asked.

"Yup. I'm on it," Nelise replied. "It's buzzing."

"Hey everyone!" Shift answered excitedly as he turned on the holo. "Where's Anta?"

"Right here, Shift," Anta replied. "I'm okay, if that's what you were wondering. But how are you?"

"We're good," Shift said. "We'll be leaving here in a few minutes. Did Angel get you up to speed?"

"Yes," Anta replied, sorrow returning to her voice.

"Don't worry about it," Shift said. "You're fine now, and we're going to get you and everyone else out of here and away from Cain and his posse."

"What are those ugly losers up to anyway?" Street asked, again turning around to see the group behind him.

"Oh man, they are howling and screaming up a storm out there. We can hear them from inside the cave. What did you guys do to them on your way out of here?"

"Nothing," Nelise said. "They started screaming the moment we came into view around the south side of the cliffs. It's like they didn't know we were there until they could see us."

"Strange," John said as he walked up to the holo behind Shift.

"Well, not that strange," Angel said. "The salt water probably covered our scent a bit. I'm sure they knew we were around, but they didn't know how to get to us."

"Cain's out there in the middle of his horde, staring straight out to sea," John said. "I bet he knew who was on that boat of yours. That's probably why they're all freaking out."

"Do you think he'll be able to figure out where we're going?" Marilyn asked. "I mean, those guys can really move. If they figure out where we're headed, there may be a landing party waiting for the ship when we get there."

"I doubt it," Shift said. Then, turning around, he yelled out, "Hey Steve, come here a minute."

Seconds later, Steve appeared on the holo in front of the five escapees. "What's up?" he asked.

"Didn't the Skins watch the boat head south?" Shift asked.

"Yeah, we could see their bodies and eyes follow you guys as you left."

"Did you ever see them turn their bodies back toward the north, as if they could see what the boat was doing?" Shift asked.

"Nope. After about fifteen minutes, most of them just started wandering around again. A small group, maybe twenty-five of them, took off running southward, probably trying to see where you were going."

"I think the plan worked," Shift said. "And, when we leave, we're taking the two boats in different directions just to confuse them more. One of us will go south and the other southeast. Then we'll both turn north after a while like you guys did."

"Sounds good," Angel said.

"You guys just keep heading toward Florida. We'll get on the boats within about twenty minutes and hope they fall for our trick. We'll meet you at Cape Canaveral not long after our original projection."

The group said their goodbyes. Anta gave a sigh as the holo closed. "I'm sorry I'm putting all of you through this."

"Dude," Street said, "this ain't your fault, remember? They already broke in and made us leave. There ain't no way we could survive on that island for long anyway. It was only a matter of time before we had to leave. Plus, your brother's pumped to see you again!"

"Okay. Then let's get there and make this happen."

33

"Okay, everybody ready?" Shift asked.

"Yeah, let's do this," John called from the deck of the other boat.

The two boats drifted away from the docks, loaded to the brim with food and provisions, along with safety and survival gear and med kits. Everything they might need to survive indefinitely, just in case their plan fell through, was stashed away in the hulls of the two boats. A wave runner was fastened to the deck on the back of each boat.

"This is pretty freaky," Carón said as he piloted the first boat into the holographic wall.

"Yeah, it is," Steve said, standing beside Carón as their bodies moved out into the fresh night air to the east of the cave.

"Alright," Shift said, "let's make our move."

The first boat turned to the south, while the second boat began to move southeast away from the island. As the first boat moved past the rocks on the south end of the island, the Skins began to wail again.

"Well, we were right," Shift said to John through his MEHD. "They didn't know we were out here until they saw us."

"We're just passing the last outcrop now," John said. After a pause, "Okay, we have visual, which means they do too."

"Well, we'll see you in a while then. Let's confuse these suckers."

Cain watched as the two boats sped off—one to the south and one to the southeast. His troops, watching from the shore, began to rock back and forth nervously, waiting for his signal. He didn't know what to do. He had hoped that something would give him an indication where they were taking Anta. But now, all he knew was that she was gone, and two other boats were leaving too. The damn salt water was messing with his powers. He had to figure out how to overcome this weakness.

Cain made the decision. He would go north with a small group of his troops. He had a feeling the perversions were too smart to just lead him where they were going. But he didn't know for sure. His ability to reason was beginning to fail him. So, larger divisions would head south. They would watch for landings. They would watch for the human perversions. But ultimately, he wanted *her*. And wherever she landed, it wouldn't take long for him to get there.

Cain gave the orders. The troops split apart and ran. They would not slow down until Cain gave them the command. He would not allow them to stop until they found Anta.

AUGUST 10
INTERNATIONAL LUNAR SPACE STATION, U.S. MOON COLONY

"Is everything operational?" Jonas asked as the small crew began to settle down for take-off.

"Yes, we are ready," Jerad replied. "Takeoff in five, four, three, two, one, go."

Jonas pushed the thruster lever forward to initiate take-off, just as Jerad had shown him during their pre-flight preparations. The engines hummed and the shuttle shook slightly as the lower thrusters roared to life. Within seconds, the shuttle was several feet off the ground and headed for the shell window through which the shuttle would pass, leaving the safety of solid ground behind.

"Awesome!" Jonas said excitedly.

"We should touch down at Cape Canaveral at about 6:00 A.M. Eastern Time," Jerad said. "Until then, I suggest everyone get some sleep."

The small crew of the shuttle stayed put as the ship glided through the window and into space. None of them wanted to miss this adventure. They didn't know whether they would ever get back into space. For Tom and Misty, who had intended to spend the remainder of their lives on the moon, this was bitter-sweet. They hadn't wanted to leave with the others, but they also knew that, if the others didn't return, they would be alone forever with the corpses on the moon.

Jonas thought about Alan, the way his body had tumbled over and over as the great winds from the German shell carried his body into the air, only to be deposited kilometers away in a crumpled heap. The scene played through his mind now, as it had done numerous times over the past few weeks. He wanted to get back to Earth—even if only temporarily—to smell the clean air and feel the ocean breeze—and to feel real gravity under his feet.

Hasani was so excited to see his sister that he didn't think he would have been able to sleep even with a tranquilizer.

Finally though, nature won, and all five of the ship's occupants fell into a fitful sleep on the shuttle's bridge. The alarms would sound when they needed to wake up. It wouldn't be long.

AUGUST 11, 4:55AM
CAPE CANAVERAL, FLORIDA

"Okay, about one hour until landing time," Nelise announced to the group of survivors gathered around the computers in the shuttle launch bay at Cape Canaveral, Florida.

The Skins had followed the later groups as they left the island. From the safety of the boats, they saw the Skins gathering in Merida, the site of the terrible shuttle disaster that had brought this plague down from the moon.

Then the Skins followed the boats as they passed by the easternmost tip of Mexico, near Cancun. They watched and listened to the Skins howl and scream at them from the shore as both boats sped out into the Caribbean. These boats, although several years old, had the speed and capacity of any new ship. The passengers were thankful for the retractable roofs that kept them out of the wind.

After rounding Cuba to the north, they sped up the eastern coast of Florida, finally landing at Cape Canaveral. There, they met Anta, Street, Marilyn, Angel, Mike and Nelise, who had already begun making preparations for the shuttle's landing. Now, just twenty minutes after arriving, Nelise was putting them to work.

"Tell us how this is going to work," Andrew said.

"It's very simple really," Nelise replied. "The ship will land automatically. Once it does, it will need to be recharged. Again, that's an automatic function. All I will do is program the charging system and it will do the rest. The wheels will need to be checked manually—that's Shift's job. He's the car guy. The outer hull will need to be inspected for any loose panels. Because I can't get the halo to work—that's the huge machine you can see out there in the bay—Carón, Steve and Street will be up on the ladder trucks inspecting those manually. Street, I'll need you to instruct Steve and Carón on that process, like we went over a couple of hours ago."

"Will do boss," Street said enthusiastically.

"Hold on," Shift said. "Why am I inspecting wheels? I thought these things used some kind of thrusters or something to keep them off the ground."

"They do," Nelise replied. "But once the ship comes to a complete stop, wheels will lower and the ship will rest on them until takeoff. It costs too much to keep thrusters operational while a ship is sitting idly. Maintaining and replacing wheels is cheaper than maintaining and recharging thrusters. And the hull can't just sit on the ground without incurring damage. Plus, a ship can be easily towed while resting on wheels, which is why wheels are used instead of any other kind of landing gear."

"I get that," Shift said, "but why do they need to be inspected? Are the wheels used during takeoff too, or just while the ship is sitting there?"

"They are used during takeoff on Earth. On the moon, with its low gravity, the thrusters easily lift the ship off the ground and it takes off. Here though, with heavy gravity, the ship is designed to get up to speed before takeoff, just like a passenger jet. The thrusters are engaged partway through the rolling takeoff and the ship lifts off the ground much easier."

"Alright, I'll inspect the wheels."

"Everybody else will begin loading equipment and cargo onto the shuttle," Nelise continued. "Of course, Anta, you will be allowed to hug your brother, but only for fifteen seconds, then back to work." Everybody chuckled.

"Have you guys seen the Skins at all?" Shift asked after instructions for landing were complete.

"No," Mike replied. "I've got all the external monitors up and running and there's nothing outside the base for miles."

"Yet," Angel added.

"Well, we need to be extra careful," Shift said. "Jon, will you help Mike monitor the surveillance cameras?"

"Sure," Jon replied.

"If anything gets anywhere near here, we'll know," Mike said. "I'll hit the MEHD alarms. Probably ought to keep the audible sirens off, right, so the Skins don't hear them?"

"Right," Shift said. "So, everyone, if your MEHD starts to vibrate, get in here, fast. While we wait, let's get all the guns and ammo off the boats and inside. Let's not take any chances."

34

"It's them," Jon whispered.

"Oh no," Mike whispered back. Then he hit the MEHD siren.

The vibration of the siren was felt on the hips of each person scattered around the base, and the people began running back to the control room.

"How did they get here so fast?" John asked as he and Shift entered the room, each trying to catch his breath. "They would have to have been running like two hundred miles an hour or something."

"That's not good," Angel said, coming through the door right behind them. The others each arrived within a few seconds of Angel.

"It doesn't matter now," Shift said. "Where are they? How close?"

"They're probably still thirty or forty miles away," Mike replied. "Our image is from satellites, not ground feeds. They've slowed down significantly in the past few seconds. It doesn't look like they know where we are though."

"I think you're right," John said. "See. Look how they're starting to spread out."

"Yeah, they look like they're searching, smelling the air. They don't look like they've locked onto a target," Shift said.

"So, do you think they'll pass us by?" Neirioui Safar asked hopefully, putting her arm around her daughter. Jon scooted closer to Suvan so that his arm touched hers.

"That might have been a possibility," Nelise replied, "except that we have a shuttle landing here in ten minutes. They'll be able to hear it soon, and by that time, they'll be closer to us."

"Ideas anyone?" Shift asked.

"Nelise, is it possible that the shuttle could land, and all of us get on and take off before we get chewed on?" John asked.

"We have to get it checked out. It has to be recharged."

"Do you think the group on the shuttle can do the hull check from inside?" Shift asked.

"Possibly, we can ask as soon as they get into our atmosphere."

"Then, that would only leave us with programming the charging system before we get on board," Shift said.

"And checking the wheels," Anta added, looking nervously at the ground.

"Oh yeah," Shift replied solemnly.

"I'll check the wheels," Andrew said.

"No, I can do it," Shift said as he moved his eyes from Anta to Andrew.

"Of course you can do it Shift," Andrew replied, "but I'm faster and fitter than you."

"True, but I'm better looking," Shift replied.

"What has that got to do with it?" Anta asked.

"Nothing," Shift said. "I just wanted to point it out." He smiled. The others tried to find the humor, but it was no use.

"Okay," Nelise said, cutting off their little argument. "Andrew will check the wheels, if we have the opportunity."

"Canaveral, do you copy?" The clear message signaled the shuttle's arrival.

"Yes, we copy. Is that you Jonas?" Shift asked.

"Yup, we're inside. Approaching now. We expect to land in about five minutes. Is everything ready?"

"Yes, but we have a little problem. The Skins are outside, snooping around. They'll hear you any second now. Then they'll know we're here. Once you land, *do not* open the doors until I tell you to. We're working out a plan."

"Okay, you'll see us land, obviously. We'll wait for your signal before we do anything."

"Actually, maybe you can help," Shift added. "After you land, can you check the hull of the shuttle from inside? We need to know if there are any problems, but it's not a great idea for us to be clowning around out there."

"Why don't you use the halo?" Jerad asked.

"We can't get the halo to work," Nelise replied. "There's something I haven't done, but I don't know what that is. Any ideas?"

"No, I've never done it or seen it done either," Jerad replied. "I'm sorry. But I think we can do it from here. By the time we land, I should know the answer. I'll get on it."

"Okay, we'll talk soon. Out."

Cain looked up, and his gaze was followed by more than 1,200 Skins, each one antsy and eager to move toward some clearer goal. The sound was growing louder, but Cain couldn't place it. Then he saw it. A ship speeding toward them through the air. It was headed straight for them, as if it meant to crash into them.

No, that wasn't right, he thought. *Where were they? Florida? Yes, a shuttle base must be nearby.* Searching the land around him, using the extraordinary eyes and ears of his followers, he saw the enormous base. Some of his troops were only a few miles from the gates. They now sensed his command. They moved eastward.

A few minutes later, they easily tore down a chain-link fence on the outer perimeter of a massive compound and began a frantic search for the perversions.

Even though he could not sense Anta, or any of the other perversions, he knew they must be here. He called Anta. He felt her response immediately.

AUGUST 11, 5:52AM
CAPE CANAVERAL, FLORIDA

"Grab her!" John yelled as Anta began running toward the door to the control room, seemingly out of control.

Street grabbed Anta around the waist as she passed by him and hugged her tight against his body as she thrashed and kicked.

"Can we risk sedating her again?" Shift said, worriedly looking at Anta from across the room. He was so scared that he completely lost focus of what he was doing. The ship was approaching and his simple job to digitally lock the shuttle's system into the computer for automatic landing fell to the wayside.

"I think we can," Angel replied.

"Yes, it's been many hours now," Marilyn confirmed. "But the dosage has to be smaller. Give me a minute to prepare the sedation."

"No. Let me just hold her," Street said, as protective as a mother bird.

"Don't let go of her Street . . ." Shift began.

"Shift, are you there?" came a voice through the message relay on the computer board in front of Shift. The attached holo lit up with Jerad's face. "Why aren't we locked onto the auto landing system?"

"Crap!" Shift said. "Sorry, we're having a problem. Doing it now. It's not too late is it?"

"Nearly," Jerad replied, "but I think we'll just make it. Okay, locked on. Just in time. We're initiating landing sequence."

Several people watched out the window as the shuttle began its descent to the runway below them on the tarmac. Then Shift turned his attention back to Street and Anta.

Street was struggling, but only a little, to hold Anta's body still. Marilyn had joined them and her battle was much greater as she attempted to hold Anta's head still so she wouldn't cause any internal damage as she thrashed her head from side to side. Not feeling the relief he had hoped, Shift walked over and approached Anta, gently laying his hand on her cheek.

"Anta," he whispered near her ear, with all the love and tenderness he could muster, "I love you, and I need you. Won't you stay with me?"

Anta fell limp almost immediately, and Street, not expecting such a sudden reaction, almost dropped her. Getting a better grip, he sank to the floor near the door. Shift and Marilyn sat down next to them and Street gently lowered her head onto Shift's lap. Street kept his eyes on Anta's still form, watching for trouble, while Shift held her head in his lap and stroked her hair.

Angel walked over to the small group sitting on the floor, crouched down, and put her hand on Street's shoulder. Street leaned his head over and rested it on Angel's hand. They stayed that way for several moments until they heard confirmation of landing.

". . . We're down. Piloting to the terminal now."

"Good," Nelise said peering out into the early morning light. "Bring her around to bay door 152. I'm sending the ship directions now. We'll be making our way to the shuttle from there. Were you able to do a hull scan from onboard?"

"Yes," Jerad replied. "Everything checks out. But we need to be charged before we can get out of here."

"Right. We have the charging system in place at bay 152. It's ready to be remotely moved into position the moment you arrive."

"What are the Skins up to?" Hasani asked. "Is Anta okay?"

"Not really," Street replied solemnly. "Cain must be calling for her or something. We've got her under control for now though."

"The Skins are on the ground, just inside the perimeter," Mike called out. "But they look like they're still searching for us. Time is running out though. They know we're here. We've got to get out of here."

"Okay," Jerad said, "we're at 152. Ready for charging."

"Entering signals now," Nelise replied. "Done. You should see the machine moving into place. Is it?"

"Yes. It's approaching now. Hold on. Okay, it's on. System says its locked and initiating charge. Hold on again. Okay, we're good. Charging in progress."

"Now what?" Hasani said through the holo.

"We're sending the jet way out to meet you," Nelise said. "Once it's connected, we'll head your way."

"We have to check the tires too," Shift said.

"Wow, who's the lucky bugger that gets to do that?" Jonas asked.

"Dr. Andrew Jones, our self-proclaimed track star," Shift replied. "While he's out there, the rest of us will make our way to the shuttle."

"Guys," Mike called. "The Skins are inside the base."

Shift and the others rushed over to the security system monitors on the back wall. The Skins were inside the base, but not inside their building; but everyone knew it was only a matter of time. They had to hurry.

"How's the jet way coming?" Shift asked.

"Locked on now," Hasani said. "Get everyone over here. We'll be waiting."

35

Cain knew the perversions were on the base. He had lost his brief connection with Anta, but he would find her again. The other perversions were evading him, but he would find them too. Their stench would uncover their hiding place. But he had to hurry. The shuttle made him nervous.

Cain's troops rushed from building to building, searching for the perversions inside the massive air base. They scrambled over rooftops and under vehicles and machines. They were like a swarm of ants, hell-bent on devouring everything in their path. Only they weren't devouring anything. They were saving their anger and ferocity for the perversions. Cain had given them free reign. They had only to bring him Anta, unharmed. Each of them knew what the penalty would be if Anta was bitten or injured.

Cain watched as his troops searched the base. Why hadn't they uncovered the perversions yet? What was going on? His grip on them was weakening, and clearly, their aptitude for the hunt was flagging as well. But he had a backup plan. He would stop the perversions one way or another. Using his unnamed power, some form of mutated telepathy and telekinesis that he'd not quite figured out, Cain directed troops stationed at hundreds of remote communications centers around the world. His power was not entirely gone. On his signal, they began destroying equipment and buildings and pulling down cellular towers, effectively shutting down communication ports the world over.

"Okay, let's go," Shift called back to the group behind him.

The arms and backpacks of every person in the group were loaded with provisions or weapons, and any personal items they still had with them. Everyone except Street. He was loaded down with Anta's still form. As they made their way toward the jet way, Andrew broke off from the group and headed down a flight of stairs. He held a 2064 Nottington semi-automatic beam rifle that would automatically lock onto its target if he had the sites even remotely close to the mark. He was only slightly comforted by that. Sweat ran down his back as he made his way down several flights of stairs toward the door which would take him out onto the tarmac.

So far, the Skins were not outside. The small group could see through the windows of the operations building as they ran toward the gate. Finally approaching bay 152, the windows began to show signs of life. Thankfully, it was only birds.

"Everything's still clear from our vantage point," Hasani said quietly though Shift's MEHD. "Nothing outside yet. Wait, the door's opening. Looks like your guy."

"Keep an eye on him," Shift said. "If you see anything approaching, even a long way off, let me know ASAP so I can get him out of there."

"Got it. He's at the rear tires now. He knows what he's looking for, right?"

"Yeah, we went through it carefully," Shift answered.

"Okay, he's moving forward now."

"Everything still look good out there?"

"Yeah, still good . . . no, not good. I can see them. They're moving very fast."

"Andrew!" Shift called out through the MEHD. "Get in here now!"

Andrew didn't hear Shift issue the warning. Communications had just gone down, but nobody knew it yet. Andrew was alone, unknowing, and the Skins were almost on top of him.

Cain could smell one now—a male. It wasn't Anta. But that meant Anta was probably close by, and he wanted her badly. He sent his army toward the terrible scent. They were almost upon it. Now he could see it through the eyes of one of his minions. His army was on the move. Only moments from now, they would have him.

Andrew saw them before they saw him. He swore under his breath and wondered why he hadn't been warned. He briefly watched, shocked by the horror of it, as the horde of demons climbed over rooftops and ran around the buildings on both sides of him. The red of their blood-stained torsos stood out in sharp contrast to the grayish-black tarmac. There must have been a hundred of them.

Then he ran.

They saw him, and their shrieks pierced the silence of the still morning air. The sound was deafening.

Andrew ran as fast as his legs would carry him toward the bay doors. If he could get there, if he could get inside, he would be okay. He rounded the front of the ship and had to veer right as the horde approached from that side. A pungent, metallic odor overwhelmed his senses and he had to choke back bile that rose in his throat, threatening to cut off his air supply.

His heart raced and his blood pumped as he approached the doors. But the horde was moving too fast—they could smell him too. They were right behind him. He turned and fired several shots into the throng as he ran backward toward the doors. Their enraged faces were the stuff of nightmares, and his fear threatened to immobilize him.

Moments later, still running backward as the throng surrounded him, he ran into the door, cracking his elbow on the hard metal casing. Still firing in desperation, at point-blank range, he reached behind him, sending sharp pain up through his elbow and into his shoulder. He was searching for the sensor. He almost touched it.

"Oh shite!" Hasani cried out as he watched the naked human-like beasts swarm over the man below on the tarmac. The man had been so close—he was almost there. But the Skins were so fast. Hasani had never seen anything like it. He'd heard what the others had told them about the Skins, but seeing it was something entirely different. Then the man rose from the ground, blood running down his neck and soaking the collar of his T-shirt. He reached out his hand, and touched the door sensor. It opened.

"They're inside!" Jonas yelled down the jet way to the people coming toward him. "Run!"

"Faster!" Shift cried out. His friends were already running. They ran faster. Some of them had already boarded the shuttle. Thankfully, Street and Anta were among them. But Mike, John and Shift were bringing up the rear.

John pushed forward with renewed strength, scooping up Suvan as he reached her. Then they were inside, yelling for Mike and Shift to hurry.

"Go, go!" Shift yelled to Mike, pushing him in the back. Mike's body was being tested. He hadn't exercised in a long, long time. The Skins were coming. Mike could hear them. He could smell them. It was awful and made him gag. That slowed him down even more. The Skins were so close.

Shift looked over his shoulder as he ran, but the Skins weren't in sight yet. They were close though. The pounding of their footsteps were loud; equal, he thought, to the pounding of his heart. They were probably entering the jet way now, just around the corner behind him. And Andrew, or whoever he was now, was probably in the lead.

"Duck!" Street yelled as he took a few steps out from the shuttle's hatch toward Mike and Shift. They both ducked reflexively as they ran. Shots rang out from in front of them and the whizzing of bullets sounded just over their heads. Screams pierced the air from behind as Skins began to fall. The noise from the guns and the screams was deafening. Soon, Shift could barely hear the pounding of his heart or the footsteps of the Skins.

"Keep running," Street yelled as he continued firing into the pack of Skins trailing Shift and Mike. As the men finally passed Street on their way to the ship, he began to back away from the oncoming mass of naked flesh, still firing at will. Among the Skins in the jet way, now lying on the floor in the clutches of death, was Dr. Andrew Jones. Beside him, Dr. Yurgi Shevchuk raced ahead, eyes bulging at the prospect of his next victim.

Street wretched as he saw his own bullets pierce the forehead of his once-friend and mentor. Dr. Shevchuk fell to the floor, blood pooling immediately under his mangled head. More Skins rushed across Andrew's and Yurgi's lifeless bodies, snapping bones with eerie cracks, as they continued to scramble toward the ship. *They're too close,* Street thought as Jonas and Hasani stepped up next to him and started to fire.

This moment would decide the fate of the human race.

More perversions appeared at the door to the great ship, firing guns at his army. They had to slow down. Cain ordered it. He could feel the pain of his brothers and sisters writhing on the ground. The pain was too great, and Cain felt it all.

Mike fell through the shuttle doors and collapsed into a heap on the floor, choking and coughing, his face pale and drawn. Shift came in right behind him, tripping over Mike and falling to his knees. Jonas and Hasani followed as Mike rolled out of the way. Finally, Street backed in and Hasani slammed his hand onto the door sensor. The big door closed on the outstretched hand of a Skin, chopping it off at the wrist.

"Closed!" Jonas called out as he and others stared at a hand writhing around on the floor of the shuttle like a severed lizard tail. Within seconds, it stopped moving.

"Lock initiated," Jerad replied through the com on the wall.

After several agonizing moments—the piercing screams of the Skins outside the shuttle doors causing several members of the group to cover their ears—the ship began to move. The small, frightened group could not only hear, but could actually feel pounding and shuffling on the sides and the roof of the great ship as Skins jumped aboard from the open jet way. It was amazing to hear, not because it was novel, but because the sound was so loud and intense despite the thickness and quality of the construction of the ship. No sound should have been heard through those walls.

Several of the humans watched out the windows as the ship backed away from the port. The Skins were falling from the smooth, round surface of the shuttle, one by one. As they hit the hard surface of the tarmac below, fragments of bone and drops of blood sprayed the tarmac around them.

Shift looked toward the open jet way. Cain was there. Unlike every previous encounter with the giant man, this time, Cain was howling with the others.

They had escaped. Anta was with them. Cain screamed to the sky as the shuttle banked slowly to the right and eventually left his field of vision. Finally, the noise from the engines died away. The only sound that remained was the heavy breathing of his army. *Heavy breathing? What was happening? Were they tired?* He would need to get to the bottom of that. But for now, he could only watch the sky and try to figure out what he would do without Anta.

36

"Andrew's gone," Neirioui said quietly to Suvan as she cradled her daughter and rocked back and forth at the front of the main shuttle lounge. "But he gave his life for us. His reward will be in Heaven."

"I know that momma, but I will still miss him."

"We all will."

Street and Angel sat side-by-side in silence in the lounge, holding hands. Street didn't have the heart, nor the capacity, to tell his friends what he had done to Yurgi. It was eating him up inside. He would never tell. They would never know.

Shift, Hasani and Anta sat in the back corner of the lounge, somberly discussing the fate of Andrew and all of their other friends and family. Anta was still breathing heavily from what had felt like a hammer-blow to her skull from the pressure of Cain's voice in her head.

"I can't lose any more of my friends," Anta said, mostly to herself. She was despondent, and the sorrow was eating her up inside.

"What happened back there?" Hasani asked. "Why didn't your man run?"

"I don't think he heard me," Shift said. "Just as I began to yell to him, my MEHD beeped off."

"Did the batteries die?" John asked, walking over to the group, even though he knew it was unlikely. Batteries on electronic equipment could last for weeks between charges and the group had been charging them at every opportunity, not knowing whether any particular time might be the last for a while.

"No. It's still fully charged. I was talking to Hasani right when the Skins got there."

John pulled his MEHD from his pocket and touched Shift's number. It connected. "Well, they work now," he said.

"Yeah, but we're not on Earth anymore. We're probably operating off some relay system on the ship, right?" Shift asked.

"Yeah, probably," Hasani replied. "Do you think the Skins could have shut down Earth communications somehow?"

"Let's talk to Mike. Maybe he can figure that out from here."

Feeling truly safe for the first time in months, the weight of lost loved ones hit most of them more strongly than ever before. The adrenaline was gone. But this time, the tears that had been shed previously were not forthcoming. Instead, many felt a depressing weight bear down on them. Most of them had difficulty even organizing the feelings and thoughts they were experiencing.

Despite the sorrow, some of them explored the ship, whispering as they found new contraptions and explored new passageways.

Dr. Bird and Marilyn Swenson had performed health checks on most of the group, and were just finishing, having found no health problems other than a highly-elevated heart rate in Mike Petrovsky and some uneasy stomachs from the lower gravity on the shuttle, which took some getting used to.

When Mike had finished his physical check-up, he checked the communications systems on Earth. He could only access communication systems in the largest cities, but nearly every accessible system was relaying operation malfunctions.

The Net was still operable though, which meant that USCAN was still up; but all cellular systems, including those operating the MEHDs, were down. Thankfully, they were no longer on Earth, so it didn't really matter. Communications on the ship, and, presumably, on the moon, would continue to function.

On the bridge, Jonas, Jerad and Nelise discussed the flight, the escape, and their luck at having no problems during take-off, apart from losing Andrew.

Several minutes later, Shift and John arrived on the bridge.

"Gentlemen, we owe you our lives."

"Yes, you do," Jonas said as he rose from his seat. He walked over to Shift and held out his hand. "But you realize that we owe *you* our lives?"

"What do you mean?" Shift asked.

"I mean that if you and your group hadn't stayed alive, the whole human race would be down to five of us. That's not much of a life if you ask me. Plus, we didn't create E-rase. You people did that. So, we owe *you* our lives, twice over."

Shift looked down at the ground, then mumbled, "I hope it was worth it."

"It was," Hasani said as he and his sister walked through the bridge doors behind Shift. "It was, my friend."

Shift turned around as Anta reached her arms up to pull Shift to her. "I love you," she whispered into his ear.

"I love you too."

AUGUST 11
SPACE

"Hey everybody, I don't want to spend any time discussing what we all already know," Shift said quietly to the group surrounding him in the shuttle's conference room. "But I do want to tell each of you how proud I am of you. We survived. And we wouldn't have done so if each one of you hadn't put your heart and soul into helping each other. That includes our new friends here." Shift pointed to his right where Jonas, Hasani, Tom, Misty and Jerad were seated, facing the group.

"Our pleasure," Jonas said, really meaning it.

"Well, we owe you a great debt for your help and sacrifice," Shift said. "Unfortunately, we don't have much to give." Shift looked over the tired faces in front of him. His expression showed how proud he was

was of them. They had accomplished so much. But the work wasn't finished. And Jonas could tell that they all knew it.

"I am going to let Jonas give us a run-down of what to expect when we get to the lunar colonies—or what's left of them."

"Thanks Shift," Jonas said. "I want to tell you what to expect and answer your questions. But first, let me tell you how wonderful it is for me—for us—to finally meet you. We've been waiting and hoping that we would have the pleasure. And it truly is that.

"Now, let me give you a physical status of the colonies. Two shells are non-functional, but we don't really need them. We will land at the International Lunar Station in the United States Colony. Everything there is in working order. Unfortunately, there are hundreds of bodies in the homes and buildings within the shell. Job number one will be to remove them.

"We've cleared all the bodies from the hangars, offices and control rooms around the landing bays, and the smell is better there; but outside the main bay doors, you will be greeted with a smell sour enough to knock you over."

"We've been there, man," Street said.

"I'm sure you have," Jonas replied, smiling sadly. He had momentarily forgotten that the exhausted people in front of him had lived through not only the death and destruction of the human race, with all of its accompanying grief and gore, but also a fight for their very lives from the Skins. He would have to remember that.

"There are living quarters inside the International Station, but they are in need of cleaning and, of course, the removal of bodies. If we start there, we could have a fairly nice place to live in just a few days. In the meantime, we can sleep, eat and live onboard the shuttle inside the bay. It won't be too comfortable, but it will do while we prepare a home in the main station."

"What's it like there," Jon Porter asked. His voice was quiet, but his eyes were alight with curiosity. Jonas imagined that this was the greatest adventure a young man could have, and he was excited for Jon, and for all of them. Suvan sat next to Jon with her hand close to his.

Suvan's mother watched them out of the corner of her eyes, hiding her smile. Jonas smiled too.

"Well, that's my favorite question of all of them I've heard over the past couple of hours," Jonas said. "So, let me tell you."

"Before you do, Jonas," Hasani interrupted, "maybe everybody should get more comfortable." Jonas looked at Hasani quizzically. Others followed suit.

"You see, I've known Jonas for several months now," Hasani continued. "He can *really* talk. Sometimes, he won't shut up." Several people laughed quietly. Only Tom, Misty and Jerad laughed out loud. Jonas reached over and punched Hasani in the arm. Then they both laughed.

"I'll be right back," Hasani said as he stood and left the conference room. He returned a few moments later pushing a cart full of food and drinks, which he distributed to the group. Once everyone that wasn't nursing an upset stomach had something in their hands, Jonas continued.

"As I was saying, the moon is amazing!"

37

We've been here for almost five days. It is as amazing as Jonas said it would be.

Our flight from Earth was without incident. Our landing was as smooth as a baby's backside. But the smell that accosted us as we left the main landing bay was worse than Jonas had prepared us for.

Back in the bunker in Mexico, the dead had only been there for a couple of weeks before Steve and Jon had most of them cleared out. Plus, the salt in the air from the sea probably acted as a sort of cleansing agent. But here, the bodies have been lying in rot for months. Many of them are just skin and bones now, but the moon's atmosphere and landscape doesn't contain all the microorganisms required for decomposition. Thus, many of the bodies are still decomposing.

We spent the first few days cleaning the dorms and living quarters in the space station. Anything that couldn't be decontaminated, was removed and burned in some very sophisticated furnaces. We also had to remove rubble from portions of the international station that Jonas and Hasani believe were intentionally destroyed in the early days of A.E. But today, we went exploring, as a group.

Nobody is quite prepared to be alone, not even those who have been here for so long. It is interesting to see the impact that the death of the entire human race is having on those of us left. From the moment we arrived, we have eaten, worked, and relaxed together. Nobody has even gone to bed at night without another person by their side, except Jonas and Jerad. Those that don't have a close friend or family member among the group sleep in a small dorm containing several bunks. Of everybody here, only Jonas and Jerad seem to be able to cope with being alone. Jerad is somewhat stand-offish anyway—not a real people-person. And Jonas had been on the moon for a couple of years already by the time the plague hit, and then he was alone for a long time. He seems pretty comfortable.

Anyway, we went exploring, with Jonas in the lead, and Hasani not far behind. We saw amazing things.

The Shell of each colony is immense and, before A.E., each housed thousands of people and their living quarters, along with businesses, laboratories, government buildings, and amusement. There are parks and wildlife, although some of the animals are dying now. And there are trees, ponds, and grass.

One large park in the United States Shell has a skate park, a fishing pond, a playground and a soccer pitch. The pond is even blue in color. Jonas explained that lights below the surface give it its blue color, since there is no blue hue to the atmosphere surrounding the moon. It is quite amazing how Earth-like the place is! The buildings are all gray, but the surrounding landscape makes up for the lack of color in the sky and the infrastructure.

According to Jonas, life in a Lunar Encapsulation Shell was, in realty, not much different than life on Earth, except that travel outside a Shell was largely restricted to the Portal System.

"All this wildlife is pretty unexpected," I said as we walked across a large patch of grass near the skate park.

"Yeah, nobody expects it when they first get here," Jonas replied, "especially since there are no natural or artificial weather systems within the Shells, so it never rains or snows. Plants receive their nourishment through fertilization and sprinkler systems not much more advanced than those on Earth."

"Where does the water come from?" Marilyn asked.

"Water was originally shipped to the Moon on massive transport ships. The water is used and reused via complex treatment plants. Additional water was shipped to the Moon, until recent events, every six months."

We learned that the temperature within the Shells is regulated to maintain a constant seventy-seven degrees, and it's never dark. Through the use of luminescent energy cores, built right into the Shells, light is regulated and maintained around the clock. Sleeping patterns are facilitated through plain, old-fashioned curtains on windows.

Then we arrived at the tubes.

"The Lunar Portal System is a series of interconnected glass-like tubes connecting the various States, colonies and outposts within the inhabited sector of the Moon," Jonas explained. "These 'tubes' are—well, they were—regulated, controlled and maintained by the IIA, the International Interagency Assembly, an arm of the IWO or International World Order. The IIA's purpose was to facilitate the productive, cooperative and safe flow of people, information, laws and orders in the lunar colonies. Part of the IIA's task was the facilitation of the flow of people and data throughout the inhabited sector of the Moon through the Lunar Portal System."

"Dude, can you dumb it down for us?" Street asked. "I mean, not for me, but for some of these other guys." I laughed as Street flicked his eyes and bobbed his head toward me a couple of times. Then others laughed too. Everyone knows that Street and I are as close as brothers, or closer.

"Sorry, I'll try. I did a lot of reading up here, and not much socializing. The tubes were, more or less, like border checkpoints. In addition to actually helping people move around, the computers that operated the tubes monitored and tracked the flow of people. Each individual intending to use any portion of a tube had his or her hand scanned prior to disembarking. Once arrival at a destination occurred, the pods, which I'll show you in a minute, wouldn't open without the same handprint. It was just a way to track where people were, and helped facilitate criminal investigations, on the rare occasion those occurred.

"The Portal System is composed of more than 750 miles of cylindrical 'tubes' floating several feet off the surface of the moon through the use of reverse polaric modulators at intervals of 0.77 miles.

"The tubes are twenty-four feet in diameter and completely transparent, including underfoot, as you can see."

We had just walked into the first tube and were admiring it from the inside.

"At each of the 0.77-mile intervals along the Portal System, there are little rooms housing ventilation equipment which ensures adequate oxygen flow throughout the tubes. The Portal is designed so that, at each 0.77-mile interval, along with the reverse polaric modulators, there's a vapor-lock system used to close off any section from the remainder of the tubes. These have been used infrequently to repair portions of the tubes that have come into contact with floating debris from outside the tubes.

"You mean like meteors?" young Jon Porter asked. There was general chuckling and head nods from the group.

"Exactly!" Jonas replied with a chuckle. "Except that more often the debris is something inadvertently left outside by one of the residents, like a wrench gone missing from a maintenance crew.

"Each of the little rooms also has a small energy storage core. The tubes were originally designed so that the flow of the pods through the tubes would actually create energy. But we've had a big problem up here storing the energy created. Most of it is lost. It's been pretty frustrating. Sometimes the tubes or lights in one of the pods will just shut off, temporarily. Then energy is re-routed and things are back to normal, usually. But sometimes, the energy loss actually causes permanent damage that has to be repaired. That's where the maintenance crews come in handy."

Jonas paused to smile at Jon, then, "Storing the energy created by the motion of pods through the tubes would have made things smoother."

"That's what Dr. Ghannam was sent here to figure out," Anta said.

"That's right. I'd forgotten about that," Shift replied.

"Who's Dr. Ghannam?" Jonas asked.

"He's the guy, well, he and his daughter, who first contracted A.E. in Egypt," Shift said.

"They were in the desert outside El-Alamein when sand-storms uncovered the sandy cave that A.E. had been hiding in for so many years," Anta added. "They were first on the scene. Then, a couple days later, Dr. Ghannam and his family left Egypt for the moon, bringing A.E. with them."

"Well, I certainly know the story," Jonas said. "And now I know the name. How interesting."

"Anyway, the Lunar Portal System ties into the main body of the Lunar Encapsulation Shell of each outpost along its various tracks. Through seamless migration of the tubes with the Encapsulation Shells, a person can travel through the tubes to nearly any destination without having to don any specialized apparatus—that means a space suit, for our younger friends here," Jonas said with a smile and a look at Jon and Suvan, and Street, who was standing behind them. "So, a person can move between destinations without ever leaving the regulated atmosphere of the Encapsulation Shells."

"Pretty cool," Mike said. "But I'm a little surprised by how nice they look. Who was the IIA trying to impress with these things? I mean, look at these little egg-shaped things. The interiors are nicer than the ones in the hovers we were flying in down on Earth."

"The design concept, although purely aesthetic, was intended to give a person traveling through the Portal the sense of space travel without space suits or apparatus of any kind. Much of the Portal is accessed via travel pods, like this 'little egg-shaped thing' as you called it. The rider sits in chairs incorporated into a reverse polaric conveyor system, free-floating within the tube. The pods can travel six abreast and, although not physically attached to any permanent apparatus, avoid collisions through the use of that same reverse polaric modulator. I'm told that the shape of the pods helps control how each pod interacts with others along the route. Who wants to give it a try?"

"You mean they still work?" John asked. "I thought you had some kind of travel ban or something and these things were shut down."

"Yes, they were shut down," Hasani replied, "but Jerad got them running again not long before we left to pick you guys up. Of course, since the handprint recognition system became a hindrance once we were all alone up here, Jerad figured out how to disable the system. Now, we just get in and go."

"I want to go for a ride," Suvan told her mom. "Can we?"

"Absolutely," Hasani replied before Neirioui could even open her mouth. "Don't worry Mrs. Safar, they are perfectly safe, and a lot of fun!"

"Not one accident has occurred since its inception," Jerad added.

Hasani looked at Neirioui, waiting for her reply. Finally, she smiled and nodded.

"*Ms.* Safar," she corrected him.

"Hold on," Anta said. "Can I ask you a couple more questions before we leave?"

"Sure," Jonas replied amicably as Jon and Suvan both frowned.

"You said that data is also shared through these portals. If that's right, then how did the shells communicate with each other after they were shut down? I mean, how did each of the shells know what was going on with A.E. after that? And, how did the five of you find each other?"

"Well, data is shared between the various posts connected to the Portal System through transparent cyberoptic communication cables imbedded into the walls of the tubes. You can see a group of them right here, if you look closely," Jonas said, pointing toward the side of the tube on his left, near the bottom.

"Even after the shutdown, data and communications still moved freely between the colonies, although there were certain 'restricted' data ports, including the "International Interagency Assembly port" to which Dr. Shevchuk's database was connected. These data ports, although running through the tubes, operated independently from the pod system. So they were never shut down."

"And you said that shells cover all of the outposts?"

"No, not all of them. Lunar Encapsulation Shells cover *nearly all* outposts in the inhabited sector of the Moon."

"I assume that, if there's a shell, there's regulated atmosphere?" I asked, filling in for Anta.

"Yes, with a few exceptions. The Shells act to maintain atmospheric pressure within a defined space. Until recently, there were six main Shells, one each for the United States, England, Portuguese-Brazil, Poland, Mexico and Burmo-Thailand, with another under construction by the Egyptian government. Now, both the Burmo-Thailand and the German shells are in ruins. There are also forty-six other Shells covering various outposts used for science, exploration, vacation, etc. All five of us were in one of those smaller shells when the plague broke out and then we lived together in a big one until we were able to duplicate Dr. Shevchuk's research and vaccinate ourselves.

"Any other questions? Okay, let's go."

As the group began to file into the various pods, Hasani pulled me aside and whispered, "She's hot man."

"Who?" I asked, feigning innocence.

"Neirioui."

"Yeah, she's not bad. Go get her spaceboy."

"Yes!" Hasani hissed as he smiled and subtly pumped his fist.

"What was that all about?" Anta asked me as we climbed into a pod together.

"Your brother has the hots for Neirioui."

"I'm sure he does."

Then we took off. Several minutes later, we entered the Portuguese-Brazil shell—the shell closest to the United States shell.

The Portuguese-Brazil shell was just like the United States shell, so we didn't stay long. The journey was the destination. The travel back through the tubes was just as exciting as the travel there. Once we arrived back at the United States shell, it was business as usual.

"Business" from here on out will include very little for most of us. We will continue to clean out the United States shell. We'll explore the other shells to locate anything of use. We'll mourn those that we've lost. But ultimately, we'll just try to live our lives, hoping for, and preparing for a chance to go home.

AUGUST 29
MIAMI, FLORIDA, EARTH

Communications were down, and any perversions still alive on Earth would have a hard time communicating with each other. That should give his army the advantage. But Cain didn't know whether any perversions were even alive on Earth any more. That should have meant that Earth was his to control.

But Cain had lost control. His ability to organize his army, or former army, had dwindled significantly over the past few days. He could no longer transport anywhere he wished. Others, stronger than he, were controlling the small groups on the other side of the world. They were younger, newer.

In Florida, his former comrades had left him alone. They were devouring the dead at such an incredible rate as to leave whole towns and cities virtually empty of the dead. And they hadn't found any surviving perversions in many days. His people wanted fresh blood. So, they had moved on, to the north. Only Cain remained in southern Florida, hoping that the shuttle would return and bring Anta with it.

He felt weak. He had noticed the same growing weakness in his oldest companions. The younger ones were still strong, but he could tell their days were numbered too. It was clear that the strength they had possessed was only temporary. It was unsettling.

And it wasn't just the physical strength that was leaving. He could see wrinkles where none had been before. His skin had begun to lose its luster. His eyes had begun to lose their focus. He was aging, quickly.

Time was not on his side.

38

"What do you think you're doing?" Carón asked Dr. Nelise Fabrisio through the mic on his suit.

"Replacing the opto-isolator," Nelise replied.

"You're putting it in backward," Carón said.

"Don't tell me how to do my job, Carón."

"I'm not. I'm telling you how to do *my* job. You shouldn't be here anyway. Let me do it."

Carón reached out and grabbed the opto-isolator Nelise was holding, yanking it out of his gloved hand.

They had been together for three straight days, working both inside and outside the Portuguese-Brazil shell and the tube connecting the shell with the United States shell. They were working on the electrical grid of the Portal System. It had gone dark four days earlier. Without constant use of the tubes, and the inability to store energy created through the tubes when they were in use, they'd been having outages for days in that area. Then, the electrical grid crashed. No light, no air flow, nothing.

As a result, the tube between the Portuguese-Brazil shell and the United States shell had stopped operating. Even its artificial gravity was off. It had been a massive hindrance to their work. Luckily, the tube leaving the United States Shell on the other side was fully operational and continuing to provide for the energy needs of the group.

But the failure of the electric grid in the Portuguese-Brazil shell and its adjoining tube was a big deal. The group only needed access to the Portuguese-Brazil shell for one purpose—but it was an important one. It was there that they were burying the dead.

Now, standing inside the Portal System, or the "tube", Carón could see that their time together was wearing them down. He didn't like Nelise and the feeling was mutual. Nelise was too hard-headed—too proud—and subject to violent anger and tantrums. He thought he was always right, just like now. And this time, as usual, Nelise was wrong. His near-mistake would have cost them days in repairs. If he had put the part in backward and turned on the system, it would have been shot. Carón did not feel like wasting any more time alone with Nelise, especially since they were stuck wearing the restrictive oxygenation suits, just in case the air got too thin in the tube while the grid was down.

"Give that back to me," Nelise said angrily, almost under his breath.

Carón barely heard the words, but could almost feel the anger in them. *Good*, he thought. *Let him be angry; but he isn't getting this part back.*

Nelise stepped forward and lunged toward Carón's hand holding the opto-isolator. Carón jumped back, floating a little in the shallow gravity inside the tube.

Nelise lunged again, and again Carón jumped back, but this time, he floated a little longer than before. Nelise was able to close the gap between them before Carón got both feet back on the floor of the tube.

As Carón landed back on the floor, Nelise rushed at him, hitting Carón's body hard and smashing him into the side of the tube. The force of the impact between Carón's oxygen pack and the wall caused a small hairline crack to form in the clear wall, but neither man noticed. With their arms interlocked, Carón lifted his feet, placing them on the wall of the tube, and pushed back against Nelise, using the wall of the tube as a launching pad. The push from his feet cracked the tube further as the men tumbled to the ground several feet away. As he rose, Carón heard a quiet hissing sound and turned back toward the wall.

With Carón's upper body turned away from Nelise, Nelise reached out, grabbed the hose connection on the back of Carón's suit and pulled. The angry, deliberate tug on the oxygen tube affixed to Carón's suit was more than the suit was built to withstand. The hose ripped loose and began to whip back and forth behind Carón as the oxygen flowed rapidly from the tank on his back.

Nelise's anger had completely taken hold of him. Carón was already off-balance from the pull on his oxygen tube when Nelise shoved him again, causing him to fall to the floor of the tube. Carón struggled to turn himself over, to face his attacker. Just as he completed the awkward turn, Nelise raised his foot and sent it crashing down on Carón's face, cracking the face plate of his helmet. Nelise raised his foot for another blow but was stopped short by a fierce hissing sound coming from the wall of the tube. It was then that he finally realized what he had done. He watched in horror as the wall of the tube split open, sucking everything around them toward the widening hole, including the tube's remaining oxygen.

Guilt swept over Nelise in nauseating waves as he watched the gentle suction—caused by the discrepancy between the air pressure of the tube and the moon's atmosphere—begin to pull Carón across the floor toward the hole. He was already struggling for breath. Nelise reached out toward Carón, but couldn't reach him. The oxygen in Carón's tank was probably already gone, and the oxygen remaining in his helmet was rapidly seeping from the cracked face plate.

At the same time, the fissure in the wall of the tube continued to grow and both men, along with their equipment and the pods around them were sucked toward the hole.

As Carón slid ever faster toward the widening cleft in the tube's wall, he struggled to regain control of the hose that was swinging wildly from the back of his suit. His panic further expended the precious air left in his suit. As he neared the edge of the hole, a pod flew toward the hole, striking Carón in the head, finally shattering his cracked faceplate and breaking his jaw.

Carón was pulled out of the tube and into the darkness, his face crumpling and his vision fading. He gasped his last breath as he floated away on the air rapidly flowing from the tube. In moments, Carón was dead. His body slowly drifted back to the surface of the moon forty or fifty meters from the tube.

Nelise continued to struggle for any kind of security inside the tube that was rapidly losing air. As he watched Carón float away, a realization of what had happened dawned. He vomited in his helmet. The violent heaving caused him to lose his balance and his tenuous grasp on the small equipment consul next to him. He slid to the edge of the hole, unable to stop his movement. Just as he was pulled from the tube, he reached out and grasped the edge of the hole with his left hand. Pulling his right hand up, he grabbed the other side of the hole, attempting to secure himself within the fragile opening. It was then, holding on so tightly that his fingers began to throb, that he understood the full implications of his angry acts. He knew he had murdered another human being.

The guilt and anguish over the act was too much for Nelise to bear. He released his right hand from the edge of the cracked tube wall and reached into his tool belt, grabbing a pair of wire cutters. Reaching around behind his own back, he cut through the hose that kept him fed with life-sustaining air. Then he let go completely and floated away on the air pouring through the tube's hole. He too, would soon be dead.

When the others learned of the tragedy later that day, they searched for the bodies. They found both within one hundred meters of the tube. The destruction of the tube and the suits was incomprehensible. What they *did* know, however, was that two more of the few remaining humans were now dead.

39

In the time the group had been on the moon, Mike had devoted a good portion of his energy to hacking into the systems that would allow him to see Earth, real-time. He had just done it. The remaining sixteen people on the moon had gathered for the big unveiling. It was time to see what Cain was up to.

"Bring it up Mike," Shift said excitedly.

Within moments, seven monitors lit up at the front of the computer bay in the International Station. Each monitor depicted a distinct location where they had run into Cain. The hope was that he might still be at some of his old haunts. He wasn't, but it didn't take long to find the Skins.

"What's going on?" Anta asked. "They're spread out all over the place. What happened to the huge hordes that kept attacking us?"

The Skins were wandering in small groups, never more than five or six together. They appeared aimless and confused, and tired.

"Look how they're staggering around," Street said.

"They're like a bunch of old folks," Marilyn added.

"Mike, can you zoom in on any of them—let us see their faces?" Shift asked.

Mike zoomed in on a group of three Skins, one male and two female, near Atlanta. The faces of the Skins were shocking. They looked like they were eighty or ninety years old. Perhaps they actually were.

"Find some more," Shift said. "Maybe these three were just old when they turned."

Mike zoomed in on a group of four Skins not more than three kilometers from the first group. They also appeared to be elderly, with sagging tissue structure and tired gaits. A few more views of different groups in the area confirmed that the Skins were definitely aging. Without the bald heads and nakedness, the small group of moon-dwellers would not have even known they were looking at Skins.

"Are they dying?" Suvan asked quietly—hopefully.

"They sure look like they are darling," Neirioui replied.

"I think you're right Suvan," John said. "They look like they're dying all right. Maybe whatever it was that turned them into freaks in the first place continued to advance their mutation. Look at this group over here. Mike, zoom in here."

The next view detailed a woman lying next to a park bench, apparently unable to get up. Next to her, another bald and barely-clothed old woman was bending over the first. As they watched, the second woman laid her head down on the first's stomach and began to lick the skin. Then she raised her head slightly and took a bite.

"Ugh, they're eating each other now!" Street exclaimed.

They watched in disbelief as the second woman began to feast on her partner. After three or four minutes, the second woman lost her balance and fell over, landing hard on her back. The two women, one now partially devoured, laid near each other as the breath slowly left their lungs for the last time.

The group sensed the moment of the Skins' deaths, only eight or nine minutes later. They appeared to die almost simultaneously; and, just as soon as the life had left their bodies, their skin began to shrivel and loosen.

"What just happened?" Jonas finally asked. "Have any of you seen that before?"

"No," Shift replied, "that was new."

Jon Porter, quiet up until now, asked, "Are they all dying? Can we go home?"

Nobody responded for fear that their hopes might be dashed by speaking them aloud.

OCTOBER 15
NEAR JUNEAU, ALASKA

"Marcus, have you seen this?" Lin Zheng asked.

"What are you looking at?" Marcus Dorian asked in return as he walked over to the small work station where Lin was sitting.

"Look what's happening to the monsters in Anchorage," Lin replied.

"It looks like they're dying. Is that real-time?" Marcus asked.

"Yeah, it's real-time."

Marcus, Lin and two other members of their staff had wisely fled the International Weather Service Headquarters in Miami, Florida in mid-February when it looked like things might take a turn for the worse. They were part of the team that successfully deployed a hurricane-busting device that dispersed Hurricane Miguel in the Gulf of Mexico, only to have the Mexican Lunar Spaceship, Gortari II, blown from the sky by a Cuban missile during its return from the moon. The Gortari II explosion, amidst the dispersing hurricane, spread parts of the space craft, its occupants and A.E. carried by one or more of its passengers, across Central Am and the southeastern United States.

Marcus knew that there was danger in remaining so close to the destruction of Gortari II after it flew into the hurricane they had just dispersed. But his death wasn't part of the plan. Over the next few days, they had hacked into, and then studied reports in a classified database set up by the IIA about the spread of Anthrax E—the "Anthrax E Database". There was much that he hadn't been told.

By February 10th, the disease was spreading rapidly through Central Am and was gaining traction in Florida. Having access to the IIA database, Marcus and Lin knew what had occurred in El-Alamein and on the moon. A few days earlier, knowing that danger was near,

Marcus had asked certain members of his staff, including Lin, whether they would leave with him to move to a more secure facility to continue their work. Lin and two other members of his staff agreed to go with him, each having no family to keep them tied down.

Unfortunately, in late February, while they were hiding out in an empty cabin in northern Montana, someone discovered their access to the database and shut them down. Since then, most of what they learned was what the news had reported—until the news stopped reporting. Marcus had learned a little from one other contact, which he did not share with Lin.

On March 5th, the two members of Marcus' staff were out foraging for supplies in a nearby town when they were accosted by a man who begged for help, coughing and choking on his own blood. Fearing infection, they had informed Marcus and Lin that they would not be returning, and pleaded with Marcus and Lin to leave Montana.

In sorrow, Marcus and Lin had packed their bags again and headed northwest. There were travel restrictions in place, but those restrictions didn't stop them from heading to Alaska. Marcus had explained that, of all places they could reach fairly quickly, the area around Juneau may be the safest place. The prevailing winds came from the sea, rather than from land due to the high mountains on the coast. And motorized access to the town was primarily by air and water. The only road into Juneau had been constructed just a few years earlier, and was difficult to navigate much of the year. If they could get to Juneau, Marcus believed they could actually be safe. So they drove the lone road through the mountains looking for some kind of safe haven.

When they arrived in Juneau, it was not to be. The plague had reached the town. Avoiding contact with all humans, and praying they had not already been exposed, Marcus and Lin sought refuge in a modern hunting cabin high in the mountains northeast of town. It was equipped with all of the devices they would need for survival—and very good locks and ventilation systems. So, they shut and sealed the doors and had not opened them since.

Then the news from all over the world ceased. The internet continued to feed bits and pieces of information, but it was unreliable. Then that stopped too. Now, the only access they had to the outside world, as far as Lin knew, was the link Lin had established with the old USCAN system two months ago. But even that was shaky. The only feeds they received reliably were from just down the mountain in Juneau and one feed from a few hundred miles north in Anchorage.

What they saw before them now was an image vastly different than what they had observed when they first hooked up to USCAN.

"So, if these guys are dying, can we get out of here?" Marcus asked, mostly to himself. Then louder, to Lin, "When was the last time you tried to connect to that IIA database?"

"It's been a long time."

"Let's try it again," Marcus suggested. He had become quite concerned for their future prospects when the communications system he had been secretly using to communicate with his contact had begun to experience problems. It was inoperable most of the time and he had not received any communication in weeks.

Lin quickly and expertly entered numbers and letters in sequences Marcus couldn't understand. She was using a rather old computer system, not the fancy ones they had at Headquarters before they left. But it seemed to be doing the job. Sequences and arrays of digits were flying across the screen as Lin performed her magic.

Finally, after about two minutes of confusion, the IIA logo appeared on the screen.

"Well, we're there," Lin said. "Let's see if we can get in."

A few moments later, the image changed and the database appeared on the screen. The last post to the database was dated July 16th, 2093, almost three months earlier. That particular post was from some colonists on the moon looking for help starting or operating a ship.

"Nice work Lin! Now, let's go back to February and read from where we left off."

"Good idea."

Lin and Marcus read into the night.

40

"Shift, come here please," Anta called out from the bedroom of their tiny apartment in the United States colony.

"What's up babe?" Shift asked as he walked from the bathroom with a towel around his waist.

"Sit down. We need to talk."

"Uhhh, okay."

Shift, uneasy at the tone in Anta's voice, sat near her on the bed, but not close enough that their bodies were touching. Anta, obviously sensing Shift's hesitation, scooted closer until their thighs and shoulders were touching. Then she whispered in his ear in a way that sent tingles up and down his spine.

"I'm pregnant."

Shift jumped up from the bed, his towel loosening and dropping to the floor at his ankles. "What?"

"You heard me."

"Yeah, I heard you. Are you sure?"

"Yes Shift, I'm sure. Marilyn checked me out this morning."

Anta let Shift stand there, naked, in silence for several moments before finally speaking again.

"Shift, hello. Are you there?"

"Uh, yeah, I'm here. Hold on."

Shift reached down, grabbed the towel, and pulled it back up, wrapping it around the lower half of his body and tucking the corner in at the waist. All the while, he continued to stare at nothing in particular, not speaking.

"Well, what do you think about that?" Anta asked.

"I think . . . well, I think . . ." Then a smile broke the corners of his mouth. The smile turned into a grin and within moments, laughter erupted from deep inside his body.

"Anta! This is absolutely wonderful! I am so happy! When are you due?"

"Mid-July."

"Are you happy?" Shift asked, more cautiously.

"Yes, I am."

"Then let's celebrate! Can we tell everyone? Let's have a party!"

Shift was so excited by the news, after it finally sank in, that he could hardly contain himself. He couldn't stop moving. His towel fell off again and Anta quickly reached her foot over and kicked it away from him. When Shift realized what she had done, he walked over and sat back down on the bed. This time, he wasn't nervous, and they did much more than just talk.

OCTOBER 29
INTERNATIONAL LUNAR SPACE STATION

The news of Anta's pregnancy was like a shot of adrenaline to the small group of survivors hiding on the moon. After the deaths of Carón and Nelise almost six weeks earlier, many of them had begun to wonder whether life could possibly continue, whether or not they ever made it back home. Now, they had come to life with the news of Anta's pregnancy.

But there was fear among them, although unspoken. Anta's blood was tainted, or so they believed. Could a human baby be healthy within her womb, or any womb for that matter? Would the baby live? And if so, what would he or she be like? Would he be sick, with A.E.? Would she be immune as a result of Anta's inoculation? Nobody talked of it, but each person thought on it. Ultimately, Marilyn could run tests on the fetus, but the baby wouldn't be exposed to air, or the A.E. in the air, until it was born. Nothing would be completely known until then. Nevertheless, their spirits were high.

A great feast ensued, albeit with processed food from the wall units of the various apartments. The only exception was fish from the pond in the park. Jon and Street had spent a couple of hours catching several fish, probably rainbow trout by the looks of them. They were cooked to perfection for the celebration.

The party continued into the night. Many of them drank wine for the first time in many months. A couple of them became intoxicated. But nobody cared. It was time to celebrate, and they did.

"John, let me help you get home," Shift said as John stumbled toward the exit to the great hall.

"Nah, I'm preeeetty good." John's slurred speech told Shift everything he needed to know about how "good" John was. His old friend was practically an alcoholic in college. Shift had seen him this way many times. Too often, John's drunkenness led to physical altercations and run-ins with the law. This time, there was no law, and it seemed unlikely an altercation would break out among the group celebrating Shift's and Anta's impending parenthood. But Shift didn't want to take any chances. He would see his old friend back to his apartment.

As John walked from the great hall, Shift followed him. To Shift's surprise, John made it back to his apartment without incident, except for a small bump into a wall that changed John's course a few degrees. Finally, John arrived at his apartment, opened the door and went inside. Shift, feeling the anxiety leave him instantly, returned to the hall to escort Anta home.

"Did John make it okay?" Anta asked casually.

"Yeah, he made it."

"Then let's go home."

"You got it babe," Shift replied. They said their goodbyes.

Upon arriving back at their apartment, both Shift and Anta plopped down on the soft bed and fell asleep almost instantly, clothed and uncovered. It had been a long day, and exciting. The news of their pregnancy ignited new life in their friends and that excitement was taxing.

Not long after they fell asleep, the alarms rang out, blaring up and down the halls and corridors of the lunar shell. The sound was deafening.

"What is that?" Anta screamed over the loud screeching of the alarm.

"The alarms! Something's wrong. Stay here."

Shift ran out into the apartment hall and was met by Mike, Jonas and Hasani who all looked as confused by the sound as Shift felt.

"What's going on?" Mike asked loudly, so he could be heard over the sirens.

"That's the alarm for a breach in the airlock system," Jonas replied. "We need to find out what happened, and fast. Mike and Hasani, go to the control room. Check the computers for codes. Find out where the breach is—go!"

While Mike and Hasani ran down the hall toward the control room, Jonas and Shift ran the other direction, toward the outside door. Jonas hesitated, then pushed open the doors. If there was a problem with the airlock system, any significant breach would probably have flushed them all out into space already; so going through the outside door and into the yard around the apartment complex would not be any more dangerous than staying in their beds.

Upon walking into the bright light of the shell, it was readily apparent where the problem lay. Not more than two hundred meters away, near the airlock bay leading to the outside world of the moon, a hover sat lodged in the bay, smoking. John was staggering toward them. Then he fell.

Shift and Jonas ran to John. He was unconscious, but he would have to stay that way for now. The two men moved cautiously toward the airlock bay. They could feel a draft pulling their clothing toward the airlock. Then they saw the smoke from the burning hover being sucked outward. Thankfully, no debris was being pulled along with the smoke. Whatever the breach was, it wasn't big enough to kill them—yet. Then they saw the problem.

"Jonas, that doesn't look good," Shift said loudly as the sirens continued to wail around them.

"It's *not* good Shift," Jonas replied.

They inched closer to what appeared to be a small crack in the shell next to the hover that John had apparently been driving in his drunken state. The images of the German shell exploding and shooting Alan into space came flooding back to Jonas. "*Is it happening again?*" He wondered.

"Shift, we need to get out of this shell, now!" Jonas yelled.

"Where should we go?" Shift asked, frightened, as they turned back toward John, still lying unconscious on the ground.

"To the shuttle bay. We can seal the doors."

Lifting John together, the two men raced back toward the apartments, where the other residents had gathered outside to stare. When they got close, Shift yelled, "Everyone get to the shuttle bay—now!"

In a panic, the small group turned as one and raced back the way they had come, through the apartments, past the great hall, and toward the shuttle bay where they had landed only a few weeks earlier.

Shift and Jonas, carrying John, brought up the rear. As they rounded the corner by the control room, Mike and Hasani came crashing into the hall and joined them. As a group, they followed the rest of their friends toward the shuttle bay.

As they skidded to a stop just inside the main blast doors, Jonas yelled out, "Is everybody here?"

All faces began to twist and turn, looking for their friends. After a few moments, a voice in the back yelled out, "Tom and Misty aren't here!"

"Where are they?" Shift called back.

Nobody answered. Nobody knew. They had left the party earlier than most of the others. Everyone assumed they had gone to bed. Nobody had seen them since.

"I'm going to find them," Jerad yelled as he headed back out the blast doors.

Just as he passed the doors, Hasani grabbed his arm and pulled him hard. "No you're not," he yelled back. "Feel the wind?"

The wind was picking up. The suction from the fissure in the shell wall was increasing.

"It could shatter at any moment," Hasani said to his friend. "You can't go out there."

"I have to," Jerad replied.

Then the sirens stopped and the moon turned upside down.

Jonas slammed his fist into the wall to shut the blast doors, but it was too late. Jerad was gone, sucked out into space with the rest of the United States shell.

41

Nobody had spoken in nearly four hours. Marilyn had initially suggested donning space suits and going out to search for Tom and Misty. But Jonas reminded them that they only had a few suits in the bay, and, if they opened the only doors now separating them from the outside, those without suits would suffocate from lack of oxygen.

When Street reminded Jonas that those not searching could hide in the shuttle, an attempt was made to open the doors to the elevator which led down to the shuttle floor, five stories below. The elevator wouldn't open. A malfunction error registered in the computers that Mike had not been able to override or repair. His best guess was that the temporary unequal pressure during the second before the blast doors closed caused some problem. But it was only a guess.

On Earth, on the Eastern Coast of the United States, the sun was beginning to rise as the moon descended behind the hills and mountain ranges on the western horizon. In the shuttle bay of the International Lunar Space Station, the only part of the United States shell remaining, it felt as though the sun would never rise again.

The elation of learning that Anta and Shift would be having a child was gone. Jerad was gone—dead. Tom and Misty were gone too, but nobody knew where they were. Probably dead.

Finally, Jonas stood, stretched his back, and walked over to the shuttle bay's communication station. He began dialing the frequencies of every shell on the moon, as he had done four times already. Starting with the major shells, he continued through the smaller outposts. He would find them, if they were alive.

For twenty minutes, the remaining twelve members of the human population, at least as far as they knew, stared at Jonas' fingers as he swiped, touched and dialed in an attempt to find the Birds. They still didn't respond. Finally, he sat back down and put his head in his hands.

"Are they gone?" Marilyn asked, on the verge of tears for the eighth or ninth time in the past few hours.

Jonas slowly raised his head. "I hope not Marilyn. They could be somewhere safe, but just not picking up the com. It's possible."

"How likely is it Jonas?" Marilyn asked cautiously.

"I don't know."

Nobody spoke again for a long time.

OCTOBER 30, 9:52AM
INTERNATIONAL LUNAR SPACE STATION

Several more hours had passed when a quiet beep was heard coming from the communication table. Jonas jumped up and stared at the table, looking for the source of the noise. A small green light was flashing next to the incoming communication sensor. Jonas pushed it.

"Hello," he said tentatively.

"Jonas, is that you?" said a quiet voice from somewhere outside the shuttle bay.

"Yes! Tom, is that you?" Jonas almost shouted in his excitement.

"Yes, it's me, but don't get too excited my friend."

"Why? What happened? Where are you? Where's Misty? Are you okay?"

"Jonas, listen please. We are together, but in body only. My dear wife was killed when the shell exploded."

The room grew quiet as Dr. Thomas Bird continued.

"When the shell exploded, Misty and I were out for a drive in one of the rovers. She wanted to see the stars and Earth. Anta's pregnancy made her so excited. She finally wanted to go home, for the first time since A.E. broke out. So we went out to see Earth. We were looking at what must have surely been the killing sands of the Sahara Desert, where A.E. first reared its dreadful head, when the alarms went off. I thought I had done something wrong. But I've been out those doors many, many times. It couldn't have been me. It wasn't me, was it?"

"No Tom, it wasn't you," Jonas replied, his voice choked with emotion.

"That's good," Tom replied quietly. "Hearing the alarm, we turned and headed back toward the shell. We wanted to be with everyone if there was a problem. We were close when the shell broke apart. The force of the blast shot our rover backward—up and out. The rover crashed. Misty was killed."

"I'm so sorry Tom," Jonas replied.

"It's okay my friend. I will be joining her soon."

"Are you hurt?" Jonas asked apprehensively.

"Yes, badly. I won't live long. Not even modern medicine can save me now."

"How do you know?" Hasani said, anxiety lacing his words, as he walked up behind Jonas. "We'll come get you. We can help you."

"Hello Hasani. Thank you for your bravery and your compassion. But you are wrong. You can't save me. I'm a doctor. I know these things." Even though they couldn't see him, the smile was evident in Dr. Bird's voice as he said those words. "But how is everyone else?"

"Jerad is dead," Jonas replied wearily.

"I am so sorry for that. I will greet him warmly on the other side."

"Thank you Tom," Hasani said.

"Now, don't cry for us. We have loved and enjoyed your companionship. We have rejoiced seeing and being with the great people who have saved mankind. God speed to all of you. I love you. Goodbye."

Then he hung up. The Birds were gone.

OCTOBER 31
INTERNATIONAL LUNAR SPACE STATION

"How does it look?" Shift asked Jonas as they peered over the railing toward the bottom level of the shuttle bay, twenty or twenty-five meters below their feet. The ship they had arrived in sat down there, gathering dust.

"Well, it looks just like it did when we left it," Jonas replied.

"Do you think you can fly it; I mean, if we need to?"

"I don't know. Jerad did almost everything last time. I didn't pay much attention. I just did what he told me. But we've got to get down there first, and that's our immediate problem."

"Bummer," Shift replied.

"Yeah, bummer."

"Well, we've got to get down there somehow. We need food and water, and we can't leave the shuttle bay unless everyone not wearing a suit is inside the shuttle. I'm afraid to see what it looks like outside the bay, but we may need to go out there. Hopefully the ship's food processors are still operational."

"Well, let's get on it," Jonas said.

Mike, Shift and Jonas spent the next two hours trying to fix the elevator which would take them down to the lower floors of the shuttle bay. Eventually, Street joined them at the elevator doors. Mike was still swiping haphazardly at the flat screen next to the doors, but Shift and Jonas sat with their backs propped against the closed doors, heads hung low in defeat.

"Please move aside dudes," Street said.

"What are you going to do?" Shift asked.

"I'm going to open the doors."

"How?" Jonas asked.

"Move aside and watch," Street replied.

"Street, don't break anything," Shift cautioned.

"I won't—probably."

Jonas and Shift stood and stepped to the side, and, together with Mike, watched as Street dug a screwdriver into the small gap between the doors. After widening the gap just four or five centimeters, he said, "Shift, hold this."

Shift grabbed the screwdriver and put his weight into it, holding the gap open. Confident that Shift could hold it open, Street grasped the two sides of the elevator door with his finger tips and pulled. As he pulled his hands away from each other, his muscles strained and a sweat broke out on his forehead. The shirt sleeve on his right arm ripped at the bicep. Fourteen seconds later, a loud pop sounded inside the elevator. The doors opened several inches in response to Street's brute force. He released his grip on the doors and they continued to open automatically.

"Whoa," Jonas said.

"I guess you haven't seen Street in action," Shift replied. "But now what?"

"Well, now I try to reset the system," Mike said.

Mike walked back over to the screen and tapped a few times. A couple quiet beeps sounded from inside the elevator.

"Well, I think that worked!" Mike said. "Who wants to get in and give it a try?"

"Uhhh, how about we send it down to the ground without someone inside first?" Jonas said.

"Good idea," Shift replied. "Can you do that from here Mike, or does someone need to push something inside?"

"Here," Mike replied, swiping and tapping at the monitor again.

The doors closed and the lift began a rapid, but controlled decent to the bottom floor. After it stopped, Mike reached over and tapped the screen to call it back up. Four seconds later, the doors opened in front of them.

"Nice work Street," Jonas said. "I wish you had come over a couple hours earlier though."

"Yeah, but then I wouldn't be such a hero, would I?" Street replied, chuckling.

"No, probably not. Let's go."

"Maybe, just one of you should go," Mike said. "We don't know what the weight capacity is. That pop sound was a bit freaky."

"Alright, one at a time then," Shift said. "I'll go first."

Shift took the elevator down to the lower level without incident. Jonas followed and stepped quickly out of the doors as they opened.

"That was a bit tense," Jonas said.

"Oh, you are very brave," Shift said, smiling.

Nobody had been inside the ship since a few days after they arrived on the moon almost three months earlier. On the outside, the ship appeared as they had left it, albeit a bit dustier. When they arrived at the ship, Jonas punched the opening sequence into the panel next to the cargo door and it opened smoothly.

"So far, so good," Shift said.

The men walked into the cargo hold and the lights came on automatically. The hold was empty, just as they had left it. But the smell that accosted them was nauseating.

"What is that?" Shift asked, gagging as he plugged his nose.

"I don't know, but it's awful."

"Well, we need to find out what the problem is and take care of it," Shift said. "I'm about to puke."

The men searched the sleeping lofts near the front of the ship first, then moved back into the lounge area. Finding nothing out of sorts, they visited the research and electronics labs, and finally the cargo hold. Nothing. But the smell got stronger as they moved toward the rear of the ship.

"I think I found it," Jonas said, pointing toward the left rear wheel chamber.

"The smell is pretty strong," Shift agreed. "Let's open it."

Jonas walked back two paces and hit the switch on the wall to open the interior wall to the wheel chamber as Shift grabbed a flashlight from the tool shelf on the other side of the hold. The men arrived back at the well at the same time and Shift turned on the light. Jonas bent down and peered inside. A thin, pale, rotting hand reached toward him.

"Whoa!" Jonas yelled, jumping back.

Then an old man slowly emerged from the well; bald, shriveled, naked, and smelling of death.

"Is that a Skin?" Jonas asked.

"Yeah, what's left of one," Shift replied. "But how did he get in here?"

"He must have climbed into the well before the wheels came up when we left Earth. Probably got stuck in the wheel well because we didn't have to put the wheels down to land here. He's been in here the whole time, just stinking up the joint."

"I guess . . ."

Shift was cut off mid-sentence as the Skin lunged at him. Shift swung the flashlight he was still holding and hit the Skin in the temple. But the blow didn't stop his forward progress. He was slow and weak, but he was alive and obviously hungry.

"Jonas, get a weapon—anything," Shift yelled over his shoulder as he continued to back away from the Skin.

"I'm looking," Jonas replied. "There's nothing in here. Wait, here's a crowbar."

"That'll work," Shift said.

Jonas brought the crowbar over, slowly, carefully, avoiding the Skin. He'd never been close to one. He'd only seen them in the videos posted on the Net from Earth in the early days and on the monitor when they picked up the stranded humans in Florida. He tossed Shift the crowbar and Shift didn't waste any time clubbing the Skin in the head. Then again. Then again.

Finally, the Skin fell to the floor, never to rise again. They were safe. But they had a mess to clean up before the others arrived.

OCTOBER 31, LATER
INTERNATIONAL LUNAR SPACE STATION

"A Skin? Here?" Street asked.

Shift told the story in all its gory detail. He exaggerated just a bit of the story for entertainment value. But everyone knew they were safe, and the story was a bit funny. Shift and Jonas answered questions, embellishing all along the way.

When there was nothing left to tell, Shift said, "So, here's where we stand. We can leave the shuttle bay, but we absolutely need suits. While on the ship a few minutes ago, Jonas took remote readings of the air outside the blast doors. There is no oxygen. That means that the containment doors and ventilation systems outside the blast doors were likely destroyed when the shell blew apart. So, we can't open the blast doors unless some of us remain on the ship while others go out in suits."

"So, either we all stay here, or some of us go out looking for additional suits and bring them back in here," Jonas added. "That way, we may be able to find a new place to live in one of the other shells. But we'd have to get rid of bodies and clean another shell first, and that would take some time. Or, alternatively, once the smell goes away in the ship, we can go on in and stay there for a while. There's food, drink and beds. We could stay there at least until we decide what to do next."

"No matter what we choose," Shift said, "nobody goes by the doors or the control board. We don't want to accidentally open the doors."

"But we need to go find Jerad and the Birds," Marilyn said.

"Yes, we do," Shift agreed. "That will be order number one."

"But once that is completed," Jonas added, "We have to have a containment plan. I've already programed the doors to be locked unless an access code is input. My thought is this: Since we don't want any accidents, I should make the process for opening these doors a two-code sequence. Then, if half of us knows one code, and the other half of us knows the other code, there will be no chance that we're all stuck in here forever unless all six or seven people who know one code or the other die for some reason. And, because it will take two different people to open the doors, there won't be any accidental, or purposeful, opening of the doors. How does that sound?"

"I like the idea," Street said.

"Me too," Hasani added.

"Well, can anyone think of a reason that plan won't work, or shouldn't be implemented?" Shift asked.

Nobody responded in the negative.

"How is John holding up?" Jonas asked quietly, to nobody in particular. Jonas was looking over at John who was sitting on the ground against the wall less than ten meters from the group. "He probably blames himself for our current situation. Is it going to incapacitate him, or is he going to be able to function as a useful member of our group?"

"You're right. He blames himself and was inconsolable after he heard about Jared and the Birds," Shift replied.

"I gave him a mild sedative and a temporary antidepressant and I'll be watching him closely," Marilyn added. "Jon and Suvan have been spending time with him too, trying to cheer him up."

"Is it going to work?" Jonas asked.

"Time will tell," Shift said. "But one thing I know; John is too valuable to let him wallow in pity or become clinically depressed. I'll go kick his butt if nothing else works."

"Let me know if you need help," offered Street with a sly grin. "I'm good at kicking butt."

"Thanks Street. I know you are," Shift replied with a grin of his own. "Now, who wants to go out there with me to find our friends and look for additional suits?"

"I do," Street and Jonas said in unison.

"Alright, let's do it. But first, let's help everyone get down to the ship. It's in real good shape, and we know it's comfortable. The wall units are still processing food and drink. There's still the smell, but I think we can get rid of it. After we get back, we can come up with a more long-term solution to our current problem."

The mood changed with that last statement. The group had become comfortable in the apartments of the United States shell. Life was starting to return to normal, albeit on the moon. Then Jerad died. Then the Birds died. Now, there were only thirteen of them, one of whom was seriously incapacitated, and the baby in Anta's womb. As far as they knew, they were the only humans left alive anywhere in the galaxy.

They needed a plan. They wanted to go home, but nobody dared believe it was possible.

42

It had been nearly four weeks since Lin had hacked into the old IIA "Anthrax E Database". Marcus and Lin had read every post, and then read them again. Soon thereafter, they began watching the USCAN feeds more closely in Anchorage and Juneau. They were now convinced that the monsters—or "Skins"—as they had been called on the database, were not only dying, but were likely already mostly dead. They saw very few moving about in either town, and those they saw were looking pretty old.

What they didn't know was whether it was safe to go outside. They learned about a vaccination on the database. They knew people had been vaccinated, and some of them seemed to be safely hidden from the Skins somewhere. But they were at a loss as to what to do about it.

"Well, we can't just stay here forever, can we?" Lin asked.

"No, definitely not."

"So what are we going to do? Nobody has responded to any of the posts I've made to the database."

"Just keep posting and keep checking, I guess," Marcus said, feigning disappointment. In reality, he held on to the belief that his contact would deliver them from their current predicament, somehow.

"I guess until someone responds to my posts," Lin said, "we can't possibly know whether it's safe out there, or how we can get hold of a vaccine, if at all. And we can't risk either of our lives on mere hope."

"Agreed."

NOVEMBER 12
INTERNATIONAL LUNAR SPACE STATION

Shift and Jonas had called a meeting in the lounge area of the ship. After wallowing in pity and remorse over the death of their friends for many days, it was finally time to make some decisions.

"Well," Jonas began, "I would thank you all for taking the time to come here, but I know that, lately, there hasn't been much else taking up our time. Of course, Mike has been busy, as you all know. I've asked him to share with us what he's been seeing the past few days. Go ahead, Mike."

"As you know, I've been watching USCAN. It has been very interesting."

Mike had been monitoring the USCAN surveillance system for weeks. He had watched as successive groups of Skins continued to age and wilt, sometimes right where they stood. He watched several episodes where one Skin ate another and then both of them shriveled and died soon after. It was as though the bad vaccine that created them in the first place was negatively reacting with itself and causing a quick and ugly death. But even the Skins who didn't turn on their fellows were still dying. It was all a mystery.

"Can you give us specifics about what you're seeing in any specific location, like the United States?" Shift asked.

"Yeah, I can. In the United States, I haven't seen a living Skin in over a week, anywhere."

"What about the rest of the world?" Jonas asked.

"Well, in the east, Africa and the Middle East mostly, there are greater numbers, but they're dying too. Really, if I were to estimate the living Skins on Earth—and remember, it's just an estimate; maybe more of a guess really—I'd say there's less than six hundred of them left anywhere."

"Wow!" Anta said. "Only six hundred? Is there any way we can actually quantify that?"

"Probably not," Mike replied. "But over the next few days, if I have a little help, we can begin to catalogue the Skins like we did with the humans back on Earth. It probably wouldn't take more than a week to get a real good estimate. And, since what y'all are really concerned about is going home, we'll start with Florida. If we want to go home, we have to be able to land safely, and live safely. So I think we should start there."

"What about northern California or back near Boston?" Angel asked. "I'm thinking about food. Northern California has all of those orchards and vineyards and had, at least, a ton of cows. And hopefully there are a few good farms near Boston, since we vaccinated herds of animals in the early days of the vaccine."

"That's a good idea," Jonas said. "But we've got to have a base to land."

"There's one south of San Francisco, I think," Jonas said.

"You know," Street said, "we can land wherever we want to land. With the millions of hovers sittin' down there unused, we can go wherever we want to go once we land."

"Duh, of course," Shift said. "What I wonder is, are there any survivors down there? If there are, maybe we could still get the vaccine to them and increase our population."

"Have you seen people alive, Mike?" Hasani asked.

"Nope. But I haven't really been looking."

"What about the Anthrax E Database?" John asked. "Has anyone posted anything there lately?"

John had said very little in the days since he crashed the rover into the shell causing it to break apart and kill three of their friends. The group had worried about his mental health. Shift really worried. It was right for John to feel guilt, but not right for him to feel such guilt that he shut down. They needed him. Several of the group reacted when John spoke by turning to look at him. Then Shift had an idea . . .

"No," Shift said quickly. "What a great idea John. Can you help me check that?"

NOVEMBER 12, LATER
INTERNATIONAL LUNAR SPACE STATION

While Mike, Jonas, Hasani, Steve and Angel went to work on USCAN, Shift, John and Anta got on the Anthrax E database. As had become the norm lately, Neirioui and Marilyn cooked and tended to other needs. Even with the limited supply of options on the wall units, Neirioui was able to come up with some amazing meals. The group feasted, regularly, on her delicious treats.

Street, really just a kid at heart, spent a lot of time with Jon and Suvan, playing games and keeping the youngsters entertained. Everyone had a place and the group functioned amazingly well. Shift often thought that, with this group, even alone on Earth, they really had a chance of survival. He and Anta shared many late night conversations on that topic.

But on this day, the database was their focus.

"Fire it up, John," Shift said.

"I haven't done this for a while. Let's see . . . oh yeah, here we go." John was in the database in a matter of moments.

"Holy Sh—sorry Anta—I mean, holy crap," John said. "Look at all of these postings from Juneau."

"That last one was posted yesterday!" Anta said. "People are alive!"

"Are they all from Juneau? Go back a bit John."

"When was the last time we posted anything?" John asked. "Or maybe, the last time the guys up here posted anything."

"Probably back in July or August," Shift replied. "Let's just go back 'til we find our last post and move forward. Let's see if anybody else is still down there."

John scrolled back in the database to July.

"Well, the last post by any of our group was July 16th. That was when the moon guys were trying to get help with the ship. Remember that? The looks on their faces a couple days later when Mike told them they just needed codes. That was awesome!" Then John laughed, for the first time in a long time. It was infectious. Anta and Shift both laughed with him. Shift hoped his friend was returning.

A few moments later, Shift asked, "Okay then, when was the next post, after July 16th, by anybody?"

"October 17th."

"Well, let's start reading there," Anta said.

The three friends spent the next few minutes reading several short posts by a couple somewhere outside Juneau. The posts detailed, briefly, their journey and what they had been doing ever since.

"So, these were the folks who broke up the hurricane that spread A.E. across the globe," Shift said sadly. "I wonder how they're feeling. They probably blame themselves?"

"*I* wonder whether they knew what they were doing," John said.

"We should answer their posts," Anta said. "They know, obviously, that had Gortari II not been shot out of the sky by the Cubans, that the hurricane wouldn't have caused any problems. Plus, if they don't know, they need to be told, that even if Gortari II hadn't been shot down, A.E. still would have spread. Right? Someone on that ship was infected. Whether the infection could have been stopped, nobody knows. But I doubt it. It's likely that nothing these two did had any real impact on anything except, possibly, speeding up the process. They need to know that."

"Agreed," Shift replied. "Do you want to do the honors? It sounds like they don't even know if there's anyone left alive in the world besides themselves. And, they aren't vaccinated. That has to change."

The group spent the next few minutes replying to the posts. Then they sat there, waiting, to see if they would hear back from Juneau. Several minutes later, they gave up and went to check on the others.

NOVEMBER 12, LATER
INTERNATIONAL LUNAR SPACE STATION

John, Shift and Anta walked into the small computer room where the others had spent the last couple of hours looking for Skins and humans. As they walked in, smiles beaming across their faces, all of the others stopped what they were doing and stared.

Finally, Hasani asked, "What?"

"Let's get everyone else, and then we'll talk," Shift replied.

After the whole group was assembled inside the computer room, and twelve faces were looking at Shift, most of them anxious with anticipation, Shift finally spoke again.

"There are others," he said calmly. "Alive."

Several people clapped briefly, and others made quiet exclamations. Overall, the group was too leery of the prospects of life to become too excited about Shift's announcement.

"Tell us about it, Shift," Marilyn said.

Shift proceeded to tell the group what they had learned. While he spoke, Mike connected to the IIA database. When Shift finally finished, Mike spoke up.

"They've replied, Shift. They can't wait to meet us."

43

"Shift!"

"What is it babe?" Shift asked, his eyes still closed and sleepy.

"My stomach is cramping—bad."

"What?"

"My stomach. I think it's the baby."

Shift bolted upright in bed and quickly turned on the light.

"The baby? What's happening to the baby?"

"I don't know Shift. Calm down though. I'm sure it's fine. Go get Marilyn please?"

"Okay."

Shift rushed from their small room on the ship and down the hall to Marilyn's door. He couldn't stand still as he knocked. Bouncing on his toes, Shift continued rapping on the door until Marilyn finally opened it.

"What is it Shift?" Marilyn asked through the small gap between the door and its frame.

"The baby! Anta thinks there's something wrong with the baby."

The urgency and fear in Shift's voice pushed Marilyn into action. She rushed back into her room and was back in ten seconds with a bag. Marilyn had been checking Anta's and the baby's vitals every morning for the past several days. All had been well.

Together, Shift and Marilyn ran back down the long hall toward Shift and Anta's room. When they arrived, Shift threw open the door and led Marilyn over to the bed. Anta was lying in a fetal position under the covers, tears soaking the pillowcase under her head.

"Tell me what's happening Anta," Marilyn said softly.

"I don't know. But it really hurts."

"What hurts dear?" Marilyn asked.

"My stomach. The cramping, or whatever it is. It's crushing me."

"Can you roll onto your back please? Is the pain coming from down here?" Marilyn asked, placing her hand onto Anta's lower abdomen.

"It's all over. I can feel pain all over my whole body," Anta replied. "But it's worse there."

"Shift," Marilyn said, "please run down to the medical station and grab the wheelchair. I'll call Angel to come help."

Shift took off, running through the ship as fast as his legs would carry him. When he returned, only three or four minutes later, Angel and Marilyn were helping Anta put a robe on. As was her habit, Anta had worn only her underwear to bed that night, and there was a small bulge where the baby was growing inside her.

Shift pushed the wheelchair up alongside the bed. Together, Marilyn and Shift lifted Anta carefully into the wheelchair and began a rapid walk through the ship to the medical station. Throughout the walk, Anta's pain rose. On two occasions, she screamed out from the pain, waking others in the ship who had been, until then, sound asleep.

When they arrived outside the doors to the medical station, the doors slid open with a soft whoosh. Shift pushed the chair over to the nearest hospital bed while Marilyn hurried across the room to where the equipment was stored.

The medical station, although highly modern and equipped with the latest technology, was small and held only eight beds. Medicine had progressed to such a degree that patients were rarely confined to beds in hospitals unless they had a serious injury. Rarely did any illness result in an overnight stay at a hospital. Until A.E. But that was also behind them, or so they believed.

Here on the ship, on the moon, Marilyn didn't think she'd ever have use for the equipment in the medical station. So, she had pushed most of the equipment out of the way and set up a small lab. She and Angel had begun, in recent days, experimenting with E-rase. They hoped to be able to determine, in some way, whether the baby in Anta's womb, or any other baby that the small group was blessed with, would be able to survive.

Marilyn rushed back to Anta's bedside pushing a medical tray on wheels. The tray was equipped with a small computer screen and several compartments holding small pieces of medical equipment and instruments. Rapidly touching the screen, she said, "Shift step to your left please."

Shift stepped to his left just as a mechanical arm lowered from the ceiling into the space in which he'd been standing. Marilyn continued to swipe the screen and input codes and numerical sequences into the computer. The arm slowly moved to Anta's side, next to her womb. A large claw extended from the end of the arm and gently grasped Anta's waist. A fine antiseptic mist sprayed just before a needle extended from the machine and pricked her skin. The needle extended through the layers of tissue, taking a reading of Anta's blood along the way. Then it continued into Anta's uterus, and, reaching the baby, took a reading of the blood of the one-month-old fetus. The needle withdrew as quickly as it had gone in.

Within seconds, Marilyn's computer lit up with arrays of numbers and letters which Marilyn utilized to interpret the data being fed from the mechanical arm to her computer.

Anta had not been in the medical station more than ten minutes before Marilyn said, "There is something wrong. But my computers can't tell me what it is. I suspect it has to do with A.E., but these computers were likely never updated with information related to A.E. They need to be updated, but I don't know how to do that."

"Should I get Mike?" Angel asked.

Anta screamed out in pain and thrashed back and forth on the bed. Shift leaned over her and wrapped his arms around her, both to hold her still and to comfort her. After a few seconds, Anta began to calm down again. Shift stood and grasped Anta's hand, squeezing tightly.

"Sorry," Anta said. "The pain comes and goes, and when it comes, it is intense."

"No problem," Shift said, emotion causing his voice to betray his outward calmness.

"Yes Angel," Marilyn said, "go get Mike, and Jonas and Hasani. Anta, I will give you some medicine for the pain, but not until I have an accurate reading of what's going on here. Please be patient with me."

A few minutes later, Mike and Angel rushed into the medical station. Hasani and John were right behind them. As Marilyn explained the problem, the remaining members of their small group began to arrive at the door. Angel quietly explained what she knew and asked them to wait outside. Then she closed the door.

Mike sat down at Marilyn's computer and began typing and swiping in an effort to find out what needed to be done to input information about A.E. into the computers. Jonas told him where to find the information they had stored on the system when they were creating E-rase. Hasani, not daring to approach his sister too closely, smiled at her and said a silent prayer for the health and safety of his sister and the baby.

Within minutes, Mike had figured out what needed to be done. He began the upload from the international station's servers to the ship. He was surprised to find the servers at all considering the state of the International Shell after the breach. Apparently, a backup of all information on the servers was stored in every major shell. Seconds later, they heard a quiet beep from the computer.

"That's it," Mike said as he moved out of the chair.

Marilyn sat down immediately and instructed the computer to scan Anta's and the baby's blood samples again.

"Here it comes," she said quietly, only seconds later. Shift stayed by Anta's side while the others closed around Marilyn and the screen in front of her.

"It is A.E.," Marilyn said. "The baby is infected and is beginning to show signs of illness. We need to inoculate the baby. Either Anta's vaccination didn't transfer to the baby, or her infected blood from her cut months ago has contaminated the baby's blood. Either way, the baby is sick."

"Will it work?" Hasani asked fearfully.

"I don't know," Marilyn said. "But I know that if we don't do it, the baby will die. This is our only chance. Do you agree with that Angel?"

"I do. Everything we know about this disease, which is not much, indicates that a human body will not likely survive once the disease has manifest itself for over thirty hours, probably less time in a fetus. When did you first feel pain Anta?"

"Just an hour ago or so. But the pain got significantly worse, quickly."

"Is there any way to tell how long ago the baby first began to show signs of illness?" Angel asked Marilyn.

"I don't know," Marilyn replied. "The computer really doesn't know what to look for. And I don't know how to tell it what to look for since we've never been in this position before."

"Inoculate the baby!" Anta screamed as another wave of pain overtook her body.

"Do it," Shift confirmed.

"Okay. Someone get John in here."

Marilyn ran over to the containment locker where they had stored pre-measured dosages of the vaccination. The dosages had been kept in syringes just in case they had needed some on the moon—in case they had found any survivors. Both child and adult dosages were in the locker, although nobody really knew if that made any difference. Plus, this was not a child. It was a fetus. By the time she returned to the bed, John was there.

"Angel? John?" Marilyn began, "how much should I give the baby?"

"I don't know that," Angel replied heatedly. "You're the doctor. Figure it out."

"I don't know either Marilyn," John said, more patiently. "What do you think?"

"I'm trying. I just . . . I don't know. We've never done this." Marilyn began to shake as she held the child-size dosage of E-rase in her hand.

Shift and Hasani both walked over to her.

"Is there any possibility that we could overdose the baby and that the overdose would hurt the baby?" Hasani asked the group.

"Not really. I . . . I don't think so," Marilyn replied. "I wish Tom were here. He'd know what to do."

"I don't think so either," John replied. "E-rase is an anti-bacterial vaccine. I think it would take a much larger dosage, perhaps the adult dosage, to cause an overdose in a fetus. So, the child dosage should be fine."

"Then let's just give the baby this dosage Marilyn," Shift said quietly. "Whatever happens, you're not to blame. We all know that. We all know that you've never been in this situation and every one of us is grateful you're here."

"I'm sorry Marilyn," Angel said. "I'm just scared. Let's give the baby the child dosage. I agree with you and John. I don't think we can overdose the baby."

Angel squeezed Anta's hand as she screamed in pain again.

"Let's go Marilyn," Shift said as he quickly guided her to the bed.

Marilyn poured the liquid from the syringe into a small cell on the side of the mechanical arm that she had just directed to the side of the medical tray. The liquid vaccination flowed from the small cell into the arm. A pointed syringe stretched out from the arm as the large claw again sidled up to Anta's side and held her down. The arm then automatically sprayed antiseptic and pricked Anta's side, slid through the layers of tissue separating Anta's skin from the fetus, and pricked the fetus.

"Now what?" Mike asked.

"Now we wait," Angel and John said in unison.

"And watch," Marilyn added.

"Just like everybody else we've ever vaccinated, we'll have to wait several days to know whether the baby is clean," Angel said.

"Until then," Marilyn added, "Anta will stay here, in bed, with all the medications I can safely give her to make her more comfortable."

Anta screamed again.

"Here's for the pain," Marilyn said as she put a small metal disc to the side of Anta's head.

Anta fell asleep almost immediately. She slept for thirty-six hours.

NOVEMBER 16
INTERNATIONAL LUNAR SPACE STATION

"How's Anta?" Mike asked.

"She's awake now, and feeling pretty good, or so she says," Shift replied.

"You don't believe her?"

"Yeah, I believe her. But she has a pretty high pain tolerance. 'Pretty good' to her could be awful to the rest of us."

"What do Marilyn, John and Angel think?"

"Anta's body is reacting to the additional dose of E-rase without complication and, as you know, the baby is still alive. So, they're hopeful."

"And the baby isn't showing any additional signs of contagion," John said, walking over to Mike's computer table.

"John," Shift said, "I am so glad you're helping out with this. I trust Angel and Marilyn, but *your* brain . . . well, you're probably the smartest man left alive."

"Ahhh, shucks," John said, feigning bashfulness. "But that isn't saying much, is it?" John smiled. So did Mike and Shift.

"Anyway, the baby looks good, at least as far as we can tell for such a small thing with a disease never before known to mankind."

"Well, I should go see her," Mike said.

"I'm sure she'd like that Mike," Shift replied. "Anyway, what are the stats man?"

"Again, it's hard to really pinpoint actual numbers, but we figure there's probably under one hundred Skins left alive anywhere in the world and not a single one alive in the northern hemisphere."

"That's amazing!" John said.

"Yeah, and I guess it makes sense that there would be none left in the north." Shift said. "The disease spread from Canada. If the Skins continued to mutate, to the point of death as we believe, then the place they started would be the first place they all died. The last place the Skins' plague hit would be the last place they died. So, the ones still alive, are they all in Africa?"

"Almost. There's a small group in Iran—maybe eight or nine of them. All the rest that we can see are in the southern countries of Africa. The Middle East and Africa were probably the last places the Skins went, and the last places to have many numbers of living humans when the Skins arrived. And now, it looks like they're the only places the Skins are still alive."

"You remember my theory that the Skins needed living human blood to survive?" John asked. "I think they are dying because there are no more humans to suck the life out of."

"That's as good a theory as any. But just how 'alive' are the rest of them?" Shift asked.

"They're all dying. There are a few in South Africa that look a little healthier, but they won't last long, I don't think. They look old, but not as old as those that have already died. Based on what we've seen with the deaths of the others, I don't think any of them will live more than a couple more weeks."

"I wonder what happened to Cain."

"We've looked for him a few different times," Mike said.

"And?"

"We found him this morning."

"Mike, you're killing me. Where is he? Dead? Alive?"

"He looks dead to me. And when he died, it looks like he was the only Skin left in Florida. It's like they all fled and left him there or something."

"Can we still see his body?"

"Yeah, let me find it. Hold on."

Others of the group had wandered in as Mike, John and Shift talked. The word was spreading. Anta and Marilyn were not among them.

"Since you're all here, let me tell you what Mike and his team have learned."

Shift proceeded to relate the conversation. When he was done, Mike said. "So, we found Cain. Here he is."

Every person in the group stared at the image on the screen. It was definitely Cain. He certainly appeared to be dead. His body had shriveled up like all the rest, but because his skin remained intact, like a few of the others, they could clearly see his features. There was no doubt.

44

"Alright Hasani," Jonas said through the Holo, "Start it up."

Jonas and Shift sat on the bridge of the ship. Hasani and Mike were in the Operations Center above the ship in the station. They had gone through all the manuals they could find and Shift had quizzed Jonas extensively on everything he may have heard Jerad say about operating the craft. They were ready to start it up.

Everyone else was gathered on the deck above the ship, watching intently. Since yesterday, when they had decided it was time to go home, everybody had been busy. There wasn't really much left to do on the moon, but some of them thought it would be appropriate to organize and make things tidy in case anyone ever came back to the International Station. None of them thought that was too likely.

The International Station was virtually worthless since the United States Shell had blown apart. Only the Mexican and English Shells had their own landing bays, and England's had never been cleaned of the dead. The Mexican Shell was an unknown. They hadn't explored it much. It was presumed that there were no dead bodies and thus, habitable at any time; but the shell was very small compared to the others. But, if anybody ever returned to the moon, it would probably be to one of those two Shells.

"Here it goes!" Hasani said excitedly as he keyed in the codes they had first located four months ago.

When the code sequence had been input, the ship quietly hummed to life. The sound was beautiful. Everyone cheered. Neirioui cried as she looked up at Hasani through the window of the Operations Center. He looked down at her and winked. "Let's go home," he mouthed. Neirioui blew him a kiss.

Within minutes, the whole group was onboard. As the ship began pre-flight maneuvers, Anta, resting comfortably in the lounge, entered the news of their successful start-up into the IIA Database. She knew that, on Earth, Marcus and Lin were anxiously awaiting news. They would be thrilled. Marcus seemed to have taken the news of other human life more casually than Anta had expected, but she could read the joy in Lin's words on the database.

"Is everybody ready to go home?" Jonas called through the ship's com system.

Answering for the group back in the lounge, Steve Porter answered, "Mr. Sampson, sir, we've been ready for a *very* long time. Take us back to Earth please."

Jonas touched screens and pushed buttons as he gently maneuvered the hovering ship to the starting block. Hasani, sitting between Jonas and Shift, started the port opening sequence. Within two minutes, the port had opened and the sweeping dark night was exposed to their view.

The ship's thrusters engaged and the ship rose into the air, shakily at first. Within a few moments, Jonas had it stabilized. Thirty seconds later it blasted out of the port to the wild and raucous cheers of thirteen very happy people. In the darkened lounge where most of them sat, Jon leaned over to Suvan and kissed her lips for the first time. Only Street saw it. He smiled. Suvan blushed, looking around nervously. But she had a feeling nobody on this ship would really be upset, not even her mother.

On the bridge, Jonas, Shift and Hasani checked and rechecked the systems to make sure Earth was their destination. Once they were sure, they went back to the lounge to be with the others. It was a time to be with their friends. It was also the time to begin planning their lives.

Anta was still recovering from the pain and turmoil of a few nights back, but she and her baby had both been cleared. As far as anyone could tell, after extensive testing, the baby in her uterus was now immune. The vaccine had worked, and with it, the hopes and dreams of several members of the group had surged. But they still didn't know what would happen when the baby was exposed to contaminated air upon his or her birth. And they wouldn't know for several more months. Plus, they didn't really know whether the air was still contaminated.

After three months on the moon, they were going home, headed for Florida. That's the place from which they had left Earth. It was the place they had some familiarity with. If they were going to land successfully, that was probably their best chance. Plus, a couple of them had some unfinished business with the body of Cain.

NOVEMBER 19
OVER CAPE CANAVERAL, FLORIDA
"Are we ready, Jonas?" Hasani asked.

"Yes, as long as there aren't any Skins on the ground waiting to eat us alive."

"Mike?" Hasani called through the holo.

"Yeah boss?"

"Stop calling me that. Anyway, Jonas and I just wanted one more confirmation that we aren't putting this ship down into a horde of Skins waiting to tear our flesh apart and gnaw on our bones. Can you confirm that we will be alone, please?"

"Yeah boss," Mike replied with a smile. "We will be alone. I checked a few minutes ago. The place is deserted except for the body of Mr. Cain."

"How about weather?" Hasani asked.

"A little cold, as expected for this time of year in Florida. However, no storm fronts and no water on the ground. We're good to go if you guys can figure out how to land this thing."

"Excellent! We'll try. Maybe you should come up here and show us how." Hasani's laugh brought a "Hmmph!" from Mike.

"Okay." Serious now. "Have everyone get in their seats please. We'll be landing very soon."

The small group of survivors sat in their seats in the lounge. They eagerly awaited the feeling of landing gear settling down upon the pavement.

"Alright everybody, about twenty seconds," Hasani said through the com system.

Twenty-one seconds later, the ship was hovering over the tarmac, coasting toward the gate from which they had hastily departed more than three months earlier. As they approached the gate, Jonas engaged the wheels which quietly lowered from the underside of the hull. They coasted the rest of the way to the gate and stopped without incident. They had arrived safely, but the apprehension of the small group was palpable.

From the computer bay, Mike turned on the outside monitors. The charging station was sitting as they had left it. The dry bones of the few Skins who had died falling from the ship as it departed littered the ground.

"Well people, should we get off?" Shift asked as they began to gather in the lounge. A couple people were already standing, but nobody moved toward the doors. It was time to leave the safety of the ship and brave the world outside, but their fear held them in place. They knew they were safe from A.E., but even though Mike had confirmed, over and again, that there were no Skins here, each of them still worried. The Skins were not to be taken lightly.

Over the past few days, Mike and the others had become confident that no Skin was left alive in North Am. The only ones they had seen moving about were far away in Africa and the Middle East. But that didn't mean they were all gone. Perhaps they were just in hiding. The group, hesitant to go outside the ship, finally drifted to the computer bay, where Mike was now sitting, looking at the world outside. Even though communications had been disrupted when they left, the power was still on. Mike had remotely connected to the camera systems on the base through USCAN.

On the various monitors set up in the bay, they could see the ship from the outside, the bones of the bodies of six Skins who had apparently fallen from the ship and died as it took off, the doors from which they had fled, Cain's body, and several other locations with only bones to show that people had once been there.

The views were depressing and terrible. The growing ease they felt looking at the Skins' dead bodies was quickly overwhelmed by a thickening sorrow that had slowly dissipated over the past few weeks on the moon. The stark reality of what they had come home to hit them.

"I can't stand to look at it anymore," Marilyn said quietly.

"It really is awful," Neirioui agreed.

The others shared the sentiments, but held their tongues.

After a few more minutes of watching the screens in silence, Street finally said, "Well, let's get out of here. I'm ready to go kick Cain's face in."

Nobody laughed, but a few felt some satisfaction in that thought.

"Maybe we should stay in here a day or two and watch the monitors, just to make sure we're alone," Steve suggested.

"I agree," Neirioui said.

"Are any of you so anxious to go out there that you can't wait another day?" Shift asked.

"It's probably a very good idea," Anta said.

Nobody rejected the idea.

"Then, let's set up monitor watches and relax a little. Get some sleep if you can," Shift said. "Mike, get the monitors set up to watch doors, hallways, large rooms, outside areas, whatever you can. Let's get them on a revolving basis and we'll all take turns watching for the next twenty-four hours. If no Skins show up in that time, we'll get out of here."

"Got it," Mike replied. "Do you want to turn the shuttle around in case we have to make a hasty retreat?"

"Not a bad idea. We'll point her into the wind and set up shop for a day. Weather looks like it will hold at least that long."

45

NOVEMBER 20, 2093
CAPE CANAVERAL, FLORIDA

"I think we should leave him alone," Anta said quietly as she reached over to hold Shift's hand. She squeezed his hand and looked up into his eyes. Her eyes were filling with tears. They were leaving the ship and Street and some of the others were anxious to have a visit with the dead Cain.

"What's wrong Anta," Shift said as he pulled her away from the group.

"I don't know."

"Can you feel Cain or something? He's dead, you know."

"Yeah, I know he's dead. Somehow, that saddens me. I have no idea why. It's like there's some connection between us that I can't explain."

"You've tried to explain it before, Anta, and told me you can't," Shift said. "I get it. Let's avoid him, okay?"

"That's a good idea, I think. But I don't want Street to touch his body either. Can we get everyone to stay away from him?"

"I don't know if we can. Cain is responsible for the deaths of many, many people. Some of our friends can't forgive that."

"I know," Anta replied. "I was just hoping they'd let it go. Maybe that's too much to ask for. Let me get far away though before it happens, okay. I don't want to feel anything or hear anything."

"Okay, I'll talk to Street. I love you Anta."

"I love you too."

After speaking with Street, Shift and Anta, along with some of the others, cautiously headed for the parking lot where they knew they would find their choice of hovers with which to leave the base.

Street, John, Mike and Angel headed down to ground level, directly beneath the terminal where the group had deplaned. Shift had convinced them to wait at least five minutes before disturbing the body. It hadn't taken much to persuade them. They each understood, in varying degrees, the 'relationship' between Cain and Anta. They respected her enough to let her get far away.

When five minutes had passed, the small group slowly approached Cain's body.

"Let me look at it first, gentlemen," Angel said. "I want to take some pictures and measurements and get some samples before you destroy the body."

With fascination equal to that demonstrated by Angel when they had encountered the first dead body so many months ago, Angel touched and prodded at the body. Street was fascinated too, but not with the body. It was amazing to watch the woman he loved—at least, he thought he loved her—react so curiously to the dead body of a Skin. Mike and John were disgusted.

"What are you doing?" Mike finally asked, holding his nose.

"What are *you* doin'?" Street asked Mike. "It don't even smell."

John and Angel both laughed as Angel stood up.

"Alright guys, I'm done. Let him have it."

Street approached Cain's body, his own body trembling with a mixture of trepidation and anger. His vehemence at this creature who had tormented his friends, especially Anta, had been pent up for a long time. Now was his chance to exact vengeance, even if Cain was already dead.

Street put his weight onto his left leg and brought his right leg back preparatory to swinging it into Cain's face. Cain suddenly struck out, grabbing Street's left leg, and yanking him to the ground.

"Ahhhhh," Street yelled as he began to kick Cain's head, and the shriveled arm that held him so tightly, with his free leg. Cain pulled Street closer.

John bolted over, pulling his gun as he ran. Cain and Street were rolling on the ground, with Cain clearly having the upper hand despite his weakened body. While Cain was not the creature he had previously been, he was clinging fiercely to Street's body, trying to sink his teeth into anything close enough.

John and Mike both maneuvered around the wrestling match, trying to find a place to shoot without injuring Street. Finally, John found an opening and slammed a foot down on the back of Cain's neck, cracking at least a couple vertebrae. But Cain continued to hold tightly to Street. John and Mike, still unable to safely get a shot off, took every opportunity to kick Cain instead. As the kicking continued, both Street and Cain began to loosen their holds. Each was getting tired. Cain's face became more and more unrecognizable as his features were smashed to pieces by the continual beating he was receiving. But he didn't let go.

Street's breathing became labored as he continued to wrestle. His strength was fading much more quickly than Cain's. Even though his face was severely beaten and swollen, Cain, now holding only Street's left arm, slowly dragged Street closer to his deformed mouth. That's when John got a clear shot and unloaded his gun into Cain's chest. Street relaxed, but Cain still moved. Street let out a blood-curdling scream as Cain's teeth sunk into the muscular flesh of his left hand. Then he passed out.

"What was that?" Shift asked, as the group stopped to listen to the sound of guns and screaming.

"That was human," Hasani replied, turning to face the direction from which they had just walked.

Shift and Jonas also turned, simultaneously, and the three began running back in the direction of the ship, pulling guns from holsters at their waists as they ran. The others followed closely on their heels. Moments later, the group rounded a corner to see Mike and Angel holding and comforting Street, who was lying on the ground cradling his hand. John was attempting to wrap a piece of bloody shirt around Street's wrist to act as a tourniquet.

"What happened?" Marilyn asked in a constricted voice, as she rushed over to help.

"Cain was alive," John said. "He was alive." His face dropped into his hands and he began to weep as the adrenaline began to wear off.

Mike crawled back as Marilyn bent down to help. Angel stood and took two steps backward before settling to the ground, sobbing.

Anta's face turned white as she stared at the mutilated body of Cain. She didn't recognize his face any longer, but she knew it was him. She actually felt his heartbeat slowly fade in his chest. Within seconds, Cain's heart stopped beating. Anta suddenly found it hard to breathe. Nobody was watching as she collapsed to the floor. The gun that she had been holding clinked on the concrete as it slid out of her limp hand. Everyone turned to look for the source of this new noise.

"Crap," Shift said, rushing to Anta. Others gathered around too.

"Her pulse is fine and she's breathing," Shift said after a quick evaluation. "It looks like she just passed out."

The relief in the faces and body language of the group was profound, and in moments, Anta's eyelids fluttered.

"Anta, can you hear me?" Shift asked as he gently rubbed Anta's shoulders and neck.

"Yeah Shift, I can. I'm fine. I think I just fainted."

"That's what it looks like. Is anything hurt? Is the baby okay?"

"I think everything's fine. How is Street?"

With that question, the group turned their attention, as one, back to Street and Marilyn kneeling on the ground next to him.

"He was bitten in the hand," John moaned.

Marilyn looked over Street's body quickly, commenting to herself, "Ok, it looks like it's just the hand; but with the speed at which we know A.E. travels through a body, if the bite is infectious, there's nothing we can do. Amputating his hand or arm won't help. Either he lives—human; or he dies, a monster." Her voice trailed off as she spoke those last words.

The group sat in silence for a few moments. Finally, Jon Porter spoke. "He won't die. He can't. Maybe the bad stuff is really weak, because Cain was almost dead." Then he cried. Suvan joined her hand to Jon's and wept with him. Jon slumped to the ground and Suvan lowered herself down too, wrapping her arms around his neck.

"I hope you're right," Steve said as he joined the kids on the ground, placing his hand on his son's shoulder.

"We can only hope and pray that is the case," Shift said. "Is that possible, John?"

On hearing his name, John shook his head swiftly back and forth, to clear away the fog that had formed since the attack. "It might be possible," he replied. "I hope so."

"Okay, since we don't know what's going to happen," Hasani said, "let's get the wound cleaned and bandaged. At the least, we can fight any potential infection, right?"

"Right. I'll do that," Marilyn said, more optimistically.

"Neirioui, can you come sit with Anta for a minute?" Shift asked.

Shift stood as Neirioui sat down next to Anta. He walked over to John and helped him up off the ground. "John, we need to figure this out. You and Angel are the only ones with any real knowledge about how A.E. works. Angel looks like she's in shock. Can we talk?"

"He was immunized from A.E.," John said quietly as they walked away. "But he wasn't immunized from Toronto's E-rase that turned everyone into monsters. You guys immunized tons of people who became Skins when they were attacked, even though they couldn't catch

A.E. We have no idea how that mutated form of E-rase progressed, or digressed over the months."

"What do you mean?" Shift asked.

"Even Toronto's E-rase immunized people from A.E., right? That's why everyone inoculated from A.E. with that version of E-rase lived. It changed them, somehow, into the Skins; but at least they lived. Then, everyone bitten, but not eaten by the Skins also changed into Skins, right?"

"Right, go on," Shift encouraged.

"So, based on what we've seen with the Skins, it seems probable that Toronto's E-rase first inoculated the people, but then continued to do something inside the recipients, transforming them into Skins. That mutation continued to progress, with the Skins becoming faster and stronger.

"Then, over the next few weeks, after we left here for the moon, we were able to watch them continue to progress, but that progression was more like aging. They seemed to be getting old very fast. As they got old, just like humans, they got weaker. That means that Toronto's E-rase didn't save them from death after all. It either changed the nature of the disease, or it only provided a small measure of protection from it."

"So what are you thinking? How's this going to turn out for Street?"

"Well, he shouldn't *die* right now, or in the next couple of weeks, if we can keep secondary infection away—who knows what germs were in Cain's mouth. The real problem is that he may become a Skin. But when the Skins got into our bunker in Boston, we saw how fast that transformation occurred after our friends were bitten. And remember when Andrew was attacked? The morphing was almost instantaneous. If Street's bite progresses like the others, the transformation should have already happened—he should already be a Skin. Since that didn't happen right away, maybe the process will happen over time and we can watch for it. Maybe he won't change at all, but if it occurs slowly, we can be prepared to take action."

"You mean kill him?"

"What else could we do Shift? If he turns into a Skin, he has to die or we could all die, right?"

"Yeah, you're right. But the thought of it sickens me," Shift replied.

"Well, let's hope it doesn't come to that. Maybe, because Cain was so weak . . . well, maybe, like Jon said, the disease inside him was weak too. Maybe Street will just get sick or something, if we're lucky. Or, even though the bite penetrated Street's skin, maybe no bacteria was transmitted because of the weak bite. I guess I really don't know."

"Do we need to restrain him just in case?" Shift asked.

"Good question," John replied. "It might be foolish not to. But since he didn't change right away, it seems more likely that it will occur, if at all, little by little over time."

"I guess we should tell the others about this little discussion."

"Okay."

John and Shift walked back over to the group. Angel had Street's head resting on her lap, stroking his forehead, and the others had stopped crying for the most part. Marilyn was holding Street's hand and cleaning it with disinfectant. Anta was sitting in a chair near the wall with Neirioui and Suvan each holding a hand. They all watched Shift and John walk up, anxiety and sorrow written on their faces.

John told them what he believed may occur. As the group processed the information, each had varying degrees of hope or misery. But the resolve was clear. When John was finished talking, he asked if there were any questions.

"How will we know what to do?" Jonas asked.

"I don't know. We'll have Angel and Marilyn monitor him."

"Do we need to restrain him?" Hasani asked.

"I don't want him to be restrained!" Angel said, choking back tears.

"We probably don't have a choice in that," Shift said.

"Is the same thing going to happen to Anta?" Jon asked, obviously thinking about Anta's tainted blood and the complications with the fetus.

"Good question Jon," John replied. "Anta's situation could be totally different. Other than her reaction to Cain's mental attacks—I'll call them that—we've seen no other indication of a reaction to the contamination, from the scratch she sustained months ago. We should hope that Street's response to this bite is as benign."

There were general nods and murmurs of approval. If they could help it, Street would live—as a human—and he would live for a very long time.

Marilyn had already cleaned and bandaged the wound by the time John completed his question and answer session. She had given him a shot of Ibuprofine and an antibiotic too. After the group's short discussion, Street began to wake. John told him his potential prognosis and the suggestion that he be restrained as a precaution. He was not pleased. Anger was etched into his face.

"That stupid . . ." Street said, clearly in pain. "If I turn, I'm going to kill myself and hunt him down on the other side. But until I turn, don't tie me down man."

John agreed that Street would not have to be restrained if he would agree to being confined for a few days and having his medical condition monitored by Angel and Marilyn. The unspoken implication was that if his condition deteriorated, he would be restrained, or worse.

46

"When will they be back?" Suvan asked her mother.

"Today; soon I hope," Neirioui replied.

The small group of survivors had set up camp in the dorms at Cape Canaveral. The dorms had housed many past pilots and astronauts. Their pictures and statements of their legacies adorned the walls in nearly every room and common space. It was a testament to what mankind could achieve, and a terrible reminder of how alone they were.

Over the past six days, two groups had left the base. Shift, Anta and Hasani had left for Juneau three days earlier. John, Steve Porter, and his son Jon had gone to Massachusetts to check out the farms where the first group had inoculated animals many months earlier. This second group was due to arrive back at the base, and Suvan couldn't wait to see Jon again. Without their MEHDS, the various groups had to rely on the Net, which was still operating, but was not always reliable. It wasn't as easy, so communication was infrequent and slow. Those that remained in Florida didn't know what the others were doing, or how they were faring.

"They're here," Mike said, leaning his head into the room where Neirioui and Suvan were talking.

Suvan jumped up from the bed where she had been lying and ran from the room. Her mother followed, slower. Her own excitement would be greater on the return of Hasani in a few days.

Suvan and Neirioui entered the common room just as John, Steve and Jon set their packs down. Suvan ran to Jon and enveloped him in a rather intimate bear hug. Suvan had recently turned fourteen years old, and was well on her way to womanhood. Jon was nearing fifteen, but the embrace by Suvan was a little uncomfortable, with his dad, and Suvan's mom so near. Steve and Neirioui carefully avoided looking in the direction of their children, but shared a knowing look.

"Well?" Mike asked. "What did you find?"

"We'll get to that. But how is Street?" John asked anxiously.

"He's great!" Angel replied. "He's still locked up; but it's been almost six days, and there's no sign of infection from either the wound itself, or the bite!"

"That's awesome!" Steve said. "That means he's probably in the clear, right? I mean, based on everything we know."

"Yes, I think so," Angel replied. "But we'll keep him locked up for a few more days. The guy is pretty pissy about it all, but I keep him company for as long as I can stand him each day."

The group laughed.

"So, tell us about the farms," Jonas said, redirecting the conversation.

"We visited all seven farms Shift had recorded. Every animal was dead at six of them. But we don't know whether those were the animals that had already died before you guys got there," John said, looking at Angel, "or whether they were the ones you vaccinated."

"The bodies were all stripped clean. Just skin hanging onto bones," Steve added. "So, unless the animals you inoculated left, they're dead."

"What about the other farm?" Marilyn asked.

"They were thriving!" Steve replied, a broad smile lighting his face. "It was the farm farthest away from any other human or animal population center. So, likely, A.E. arrived there, if at all, much later because there was so little contact with the outside world."

"Yeah, it was like A.E. was never even there," Jon added, attempting to insert himself into the adult conversation. "I mean, there were cows, chickens, pigs, sheep, horses. There was even a couple of llamas!"

"I forgot that it was you who took care of the animals in Cabo Rojo," Angel said, acknowledging Jon's input. "You may inherit yourself a farm, if you're not careful," she added, smiling.

The others laughed.

"How were the animals eating and drinking?" Marilyn asked. "Well, mostly, I wonder what the chickens and pigs ate. I get all the others."

"The chickens were all in a barn . . ." John began.

"Yeah, we put the chickens in the barn," Angel said. "And dumped the chicken feed all over the ground. We didn't know how long we'd be gone, but they had plenty, obviously, or they'd all be dead. And we put the pigs in the field with the orchard. There were lots of young trees there with fruit starting to grow low on the branches. We assumed that they may be very hungry for a while, but when the fruit matured, that might feed them. I guess we were right."

"Well, it's good that you found them before winter set in," Marilyn said. "What would they have eaten? What would any of them have eaten when the snow fell?"

"They would have died," John replied.

"Then I'm glad we made it home in time," Jonas said.

The news was good. They would have meat. Now they hoped they could live long enough to enjoy it.

NOVEMBER 26
NEAR JUNEAU, ALASKA

"Is this the right place?" Anta asked as they approached the cabin high in the snow-packed mountains, several kilometers east of Juneau.

"Well, it's the coordinates they gave us; and unless the Net's gone on the fritz, this has to be the place," Hasani replied, shivering even with the heater going in the hover. It wasn't usually quite so cold in November this far south. The windows were fogged and hard to see through, but the GPS coordinates brought them to this location. Having never been here before, that was all they had to rely on.

"Let's go knock," Shift said. "That'll probably scare the crap out of them."

"You two go ahead," replied Hasani. "I'm afraid if I let the hover shut down, we may not get it started again."

"Good idea Hasani. We'll try to be quick."

Marcus and Lin knew the group had landed in Florida. A post to the IIA Database confirmed the same. When Shift had asked for their address, it seemed kind of funny. Like friends were just coming for a visit and needed directions.

What Marcus and Lin didn't know, was that anyone was coming so soon. They had expected someone to show up to inoculate them at some point, but nobody had said when that would occur, because nobody knew how long it would take to get to Juneau and cellular communication systems were down.

Shift and Anta struggled along a slight depression in the snow that appeared to be a winding path, toward the front of a small, modern cabin tucked into the trees and half-covered by snow drifts. The cabin was constructed of dark brown, faux wood. Three large windows looked to the west over a small, wooded valley.

A picnic table was mostly buried under snow on the side of the cabin next to a small shed probably containing landscaping or gardening tools. From that table, its occupants would have had a beautiful view of the sea in the distance, but not on this day. A stiff breeze flowed through the bare trees, causing them to sway back and forth over their heads, and a dark sky above threatened more snow.

Shift raised his hand and gently rapped at the half-exposed door.

Shuffling sounds could be heard from inside. Something banged against the floor; perhaps a chair being knocked over.

"Startled them all right," Shift said with a smile.

After a few moments of silence, Anta began to feel a little guilty. "I'm going to call them. This isn't very nice."

Shift nodded.

"Hello in there! Marcus, Lin. It's us, Shift, Anta and Hasani, from the moon."

More noises, but this time the noises were less muffled and came toward the door.

"Who is it?" a female voice called out.

"Shift, Anta and Hasani, from the moon," Shift called out, laughing. "We've come to rescue you!" Anta joined his laughter. This was a joyous occasion, and Marcus' and Lin's trepidation would only last a few more moments.

A few seconds later, a male voice called out, "Can you prove it?"

"Um, not really," Shift replied. "What do you propose as proof?"

"I'm not sure really," said the man behind the door. "Maybe you could tell me what technology we used to dissipate the hurricane. Hasani asked me some questions about it through the database."

"Hasani is back at the hover, keeping it from freezing," Anta replied. "But he told me it was WDD, right? Wind dispersion and diffusion."

"That's right. Do you have the vaccine with you?" the male voice asked, getting right down to business.

"Yes, so it's safe to open the door," Anta replied.

"What about the Anthrax E? How do we keep from being contaminated?"

"Not a problem. If you receive the injection within the twenty-four-to-thirty-hour incubation period, there's no risk of contracting the disease."

The door hinges creaked as the door was pulled slowly open from the inside. Snow cascaded into the cabin from the drift. Two faces, healthy but nervous, looked out from the darkened room into the daylight outside. The faces on the outside were beaming as the two faces from the inside revealed that they were connected to heads and bodies, now crossing the threshold into the suffused light from the overcast sky.

Marcus and Lin hadn't been outside in a very long time, and they had kept the drapes closed most of the time, fearing that the monsters that had roamed down in Juneau might come around and see them. As their eyes adjusted to the natural light, they backed up to allow Anta and Shift to lumber into the cabin, stomping snow off their boots and wiping it from their clothing. Marcus and Lin were quickly wrapped in hugs from the two strangers, saviors really.

"I can't believe you're really here!" Lin said excitedly as the crush of hugs began to lighten.

"I really believed this day would never come," Marcus added. "We are so glad to see you. How many doses do you have with you?"

Anta wondered at Marcus' question, but she let the thought slip away as Shift spoke.

"Enough for the two of you," Shift said as he pulled a small rubber pouch from the pack on his back. "Time to inoculate! I hope you're ready!"

"Oh yes, we're ready. So very, very ready," Lin replied, rolling up her sleeve. Then she walked back into the small cabin, leaving the path clear for the others to follow.

"We should close the door," added Marcus, with a laugh as he looked at the pile of snow in the doorway. "And let's eat. You guys look like you could use a rest. But let's get this over with first," he added, pulling up the sleeve of his t-shirt.

"Yes to everything," Shift replied. "But Hasani is still in the hover . . ."

"Oh, yes. We can solve that little problem. But I don't really want to go out there without the shot first."

"I don't blame you," Shift replied. "Come sit down."

After Marcus and Lin had received injections, Marcus walked back to the front door and picked up a long cable and some equipment on the floor. "It's a little old-fashioned, but it still works."

"What is it?" asked Anta.

"It's a portable electric engine warmer," Lin responded as Marcus handed the equipment to Shift and went for his winter gear. "They've been used, in one form or another, for a couple hundred years in Alaska."

After pulling his winter coat and gloves on, Marcus took the heater from Shift and headed out the door with Shift trailing him. They soon returned with Hasani, all three laughing at something that was said, to find the snow cleared from immediately in front of the doorway, with a rough slope cut for access. They entered the cabin to find the women warming water on the stove and setting food out on the table.

The small group shared a pleasant, simple meal. Both groups shared their stories. They all laughed, and cried. Finally, several hours later, Marcus and Lin showed the others to the spare bedrooms. Neither Marcus nor Lin could sleep. Tomorrow, they would be leaving this temporary home and traveling into the world. For the first time, they would see, first-hand, the extent of the damage caused by A.E.

After Lin finally dosed off, well past midnight, Marcus opened the com port on his watch.

They're here, he typed, *we'll be leaving in the morning.*

How many doses do they have with them? he read in response.

I don't know. They wouldn't say.

Then stay close to them.

NOVEMBER 30
CAPE CANAVERAL, FLORIDA

"It's so good to see you again," Neirioui said quietly to Hasani after most everyone else had gone to their respective beds for the night. "Those people seem very nice."

"Yes. We're lucky to be part of such a wonderful collection of people, aren't we?" Hasani replied.

She scooted closer to Hasani and slipped her hand into his. "I've been wanting to do this for a very long time," she said as she leaned closer and parted her lips.

Hasani closed the gap and their lips met for the first time.

47

"Get those stupid animals into that train!" Street yelled above the cacophony of noise surrounding the men.

"I'm trying," John yelled back. "Shift, you gonna help, or what?"

"Dude, I've only got two hands man. This little prodder thing isn't working."

"Gentlemen," Jon Porter yelled over the noise, "this isn't really that hard. For guys that outlived A.E. and the Skins, you three are such wimps."

Jon smiled as the three men laughed and tried a little harder. The day was bright and beautiful, if not a little chilly. But the fresh air of the countryside, away from the smells of the corpses that littered the cities and towns, was wonderful. Jon tucked his chin into the top of his coat to keep it warm as he moved from side to side, herding the animals.

Six weeks earlier, the group left Florida and traveled by hover to the one farm in Massachusetts where John, Steve and Jon had located the previously-inoculated and living farm animals. Various members of the group had traveled to and from the farm in the two and half months since the discovery. Now, they were all living there, tending to the animals. But there wasn't enough room.

A decision had been made to move their plantation from Massachusetts to Boise, Idaho. They wanted to be closer to the

California coast, in farm country with plenty of water and room to grow. Since that time, a couple different plans had been made, then scratched, for transporting the cows across the country. The best plan, the one they were currently attempting, was to just remove the seats from a mag train and push all the cows on board. Sure, the train would be ruined, but there wasn't really much use for it these days. They would come back for the other animals later.

The real problem had been herding the animals the nine miles from Queen Lake to the station in Athol. Street, Shift, John, Jon and Suvan had taken on the assignment. The others were already on their way to Boise to find a permanent home. Dr. Jonas Sampson had been to Boise for business a couple dozen times—mostly to lecture at Boise State University. So, he knew the area a little. Well, he knew where the best bars were; or at least, where they had been.

"So, are we going to make it today, or what?" Jon called out.

"You're such a hardass," Suvan said, smiling, as she watched Jon lecture the grown men.

"Well, I've got to be with these clowns, don't I?"

MARCH 25
BOISE, IDAHO

"Okay boss, where do we start?" Hasani asked Jonas as they pulled up to a service station at the eastern edge of Boise, not far from the Boise International Airport.

Like almost every other town and city across the northern United States through which they had traveled, Boise's infrastructure was largely intact, and its buildings whole. But A.E. had consumed the human population and most of the animals too. The Skins had probably caused their fair share of chaos in Boise too.

In every town, the evidence of death was visible in the homes and buildings they passed. Dry bones were strewn across lawns and parking lots, and rotting clothing and trash was pressed against walls and fences where the wind had left it. Boise was no different.

"Well, I know there's good farmland on the other side of town," Jonas said. "A place called Sunny Slope. That's where I want to go, just to check it out. If it isn't any good, there are a few small towns up in the hills above Boise, but they probably get more snow than we'd like in the winter."

"Sunny Slope sounds like a nice place," Neirioui said.

"It certainly *was* a nice place before A.E. Some of the students and faculty from Boise State would go fishing on the Snake River that runs right along the base of the hills. I joined them a couple times. It was a peaceful little place. The suburbs hadn't expanded that far when I was there last. If that's still the case, Sunny Slope promises to be a pretty great place!"

"Off we go then," Hasani replied.

MARCH 26
BOISE, IDAHO

"How are we supposed to get to this place?" Shift asked. "We're not herders you know."

"That's what I hear," Anta replied, her voice betraying the smile on her face.

Shift and Anta were talking on a telephone—a land line connected to a small, old café in Boise. When Anta and the others had arrived at Sunny Slope, Mike found a farmhouse with the landline still connected, then traced the line digitally up the network until he located the phone numbers of both the farmhouse and the café where Shift and the others were waiting, near the train station.

Anta had sent Shift an old-fashioned email yesterday morning, which Shift received on an old smartphone connected to the wifi at the train station in Athol. Even though cellular communications were down, the Net was working just fine for now, and so was wifi, at least in some places.

"You've got to take the train out to a place called Caldwell. From there, it's about a ten-mile trek across mostly farmland. If you stay on the paved roads, the traveling should be much easier."

"Can you send some people out to help us herd? Getting these stupid animals to the train in Athol was no picnic."

"Sure, we can be there in ten minutes. How much time do you need?"

"I don't know. Give us forty-five. Thanks babe!"

MARCH 26, LATER
SUNNY SLOPE, IDAHO

"This will definitely work," Shift said as he gazed out over the grassy farmland that gently sloped down to the Snake River. He and Anta were standing on top of a small rocky bluff that overlooked the river, watching the sun set in the west. An iron cross was planted firmly in concrete at the top of the rise next to them. It was rusted and dented, but still held firm. A plaque called the hill "Lizard Butte". A diminutive engraving at the bottom of the plaque, attributed to someone whose name had been scratched out, said: "Your destination is where your next journey begins."

On the land all around the hill, apple, pear, cherry, apricot and peach trees were choked with the first blossoms of spring. Farms with large gardens that needed tending were dotted sporadically along the sides of the few dirt roads leading off the main highway through town. White picket fences and rock walls encircled vast patches of grassy grazing land, just now beginning to green in the warmth of the spring sun. The river was wide, filled to the brim with the run-off from winter snows from as far away as Two Oceans Plateau in western Wyoming, a distance of more than four hundred miles.

Across the river to the southwest, the small town of Marsing, with its various shops and stores, looked like a dream in the dying light. While it had never been a large or wealthy town, recent gold strikes in the Owyhee mountain range to the south of town had led to several beautification measures and the construction of several boutique hotels and posh homes throughout the area. They would need to visit the town soon to see what supplies remained. Less than a mile away, it would probably become the center of their new home.

"It's beautiful, isn't it?" Anta said, absentmindedly rubbing her swollen belly.

"Absolutely! Have you got us a house picked out yet?" Shift asked.

"No. I wanted to do it together."

"That's a great plan!"

48

"Shift, get Marilyn! It's time!" Anta called out through the back door of the small farmhouse in which they had made their home.

Shift was in the garden, pulling weeds. Over the past three months, he had repaired fences, built a small barn, planted a garden, and learned how to tend chickens, at least well enough that he wouldn't kill them accidentally. This new life was a lot of work, but he was happy.

"What? Now? It's too early!" Shift called back.

"Just get her please. Everything will be fine."

Twenty minutes later, Marilyn and every other person in the small community of Sunny Slope had arrived at Shift and Anta's home. A baby was going to be born. He was coming early. Each person there, especially Anta, was nervous and afraid. But they were also excited. This was the moment they had been waiting for.

Although others had become romantically involved over the past few months, nobody had dared to conceive a child. Today, or soon, they would know whether human life would continue. Within hours, they hoped, they would know their fate.

"Please back up," Marilyn said.

"Yeah, seriously people. Don't you have any respect for Anta's privacy?" Street added, glaring at the small crowd crushing each other in the doorway of the bedroom.

"Uh, Street, you too buddy," Shift said carefully. "You should probably leave the room too."

"Oh, yeah, I guess so. Sorry Mayor. Sorry Anta."

"No problem, Street," Anta said, smiling.

"I'll be right out here, on crowd control. Nobody will bother you until you say so."

"Thanks dude," Shift said. "And stop calling me Mayor."

"I'll stop calling you that after I beat you in the next election," Street replied, smiling.

Four and a half hours later, the silence in the small farmhouse was broken by the healthy wail of a baby boy, muffled by the heavy wooden door separating the two rooms. The group erupted, many of its members jumping to their feet and heading toward the bedroom door. It wasn't as if they didn't understand the privacy issue. The excitement and anxiety was just too great.

Street blocked the door. "Don't get any closer," he growled.

They backed away, but the voices didn't die down for a while. Twenty-five minutes later, the bedroom door opened and Marilyn stepped out, closing the door quietly behind her.

All voices quieted. The room was silent.

"He is healthy, for now," Marilyn said, "but John and Angel will now take his blood over to the lab for analysis."

"We should know within the hour," John said as he walked toward the front door holding a small vile filled with the blood of the new infant. Angel followed.

Even though John had tested the baby's blood several times before he was born, everybody knew that this was different. All prior tests monitored the baby's continued fight against the deficient E-rase produced by Toronto which Anta had received via a small cut in her finger during that first battle with the Skins. The baby was easily winning that fight, just as Anta had.

Now, however, the baby had breathed air. They knew, from testing done just two weeks earlier, that A.E. was still floating around in the air at Sunny Slope, and, they supposed, everywhere else too. Now that the baby had taken that contaminated air into its lungs, and thus, into its bloodstream, they could test the blood to see if Dr. Shevchuk's vaccine, injected months earlier, was able to fight A.E. and win. If so, testing would continue for several more months just to be sure.

Over the next fifty-two minutes, only whispers were heard in the living room of the small farmhouse. The people gathered there had each stood, at varying times, and left the room to get fresh air, only to return to await the results that John had promised nearly an hour earlier. Even though only ten people occupied the small living room, the air was stuffy and claustrophobic.

Finally, fifty-nine minutes after they had left, John and Angel returned to their anxious friends. Street knocked on the bedroom door and called to Marilyn. She opened the door to allow Shift and Anta to hear the conversation.

The air was silent and still. The humidity in the small living room was suffocating. Even with the air conditioner running on high, sweat trickled down faces and backs. Time moved very slowly as John unfolded the piece of paper he was holding. A fly landed on the sheet of paper and he absentmindedly brushed it aside with his hand.

Hasani clasped Neirioui's hand tightly. Jon and Suvan, sitting across the room, also held hands. Angel stood, walked over next to Street by the bedroom door, and wrapped her arms around his wide waist. Mike couldn't stop his knees from shaking.

Anta, lying in the bed in the adjacent room, held her new baby, Yurgi, against her breast as Shift smoothed down her disheveled hair. Not since that wonderful day, over thirteen months earlier, when Dr. Yurgi Shevchuk had announced the successful creation of a vaccine, had they been this nervous and excited.

"Hey," John began, not quite as eloquently as Dr. Shevchuk had begun so long ago, "we have the results." John's face was a mask. His emotions, whatever they were, were not visible—just the way he had planned it.

A few seconds later, John continued, "we have a healthy, wonderful baby! The vaccine is fighting A.E. just as we had hoped!" Then he smiled, that contagious smile that everyone loved.

Just as many of them had done over a year earlier in that lonely bunker near Boston, the group celebrated. Street provided high fives and butt slaps to most everyone in the group. Shift leaned over to Anta and kissed her lips. His tears fell onto Anta's cheeks, mixed with hers, and then dripped onto the forehead of baby Yurgi.

At the back of the room, hidden behind several others who were celebrating the glorious news, Marcus typed into his watch: "It worked. The baby will live." Then he touched the "send" icon.

SEPTEMBER 20, 2094—SHIFT

Baby Yurgi is three months old. His health is fine. Our family is happy. Our people are happy. We have food, water, health and safety. While loved ones are missed horribly, each of us finds peace in knowing that we are a part of the epic story of the continuation of human life on Earth.

Yurgi won't be alone either. He will have a cousin. Neirioui is pregnant. Hasani, my new brother, is thrilled. We all are.

Life may be hard, but only as hard as it has been over the past few months. We're still working on maintenance issues with electrical power, home heating and other technologies. We don't know how long the Net will continue working, but there are tons of books online and we are downloading and printing everything we think we will need in the future. There is still a question about how other newborns will respond to A.E. Anta's case was a little unique. It's hoped that, unlike baby Yurgi, whose mother's blood had been contaminated, future children will be born immune as a result of the inoculations of their mothers. If not, however, we may need to reproduce the vaccine for future generations.

We will continue to rebuild. People will again populate the Earth, but it will be a slow process. At least we know, finally, that life will continue.

49

"Happy Birthday dear Yurgi. Happy Birthday to you!"

Sitting on his mother's lap at a picnic table on the deck in the backyard of the Bader's small home, little Yurgi Bader bent over his chocolate cake and blew hard, just like his mom had shown him earlier that morning. The lone candle shifted in the soft breeze and went out.

"You did it!" Anta said, squeezing her son tenderly. A happy smile lit his small, one-year-old face as everyone around the table clapped and cheered.

"Happy Birthday son," Shift said, bending down to kiss him on the forehead.

Anta and her husband, Shift, had cried tears of joy twelve months earlier, the day Dr. John Silitzer and Dr. Angel Robertson walked into the front room of Shift and Anta's new home with the test results of their newborn son's blood. The others had cried with them. Life would continue.

Since then, two other children had been born, immune to the effects of A.E., and were now each as healthy as the last. Neirioui Safar and Hasani Chalthoum had a beautiful little girl ten months after Yurgi was born, followed a week later by another girl to Mr. Threet "Street" Kimball and Angel Robertson.

Now, the group had eighteen.

While birthday cake was cut and passed around, Yurgi hopped off his mother's lap and wandered over to a shady spot on the deck where his future playmates, Sami Chalthoum and Echo Robertson, lay side-by-side in a small portable crib. They were no fun. Moments later, Yurgi wobbled away on unsteady legs to chase the chickens who had carelessly sauntered into the yard again.

The day was beautiful. In fact, life was beautiful. Though the devastating effects of A.E. were still felt and seen everywhere they went, new life had revealed itself again during the group's second spring in Sunny Slope. The cattle and other animals, shipped by train across the country over a year earlier, had thrived on the grassy hillsides.

A few baby animals had been born again this spring, immune, just like Echo and Sami. There had been no need to inoculate the new arrivals.

Pigs lazed about, enjoying the warmth of the sun on their pink skin after the previous night's thunderstorm; and chickens produced eggs in abundance. The copious fruit trees of Sunny Slope continued to produce more than enough for the small group's needs.

"Yurgi! Do you want some cake?" Anta called from the small porch.

"Yes!" he squealed. He stood slowly and tottered back from where he had sat down to play with a dandelion.

"Shift," Street began as he pulled his friend away from the group, "It's time we went down to Brazil."

"Yeah, it probably is," Shift replied. "Anta has dreaded this, but I don't see how we can keep putting it off."

Six days earlier, the computer in Mike Petrovsky's lab had registered noises—static mostly—coming from somewhere in Rio de Janeiro, Brazil. Mike spent hours slowing down and speeding up the recording, trying to hear any sound beyond the static. Finally, he heard one word: "Idaho." After numerous failed attempts to speak with anyone by whom that word may have been uttered, and reviewing scratchy and unreliable feeds from USCAN, Shift decided they would need to investigate in person.

Mike had not been able to pinpoint the exact location from which the word had emanated, nor had he been able to determine who, or what, had said the word. But the noise had come from somewhere near the center of the city.

Mayor Shift Bader kept a large quantity of the original doses of E-rase, the vaccine that had ensured this small group's survival, under lock and key in a safe room at his home. For the past two years, nobody but Anta, Shift and his friend, Dr. John Silitzer, had access to the safe room. They didn't know whether they would ever need the vaccine again, but if they did, it was available. The vaccine had been in the cooled safe room, untouched, for over a year, save for monthly testing to ensure its continued potency; but if, or when they went to Brazil, they would take the vaccine with them.

Now, despite some trepidation about leaving the group, Street was getting restless. He finally gathered the nerve to speak to Shift about it, while Anta was busy with her guests.

"*If* you go, who do you want to go with you?" Shift asked.

"That's easy," Street replied. "You and Jon."

"Jon? You think Steve, or Suvan, would actually sanction that?"

"Hey, he's his own man, right? He's not a kid anymore, and I trust him with my life. So, yeah, that's who I want to go."

Jon was definitely not a kid anymore. At seventeen years old, Jon Porter stood an imposing six foot three inches in height and weighed nearly 210 pounds. His strength had grown tremendously as he farmed the land around Sunny Slope. And he was not afraid. Of all the adults in the group, Jon had been the only one in favor of conducting long-range searches for human survivors after their arrival in Sunny Slope. When they first arrived in Sunny Slope, at just fifteen years old, he had pushed the group to go looking for survivors on several occasions. And he, along with Neirioui and Suvan Safar, were the only people known to be naturally immune to A.E.

Now, he carried a lot of weight, both politically and physically. His opinions mattered. And the people loved him. But Suvan Safar loved him most. And Jon loved her back; at least, he thought it was love.

"If you can convince Steve, and Suvan, to let Jon go, then I can probably convince Anta to let me go. But you, my friend, may have the most difficult time. Angel is one tough mother. So, good luck with that."

Street laughed. He loved his wife. And she *was* one tough mother, as of two months earlier. Even though Echo was born healthy, the birth nearly took Angel's life. Dr. Marilyn Swenson believed that any other person would have succumbed to the loss of blood that Angel suffered in those first few hours after Echo's birth. But not Angel. She had a daughter to raise, and a man to love, for the first time in her life. She was not going to let that come to an abrupt end; especially not after surviving A.E., the Skins and a trip to the moon.

Angel's intensity and fire continued to push her to greatness. Her home was the finest in the community; and her garden was thriving beyond expectations. She even had Mr. Threet "Street" Kimball wearing clothing other than tank-tops and jeans. She was respected in the small community and loved for her passion. And Street adored her. She was the mother he never had, the friend he'd always wanted, the lover he'd dreamed about, and the mother of his child. Above all, that was the thing that mattered most. Echo was a beautiful girl, just like her mother, and Street was wrapped around her finger.

But Street knew he would have no difficulty convincing Angel that it was time to go. He and Angel had spent the last three nights discussing this very topic. Her fascination with the effects of A.E. so many years ago had worn off. She wanted Street to go. She would miss him, but she was smart enough to know that they had a responsibility to find anyone still living and help the human race survive. But Shift didn't know that.

"Okay boss, I'll work on Angel, and I'll talk to Jon. You go do your job and get Anta to agree. It's time to go."

"Alright, but I'll wait until the party's over to talk to her, if that's okay with you. I'd like a piece of cake."

"Sure boss," Street laughed.

Shift smiled as he walked over to Yurgi who was sitting in a high chair at the table, frosting all over his little face. He held his hands out when Yurgi turned to look at him. Yurgi smiled and giggled when he saw his daddy. The future looked bright. It was a new world—one full of promise and hope.

EPILOGUE

"Is everything ready?" Shift asked. Lilly, sitting next to him in the cockpit of the small plane, turned her head to look at Shift.

"Yes. Ten seconds to lift off. Will you tell the folks back there to make sure they're buckled?"

Shift leaned back and twisted his head so he could see the eight other people in the rear of the plane. "Buckle up everyone. We're out of here in a few seconds."

Lilly pushed the throttle forward. The plane was old, and still ran on fuel, but she had figured out how to pilot the craft. As she moved the plane out onto the runway at the Carlos Jobim International Airport, past large ships and smaller jets that had been sitting idle for more than two years, a tear formed in the corner of her eye. She wiped it away with the back of her hand and then pushed the throttle all the way forward.

The airport sat on the western edge of a small island in Guanabara Bay. While the exterior of the buildings on the grounds appeared well-preserved, the tarmac at the large airport was rutted and cracking. Roots from Guapeba trees and other plants had spread across and under the tarmac in several places, causing upheavals in the once-flat airstrip. Prior to their flight, the small group had walked the runway and cleared the plants and roots that crossed the path their plane would take, but it was still precarious. They had marveled at the damage which had occurred in just two and a half years of disuse.

The small plane lurched once, twice, and then began a swift acceleration. It bumped over cracks and gouges in the concrete runway, but finally left the ground. Shift exhaled, releasing the breath which he had involuntarily been holding.

"Whoa," Shift groaned from the co-pilot seat as the plane began a steep ascent from the hot tarmac. He wasn't serving any function sitting in front with Lilly, but the plane only held ten people, including a pilot and co-pilot. He had eagerly volunteered to sit up front with Lilly. Now, as the ground began to drop away, his stomach tightened and he had to close his eyes. He had never flown on a plane this small.

"I'm going to keep it low so I can follow landmarks," Lilly said. "Probably only four or five hundred meters off the ground. I don't know any other way to get us to Idaho."

"That's fine with me," Shift replied, holding his stomach.

Less than ten minutes into the flight, Street called up from the back. "Do you guys hear that noise? Is that the plane?"

All talking ceased as people strained to hear what Street had heard. Lilly checked her gauges. Everything looked fine there. Several people looked out the windows. The sound seemed to be coming from outside the plane.

"Oh crap," Jon said moments later. "Is that Franconi's ship?"

"Woah" Nic called out, looking in the direction Jon was pointing. "He's headed straight for us."

"Evasive maneuvers Lilly," Shift said. "If that's even possible in this thing."

"I'll try to . . ."

Lilly's words were cut off as a loud explosion rocked the rear of the plane. The plane dropped instantly, nose down, toward the ground. It began to spin as the left wing separated from the main body of the ship.

"Hold on to something!" Lilly yelled as she attempted to level out the plane before impact with the ground.

Within moments, the ship crashed through the dense upper canopy of the Tinguá Biological Reserve north of Rio de Janeiro. As it broke through sinewy vines stretching between Murumuru palms and other large trees, pieces of the plane severed off, leaving a trail of debris 250 meters into the undergrowth. Fire engulfed the rear of the small plane as it finally came to rest in a small clearing.

A loud explosion brought Shift to consciousness. He had no idea how long they'd been on the ground, but he could hear fire crackling nearby and smoke filled the cabin. Lilly sat next to him, still buckled into the pilot seat. A thick branch had smashed through the front window and impaled her chest. Blood pooled on her lap and ran down her legs and onto the floor of the plane. She wasn't breathing. Shift knew he had to help the others—unless it was already too late.

PREVIEW: NOW WE SURVIVE

The Cuban sat alone in the dark room, sweat dripping down his spine. His white cotton shirt clung to his bulky midsection, even as his stomach grumbled in anticipation of his next meal. His third cigarette had burned down to its filter and he pressed it into the ash tray on the table beside him. The humidity and smoke in the small room was suffocating; but he had to tell the story. The world had to know what happened. The guilt was tearing him apart.

After several long minutes, the old intercom system crackled to life.

"Good morning sir, could you please verify your name?"

"No. I told you I wouldn't say who I am. My name stays out of this."

"That's fine," the voice replied.

"And don't turn on the lights," the Cuban added. "If my face is shown, I'm as good as dead."

"I understand. I also understand you have some information concerning the destruction of Gortari II yesterday. Is that correct?"

"I do. I know everything about it."

After a short pause, the voice coming through the intercom system said, *"Why don't you start from the beginning."*

"Okay. About two weeks ago, I was contacted by a high-ranking official within the IWO. He solicited my help with a project that would, as he said, help Cuba peacefully assimilate into the greater world society. He told me that my help would be invaluable. I asked him why he thought I would want Cuba to assimilate into the IWO. He said he had an extensive background portfolio on me and threatened that if I didn't cooperate, he would disclose my background to Cuban authorities."

"Did that worry you?"

"I'm not going to talk about that. My background has nothing to do with this. Anyway, I agreed to help and then didn't hear from him again until yesterday."

"What did you hear yesterday from this IWO official?" the voice asked.

"He asked me to help shoot down Gortari II. He said that . . ."

The Cuban stopped speaking as a quiet sound arose from the other side of the door to the small room. It sounded like a ticking clock, but he hadn't heard one of those since his childhood.

Suddenly, a violent crash filled the air and the heavy, metal door flew from its hinges, crashing against the table at which the Cuban sat. The table shattered, a sharp wooden edge cutting the Cuban's leg, the blood dripping to the floor.

Light poured into the room from the hallway. The light was so bright, and the man's senses were so dulled from the explosion, that he couldn't see anything more than the shape of a human figure standing in the doorway.

The figure approached the frightened man. As the figure neared, the Cuban could see that a mask covered the stranger's entire head. The stranger lifted his arm and stuck the cold barrel of a gun to the Cuban's forehead.

"Wh-what are y-you d-doing?" the Cuban stammered.

"This is from our mutual friend," the man replied quietly. "He said you need to stop talking."

The stranger pulled the trigger and the Cuban fell to the floor, dead. A wisp of smoke rose from the barrel of the gun as the stranger fled.

JULY 7, 2093—YEDIÖREN, TURKEY

"Run girls," Hasan Tabak yelled, as the monster dug her teeth into the soft flesh of his thigh. *"Run!"*

It was unclear how it had happened, but the Skins—that's what the Americans had called them during a hasty conference call a few days earlier—had found them. The small research team was secluded in an underground bunker in the hills on the western shore of Çamlıdere Baraj Gölü, a large man-made lake 90 kilometers north of Ankara, Turkey. Not only had the Skins located them underground, but they had actually found a way in. Now, the scientists and politicians that had hidden there for so long, believing they were safe from Anthrax E, were rapidly falling to the terrible ferocity of the monsters.

"Dad!" Sena screamed as her father fell to the ground. Within moments, he stopped thrashing and became completely still. Then the woman, or whatever she was, lifted her head and stared at the two young girls. She cocked her head to the side, but made no further movements. They had heard reports from others around the world that the Skins attacked, unprovoked and without thought. They had also heard, however, that some of the women were less brutish. Now, in this place, this lone female hesitated.

"Move slowly," Sena whispered, gently tugging the hand of her sister. "Very slowly. Don't lose eye contact. Whatever you do, keep your head up."

"Okay," Dilan whispered in reply, her voice shaking from fear.

The tears that had formed in Dilan's eyes almost instantly when their father was attacked moments earlier had already dried up. Sena could not believe that Dilan had already overcome the grief, but certainly, her fear was stronger than any sorrow she could possible feel at that moment. Sena knew, because she felt the same way.

The girls slowly backed away from the monster still staring at them. Behind the naked woman, others continued to tear down doors, hungrily seeking out the remaining humans. Sena did not point it out to her sister, but she could see some of their friends rise from the floor in the distance and join the pursuit. For now, however, only one Skin was paying them any attention.

They continued their slow, methodical retreat toward the main entrance to the bunker. Their progress was cut short when Sena ran into the sealed doorway to the decontamination chamber. She knew exactly where she was and slowly reached up to her left, just above her shoulder, and touched the keypad.

The sound from the doors opening awakened the Skin. In a mad rush, she screamed as she practically flew toward the girls. They jumped back into the chamber and Sena slammed her hand into the keypad on the other side just before the Skin reached them. The door closed on the woman's hand and wouldn't close the rest of the way. As Dilan cowered in a far corner of the chamber, the nearly-naked flesh of the bloody woman slammed into the outside wall of the chamber over and over again.

Sena looked around and grabbed the only weapon she could find, an oxygen tank used with the protective suits that were stored just inside the bunker from the decontamination chamber. With fear spiking her adrenaline, Sena beat at the hand of the screaming woman with the metal cylinder until the hand severed from the woman's wrist and fell to the floor. Sena gagged as she watched the fingers on the detached hand twitch thrice as the door closed the rest of the way. Then the machines began to swirl around the girls, decontaminating them before opening on the other side.

AUTHOR'S NOTE

Thank you for reading *Tomorrow We Rise!* I hope you enjoyed reading the story as much as I enjoyed writing it.

As with so many products for sale today, much of what drives future sales are positive reviews from people like you. If you have a couple of minutes, I would appreciate your honest feedback through a product review on Amazon. It's easy: just login to Amazon.com and click on the "Orders" tab. Then, find my book and click on the button that says "Write a Product Review".

If you didn't purchase the book through Amazon, but would still like to leave a review, search for the name of the book(s) on Amazon's website. Click on the book's title then scroll down to the Customer Reviews section. Click on "Write a Customer Review". You can leave a separate review for each of the three books in the series.

Thanks again!

I wrote *Tomorrow We Rise* because I wanted to see what might become of people after a crisis ends. I've read too many books that end just as Book 1 (*Today We Die*) ends. The vaccine is created. Life will continue. Hurray! But then what? Few books go on to explain the "then what" of a tragedy.

So, I wrote it.

Tomorrow We Rise may not be the final chapter in mankind's struggle for survival, but it gave me an opportunity to explore what life might be like when the population of the world shrinks to near zero. The third and final book of The Killing Sands series—*A New World*—

will attempt to bring the story full circle. I hope you'll read it too. I don't want to leave anyone hanging.

As with *Today We Die*, in writing *Tomorrow We Rise* I utilized the skills of many people. My dad, Steve Wilde spent many hours helping me edit and polish *Tomorrow We Rise*, at the same time as writing his own book. Of course, he's retired, so he has a bit of time on his hands. ☺

Ron Beach, Jamie Richens Kirkham, Susan Niedert and Jacob Cooper again provided valuable reviews, edits, financial support, emotional support, and occasional kicks in the butt when I messed up.

Finally, my wife (Chandi) and my daughter (Sage) accompanied me to the Bahamas where I took the photograph for the cover of *Tomorrow We Rise*. They suffered through a terribly sunny and peaceful trip. It was quite the sacrifice.

ABOUT ME

I'm sure nobody really wants to read about me again—I'm not that interesting. But just in case I'm wrong, or you didn't find the time to read about me after reading *Today We Die*, please read on.

I grew up in Taylorsville, a suburb of Salt Lake City, Utah. My teenage years were spent skiing, golfing, mountain biking, hiking, camping and dating. After high school, I spent two years in Scotland on a service mission. During college, I met and married Chandi, and we started a family.

I graduated from the University of Utah with a bachelor's degree in mass communications in 2003—Go Utes! Since my only job prospects with a degree in mass communications included writing obituaries and teaching mass communications to others, I went to law school in San Diego, California. Boogie boarding became my favorite pastime. I graduated from law school in 2007 and was offered a very nice job at a small firm in St. George, Utah, in the southwest corner of the state. Now, I practice law in both California and Utah.

My family and I have lived in St. George for ten years now. It's hot and incredibly scenic here and my life couldn't be better. I'm a husband and a father of six. My wife and kids are amazing and keep me busy and young-ish. My wife is still as beautiful as she was the day I met her—eighteen years ago. I'm a lawyer, a pianist, a percussionist, a Sunday School teacher, a soccer dad, an armchair quarterback, an outdoor enthusiast, and now, an "author". In the very little free time I have, I camp, cliff-jump, kayak, golf, do yardwork, and hike with my family. On the rare occasion I have free time after all of that, I write.

Keep up with me at *www.danielpwilde.com*, *www.facebook.com/danielpwildeTKS*, or e-mail me at *danielpwilde@gmail.com*.